DATE DUE		
DEC 26 2001			
FEB 23 2002			

The Measure of the World

The Measure of

THE WORLD

A Novel

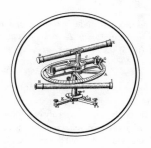

DENIS GUEDJ

Translated by **ARTHUR GOLDHAMMER**

The University of Chicago Press   Chicago and London

Originally published as *La Mesure du monde,*
© Éditions Seghers, 1987; Robert Laffont, S.A., Paris, 1997.

The University of Chicago Press gratefully acknowledges a subvention from
the government of France, through the French Ministry of Culture, Centre
National du Livre, in partial support of the costs of translating this volume.

Other books by Denis Guedj include *La Gratuité ne vaut plus rien: Et autres
chroniques mathématiciennes* (1987), *La Révolution des savants* (1988), and
L'Empire des nombres (1996). *La Mesure du monde* (1987) was awarded the Prix
d'Institut in 1989.

The University of Chicago Press, Chicago 60637
The University of Chicago Press, Ltd., London
© 2001 by The University of Chicago
All rights reserved. Published 2001
Printed in the United States of America
10 09 08 07 06 05 04 03 02 01   1 2 3 4 5

ISBN: 0-226-31030-2 (cloth)

Library of Congress Cataloging-in-Publication Data

Guedj, Denis.
    [Mesure du monde. English]
    The measure of the world : a novel / Denis Guedj ; translated by
Arthur Goldhammer.
      p. cm.
    ISBN 0-226-31030-2 (cloth : alk. paper)
    I.   Goldhammer, Arthur.   II. Title.
PQ2667.U3555 M4713   2001
843'.914—dc21

                        2001000488

PREFACE

It all began with one sentence: "In order to determine the length of the standard meter, astronomers Pierre Méchain and Jean-Baptiste Delambre traveled from one end of France to the other between 1792 and 1799 and measured the length of the meridian." I began quivering with excitement. Hadn't the monarchy come to an end in the summer of 1792? And hadn't the Consulate begun in the fall of 1799? Brumaire and all that . . .

And between those two dates: the Republic!

So, in order to set before the world a new unit of measure, two astronomers had measured the entire length of France, and their work had lasted the entire length of the Republic. They had taken the measure not only of French territory but of French history. But who remembers that the law that gave birth to the meter as an official unit of measure called it a "republican measure"?

History and geography had joined forces to give the world a unit of measure.

The sentence in question appeared in a book on metrology that I was reading one day while leaning against the door of a subway car in the Metro between Monceau and Barbès. The train had reached the point where it emerged from underground into the open air. In an instant the train had become airborne.

Immediately I visualized the story as a film—a film I am still eager to make.

No sooner did I reach home than I set to work. My dictionaries and encyclopedias left me with more questions than answers. The next day I set off for the library.

What I discovered went far beyond what I had innocently imagined on reading that sentence in the book on metrology—indeed, far beyond what I had hoped for.

My first order of business was to learn as much as possible about the history. The story of the meter seemed to have escaped the attention of novelists despite their endless search for new subjects. It also seemed to have escaped the notice of historians, who had shown little interest in the event despite its importance and consequences.

I wanted to learn as much as possible, and I wanted my information to be as accurate as possible. There is no substitute for the facts. Experience teaches us that truth is often stranger than fiction. And there is no substitute for original documents if one is lucky enough to find them. Thus, I scoured the Bibliothèque Nationale, the Archives de Paris, provincial archives, the archives of the Observatoire, the Bureau des Longitudes, and countless other repositories of documents almost two centuries old.

From morning till night I was immersed in another world, and when the bell rang to signal that the time had come to turn in my boxes of documents, I found it difficult to disentangle myself from my work. When I left the reading room of the Bibliothèque Nationale, it was already night: I had missed the day because I had spent my waking hours entirely in the past.

I discovered the poignant, mysterious letters that Méchain wrote to Delambre over a period of seven years, and I read Delambre's generous and patient replies. I delved into notebooks written with an admirably pure hand; I reviewed long series of measurements; I read notes on the condition of the sky and the quality of the sunlight, on the density of the clouds, which interrupted a series of measurements that was already well under way, and on the texture of the halos that surrounded some of the *signaux,* or targets, that the astronomers used in their measurements. I admired the precision of the sketches depicting the shape and exact location of various of these targets.

I followed the movements of the two astronomers on the map and observed the progress of their operations. Delambre worked his way north, in flat land where the lack of relief caused problems, while

Méchain worked his way south, where the excess of relief brought problems of another kind. I leapt from Dammartin-en-Goële to Dun-sur-Aron, from Culan to Morlac. At a glance I recognized Mount Bugarach and the Black Mountain, the fortress of Bellegarde and the Tower of Sermur, the Puy Violan and the Puy d'Aubassin. Soon the epic held almost no secrets for me, at least on the map. In reality, of course, secrets remained—fortunately for me.

Since relief is one of the dimensions that lend drama to history, how could I not go in person to inspect the terrain?

The task that I had set myself was at once the work of a historian of science and the work of a novelist. I had to see what was happening, to imagine each scene as concretely as possible, to see what each place looked like, to understand how the astronomers had felt. I had to see what they saw and to describe what they described in order to capture it.

My work turned out to be remarkably similar to the work of Delambre and Méchain. I felt that we were working together. For similar reasons, they and I both needed to find the right "point of view" and the proper lighting. We had to wait for the right light with our eyes glued to our instruments. In the middle of the night too, they had carried out measurements on mountaintops by illuminating their targets and using reflectors to focus the light.

When I climbed stairs that Delambre had climbed and followed in Méchain's footsteps up mountain trails, I found myself breathing as hard as they must have breathed. I asked myself how many steps Delambre had climbed in the course of the expedition: in the tower of Rodez, in the dome of the Pantheon, in the cathedral of Bourges, and in dozens of small village belfries.

I visited the stations where they made their measurements. They invariably chose extraordinary "points of view." This was hardly surprising, since the quality of the triangulation depended on it. Their assistants Tranchot and Bellet spent weeks scouting out the best sites.

What a magnificent story! An adventure to begin with, with arrests, chases, accidents, difficulties, snow and cold, fires, churches struck by lightning, scientists mistaken for spies, royalist émigrés, beggars, charlatans, and sorcerers.

It was to be an adventure set in the middle of the French Revolution. Its story was to revolve around two scientists forced to do their work in the most turbulent of times. What an opportunity to set a true story against a historic backdrop, a story of men and ideas, of science and society, in which concepts were as important as actions.

The story also has its deeper, more serious, more tragic side. If there were many adventures along the way, what was really at stake here was a quest to define a unit of measurement suitable "for all people in all ages," in the words of Condorcet, a quest undertaken when revolutionary unrest was at its peak. That unit was supposed to be taken from Nature and endowed with the virtues of Enlightenment philosophy and the values of the French Revolution: equality, universality, objectivity, and permanence, all illuminated by the light of Reason.[1] A sort of geodetic Grail, in other words. It was mainly Méchain who interpreted this as a mandate to search for a degree of perfection that was impossible to achieve. He would not survive the effort.

❖

Nearly everyone knows what a meter is—in most countries other than the United States, it is a unit that people deal with every day. But almost no one knows for sure how it was created or what incredible effort it took to determine its precise length. The history of the meter is therefore, in the proper sense of the word, a *revelation.*

Beyond this revelation, why did I find the story so fascinating? What was it that filled me with such passion for such a long period of time? Will I ever know? I remember, in any case, that some things about it appealed to me right off. For one thing, there was the fact that the story is set not in a place or region but *along a line.* It was a line that became a story. Let me explain what I mean. The seizure of the Bastille, the Battle of Waterloo, the smashing of the vase of Soissons, and the barricades of May '68 were events with specific locations, whereas the epic tale of the meter was an event distributed along a line, a very rare thing.[2] That line was more than six hundred miles long. By its very nature the subject forced me to deal with an event that unfolded in space and time, hence with "history" by definition.

1. This is the subject of another book of mine, *Le Mètre du monde: Histoire politique, scientifique et philosophique de l'invention du système métrique décimal* (Paris: Editions du Seuil, 2000).

2. The recent eclipse of the sun was a similar event, whose linear character may help to explain some of the enthusiasm it aroused.

What is more, it was an invisible line, not a line inscribed on the Earth's surface. It was not a road like an interstate highway or a structure like the Great Wall of China or even a line like the Maginot Line. It was rather a mythical line: the meridian of Paris.

This imaginary line, this expression of the size and shape of the Earth, was to be transformed through the story I wished to tell into a unit of measurement by which everything on Earth could be measured.

With respect to the nature of events and their effect on us, moreover, the transition from point to line is not without significance. If you're at one point on a line, you can't be at some other point. This limitation is a source of fascination.

Since we cannot be everywhere at once, we are obliged—happily—to travel along our imaginary line. If we wish to measure, we must move.

◆

For me, working on this history was the occasion of a second revelation: I discovered the French Revolution of my dreams. Often tragic, sometimes generous, the Revolution was an adventure of the mind that sought to remake the world, give names to things, and so on. Out of a powerful desire for happiness, men conceived the ambition to create a new world. Some magnificent figures lent themselves to the effort, among them Condorcet, Gilbert Romme, and dozens of other men and women whose names I discovered in the course of my work. In countless speeches and texts written in the heat of events, they revealed a superb gift for language.

Take Barère of the Committee of Public Safety: "It would be a fine thing to see the National Convention, immobilized amid tempests, show some concern for the eternity of the republic by taking an interest in great monuments, in ports, canals, public highways, and public works destined to impress upon the soil of Europe the indelible trace of its proclamations of the rights of man and the citizen."

Or this text from the Académie: "The Académie feels that, in working for a powerful nation, obedient to the orders of enlightened men whose views encompass all men in all ages, it ought to concern itself not so much with what is easy as with what most nearly approaches perfection."

I also learned just how much the Revolution had "needed scientists" and how enthusiastically most scientists had answered the call. The Revolution also influenced the expedition indirectly: it led to war, scarcity, restrictions on movement, and disruptions of the currency that complicated matters for Delambre and Méchain.

The Revolution built scaffolds to execute its enemies. By contrast, our scientists built scaffolds when suitable high ground or other vantage points were not available for their work. They climbed these structures in order to see those faraway "targets"—belfries, towers, mountain peaks—whose relative location they wished to measure.

In advancing along the meridian, our astronomers thus proceeded from one high point to another. Meanwhile, down below, the Revolution also proceeded. It had conceived the project of defining the meter and continued to support it as the Constituent Assembly gave way to the Legislative and the Legislative to the Convention. Commission succeeded commission, order succeeded decree. The silence of the mountains and the calm of the bell towers alternated with the boiling passions of the day.

In order to retrace the travels of Méchain and Delambre, I set up an organization, looked for subsidies, found them, and put together a whole team to embark on an expedition. This was the origin of Operation Meridian.

On May 15, 1989, in Dunkirk, we carried out our first measurement. Perched atop the belvedere of the Intendance, a dozen or so individuals took part in measuring the angle between Cassel and Watten, with help from the engineers of the Institut National de la Géographie. And from there the operation continued day after day, from one triangulation site to the next.

People were excited by the idea of participating in an expedition in their own backyard and of identifying a nearby summit or steeple as a historic site that had once been part of a passionate adventure. This was one of the secrets of Operation Meridian, a veritable expedition into the heart of France. This was no South Sea voyage or exploration of the forests of the Amazon or the frozen wastes of the North Pole or the vast Sahara. It was the Cantal and the Pas-de-Calais, the Cher and the Aveyron. People said to themselves, "Important things took place near where I live." For those who took part in the adventure as for those who read about it, history became embodied in geography and the local terrain suddenly became the theater of a suspenseful drama.

In one hamlet a banner was hung over the small road leading into town: "Welcome to the Meridian." Long tables were filled with food and bottles of wine in the village square. All the villagers assembled, and the mayor delivered an emotional speech in which he recognized the connection between "his" earth and the Earth and exhibited the pride he felt in the fact that his little piece of France had been a part of History with a capital *H.*

On June 14 the last measurement was carried out from the tower of Montjuich in Barcelona. More than fifteen thousand people had taken part in Operation Meridian. Nothing had been able to stop that onrushing truck. And yet, whenever I meet readers of this book, I still hear the same heartbreaking remark: "You know, as I was reading, I kept saying to myself, this would make a terrific movie." You don't say. And I tell them that originally I had written this novel as a screenplay. But that was before I had taken the measure of the world.

— *I* —

June 24, 1792. The Tuileries still bore traces of the human tide that had just washed over them: discarded food wrappings, deposits of excrement, bits of rag, trampled flower beds. A handful of gardeners gauged the damage, deliberately turning their backs on the sapling that a procession of marchers from the *faubourgs* had planted three days earlier over the objections of the king's guards. It was a fine tree, which would survive until at least the end of the century if nothing—neither stroke of lightning, ax blow, fire, nor parasites—interfered with its growth. Pinned to its trunk was a tricolor cockade in all its splendor.

At the end of the drive, parked back-to-back in front of a wing of the palace, stood two heavily laden berlins, ready to depart. Identical but for their color—one was green, the other bronze—each was fitted out in the rear with an enormous, oddly shaped trunk. In the vicinity of these two carriages a small group had gathered: Lavoisier the distinguished chemist, Condorcet the philosopher and deputy of the Legislative Assembly, and the Chevalier de la Borda, a physicist. With them stood a woman and her three children.

This small group had gathered to bid farewell to Citizens Pierre Méchain and Jean-Baptiste Delambre, who were about to depart the capital.

"So then Méchain," Delambre greeted his partner. "The south for you, the north for me."

"So says the Assembly," the other man replied.

"And I'm staying in Paris," Lavoisier gloomily remarked as he handed each man a small strongbox containing letters of credit and pieces of gold and silver. Then Borda handed each traveler a briefcase containing passports and letters of recommendation signed by the king.

Thérèse Méchain tried hard to hide her anxiety. Dignified and silent, she remained aloof from the others. But as Delambre approached to take his leave, she could no longer contain herself. "If only you were going with him!" she blurted out. At this point Condorcet joined the two of them. He would stay in constant touch with both travelers, he reassured Mme Méchain, and would share any news with her the moment he received it.

Méchain climbed into the bronze carriage, Delambre into the green. Their eyes met. Did they really glow, as they seemed to, with the excitement of departure, or was the gleam merely a reflection of the bonfires of Saint John that had illuminated the heights of Montmartre for the past several nights?

"To Rodez! To Rodez!" both shouted simultaneously.

The two berlins shuddered into motion at the same time, heading off in opposite directions.

For Lavoisier this day marked an anniversary. Nine years earlier he had gone to work as usual in his laboratory at the Arsenal. That morning, by combining flammable air and vital air in a sealed bell jar in precisely calculated proportions, he had created—water! A few drops—of matchless purity—had formed beads on the glass walls of the jar. Water from the inception!

Out of gases had come water! Hence one of the four elements that according to ancient myth made up the world was in fact a compound substance. This discovery spelled the end of man's belief in primary elements, in aristocratic substances that outranked all the rest. A revolution! As he left the Palais des Tuileries, Lavoisier, remembering that he was one of the fathers of the Republic of Matter in which all substances enjoyed equal rights, could not suppress a momentary fear that another Republic, this one not of Matter but of Men, was even now being born.

Alongside him walked Condorcet, whose sympathies were precisely the opposite of Lavoisier's. As a *philosophe,* the sole surviving Encyclopédiste, and president of the Legislative Assembly, he hoped that the Republic's time had come: better a sovereign who is absent, as he put it, than a sovereign who is present. As for Borda, despite his devotion to the monarchy, he had fought with the American "insurgents" in their battle to free themselves from the English crown.

The three men had not gathered in the courtyard of the Tuileries to debate the best form of government, however. They had come as over-seers of a mission that the Assembly had authorized and the king approved. Why, then, was Thérèse so apprehensive?

It was not the first time her husband had been sent on a mission. But so much had happened in the past three years! Why, the very buildings of the Tuileries now had new names, and their occupant a new title. What had been the Pavillon de Marsan on the north side was now called Liberty. The pavilion in the center had been dubbed Unity, while Flore, to the south, was now Equality. Over all three buildings a tricolor pennant now flew day and night. As for the king of France, his title was henceforth "king of the French," and people now called one another "Citizen" and the old constable's corps, the *maréchaussée,* had been re-named the Gendarmerie Nationale. Just a week earlier, and only a few feet from this very spot, a great bonfire had been lit, and into it had been tossed the "playthings of the nobility": an enormous batch of letters patent and parchments attesting to the nobility of dukes, marquis, vis-counts, and counts had been set ablaze at the foot of the statue of Louis XVI, which the flames had licked for hours. The *patente,* a new tax on professionals, had been enacted, and throughout France the right to own so much as a single slave had been abolished. Meanwhile, the Sor-bonne had been closed, and Corsica had been opened up to the Conti-nent. The bridge at Avignon had become French. And steps had been taken to root out the dialects and patois that prevented citizens from un-derstanding one another, or so it was claimed.

If variety of dialect was undesirable, so was diversity of weights and measures. Wood for the fire was sold by the cord, charcoal by the ham-per, peat by the basket, ocher by the barrel, and framing timbers by the mark or joist. Fruit for cider was sold by the *poinçonnée;* salt by the *muid, sétier, mine, minot, boisseau,* and *mesurette;* lime by the *poinçon;* plaster by the bag. Wine could be bought by the *pinte, chopine, camuse, roquille, petit pot,* or *demoiselle.* Spirits were sold by the *potée,* wheat by the *muid* and *écuellée.* Fabric, carpeting, and tapestries went by the square ell. Woods and fields were measured in *perches carrées* and vineyards in *dau-rées.* An *arpent,* or acre, equaled twelve *hommées,* an *hommée* being the amount of land one man could till in one day. So was the *oeuvrée.* Apothecaries weighed in *livres, onces, drachmes,* and *scrupules.* A *livre* was equal to twelve *onces,* an *once* was eight *drachmes,* a *drachme* three *scrupules,* and a *scrupule* twenty *grains.*

Lengths were measured in *toises* and *pieds de Pérou,* one of which was equal to one *pouce,* one *longe,* and eight *points du pied du Roi:* this "king's foot" was that of Philicteres or of the king of Madedonia or the king of Poland; and there were also feet of Padua, Pesaro, and Urbino. The king's foot was approximately equal to the old foot of Franche-Comté, Maine, and Perche, although surveyors still used the foot of Bordeaux. Four of the latter were close to one *aune,* or ell, of Laval. Five made up the Roman "hexapod," which was equivalent to the *canne* of Toulouse and the *verge,* or rod, of Norai. This was the same as the rod of Raucourt as well as the *corde* of Marchenoir en Dunois. In Marseille the *canne* used to measure line was longer than that used to measure silk by roughly one-fourteenth. Imagine the confusion with some seven or eight hundred different units of measurement throughout the kingdom.

"Deux poids et deux mesures!" Two weights and two measures: the slogan captured the very essence of inequality, the notion of a "double standard." The Revolution, responding to grievances expressed not only by villages throughout France in 1789 but also as early as the Estates General of 1576, which had insisted that "everywhere in France there should be but one yard, one foot, one weight, and one measure," decided to enforce uniformity. It established a single standard system of measurement, thus facilitating trade and encouraging greater honesty in commercial transactions.

◆

After leaving the Tuileries and passing without difficulty through the customs barrier around Paris, the bronze berlin headed due south across the countryside. Inside, with windows open and curtains lowered to allow a cool breeze to enter, Méchain sat comfortably and observed the man opposite him, who had already fallen asleep.

For Méchain had not set out on this mission alone, any more than Delambre had. Each was accompanied by an assistant: Citizen Bellet for Delambre, and Tranchot for Méchain.

Tranchot had the reputation of being a stalwart country fellow, strong-willed but competent. His familiarity with mountainous terrain would be invaluable when it came time to brave the Catalan peaks, the Pyrenees, the Corbières highlands, and the Montagne Noire. Méchain, staring at his companion's small hands as they lay idly on his thighs, guessed that they would prove agile and strong. Watching Tranchot as he slept, he sensed that this was not a man who worried overmuch about his inner weather. That was exactly what he wanted. The coach drove through a village. Méchain glanced outside and saw puzzled looks on the faces of the inhabitants. Was it the unusual construction of the carriage that drew their stares? Méchain settled into a comfortable position and set a small collapsible table into position. He then spread out a map of Catalonia and began to study it.

The carriage braked so suddenly that Tranchot was thrown from his seat onto the seat opposite, pinning Méchain's arm. "Citizens, your passes." The order of the officer of the National Guard who now appeared before them went unanswered. Méchain looked down at the smashed table, rubbed his sore arm, and picked up his map, which he tried absent-mindedly to smooth. The officer repeated his order. Dazed, Tranchot picked himself up. Through the window he caught sight of a rifle barrel glinting in the sun: the carriage was surrounded. Méchain remained silent while Tranchot tried to explain the nature of their mission to the officer. The officer listened politely but gave orders to search the carriage. Méchain, striking a hostile pose, seemed determined not to collaborate with the men carrying out the search. But Tranchot, who understood the reason for these checkpoints, displayed no ill will, for he knew that dozens of aristocrats and prelates were fleeing the country every day, taking their fortunes with them.

The search turned up neither arms nor jewels: only two letters of credit addressed to Spanish bankers. The soldiers were about to let the berlin pass when one of them discovered twenty sealed letters in a briefcase that had fallen under one of the seats. The officer wanted to open them, but the soldier objected, pointing out that the Constituent Assembly had issued a directive prohibiting the breaking of official seals unless an elected municipal official was present. The officer accepted this and sent someone to the nearby village of Essonnes to find the *procureur-syndic,* roughly the equivalent of a mayor.

Upon his arrival, the *procureur* took one of the letters, broke the seal, and at the request of the soldiers read it out loud: "The king recommends to the administration of la Creuse Messieurs Méchain and Delambre, astronomers of the Academy of Sciences."

"Where is this Delambre?" asked the officer. Since Méchain was still refusing to speak, Tranchot explained that Delambre was at that moment headed toward Dunkirk, while he and Monsieur Méchain were on their way to Barcelona. The official continued his reading: "Louis, by the grace of God and the constitutional law of the State King of the French: To all, now and to come, greetings."

Since the letter had been signed by the king, the majority of the guards agreed that the berlin should be allowed to pass. But one spoke up to point out that there were twenty more letters whose contents had yet to be examined. The *procureur* broke the seal of a second letter. It was addressed to the département of Aveyron. A third, to the département of the Tarn. A fourth, to the département of the Pyrénées-Orientales. The contents were identical.

The letters whose seals had been broken were spread out on one of the trunks that had been removed from the carriage. Those that remained sealed were neatly arrayed on a second trunk.

A driver whose oxen were grazing in a nearby field came over to see what was going on. A group of peasants on their way home from the fields joined him, abandoning their wagons and carts along the road. Several private carriages also stopped, and their occupants joined the swelling crowd of onlookers. As the letters were read everyone listened attentively, and they quickly realized that each new missive simply repeated the contents of the previous ones. Sitting off to one side, Méchain seemed to take no interest in the proceedings.

By now six letters had been read. Some of the assembled wanted to hear them all. Fifteen remained unopened. Suddenly the astronomer stood up. Brushing aside the curious, he marched straight up to the *procureur-syndic* and stated flatly that all the letters were identical. He then proposed a way of expediting the procedure. As an expert mathematician and specialist in the laws of probability, he suggested that a letter be chosen at random. If it was identical to the others, he should be allowed to proceed; otherwise he should be arrested on the spot. The spectators approved of this proposal because it meant that they would learn the outcome of the incident without having to stand around for hours in the middle of nowhere.

Everyone drew closer. The children were told to hush, and silence settled over the crowd. Tranchot took up a position alongside Méchain, his back to the carriage. The decisive letter was in the hands of the official, who slowly removed the seal. After quickly reading it over, he smiled: "The king recommends, etc." A shout went up. Tranchot squeezed

Méchain's arm in a friendly way, and some of the onlookers hastened to congratulate them.

◈

"The longest geodesic measurement in history, as Borda called it, is off to a bad start," Méchain grumbled as he climbed back into the carriage. A navigator, physicist, and inventor of instruments, Borda had just perfected a marvelous new device, a repeating circle. Two of the three existing specimens were packed away in Méchain's trunks.

How long would the expedition last? The optimists were saying a year. Méchain thought it would be at least two. The truth was that nobody really knew. Not the deputies in the Assembly who had sponsored the project, nor the scientists of the Academy who had discussed the principles involved, nor the members of the Commission on Weights and Measures who had done the planning. Sitting in the gallery of the Constituent Assembly and, later, the Legislative Assembly, Méchain had dutifully attended to the speeches of Talleyrand, Condorcet, and Prieur of the Côte-d'Or. He remembered his emotion when Condorcet, speaking to a chamber full to the bursting point, had dedicated the expedition "to all nations and all ages." Now there was a fellow who knew how to turn a phrase, but Lord, what a terrible speaker! Méchain could remember what he said almost word for word: "In carrying out this measurement, which is destined to enlighten all mankind and bring nations closer together, we must choose the right course: not that which is easiest but that which will yield the most perfect result possible."

What measurement was he talking about? Why, nothing less than to determine as precisely as possible the length of the meridian between Dunkirk and Barcelona. This was the daunting task that Méchain and Delambre, both astronomers and members of the Academy, had been chosen to carry out. They would start at opposite ends of the meridian and work their way toward Rodez, where they would meet at the conclusion of their work.

◈

Unity in language, unity in government, unity against all enemies foreign and domestic: for three years everyone had been obsessed with unity, abhorred the arbitrary, and felt universal.

Measurement is quantity: that is why it exists. But people wanted it to be "quality" as well, hence universal, eternal, and invariable. Anything that stands alone, that depends on nothing else, that is arbitrary, is not fit to be adopted as a permanent standard, they insisted. As proof they cited the long history of humankind.

It had therefore been decided that any new unit of measurement must for the rest of time be intimately linked to changeless objects rather than to anything dependent on the vagaries of human decisions or events. What possessed the requisite qualities other than Nature? And what in Nature was more apt than the terrestrial globe itself to guarantee constancy, universality, and eternity?

Everything was in place: the time, the men, the institutions, and the technical resources. This, then, was the solemn moment of definition. It was proclaimed that the new unit of length would be a piece of the globe: "one forty-millionth of the circumference of the meridian."

Méchain tried to relax. He stretched out his legs. This berlin was comfortable indeed! Borda had overseen every detail of its design. A marvel of ingenuity: There was a folding table with extensions that could be used as a work surface. The well-upholstered seats could be converted into beds for two. Niches fashioned in the wooden walls served as storage compartments for various instruments: a traveling thermometer, a clock calibrated in seconds and another equipped with an alarm, two capillary hygrometers, two barometers, a compass, a small level, and two pocket magnifying glasses in their patent leather cases. A compartment in the ceiling held a bundle of maps. Borda had thought of many other clever systems as well, but Lavoisier, the Academy's treasurer, had put a stop to any further expenditure of funds.

The berlin was once again moving along at a good clip. Essonnes receded into the distance. Seated next to the coachman, looking down on the horses' hindquarters glistening with sweat, Tranchot admired the perfection of the mechanism that was transporting him to Spain. The first of the three-horse team raced ahead into the thickening dusk, and the two other horses followed blindly. The coachman dozed but kept a loose grip on the rawhide reins.

Tranchot had been upset by Méchain's behavior, at first irritated by his lack of emotion and then angered by his dejection, but in the end he had been won over by his companion's sudden burst of energy and skill in extricating them from an unpleasant situation. Méchain had the reputation of being a man who kept to himself. Like the pair of horses in the rear of the three-horse team, he and Méchain had no choice but to march in step. For months, perhaps even years, they would be sharing everything: the same jobs, the same meals, the same carriage, and more often than not the same bedroom. A regular marriage! The thought made him smile. A consensual marriage, he had to admit.

Was that Méchain's voice? It was hard to hear because of the wind. Tranchot turned around. Leaning out the window, the astronomer was shouting at the top of his lungs, but it was impossible to hear what he was saying. The carriage slowed to a stop, and Tranchot leaped down. Without opening the door, Méchain ordered the coachman to turn around. "We're going back to Paris! To be arrested, checked, and searched every step of the way! As if the natural obstacles weren't enough! I've decided to postpone the expedition."

"But th-that's impossible," Tranchot stammered. "Delambre has already left. *He* won't be turning back." The last sentence was uttered in a deliberately provocative tone. "And besides, Captain Gonzales will be waiting for us at the Spanish border. There won't be any second chance. If you put it off, you sink the mission."

"It's already sunk. You saw what happened. You saw how they treated us."

"All they did was check up on us and slow us down by a few hours. But we were allowed to continue."

Calmed down, Méchain grumbled a few more words, addressed more to himself than to his assistant. "We won't succeed unless we can count on the help of local officials, policemen, and ordinary citizens. We'll need carpenters, wood, porters, animals at every step of the way. No, it's impossible. The expedition has to be postponed."

"You don't understand, then," Tranchot erupted, emphasizing every word. "Things are not about to calm down! This is not a riot or peasant uprising. This is a revolution. If we go back to Paris, we won't be able to get out again for years."

◈

Night was almost upon them. The next way station was still leagues away, but the bronze berlin had not moved. The coachman, sitting in the grass, his pipe in his mouth, was waiting for Méchain to make up his mind: would it be north and back to Paris, or south? He stood up. "Not to butt in," he said to the astronomer. "I don't make a habit of sticking my nose into other people's business. But I think he's right. What's happening now isn't going to be over tomorrow, believe me. And it's a good thing, too."

The astronomer climbed back into the carriage and called Tranchot, who was pacing up and down the road to calm himself down. "So what do we do?" the coachman asked. Méchain pointed to the south. "Head for Catalonia," he said.

The moment the berlin started to move, Méchain swore an oath to himself not to return to Paris until the meridian had been measured.

◈

Montargis, Bourges, Montluçon, Brive, Rodez, Albi, Castres, Carcassonne, Perpignan. The berlin was not halted at any other checkpoint. It proceeded straight on to the Pyrenees and the border. A week to the day after the incident at Essonnes, the travelers crossed into Spain, where Captain Gonzales greeted them.

Gonzales, an astronomer and officer in the navy of His Majesty King Charles IV of Spain, had been sent to accompany the foreign experts on their journey through Spanish territory. Naturally he had been instructed to keep an eye on the two foreigners—not just foreigners, but Frenchmen!—but, beyond that, he was also to take part in their scientific expedition, which Spain had been invited to join and from which it hoped to derive numerous benefits.

Contrary to what Méchain and Tranchot had told the officer in Essonnes, the green berlin had not headed straight to Dunkirk. At the first stop, in Dammartin-en-Goële, Delambre had learned that the collegiate church in the village had just been bought by someone who intended to demolish it before winter arrived. But the church steeple was one of his primary targets in the Paris region and as such irreplaceable. Changing his plans on the spot, he decided to begin operations in the vicinity of Paris at once. This would have the additional benefit of allowing work to be completed on certain instruments that were not yet ready to go: the fourth repeating circle, on which the craftsman Lenoir was putting the finishing touches, as well as a reflector and several parabolic mirrors. Bellet eagerly awaited their arrival, as one of his jobs was to maintain and repair the astronomical instruments and clocks.

Once the decision was made to postpone the trip to Dunkirk, the astronomer and his assistant began crisscrossing the Paris region from north to south. In Montmartre, instead of the steeple with a clear view in all directions that they were expecting, they found nothing but a ruined tower from which no observation of any sort could be made. By contrast, the tower in Montlhéry was astonishingly well preserved, but its walls were too thick and its shape too irregular to make a good target. Delambre had a tower built to his specifications. It was destroyed the very same day. The next day, the municipal *procureur* had it rebuilt at the expense of the man who had committed the crime, but a few days later the replacement was knocked down by a person or persons unknown.

Even though the steeple of Saint-Martin-du-Tertre, north of Paris, had been rebuilt fifty years earlier, it was so dilapidated that all the bells but one had been removed from the belfry; it shook the timbers and masonry each time it was rung. The summer wore on. In Jonquières,

Delambre and Bellet attended a celebration marking the anniversary of the fall of the Bastille. In the midst of the ceremony, a villager approached the astronomer and whispered that he knew someone still alive who had witnessed an earlier expedition led by Cassini of Thury. Delambre, excited, asked that the man be brought to him at once. The elderly gentleman came and began recounting his story. Fifty years had passed since Cassini had mounted his expedition. Once the old man started talking, he could not be stopped: not a single detail was omitted. In those days, he said, he had still been spry enough to carry heavy timbers up to the top of the mill that Cassini had chosen as a target. That mill had since collapsed, however, and nothing remained but a heap of stones. A half a century! Delambre, who had read an account of the Cassini expedition written at the time, was delighted. But the man's words did not have altogether the desired effect on the crowd. People began to murmur. Ignoring this reaction, the astronomer and his assistant set to work. Then the officials of the local government arrived as a group. In sober terms the mayor explained the villagers' worries about what was going on and asked the two men to suspend their operations until the departmental administration gave its approval.

Delambre left immediately for Beauvais, where he was received that same day by the president of the Oise *département,* who fortunately had been a member of the National Assembly, indeed had presided over that body when it had voted on one of the decrees pertaining to the measurement of the meridian. When the astronomer returned to Jonquières with an enthusiastic recommendation from the departmental authorities, he met with a warm reception, and from then on his stay in the village proved both pleasant and profitable. Everything seemed to be falling into place, especially after a solution was found to the problem of the Paris station. After inspecting the dome of the Invalides and the Pantheon and, one more time, the summit of the Butte Montmartre, Delambre had discovered a belvedere on the latter that was just what he needed.

❧

Borda and Delambre were walking along the Seine toward the Quai Conti. Borda was repeating to his companion a riddle that Mlle de Lespinasse liked to put to guests in her salon: "This man's mind can be described in terms usually reserved for God: it is infinite and present, if not everywhere then at least in everything. Just and nimble, powerful and subtle, clear and precise, his mind has the facility and grace of Voltaire, the savor of Fontenelle, the wit of Pascal, and the profundity of Newton. Of whom am I speaking?"

"Condorcet!"

"Correct. How did you know?"

"Simple: like Voltaire he is a *philosophe* not afraid to use his tongue, and like Voltaire he has also made himself a goodly number of enemies. Like Fontenelle he is an academician, indeed perpetual secretary of the Academy. And like d'Alembert, he contributed to the *Encyclopedia*, whose mathematical sections he rewrote in their entirety."

"What you say sounds like an obituary," Borda remarked.

"You're the one who proposed the riddle. Do you know how many mathematical articles there are in the *Encyclopedia?*"

"No."

"Neither do I. But let's continue. Like Pascal, he is a mathematician, but he goes Pascal one better by attempting to apply the theory of probability to courtroom testimony, elections, and decisions of all kinds."

"But wasn't Pascal's wager also a kind of calculus of probabilities?"

"God does not play dice! Neither does Newton, who if I remember correctly was the last piece of your puzzle."

They had reached the Hôtel des Monnaies, where Condorcet lived.

◈

"On the pretext of measuring a few degrees of meridian, these academicians have persuaded the ministry to give them a grant of a hundred thousand écus to cover their costs. A nice little pie, which the brethren will share among themselves."

"You see, not everyone agrees that the expedition is a good idea!" exclaimed a delighted Condorcet. "I prefer it that way. Unanimity is always a mask for tyranny."

When Delambre, accompanied by Borda, entered the Condorcets' salon, a pretty woman was reading an article by Marat that had appeared in *L'Ami du peuple*. With his usual fury the author denounced "the mania for systems, which has led physicists to attempt to reduce all natural phenomena to a single cause."

"What's surprising about that?" asked a man with a Prussian accent. "Marat has never been for unity! He is consistent at least: he opposes unity even in physics."

"Marat is against unity, Condorcet against unanimity. And I'm against uniformity," laughed a young man with a marvelous American accent.

The American was Thomas Paine, the hero of the War for Independence. The Prussian was a wealthy baron who had given up everything, including his name, in order to throw himself body and soul into the Revolution. "He now calls himself Anacharsis," Borda pointed out to Delambre, who had never been in this salon before. "And the beautiful woman is our hostess, Sophie." Condorcet stood next to her holding a ravishing child, Eliza, who blew everyone a kiss before her father carried her away amid laughter. Delambre watched them disappear, amused to have surprised his colleague in the role of husband and father.

All that Europe boasted in the way of intelligence and art gathered in the salon of Sophie Condorcet: the English economist Adam Smith; the German storyteller Jakob Grimm; the French poet André Chénier; the scholarly monarch of Denmark, a great disciple of Rousseau; the physician Cabanis and his young colleague Pinel, who took care of the insane. And many others.

Some time passed before Condorcet noticed the presence of Delambre. In this house things were done simply, so guests were not announced when they arrived. The *philosophe* called for silence so that he could introduce the astronomer to his other guests. Delambre was immediately besieged with questions. Why choose a meridian? Why this one rather than some other? Why Dunkirk and Barcelona? A very small lady asked, "Why one forty-millionth of that meridian and not—oh, I don't know—one three thousand four hundred and twelfth, for instance?"

Delambre made a sign with his hands to halt the avalanche of questions. Desperately looking around for Borda, he found him standing off to one side, obviously enjoying the scene immensely. Begging for help with his eyes, the astronomer watched as his companion ostentatiously moved off to the buffet with a malicious smile on his lips.

Thus it was without Borda's help that Delambre answered the other guests' questions. He explained that this meridian had been chosen because it was the one that passed through Paris and that several attempts had therefore already been made to measure it. The most recent of these, half a century earlier, had been the one led by Jacques Cassini of Thury. "His work inspired us, and we hope to use some of his results. Unfortunately, a mill that he used as a target in the village of Jonquières has already turned out to be of no use to us. As for Dunkirk and Barcelona, we chose those two cities because both lie on the meridian at sea level, which will simplify all the calculations." Sophie brought him a glass of liqueur, and Delambre rose in the hope that he might be allowed to drink in peace. But someone pointed out that he had yet to answer the question about the forty-millionth part. "Antiquity loved games, so much so that in the Aswan region of the Nile, the unit of length was known as the 'stadium.' Eratosthenes measured the distance from Aswan to Alexandria, and from that he deduced the circumference of the Earth: 250,000 stadia, which is roughly equal to forty-million *demi-toises* of Peru," Delambre replied, just before emptying his glass with one swallow.

"You want the new unit of measurement to be universal, yet you are defining it without the cooperation of any other country. This seems contradictory," someone observed. At this point Condorcet joined the discussion: "France has done everything in its power to persuade other countries to join in the effort. The Constituent Assembly issued a decree calling upon the king 'to write to His Majesty in Great Britain' asking that members of the Royal Society of London be sent to accompany their French counterparts. Louis XVI wrote the letter, but the English thumbed their noses. Since the taking of the Bastille, London, Berlin, Vienna, and Moscow are treating Paris as though it had the plague. But Europe cannot stop France from realizing her dreams. Since governments and peoples are not one and the same, we made up our minds to do without the assistance of the former." Condorcet then quoted the Assembly decree from memory:

> There is no need, in our judgment, to await the concurrence of other nations either to choose a unit of measurement or to begin our operations. Indeed, since we have eliminated all arbitrariness from the determination and rely only on information equally accessible to all nations, there are no grounds whatsoever for the reproach that we wish to establish some sort of preeminence.

In short, if memory of these efforts were to disappear and only the results were to remain, those results would reveal nothing of which nation conceived the idea or carried out the measurement.

Anacharsis Cloots, who in his own mind had erased all borders from the face of the earth, seemed overjoyed. He hurried over to embrace Condorcet. Delambre went out onto the balcony. Below him flowed the Seine. Borda suddenly appeared at his side. "I've got it," he shouted. Delambre stared at him quizzically. "The meter! We'll call it the *meter!*" And then he vanished as suddenly as he had appeared. Delambre was surprised that Borda had chosen a Latin root. Both men had a passion for Greek and differed about only one thing: Borda preferred the *Iliad* and Delambre the *Odyssey.* The lights of the Tuileries danced in the calm waters of the Seine. Tomorrow the astronomer would leave Paris for Dammartin-en-Goële.

— *3* —

The narrower the steeple, the better the target. The steeple of the collegiate church of Dammartin-en-Goële was just right. Climbing the endless spiral staircase, Delambre felt as though his body were being twisted into a corkscrew. Pausing to catch his breath, he told himself that he would have to get used to these interminable climbs; then he started up again. All of a sudden he emerged into a dazzling, almost painful light. An ocean of fire surrounded him, sun and wheat melded together in a single molten mass. Squinting against the brightness, he scanned the horizon around the campanile: wheat everywhere! In places clouds seemed to rise up out of the earth. It was harvest season, and the air was thick with stubble swept up by the wind. Two words summed up the plain of Goële: rich and monotonous.

Blue with distance, a crown of hills and buttes marked the horizon. It was if the church had been erected at the exact center of a vast amphitheater. Far off stood the round-backed hills of Coupvaray, Caretin, and Chaumont; the arches of Ecouen and Montmélain; the shrugged shoulders of Saint-Christophe; the plateaus of Sannois and Calvaire. Far off to the south, invisible to all but an experienced eye, rose a vague eminence: Montmartre. Closer in, but invisible, lay Ermenonville, where Rousseau lay buried on the Ile des Peupliers. Since the beginning of the Revolution people had been flocking to his grave.

"And that tower over there—do you know that one?" Delambre suddenly turned around. The carpenter, who had come in without making a sound, was standing behind him, pointing.

It was the tower on Mont Epiloy, which the astronomer knew quite well. The carpenter seemed surprised. "I'm from Amiens," Delambre said. In all the Somme was there anyone who did not know the famous tower in which Joan of Arc had been held captive?

In a belfry of course one finds bells. Until now Delambre had never been close enough to touch one, and those before him now seemed gigantic. Placing his hand on the bronze, he thought he could feel vibrations, which it amused him to think of as vestigial sounds somehow trapped in the metal. When he leaned on the bell, it didn't move. He was about to push harder when he caught sight of the carpenter, who stood balanced on the tower's main beam apparently enjoying the astronomer's futile exertions. An enormous oak beam supported both bells. It was so stout and so deeply embedded in the stone wall of the belfry that it seemed nothing could ever dislodge it. The carpenter leaped nimbly onto a narrow ledge, where the astronomer joined him by climbing a swaying rope ladder. Though not actually dizzy, Delambre felt uncomfortable. The moistness at the back of his neck was a sure sign. After testing the trusses and rafters, the carpenter pointed to a purlin.

"Although it's been here for a couple of centuries, it's still as sound as a ship's mast. We'll build the scaffold here."

Delambre noticed that the word he used was *échafaud* and not *échafaudage,* or scaffolding, which struck him because *échafaud* was also the word for the structure that supports a guillotine or gallows. "Fire's the only way to do it, and even then . . . Hellfire." With a loud laugh that echoed through the belfry, the carpenter continued to make his way along the groaning girders.

Delambre decided to go down to the Auberge de la Grosse Tête, ignoring Bellet's ironic remark that the name of the inn (which means "Big Head") was somehow connected with the academician's intelligence. The food was good, and the room, which overlooked the village square, comfortable. The servant who showed him to his room, a girl with a shrill voice, pointed out the spot where several men had not long ago been hanged and left dangling in front of the mill that also served as a courthouse.

The square was also where the news was discussed every evening. There was always someone who had spent the day in Meaux or Senlis, or perhaps a traveler on his way from Soissons to Paris, who could be counted on to share what he had gleaned with the people of the village. Anyone coming from Belgium or the border region was likely to be bombarded with questions about how things were going at the front: France was at war with the king of Bohemia and Hungary.

The most widely discussed event of recent months, the one that had unleashed the warmest passions and triggered the bitterest disputes, was the invasion of the Tuileries by the inhabitants of the *faubourgs*. Intruders had even forced their way into the royal apartments. There was pity for Louis and the little dauphin, but none for the women: no one had a good word to say about the mother or the daughter. Someone said he had heard that the invaders had not been disrespectful to the royal family and that no damage had been done to the palace, to which an elderly man replied, "But still!" Many grave-looking people murmured their assent, but others pointed out that not so very long ago everyone in the village had joined in sacking the nearby castle of the Condés. Yet that, it was objected in turn, had been done only to burn the records of the Condés' seigneurial rights, and in any case "the king isn't the same as the nobility."

One detail had captured everyone's imagination: the red cap. It was generally held to be a good thing that Louis had been made to don the Phrygian cap of the revolutionaries, and the thought of "the Austrian woman's husband" wearing such headgear had unleashed a gale of laughter. "A cap over a powdered wig! A cap over a powdered wig!" one man chortled. But another angrily insisted that the king had been disgusted by what he had been forced to do. A peasant who had thus far been silent now came forward. "Disgusted? I wear a cap, and I'm proud of it." Then the servant from the inn, the girl with the shrill voice, spoke up. She had it on good authority, from her cousin who had been there, that a beautiful woman had walked right up to the king and shouted at him, "Listen to us! That's what you're there for, to listen to us!" This news stunned the crowd, and in the ensuing silence someone muttered, "It's true. That's why he's there, to listen to us."

❖

Wedged between spire and bells, the scaffolding filled the entire belfry, which gives you some idea of its size. "Up here nobody will bother us. People are far too lazy to climb all those stairs. Height has its privileges: you can be alone right in the center of town!"

Absorbed by the business of setting up the repeating circle, Delambre only half paid attention to the carpenter's idle chatter. Placing himself behind the instrument, he released various safety catches, thereby allowing the telescope to move freely. Wrapping his hand around the barrel of the instrument, he aimed it to the north and grasped the knurled focusing knob, which turned easily at the touch of a finger. Slowly the turret of Clermont emerged from the hazy void.

Bellet had watched his every move. Delambre now stepped aside so that his assistant could take a look. Mechanically brushing back the lock of hair that fell across his forehead, Bellet leaned forward and peered into the lens. Then he muttered something like, "Perfect, perfect—perfectly clear."

Soon the light had grown too dim to continue. Delambre locked the telescope in place. How many more measurements like this one would there be before they reached Rodez? Bellet replaced the lens covers and threw a spotless cloth over the instrument. The carpenter stared out for a moment through the glowing aperture of the belfry and pointed to the horizon. "We are the last to see the sunset," he said proudly. Then, suddenly, he pricked an ear. "Listen!"

A strange silence invaded the tower. Bellet stopped stowing the instrument. Delambre and the carpenter stood still. Delambre could hear a welter of noises. The sound seemed to come in waves, as if breaking against the tower, but muffled, filtered by the distance and yet distinctly audible: there was the sound of a cart rolling over cobblestones, the neighing of a horse, children shouting, a squeaking gate, many marching feet. Though recognizable, the sounds seemed somehow unreal. The carpenter leaned forward as if to hear better. Delambre moved to his side. Down below, on the square, tiny people gathered in shifting groups as night fell.

<hr />

And so it was every night of that July until one day an unusual sound caught the attention of the astronomer and his assistant: the roll of a drum. Bellet ran to the wall to see what was going on. "Come see!" he shouted in a state of excitement, squirming about so much that he caused the scaffolding to shake.

"You're blocking the view! Go down and see what's going on instead of standing there like a lump in front of the equipment."

Bellet was already on his way down the ladder. Emerging from the darkness and silence of the nave into the light of the tumultuous square, he felt momentarily disoriented. Drums rolled again, and then came a metallic explosion of trumpets. The marchers were coming to the square.

Four men moved slowly forward holding a muslin banner stretched between two enormous standards. On it were clumsily inscribed the words "Liberty" and "Equality." Folds in the fabric partially concealed a third word, making it illegible.

Behind them came the mayor and various representatives of the local populace: men of substance in cotton breeches, peasants in wooden shoes, artisans in hemp tunics, merchants in leather shoes. They marched in silence but could not refrain from signaling to their families along the route, only to resume their sober composure immediately.

No one smiled when the mayor failed in his first two attempts to mount the podium that had been erected near the Tree of Liberty. Quickly he smoothed his wrinkled sash and then turned to face the crowd: "CITIZENS! THE FATHERLAND IS IN DANGER!"

This sentence, hurled like a thunderbolt into the cathedral-like silence, had an immediate effect. The crowd shuddered as if buffeted by a wave. Bellet felt welling up inside him an emotion he had never felt before, a mixture of resolution and melancholy. The crowd stood transfixed, and in its immobility there was something primitive, animal. "In danger!" That phrase, shrewdly chosen by the deputies of the Legislative Assembly who had drafted the speech, immediately aroused a sense of urgency in every member of the audience. Every man and every woman heard it as a call for help: the Nation was calling upon its citizens to save it.

The mayor took the text of a proclamation from his pocket and began to read:

> Substantial numbers of troops are advancing toward our borders. The enemies of freedom have taken arms against our Constitution. CITIZENS, THE FATHERLAND IS IN DANGER! To those honored to be the first to march in defense of all they hold dear, we say, Never forget that you are Frenchmen and that you are free. Let their fellow citizens look to the security of people and property on the home front. Let the people's magistrates remain vigilant. With the calm courage that is the mark of true strength, let everyone await the law's signal, and the fatherland will be saved!

Wiping his brow, the mayor relaxed as though in revealing the contents of the proclamation to his fellow citizens he had relieved himself of a terrible secret. With a sweeping gesture of his hand, he proudly announced that "this same proclamation is even now being read in every village in France."

This news was greeted by a huge ovation. In an instant the mounting tension was released. Everyone began talking at once. To know that at that very moment people in Marcilly, Plailly, Juilly, Mesnil, and Ermenonville were gathered on their village squares listening to the very same appeal, to feel the vast fabric of the nation being woven as they spoke, produced a kind of intoxication that made people's faces turn red and their eyes glisten. It was a tragic intoxication that said, "Give us liberty or give us death!"

The innkeeper set up a table and chair on the podium. A municipal official took the place of the mayor.

"Enlistment may now begin," the official announced, setting a large ledger on the table before him as he did. "Anyone who wishes to volunteer should come forward to enlist. No need to own a uniform. Men may go into battle in their work clothes."

One man was already standing in front of the podium, waiting quietly. He wanted to be the first to sign up, the first to leave for the front.

From his observatory, the astronomer had watched the procession march into the square. When the mayor began to speak, Delambre could hold out no longer. By the time the municipal councilor called for men to enlist, he had joined the crowd. When he failed to spot his assistant, he went looking for him. After wandering about for some time, he finally caught sight of him. Bellet was bending over the enlistment book, quill in hand, ready to sign. Delambre rushed over and grabbed his hand.

"Bellet, what are you doing? Are you mad? Wait, don't sign up. Not right away. I beg you to reconsider."

He took his assistant off to one side and spoke to him in a gentle voice. "I understand your feelings. You think that going off to fight is more important than finishing our work. With the fatherland in danger, how can we possibly stay up in our belfries making measurements as if nothing were happening—"

"What I think is that if we're invaded, there won't be anything left to measure. If the English take Dunkirk, your expedition is finished."

"*My* expedition?"

"That's not what I meant."

"Remember the words of Condorcet: 'For all nations and all ages!' Measurement is universal, it doesn't depend on events."

"But it does, whether you like it or not," Bellet replied. The two men faced each other.

"If Dunkirk falls," Delambre screamed, "if Perpignan falls, we'll go right on working. We can't stop."

❖

August came. On the square in Dammartin there were far fewer men than before, and in the inn as well the crowd had thinned. One morning Delambre, tired of waiting for the air to clear so that he could see the target in Montmartre that he had spent so much time searching for, made up his mind: since the target refused to be seen by day, they would observe by night. Bellet would set out immediately for Montmartre, and when night fell he would light a specially designed reflector lamp so that Delambre, perched in his bell tower, could make his measurement.

"All right, then," the astronomer remarked. "We're agreed that you'll light the lamp two hours after sunset. Not a moment before. If all goes well, I should be able to see it at an azimuth of approximately—" The rest of his sentence was swallowed up in a monstrous din. A vigorous tug on the bell rope beneath their feet had set the bells tolling, much to the consternation of Delambre, who was beginning to find them unbearable.

Bellet was loading the reflectors into the carriage when his attention was drawn to a crowd gathering in the square. A man, bare-chested beneath his leather apron, had climbed onto a bench and was addressing the villagers in stentorian tones: "On me the threats have the opposite effect. It seems like if you scratch the Tuileries or rub the king's noggin a bit too hard, the Austrians and the Prussians—" He struggled to find the right words. "What was it they wrote?" he asked the young men in wire-rim glasses who stood beside him. The man took a newspaper from a sack of the sort that hawkers used to carry their wares. "They wrote"— he had trouble finding the sentence—"oh, yes, here it is: they wrote that 'they will exact a vengeance that will be remembered forever.'"

"Right, that's it," the speaker resumed. "Remembered forever."

At this point the hawker climbed up on the bench himself, unfolded his newspaper, and read out loud. "They say that the citizens of every French village, city, and town must immediately surrender to the Austrian and Prussian troops. That anyone who tries to defend himself will be made an example of. That houses will be demolished and burned and that Paris will be occupied and turned upside down."

The man in the leather apron exploded. "Did you hear that? The more I hear, the angrier I feel!"

Bellet practically snatched the newspaper from the man's hands. It was the *Chronique de Paris.* The banner headline read: "ULTIMATUM FROM THE COMMANDER-IN-CHIEF OF THE PRUSSIAN ARMIES. *Brunswick's Incredible Threats!*" As he read he tried to remain calm. Immediate surrender . . . Paris occupied and turned upside down. He was so tense that he tore the paper. If we are defeated, he thought, France will be destroyed. He knew how powerful the foreign armies were. He also knew that most French officers had deserted and that the troops were short of weapons and ammunition. The words of the municipal official still rang in his ears: men may go to battle in their working clothes. Which meant that there were not even enough uniforms to go around. To judge by the volunteers who had left for the front, there could be no doubt about the outcome of the war. None of them had so much as held a saber or fired a cannon, and they were being sent into battle against professional soldiers! Bellet's heart fell at the idea that everything he had believed in and hoped for might be destroyed. Tears came to his eyes: tears of helplessness.

As he walked away, he heard the speaker address the crowd once more. "And do you know who's in command of the émigrés fighting at Brunswick's side?" Bellet turned around. "Louis Joseph, the former prince of Condé!" the man shouted, bearing down on every word. "The count of Dammartin, lord of our village!"

Everyone knew the count. As recently as four years ago he was still lord in these parts, and when his carriage had passed through the village on the way to his castle, people had bowed down and doffed their hats. Angry shouts were heard, shouts of fury, rage, spite, and shame. The very name Dammartin had been linked to the name Condé for centuries, and the disgrace would fall on the village and its inhabitants.

❧

It took five hours to get to Paris. As Bellet climbed into the berlin, a man called out to him. "Are you going to Paris?" It was a fellow he had often seen around the inn.

"I have to be in Montmartre by this evening."

"They say that the people of the *faubourgs* are going to march on the Tuileries to let the king know what they think. I'd like to join them, but I'd have a devil of a time getting there on foot."

The man sat down beside Bellet. The coach began to move. A woman came running toward them.

"Take this, Louis," she said, holding out a loaf of bread to the passenger. "They say that in Paris there's nothing left to eat."

The man leaned out and took the bread.

"Don't worry. I'll be back tomorrow." Then he turned to Bellet. "That's Louise. I'm Louis. Obviously we were made for each other. But what am I supposed to do now with a name like Louis? I'll have to change it, because that's the king's name. So what do you do for a living?"

"I'm an engineer."

"I'm a saddle maker." He sat silently for a while, thinking. Then he said, "Heavy rigs. Tough saddles. Sturdy harnesses. Beasts of burden are my business, and you can bet they'll be around for awhile. In Senlis there were three saddle makers. Only one's left. They used to think of themselves as top of the line. Fancy horses, that's what they dealt with."

A rhythmic clacking sound cut him off. In a field alongside the road a strange machine was moving through a cloud of thatch. It was a kind of mill, pulled by a single animal. Bellet ordered the carriage to stop.

The machine contained two large, rapidly rotating cylinders covered with small blades. A small boy led the animal, while a man followed along behind directing the hay into a hopper that collected one enormous bale after another. Bellet had never seen anything like it. The noise was intense. Under the blazing sun the man looked like a wicker mannequin, his body a mass of chaff, stubble, and hair all mixed together. The bale was forced toward the cylinders, grabbed by a large pair of jaws, and instantly chopped. Just below this, grain flowed crackling into a milling device, which ground it to a specified degree of fineness.

"That's a reaper," Louis remarked when Bellet returned to the carriage. He held out the loaf of bread, from which he had already taken a bite. "It's the latest thing. Seems that it comes from England. They're using it on land that used to belong to the Condés."

Upon hearing once again the name Condé, Bellet felt a surge of rage. He was angry that he had listened to Delambre and not enlisted. "So you didn't join the volunteers either?" he asked suddenly. Louis bowed his head and mumbled an answer. "I'd've gone, but I have three little ones, and the missus didn't want me to. How about you?"

"Me?" Bellet stammered. "I'm in the same boat."

Louis's eyes lit up for a moment. "Your missus didn't want you to go either?"

"In a manner of speaking," Bellet answered with a smile.

Darkness invaded the bell tower. Leaning against the opening, Delambre gazed off in the direction of Paris. A moonless night had descended on the capital. This was the moment.

Pointing the telescope toward Montmartre and the spot where Bellet was supposed to light his lamp, he began his observations. Nothing! No fire, not a sign of life. Surprised, he checked his instrument and reset the spotting scope. Everything was as it was supposed to be, but Montmartre was still invisible. No doubt Bellet had been delayed. Perhaps it had taken him longer than expected to set up the equipment.

Several times during the night Bellet returned to his instrument, but still he saw nothing. Not a trace of light! Annoyed, he brusquely swept the horizon. A brilliant light appeared in the eyepiece. The astronomer had never seen anything like it. The light was unmistakably real and emanating from the center of Paris. Delambre stood for a long time with his eye riveted to the instrument. Finally, he decided that figuring out the cause of the light was beyond him, and he went off to bed.

After a while the disturbance outside became so loud that he woke up. Cursing, Delambre turned over and tried to muffle the sound of voices by sticking his head underneath the pillow. Finally he gave up and opened his eyes. Despite the curtains sun was pouring into the room. He got up, pulled back the curtain, and opened the shutter.

A crowd of fifty or so villagers had gathered around the mail coach. Others came running through the narrow streets to join them. Everyone was excited. A man passing below his window shouted up to Delambre: "It's the Tuileries! The Swiss fired on the crowd. Thousands of people are dead. They say that the king is prisoner in the Temple. The Tuileries burned all through the night."

Delambre closed the window and pulled the curtains. As he settled back into bed, his eyes half closed, he muttered, "I hope it wasn't Bellet who started the fire."

❦

The next day the astronomer began to worry about his assistant's absence, even though he had been told that dozens of coaches had been held up at the gates of Paris. He passed the collegiate church without so much as a glance up at the steeple and went directly to his room to read the *Chronique de Paris*. As usual, the front page contained a report on the meeting of the Assembly written by Condorcet.

> Night of August 9–10. During the night the tocsin was sounded. The Assembly met at midnight. It heard petitioners from several Paris sections say that people were in an uproar because they believed that the court had gone over to the counterrevolution. A municipal official announced that the king, queen, and royal family wished to appear. The king entered, followed by his wife, his son, his daughter, and Mme Elisabeth. He stood next to President Vergniaud and said, "I have come before you to prevent a great crime, and with you I feel that I am safe."
>
> M. Carnot asked how the Assembly planned to deliberate, since the Constitution stated that there could be no deliberation while the king was present. It was decided that the king and his family would move to the stall normally occupied by the Assembly scribe, which is separated from the main hall by a grille. Suddenly cannon fire was heard from the direction of the palace.
>
> The king stated that he had ordered the Swiss not to fire. The cannon fire intensified. It was accompanied by a good deal of musket fire as well. The king, his family, and the deputies listened in silence. A speaker asked that persons and property be placed under the protection of the law. This motion was greeted with applause and promptly passed. Another speaker asked his colleagues to proclaim *Vive la liberté! Vive l'égalité!* All the deputies rose and did as they were asked, with their arms raised to heaven. It was announced that the palace had been forcibly entered.

Delambre feverishly turned the page and devoured another article that recounted what had happened at the palace:

> The awakening of the people was awesome, and for once it is possible to say without fear of exaggeration that they rose as one. This was not a rebellion that could be put down with a few volleys but a general insurrection, a real revolution in the revolution, which nothing could resist.

By nine o'clock anyone or anything capable of carrying weapons was headed for the Tuileries. Citizens were saying out loud that they wanted the king toppled from his throne. No one expressed any intention of doing him harm. Grenadiers in two notoriously royalist battalions had made it known to their cannoneers that they would be shot if they refused to fire on the people. The same grenadiers rallied the Swiss Guards and told them to fire on anyone who moved.

No sooner had the king reached the Assembly than the carnage began. The Swiss fired from the windows and even the ventilators. Unarmed and poorly armed citizens fled. Brave guardsmen from Marseilles and Brest rallied, and Parisians, mostly from the Saint-Antoine and Saint-Marceau districts, marched behind them. Cannon fire was answered with even fiercer fire. National guardsmen were seen racing after cannonballs that had been fired from the Tuileries and firing them back at the palace. When the marchers reached the Carrousel, they were hit with heavy fire. Royal guardsmen lying in ambush in their barracks fired volley after volley into the crowd, killing hundreds of people. Soldiers from Marseilles pressed forward and hurled sacks of powder through openings into the barracks, setting off explosions. A fire broke out immediately, producing great quantities of smoke.

In the end the defeated Swiss Guards laid down their arms, but not before a great many *fédérés,* Marseillais, and Parisians had lost their lives. Despair was at its height, and except for a few Swiss Guards who were spirited away from the scene, all were massacred. Many were taken to the communal offices and executed.

The Carrousel burned all night long, and if not for the efforts of the National Guard the fire would have spread throughout the palace. Within a short time the Tuileries were invaded. The furniture was carried off to the various sections of the city. Thieves were executed, but in the confusion some innocent people paid for the crimes of others. A number of precious items were saved. Special mention must be made of the unselfish action of M. Collard de Trone, a cannoneer of the Petits-Pères and a native of Caen. After discovering the sum of 1,500 louis in the queen's desk, he deposited the funds with the Commune. He also found two letters addressed to the queen, which we will publish in the coming days.

Statues of Louis XVI, Louis XV, and even Henri II were toppled. Three citizens were killed when a bust of Louis XV fell on them.

Delambre's head ached. He got up and walked about the room, at once relieved and anxious. Relieved as one sometimes is when a long-gathering storm finally arrives, and anxious because he never imagined that it would arrive with such violent force. He returned to the newspaper: "The telescope mounted on the walls of the military school observatory by the astronomer Lalande was seriously damaged by men who had entered the building in search of arms." A brief notice printed just below also caught his eye: "Handsome two-room apartment, very nicely furnished, with a superb view of the river, suitable for a single man and his servant. Also appropriate for a deputy. Apply to M. Gifon, hardware dealer at 11, quai de la Mégisserie, at the corner of l'Arche-Marion, near the Pont-Neuf."

"I'm not a deputy," Delambre thought, "but I would prefer that apartment to the one I have now on the rue de Paradis. A view of the Seine, two rooms, suitable for a bachelor. If my salary is increased, I could live on the river opposite the quai de Conti and Condorcet." And then he fell asleep.

❧

Bellet finally returned two days later, having been detained all that time at the gates of Paris. Since the Montmartre tower could not be used, Delambre decided to use the dome of the Pantheon instead.

The green berlin was about to leave Dammartin-en-Goële when Bellet noticed a woman in black crossing the street. It was Louise. She had waited for her husband in vain: Louis the saddle maker was among the thousands who had died on the night of August 10.

4

Before leaving Dammartin, Delambre had dispatched the carpenter to build a target platform on the old Montjay tower a few leagues from the village. But he soon returned—much too soon. Even before he could unpack his tools, the citizens of Montjay had gathered and ordered him to stop work. The law had been respected: the townspeople had obtained a formal injunction before confronting the workman with their demand. Delambre took this legal document and immediately set out for Meaux. But times had changed: the authorities no longer had the power or in some cases even the desire to restrain the populace. Delambre was told that it was no longer possible to issue orders to the people. One could only assure them that there was no cause for alarm and urge that the work be allowed to proceed. Delambre was given a letter filled with such assurances for the mayor of Montjay, and the curé agreed to read it before his Sunday sermon. This proved to be a mistake: it had been some time since anyone took as Gospel what priests said from the pulpit. The fact that the priest read the letter only stiffened resistance to Delambre's wishes. The people of Montjay enlisted the support of other nearby communes, such as Lagny, and promised to answer force with force. Their agitation mounted as the situation in Paris grew tenser by the day and as the surrounding countryside became increasingly nervous.

Anxiety was the order of the day, and anxiety engendered suspicion. Suspects were everywhere. But suspicion was not indiscriminate: some people were suspect, others not.

In Paris, for example, a man named Chappe erected with his brother's help a curious contraption atop the hill of Ménilmontant in the Parc Saint-Fargeau. It consisted of a wooden frame with shutters that could be opened and closed at will. The brothers claimed that the purpose of this device was to communicate over long distances. But this only begged the question. With whom were they communicating? And what was the content of their communication? And the answers to these questions were obvious: they were transmitting intelligence to allies of the queen who were preparing to destroy Paris. Brunswick's angry words still resounded in everyone's ears. The "optical telegraph" was immediately set ablaze, and although there was a move to toss the brothers Chappe into the flames as well, they managed to escape with their lives.

From similar causes, similar effects: Delambre and Bellet were not permitted to carry out their measurement in Montjay. And the only reason why the mob didn't set fire to their equipment was that they had not been allowed to set it up in the first place.

<hr/>

Since Montjay was now unavailable, another site would have to be found. Thus far that morning our travelers had encountered four barricades. Access to each new village was blocked by a dozen men, mostly armed with pikes. Some wore the regional peasant dress, while others were in uniform, either the official uniform of the National Guard or the unofficial one of the sansculottes: a brown cloak with a red collar over homespun trousers. Every chest sported a cockade, either pinned to the man's jacket or fastened to his blouse. Emotions ran high. Everywhere municipal councils were meeting in permanent session. Delambre and Bellet were hauled before these local assemblies and asked to show their passports and explain the nature of their mission. They were then asked to produce their travel permits, which they did reluctantly every time because they knew what would happen next. As if in a nightmare the same scene repeated itself in village after village. It was similar to what Méchain had experienced two months earlier, as Delambre knew from a letter his colleague had sent to the commission.

A municipal official took his pass. "The authorities request that assistance be provided to Monsieur Delambre in procuring wood and other materials needed for the construction of targets: poles, reflectors, and scaffolds."

"Scaffold! He said scaffold!" The mob began to cackle, and the laughter was punctuated by the loud noise of rifle butts pounding the ground. As pikes danced above his head, Delambre tried to retreat. The mayor, not amused, shot a reproachful glance at the man who had blurted out the jibe and then resumed reading. "The authorities further request that assistance be provided in setting up targets atop belfries, towers, and castles. They also ask that Monsieur Delambre and his assistants be allowed to proceed with their observations undisturbed and that the structures they erect be left intact." Suddenly, a sansculotte who was reading the text over the mayor's shoulder, shouted: "But it's signed *Louis!*" A groan went up from the mob, which closed in on the travelers in a menacing way.

"But it's the Assembly that voted to approve the expedition!" Bellet protested.

"It's the signature that counts! And anyway we accept only passes from this district," the mayor replied.

Unable to contain himself a moment longer, Delambre exploded. "Our passports are in order. We are on an official mission. I was sent by the Academy."

"The 'Cademy? The 'Cademy! There is no more 'Cademy. We're all equal now!" the sansculotte angrily exclaimed.

A few moments later, however, they were allowed to proceed on their way, though not without dire warnings of far worse troubles to come.

"What is that roof over there on the horizon that looks like a pyramid?" Bellet asked as he surveyed the countryside. It was the Château de Belle-Assise, which as it happens was conveniently oriented and nicely hidden in the forest. The two travelers headed for the castle, which they found empty and silent. Unnoticed, they were able to carry out their measurements in peace.

With the instruments safely packed in their cases once again and the baggage loaded, the two travelers were about to leave the castle when a detachment of National Guardsmen from Lagny arrived to search the premises, where arms had allegedly been stored. Instead of arms they found the green berlin with the astronomer and his assistant inside. The two men were recognized, and with the incident at Montjay still fresh in everyone's mind, they were detained and forced to walk across the countryside in a driving rain.

The troops and their prisoners quietly made their way through the woods. Night had fallen, and lightning illuminated the sky.

"A hell of a storm!" shouted one of the guards. "And the hay still out in the fields."

Everyone fell silent. "Too bad you're not a couple of pretty girls," one of the soldiers ventured. When the others stared at him in silent disapproval, he stammered, "All I meant was that there used to be a custom in our neck of the woods, over by Lagny. If a fellow met a girl alone after dark in the open country, outside the city limits, he could force her to make love, and the girl had no right to protest. That's the way it used to be."

"You hear that, Bellet?" Delambre called out to his invisible companion.

"I always knew that we were lucky," a hoarse voice replied. Bellet was soaking wet. There hadn't been time for him to grab his overcoat. The sansculotte beside him removed his cape and threw it roughly over Bellet's shoulders. The recipient of this gift tried to shrug it off.

"Take it, I'm telling you. I'm used to the rain."

The sansculotte took off his soaking-wet cap and wrung it over Bellet's head. As water cascaded down his cheeks, he laughed loudly. "I never bathe any other way," he said.

Everyone burst out laughing, including Delambre. Everyone, that is, except Bellet.

"You're not in prison," they were told upon arriving at the Auberge de l'Ours in Lagny. "Just protective custody." Nevertheless, two guards were posted at their door throughout the night. To protect them or to prevent them from fleeing?

Bellet, his hair still wet, lay stretched out on the bed in a nightgown borrowed from the innkeeper. His eyes were shut tight. Delambre felt that he must alert Paris to their situation at once. But whom could he notify? The Assembly? The Commission on Weights and Measures? Or Condorcet himself, who in the days since the Tenth of August had become one of the most important men in the country? Delambre preferred not to travel to Paris himself, because he felt that everyone there would insist on postponing the expedition until later. Once operations were called off, however, it was unlikely that they would resume any time soon.

Bellet sat bolt upright. "They've requisitioned our horses, confiscated our instruments, and seized our carriage. God knows where our papers are. And I have a fever."

"You don't have a fever," Delambre insisted. His tone was that of a man for whom even a white lie was intolerable.

The door opened, and the guards came in with trays of food. Delambre, recognizing the sansculotte who had challenged him on the subject of the Academy, went straight up to the man and said, "Sorry to disappoint you, citizen, but the Academy has not been abolished." At first the man seemed at a loss for words, but eventually he found the perfect comeback: "If it hasn't been abolished yet, it will be, you can rest assured of that. So sleep well, citizen. Tomorrow is another day."

"Sleep well? The way things are going we'll soon be in the Conciergerie, where we'll have all the time in the world to sleep," Bellet muttered.

In the course of their travels they had witnessed the growing tension in the country and seen fear take hold of the population. In less than two weeks the military situation had become critical. On August 16 the Army of the North had been forced to retreat. On the 19th, Lafayette, once the idol of Paris, had gone over to the enemy. On the 23rd, Longwy had surrendered, leaving the east undefended. On the 30th, Verdun had fallen, clearing the way for the Prussians to enter Paris. Treason! People saw it everywhere, and they were not always wrong.

Imprisoned royalists were known to be rejoicing at the approach of the enemy armies. The powder keg was smoldering, and it wouldn't take much to set it off.

As Delambre and Bellet sank into sleep at the Auberge de l'Ours in Lagny, Paris, just a few leagues away, was enduring one of the darkest nights in its history. Prisoners at the Conciergerie had their throats slit, others at the Châtelet were put to the sword, and still others were massacred in the prisons of La Force and L'Abbaye. Heads were again paraded through the streets on pikes. The date was September 3, 1792. On that day Paris was hideous, as hideous as it had been two centuries earlier on the morning of Saint Bartholomew's Day after a night of massacres ordered by the ancestors of the very people who were today being murdered with comparable savagery.

Who committed these atrocities? A few hundred men, five hundred at most. Like the garbage that collects in the eddies of a brisk current, they found each other on their own. No one supplied them with arms. Some may only have dreamed of committing such crimes and were horrified to learn that a massacre had actually been carried out. But a massacre it was.

"Already the pools of blood spilled by this pack of brutes are polluting a revolution whose goals were once prosperity and justice," thought the mayor of Lagny when, at daybreak, he received the sinister news.

Aware that someone was shaking him, Delambre awoke in a fright. The mayor urged him to dress quickly. Bellet took longer to open his eyes, but the mayor seemed so keen to have them out of there that he dressed even more rapidly than Delambre. People gathered in the street and then fanned out to reconnoiter the highway. The mayor led Delambre and his assistant to a hiding place and advised them to stay put. If he failed to return soon, he said, they should try to escape. But he did return and took them to their carriage.

❖

They hitched up their horses and drove with the mayor to Saint-Denis. "By nightfall," the mayor told them, "you will either be free men with new passports or you will be in prison. But everything will be done according to law."

Two mounted gendarmes escorted them through the swelling crowd. The carriage approached the basilica, which contained the remains of Dagobert and Saint Louis, Philip the Bold and Philip the Fair, John the Good and Francis I. But the church was surrounded by a sea of people, and it became increasingly difficult to make any headway through the crowd.

"Death to aristocrats!" "Long live the Nation!" "Hang the traitors!" Faces were pressed to the windows. The square was chockablock with people: soldiers from every corner of France, dead tired and asleep in the dirt during a brief rest stop on their march to the borders; confused volunteers, urged to fight but still awaiting arms that never seemed to arrive; and countless inmates of the workhouse, beggars rounded up on the streets of the capital and obliged to spin cotton for the state. Wild rumors ran through the crowd, which broke up into small groups only to coalesce, denser than ever, a moment later.

With a final shudder the berlin ground to a halt, unable to proceed.

The mayor loaded his pistol, hid it under his jacket, and donned his tricolor sash. Then he set out to seek reinforcements, but only after ordering his two passengers not to leave the carriage for any reason. "Here at least you'll be safe."

He opened the door, forcing the crowd back, and stood on the carriage step. "Citizens," he said, "these men are under the protection of the public authorities. I will not allow atrocities to be committed here like the ones that have polluted Paris and dishonored the nation."

He climbed down into the crowd. His tricolor sash was swallowed up by the soldiers' blue uniforms. A man leaped forward: "People everywhere are using patriotic costumes as a disguise to protect traitors. They deceive citizens by pretending to speak in their name. This is a royalist district, a *feuillant* district. Don't trust anyone!"

Another voice chimed in. "A hundred rifles!" it shouted. "A hundred rifles." Last night, the man explained, on the road to Lagny, a carriage full of aristocrats had been searched and more than a hundred rifles had been found. He then pointed at the berlin. "And this one—this one is probably also full of rifles."

Two men immediately set about unloading the baggage. Just as the case containing the instruments was about to be forced open, Delambre leaped out of the carriage. "Don't touch that crate. The instruments inside are precious."

"Precious?"

"I mean precious—for science. You can open it, but be careful!"

The crowd pressed close, curious to see what was inside the crate. Lenoir's instruments, still brand new, had never looked more sumptuous, especially the long telescope with its gleaming gold fittings.

"A military field-glass!"

"No, an astronomical telescope," Delambre corrected.

"A fine gift for Brunswick and Condé!"

Delambre protested that they were scientists, that they had no intention of leaving the country and were on their way to Dunkirk for the purpose of doing scientific work.

"Dunkirk! That's where we're headed," shouted a group of volunteers. "Come along and fight with us."

It was decided that the prisoners should be interrogated on the spot. Delambre took a step backward, Bellet opened the door of the berlin, and a gendarme cocked his weapon and aimed it at the crowd with a warning that the two passengers were under the protection of the authorities and no one should lay a hand on them.

"Quick, Bellet, the circle!" Delambre shouted. "Take out the circle."

At the same time a detachment of national guards with rifles on their shoulders hastened down a nearby street toward the square. In front of the troop, marching almost double-time, was the mayor of Lagny, who urged the soldiers to hasten their step.

Meanwhile, back at the carriage, another gendarme had come to the assistance of his colleague. The crowd had pulled back enough to allow the repeating circle to be set up on its sturdy stand. Bellet tightened the last screws.

Delambre then lectured the crowd at the top of his lungs. "Nowadays everybody knows that the Earth is round, almost spherical in shape. If you were to take a thread and stretch it from one pole to the other, that would be a meridian. Beneath the feet of each and every citizen passes a meridian. Just as every citizen is equal to every other, so, too, is every meridian. We have chosen to measure the one that passes through Paris." He then pointed to the repeating circle. "This is a new measuring instrument. It is the most precise instrument of its kind ever built."

A young man wearing trousers and an ample white blouse stepped forward from the group of volunteers. In his hand he carried an old rifle with a bayonet, identical to the rifles carried by his comrades. "I'm a surveyor by trade. Measurement is something I know. I have nothing against these citizens, but I can tell you that I've never seen an instrument like this. In any case, you don't use a thing like that for measuring distance, that I'm sure of. You use a surveyor's chain."

"Hooray for the surveyor! Kill the fraud who claims to be a scientist!"

Dismayed by these words, the surveyor tried to make himself heard above the din. "I didn't say they were traitors."

Upon hearing shouts at the far end of the square, the mayor of Lagny broke into a run. Followed by the detachment of guardsmen, the mayor was astonished, upon reaching the carriage, to find Delambre, pencil in hand, drawing blue triangles that intersected green circles on either side of a broad red line drawn across a map of France nailed to the back of the berlin. The red line represented the meridian of Paris, the green circles the stations chosen for the measurements.

"Saint-Denis is here," Delambre announced. "And up here is Dunkirk. Way down here, this point, is Perpignan. Even farther down is

Barcelona, in Spain." The shouting had stopped; people in the crowd were now paying close attention. "When you want to measure great distances, you can't use a surveyor's chain. The problem here is not to measure a field but to calculate the distance from Dunkirk to Perpignan. In other words, to determine the length of France."

Someone shouted, "The Prussians are in Longwy, the uhlans in Verdun. If they keep it up, there won't be anything left for you to measure."

Delambre walked over to the repeating circle. "With this instrument, we can measure angles, and from angles we can calculate distances. This is what we plan to do. First, we'll locate a series of elevated points: peaks, steeples, and towers scattered about the meridian. Using those points, we'll establish a series of triangles."

Bellet now held up a long flat rule, or measuring stick, and showed it to the crowd. "Then, with this other instrument, we'll measure one distance, just one, a 'baseline.'"

"Now that at least looks something like a surveyor's chain!" the surveyor gleefully exclaimed.

"It is one, in fact, but it's more precise," Delambre remarked. "If you know two angles of a triangle and one side, you can calculate the other two sides. And proceeding from one triangle to the next, we can then figure out the length of the meridian."

Delambre released the telescopes on the repeating circle. The gendarmes lowered their weapons, and the mayor of Lagny smiled.

"The two telescopes are independent. You aim one at one target, the other at another target," Delambre explained. He then signaled to the surveyor to come over and try it out for himself. "Here, have a look."

The surveyor hesitated. Urged on by his comrades, he cautiously bent toward the instrument and aimed the telescope at the basilica's spire, which stood out clearly against the sky.

Everything looked blurry!

"You have to focus it," Delambre whispered in a voice that only the surveyor could hear.

5

At that very moment, three hundred leagues from the howling crowd around Saint-Denis, Méchain, submerged in the silence of the Catalonian mountains, aimed his telescope at the sierra of Montseny with consummate skill. Quickly, efficiently, precisely, he manipulated the instrument with an astonishing dexterity that Tranchot, seated in a niche in the rock nearby, quietly admired. An improperly secured barometer began to teeter. With one quick motion Méchain caught it and prevented it from toppling over. It was impossible not to admire the change in him. Was this the same man who had been ready to abandon the whole mission just two months ago? He seemed to move with newfound freedom and grace, and his face had taken on a handsome tan. Indeed, he was looking more and more like the natives of the mountainous region in which they were now working.

Carpeted with thick forest, the sierra of Montseny stood out from the surrounding mountains by virtue of its twin peaks, which seemed not to rise side by side so much as to face each other in endless dialogue. Captain Gonzales sauntered over and asked the astronomer if he knew the name of the peak at which he had just aimed his telescope. Méchain nodded. It was Homa-Morta. Gonzales had just come from Barcelona. The tents would be ready within the week, he proudly announced. Méchain had sketched a design, and Gonzales had found a man who could do the work more quickly and at lower cost than anyone else. Then it would no longer be necessary to leave the summit every night. They would sleep at the observation station. No more filthy rooms, needless effort, and wasted time. Come nightfall the members of the expedition would no longer be obliged to risk their lives on treacherous mountain paths. Méchain complimented Gonzales on his quick work.

A few days later the finished tent was hauled up the mountainside. Soon it could be seen silhouetted against the Catalonian sky: a cone topped by a large sphere that served as a target for their instruments. A long wooden center pole was set vertically like a mast, held up by ribs affixed to its top end and covered with bleached canvas. The lower end was trimmed with a wide band of ribbed twill to keep out the wind. Three additional poles were attached to a circular base. The bottom of the canvas was fastened to the base by means of rings and stretched with iron stakes.

◈

If you want doors to be opened to you in a remote Catalonian village, you had best not travel in the company of two French scientists and an officer of the king of Spain. Castilian was the official language of Spain, the language of the king and his government. But there was no point addressing a villager or peasant in that tongue: the man's face would immediately go blank, and he would turn his back on you and walk away. When Gonzales spoke to people in Catalan, however, things began to happen. As the captain was only too happy to point out, the people of the region referred to God not as "Dios" but as "Deu." So "Deu" it was. Gonzales's help was therefore indispensable when it came to negotiating with the villagers, hiring porters, and discussing the day's chores with the workmen. What is more, the captain knew every nook and cranny of the region. Méchain therefore prized his assistance, even though he had been sent by the Spanish authorities to keep an eye on them. In his zeal for science, however, Gonzales soon forgot his political mission.

In Spain, French was looked upon as the language of learning and good manners. Gonzales was a nobleman with a keen interest in astronomy and therefore perfectly at ease in French, which he spoke almost without accent. Had it not been for his inimitable way of pronouncing the letter *s,* he might have been mistaken for a Parisian native.

◈

As the sun sank, Méchain began to move more rapidly. At the end of each day he always went into a frenzy in the hope of cheating time of one more measurement before nightfall. Notre-Dame-del-Monte, Puig-se-Calm. Each measurement consisted of a series of operations, always carried out in the same order. Méchain took obvious satisfaction in his ability to move seamlessly from one operation to the next: aim and secure the first telescope, aim and secure the second, release the first, rotate the circle. This series of actions might be repeated ten, twenty, even a hundred times, for repetition was the very principle of the "repeating circle," its simple but ingenious secret. As its inventor, the Chevalier de la Borda, had discovered, the more often the measurement was repeated, the more precise it became: by multiplying the number of measurements, one could divide the magnitude of the error.

A short distance away Gonzales was talking to Tranchot. Méchain tried not to let himself become distracted, but the captain's slow drawl made him forget what he was doing.

"People from hereabouts will tell you that a very long time ago the sierra was covered by a forest so thick that it was impenetrable. Each year, when the good weather returned, young people would try their luck, but none ever returned. At the foot of the mountain stood a tiny village, and in that village there were two friends, one of whom suggested that they should venture into the forest together. Soon they set out to do just that. One of the men, who claimed to know the way, went first. Every night he climbed to the top of the highest tree, took his bearings in relation to the stars, and decided what route to follow the next day. The other, a trusting fellow, followed. They penetrated deeper into the forest than anyone had gone before. Then, one night, there were clouds, and things seemed not quite right. The stars—how shall I put it?—seemed not to be in the right places anymore. It was impossible to take any bearings. The scout climbed down from his perch. Would he alert his companion? He knew perfectly well that they were lost, that he had made an error. But where? When? He said nothing, held his peace, and continued on his way.

"Weeks later, the village was awakened by shouts. Everyone rushed outside. It was a ghost—no, a man, staggering out of the forest on his last legs. The villagers drew back to let him pass. Finally he collapsed in a heap by the edge of the fountain in the village square. It was one of the two explorers: not the scout, the one who knew that they had gone astray, but the other, the one who followed. How had he managed to survive and find his way home? The mystery remains unsolved to this day. The man lay stretched out on the ground, apparently dead. The villagers carried him to his home. In fact he was still breathing. In his delirium he told the whole story. Ultimately he recovered but never spoke again. Had he gone mute or chosen to remain silent?

"The next summer it was very hot in the valley. It must have been a torrid August, like this one. Suddenly the entire forest burst into flame. No one had ever seen anything like it. All the people in the village—men, women, and children—gathered in the square and stared, transfixed. But to everyone's surprise the mute was nowhere to be found. They looked all over for him, but he had disappeared. A small boy said that he had seen the man enter the forest. No one ever saw him again.

"The forest burned for days on end. The mountain had vanished into a vast cloud of smoke. One night the blaze ended. The next morning, the villagers could again see the mountain. It was completely bare, and at the very top rose two peaks that faced each other, still enveloped in swirls of smoke. Moments later a voice broke the silence. It was the voice of an old peasant: 'That's the Homa-Morta,' the voice said. 'The man who died of silence.'"

Suddenly Méchain turned toward them. "Why two peaks?" he asked in a tone that was almost aggressive. Speaking as slowly as ever, Gonzales responded. "One stands for error, the other for truth, but we don't know which is which!" This was followed by silence until Méchain shouted "Signature, signature!" Tranchot and Gonzales rose in response, but rather reluctantly because both remained under the legend's spell.

◆

Every page of the expedition's record book was signed by each member of the expedition or by outside witnesses enlisted to certify that the recorded measurements had indeed been performed as described. No subsequent changes were permitted. The signatures authenticated the records to the scientific community and to all posterity. Signing the book had become a ritual, and Méchain took steps to make sure that it retained its sacred character. This evening ritual marked the end of each day's work. Affixed to often incomprehensible pages of calculations and observations, the scrawled names reminded everyone of the mission's goals, including the porters and workmen who often witnessed the ceremony. The signing bestowed meaning on their daily exertions. Everyone was aware that the signatures radically transformed the status of the document.

On this particular evening, Gonzales, Tranchot, and Méchain, alone at the summit, affixed their names to the daily log. The next day they went their separate ways. Tranchot headed straight up the sierra of Montseny to set up the next target. Gonzales, laden with baggage and instruments, led a small caravan to Puig-se-Calm, where a new base camp was to be built. Meanwhile, Méchain headed off to Montserrat to reconnoiter the area and lay out the triangles to be measured next.

❧

Montserrat: serrated mountain, a colossal block of granite sawed through by the waters of the Llobregat. Like an accomplished sculptor, the river had lovingly sculpted the rock, forming perfect columns, fingers pointing skyward to form a stone hand of many joints. Through a clearing in the woods Méchain caught sight of it, poking at the sky.

After parking the berlin and leaving his horse with a groom, Méchain set out on foot, at first accompanied by groups of Benedictine monks on their way to the abbey. At the crossroads the monks left him and quickly vanished, however, and Méchain found himself alone. A gentle slope took him away from the village, but soon he came to a staircase so steep that it made him dizzy.

Hundreds of stairs! How many pardons for how many sins were granted to the penitents who cut those stairs into the rock? The infinite is not of this world: the staircase did eventually end. It had taken him from the surface of the earth to the middle of the sky, or so Méchain thought for a moment, until he saw the rest of the path ahead of him: a terrifying trail skirting a bottomless crevasse. But there was no other choice. Within a few steps he had caught his breath and plunged into semidarkness. Beneath his feet the precipice dropped off so sharply that it made his heart pound, while the sun caused the ominous row of granite needles above to glow bloodred. All around him rose crenellated walls topped by bunkers and flanked by impregnable bastions. He felt as though he had wandered into the ruins of a gigantic medieval fortress. He could have kicked himself for not starting out sooner. Fragments of the legend that Gonzales had recounted came back to him unbidden, leaving him with a vaguely uneasy feeling. Something in the story of the Homa-Morta had bothered him. Was it the silence of the scout? The fire? The unacknowledged error? Something startled him. A sound! Was it an animal? Boars were said to roam these hills. At last he spotted a tiny structure embedded in the rock ahead. It hewed so close to the shape of the mountain that if not for his preternaturally keen eyesight he might have missed it altogether. So these were the celebrated hermitages he had heard so much about! Anyone who would live at these altitudes would have had to adopt the ways of the birds. He would have had to soar! Just ahead, standing in the scrub and almost one with the landscape, a wiry old man with an enormous snow-white beard stared suspiciously at the importunate intruder. A moment later the dark shadow had vanished, swallowed up by the rock. Méchain hurried on. He was a good hiker. Soon he reached San Geronimo, the highest point of Montserrat. A tiny chapel almost filled the flat summit. Méchain dropped his knapsack and sat down. When he looked up, a dizzying spectacle awaited him: a colossal organ of stone whose gleaming pipes reached all the way to heaven. Now and then the wind, skimming the cliffs, emitted a crude music, a sound like that produced by blowing into a conch shell. Méchain sat there for an hour or two, forgetting the purpose of his journey. He spent a good long while admiring the vast and sparkling Mediterranean, which seemed almost close enough to touch. All at once the chill of dusk was upon him. There was no time left for observations, no time to make his way back down before darkness fell. He had never spent an entire night in a chapel before.

He pushed open the door. Behind the altar a black Madonna wearing a golden crown held a stern-looking child in her arms; she seemed to stand guard over the chapel's shadowy interior. To Méchain the expression in the ebony Virgin's eyes seemed tragic and gentle. Feeling uneasy, he quickly lit two half-used candles and an old oil lantern.

In the resulting light the black saint seemed impressively serene. What strange people, these Spaniards, to worship an imported Virgin! "Is she a vestige of the Moorish presence?" Méchain asked himself. "White God and Black Devil?" And then he immediately fell asleep.

A muffled chant seemed to reach his ears from afar. Méchain caught sight of a majestic staircase, which he climbed without difficulty. The chant grew louder. A door opened onto the great hall of the Academy, magnificently illuminated for the occasion. Méchain approached the podium, preceded by an usher carrying a huge book. It was Méchain's work on the comets, which was hailed as one of the most important books ever published. Then he opened his eyes. To date he had written no book and knew that he never would. Through a tiny window a ruddy dawn entered the chapel. The chant persisted. Méchain hastened outside, still barefoot. Already the highest peaks were aglow. From the valley below, sunken in fog, rose the somber, distant voices of the abbey's monks as they sang matins. Penetrating the clouds and seemingly filtered by them, the sound that reached the astronomer's ears possessed a mysterious purity. He spent the morning marking locations and then headed back to Puig-se-Calm. The summer was nearly over, and fall was on its way.

~~~

September 22, 1792. Horizon clearly visible, no reflection on the targets. Around noon, after the fifteenth observation, the wind rose with such force that it was impossible to continue. Later that afternoon it abruptly stopped, and measurements resumed.

Distance to the zenith of Montserrat.

Target clearly visible. We aimed at the peak of the roof of the small chapel on the summit of San Geronimo. The series of twelve measurements yielded 89°51′56″.

Méchain, sitting below the summit to protect himself from the wind, was finishing the daily report when the sound of a bottle being uncorked made him turn around. Gonzales, dressed in an impeccable uniform as if on parade and with a blue gentian in his lapel, held up a labeled bottle of wine. Behind him, Tranchot, who was just as elegantly turned out in clothes he'd managed to dig up God knows where, held out a plate of small sausages with lots of pimento. He warned the astronomer that these might be a bit on the spicy side, but Méchain, ignoring the warning, felt as though a fire had been lit inside his mouth.

Seen from outside, the tent looked like a large paper lantern that had been hung up in empty space. Tranchot solemnly lifted the flap and signaled Méchain to enter. What a change! Everything had been neatly stowed. The poles had been decorated with gilded branches, and Catalonian fabrics had been laid over the canvas. One chandelier sat on the ground, another hung from the tent pole. It looked like the tent of a sultan. The crates they used to transport the repeating circle had been pressed into service as a dining table and covered with a white cloth on which three plates of genuine porcelain had been set. And there were even glasses, which Gonzales now filled. "Let us drink in honor of this day, for today throughout the world the hours of daylight are equal to the hours of night," he said. So that was it! "Of course, the equinox!" Méchain exclaimed. Had he not recorded the date in the register: "Today, September 22"? Gonzales was a naval officer, and on this day, aboard ships the world over, sailors were in the habit of celebrating. He, at least, had not forgotten. Méchain raised his glass. "Let us enjoy it while we can," he said. "By tomorrow the night will already be longer than the day."

This was the first chance they had had to truly relax. For three months they had not had a moment's rest. Plenty of wine was drunk, and the food was excellent. Without a doubt it was the finest meal that had ever been served at that altitude. How the devil had Méchain's two companions managed to get hold of all that food, carry it up the mountainside, and cook it without his having noticed a thing? Now he knew why, much to his annoyance, they had been coming and going all afternoon.

Méchain was known as a quiet man, not secretive or shy but reserved. Withdrawn, impeccable in his manners, and generally aloof, he had never felt close to his fellow workers. Tonight was different, though. Tranchot had never heard him talk for as long or as freely as he did now. He thought it might have been the wine. Fascinated, he listened as Méchain spoke of stars and comets, eclipses and planets, of the observer's patience and the calculator's perseverance. For days or even weeks, he said, an astronomer could work as though nothing existed for him but pen and paper. Then came the supreme moment of confronting the universe, of testing one's conjectures against the order of the world. Would the star be where it had been predicted to be? Would the eclipse take place? Would the comet appear?

A hunter, Tranchot likened the pleasure the astronomer described to the delight he felt when his quarry finally appeared after hours of patient waiting. To predict what would happen in the privacy of one's own observatory and then see it actually come to pass: that, Méchain confided, was the great prize, the careful calculator's revenge upon the genius and his flash of insight.

But Méchain was not the only one to talk about himself that night. Tranchot, the geographer, spoke of having fallen in love with Corsica during the years he had spent working there on his superb map of the island. And Gonzales, the sailor, spoke of the skies of the Americas, the swells of the Atlantic, but above all of the beautiful women of the Pacific isles.

Méchain then went outside and took a walk around the tent. It was a strange life he was leading. The thought brought a smile to his lips. Most of his time he spent in cramped quarters, always short of space even in the midst of immensity. For a long time he stared at the sky, shaking his head as he peered out into space. "The moon revolves around the earth, the earth around the sun. Wherever I look, I see only hierarchies," he muttered to himself. Without turning around he said, "You see, Tranchot. The equality you were speaking of a while ago lasts but a single day. If you tried to enforce it, you'd stretch that day out to the length of a year." Tranchot said nothing.

One bottle remained unopened. Gonzales stood up. "Let's drink to friendship between our two countries." As he said this, he embraced his two companions. A gloom came over him: he knew things that the other two men did not.

While in Barcelona, his superiors had informed him that relations between France and Spain were deteriorating rapidly. "The French disease": for many years the phrase had been used throughout Europe to describe a dread malady, syphilis. But lately it had been attached to an even more terrible scourge: the Revolution. More terrible and more contagious: already it was threatening to spread across the Pyrenees. From Barcelona to Figueras thousands of copies of the Declaration of the Rights of Man and the Citizen in Catalan were already in circulation. To add insult to injury, the translation had been done by a man named Damiens, the grandson of the Damiens who, forty years earlier, had stabbed Louis XV in his right side with a dagger. Such was the information, at any rate, reported by the spies of His Majesty Charles IV of Spain, who, on the basis of these allegations, was preparing to wage war on France. He was being egged on by the royal families of the European nations allied against the Revolution as well as by hordes of French émigrés who had taken refuge on Spanish soil.

Gonzales also concealed from his companions the fact that his superiors had ordered him to be prepared to abandon the expedition on a moment's notice, if and when the time came.

The three men left Puig-se-Calm. Heading north, they pitched their tent on another summit nearer the border. Arriving late in the afternoon, they had time only to set up camp before night fell. The night, like many previous ones and no doubt others still to come, ended for Tranchot with an irresistible urge to urinate. No matter what the altitude or the season, he always jumped up from his bed and went running to relieve himself. This morning, however, he had the odd sensation of jumping into a cushion of feathers. Somewhere out there in the mist was a precipice, but where?

Feeling his way like a tightrope walker, he took a few steps forward. He couldn't just relieve himself at the door of the tent! Then he tripped over a rock, swore, pissed blindly into the dark hoping to avoid the wooden base of the target, and finally returned to the tent, pulling the flap tightly closed behind him.

Méchain, accustomed to scanning the heavens for improbable comets, and Gonzales, used to waiting while his ship lay becalmed on the high seas, got along easily, but Tranchot found life among the clouds unbearable. He hated the sly way in which objects hid themselves until you were right on top of them and vanished again the moment you stepped around them. You could be having a conversation with somebody and a puff of cloud would come and swallow the person up, cutting you off in midsentence. The hardest thing to live with, though, was the quality of the silence: sounds were not just muffled by the clouds but literally swallowed up.

Tranchot felt he had gone deaf as well as blind. This sensation left him only when he was inside the tent. And even there a halo surrounded the lamp, creating an eerie mortuary glow that accurately reflected Tranchot's state of mind even though he, as a man of the north, accepted fog as an ordinary natural phenomenon.

After three days of being almost totally shut up, Tranchot exited the tent and refused to go back inside as long as there was daylight. He wanted to be the first to announce the end of this torture, so he planted himself at the edge of the platform and watched.

Méchain settled comfortably inside and reread all the notes he had taken since arriving in Spain. Then he organized his observations and began a series of calculations. As he was completing a lengthy computation, he heard a shout and lifted the flap of the tent. A small patch of blue sky was already disappearing from view. He had just time enough to see the gash in the horizon close and the stubborn opacity return. How long could this go on? Food was beginning to run short. A short while later there was another shout. Méchain did not move. Tranchot, still on the lookout, had seen a flash of sunlight. Aiming the telescope at the spot where the cottony armor had been slashed, he could make out three patches of color, which seemed to be flapping in the wind. Was it a mirage due to the high altitude?

No, it was the fortress of Bellegarde, and the three patches of color belonged to the tricolor flag that flew from its tower. Straddling the frontier, the fort enjoyed the honor of being the expedition's first target on French soil.

◆

Gonzales did not make the journey. He was to wait for his companions in Barcelona. The berlin passed a tiny military cemetery set in a clearing in the woods. There were few grave markers because the last war had ended more than a century earlier. Exhausted, the horses came to a halt at the top of the hill, just outside the fortress of Bellegarde.

Méchain could not have hoped for a better observation post. The flag that Tranchot had spotted through the telescope flew from a tower, and from atop that tower it was possible to observe anything that moved on either side of the border in the Catalonian plain below. On one side stood Figueras, on the other Perpignan, their next destination. Once again the berlin shuddered into motion.

◆

To reach the square in front of Perpignan's *hôtel de ville* they drove up a beautiful new avenue wide enough for two carriages to pass. A swarm of itinerant merchants hastened to greet them. Tranchot bought himself a pair of boots known locally as *espardenyes en corde,* which laced all the way up to his calf. Méchain purchased a multicolored wool scarf for Thérèse. Tranchot wanted to try on his new boots at once. Before he could finish lacing them up, however, he heard Méchain gasp. "Tranchot! Tranchot! Do you see what I see?" Looking up, he saw Méchain staring at the Hôtel de Ville. Two words had been engraved in gold letters on the pediment: "French Republic."

At the same time an animated discussion was under way inside the building's great hall.

"Where shall we put the Spanish?"

"On the west side."

"And what about the English?"

"What can I do? It's not my fault that pyramids have only four sides!"

"Méchain!" Llucia, the mayor, rushed to greet the astronomer as he entered the building. "Everyone thinks you're in Catalonia!"

"I was there only yesterday."

The discussion that Méchain's arrival had interrupted had been about the model for a monument in the shape of a pyramid that was to be erected on a massive circular base. The plan was to build this monument on the beach at Port-Vendres, two leagues from the city. It was to feature the text of the Declaration of the Rights of Man and the Citizen in four languages: Spanish, Catalan, English, and French. The discussion was about which language was to go on which face.

Llucia introduced a number of people: a couple of soldiers, an architect, and a group of newly elected regional delegates. One of them, named Arago, the mayor of the small town of Estagel, asked the astronomer about his work. Llucia meanwhile had re-joined the others in the discussion about the pyramid when he was informed that the coach for Paris was about to leave. The mayor told Méchain that he was off to the capital to speak to the Convention."

"The Convention?" Méchain inquired.

To the astronomer's astonishment, Llucia recounted the most recent events: the Legislative Assembly had dissolved itself and been replaced by a new assembly, the Convention. "Perhaps you know that we are now living in a Republic?" someone asked ironically.

"I've only just found out," Méchain replied.

What candor! What naïveté! Llucia was about to make a comment to that effect when he recalled his own stupefaction at the news a few weeks earlier. Standing where he was standing now, he had absent-mindedly opened a letter from Paris only to read the following:

The inception of the Republic was marked on September 22, the day on which the sun, having arrived at the true autumnal equinox, entered Libra at 9 hrs. 18 mins. 30 secs. AM at the Observatory of Paris.

France is no longer the property of an individual. You will, Sir, proclaim the Republic in your *département*. Proclaim fraternity, which is but another name for the same thing. Publish this decree with all deliberate speed and see to it that it is read in all the municipalities of your *département*.

Frenchmen, you have until now been mostly bystanders in events that you had no part in planning and whose consequences you could not foresee. From now on no man shall recognize any master other than the law.

The letter was signed "Rolland, Minister of the Interior." Eighty-six identical letters had been sent to each of the country's *départements,* as the new administrative divisions were called.

The emotion of that moment had yet to dissipate. Llucia could not conceal this from Méchain in relating the facts. When Méchain heard the terms in which the Republic had been proclaimed, he felt a surge of pride: What a fine homage to astronomy! What is more, the text even mentioned his own residence, the Observatory of Paris! He immediately remarked that the country had gone from monarchy to republic on the very day that the sun had passed from one hemisphere to the other. Puzzled by the astronomer's blank expression, Arago asked him a question. "Where were you on that day, Méchain?"

"In the mountains. In the mountains," he answered quietly, remembering the meal with which he had celebrated the equinox.

For a moment there was silence, and Méchain was like a mirror in which the terrifying condensation of time could be seen in reflection: two months away from society and it was as if he had just arrived from another planet!

◆

Mindful despite all this of the reason for his journey, Méchain announced that in pursuing his work on the mountaintops, he would be obliged to erect stations that resembled tents. There was a danger that these might alarm the populace, and it would be unfortunate if any harm were to come to members of the expedition, which included a Spanish officer by the name of Gonzales. "We will begin with Bellegarde," he added.

"Bellegarde! That's where the Spaniards will attack! It would be safer to postpone your measurements until later."

Méchain turned white. Llucia, pretending not to notice, went to his desk and scrawled a few words on a piece of paper, which he then handed to Méchain. "But in times like these," he said with a strange smile, "is it really wise to play it safe?" He had given Méchain the pass he needed.

Méchain indicated that he would make several reconnaissance forays on the French side of the border before returning to Spain, where most of the triangles had already been measured but a number of observations remained to be carried out: measurements of the latitude of Barcelona, of February's lunar eclipse, and of the passage of a comet.

"A comet! Did you know that our enemies insist that the Republic will pass as quickly as a comet?" Llucia interrupted.

With a malicious smile on his lips, Arago then spoke: "Don't they say that comets come back again and again, returning to the same place in the sky at regular intervals?"

"Indeed. But it took 76 years for Halley's comet to return."

"We'll wait! We'll wait!" Llucia and Arago exclaimed together with a loud laugh.

◈

A few minutes later, Llucia climbed into the stagecoach that was about to depart for Paris. Méchain handed him a letter and a package. The package contained the Catalan scarf, which was to be delivered to Mme Méchain at the Observatory. The letter was for Condorcet.

"I'll see him at the Convention," Llucia interrupted, as Méchain began to recite Condorcet's address. Leaning out the window, he said, "I wish you good luck on the peaks." For a moment he looked as though he might be trying to imagine the astronomer at work. "Can I tell you something in confidence? You won't take offense?" He lowered his voice. "There are so many exciting things happening on earth right now that I don't envy you working so close to the sky."

"We began measuring the meridian under the monarchy. We shall continue under the Republic. Who knows what regime we'll finish under?" Méchain replied in the same low tone. "The globe, whether it be royal or republican, is still slightly flattened at the poles."

"Well in that case, citizen astronomer, I would rather it be slightly flattened at the poles *AND* republican."

— *6* —

One week later, Llucia arrived in Paris. Before going to see Condorcet, he stopped by the Observatory and introduced himself to Thérèse. His thick southern accent made her laugh. When he handed her the package that Méchain had given him, she set it down on the table without looking at it. But after making small talk for awhile, she could stand the suspense no longer. Tearing open the wrapping, she was delighted to find the Catalan scarf inside. Flirtatiously she wrapped it around her shoulders, drew the ends together over her breasts, and held the scarf taut with her hand. Then she peppered Llucia with questions: "Méchain? Méchain? Méchain?" He answered eagerly.

With Condorcet, however, Llucia was less fortunate. The object of his visit, he was told, had just gone out "with Madame and the little miss." Where had they gone? "To visit Citizen Lavoisier, Boulevard de la Madeleine." And where would they go after that? "To the Convention in the afternoon." Llucia decided that he would look for them there.

<hr>

A small metal cylinder floating in a bathtub: that was what Condorcet, his wife Sophie, and little Eliza discovered upon entering Lavoisier's laboratory. Leaning over the tub with his sleeves rolled up to his elbows, the chemist was carefully scraping the surface of the cylinder with a wire to remove clinging bubbles of air. Liberated bubbles gathered in bunches at the water's surface. "Are you chasing bubbles?" asked Eliza, who seemed enchanted by this game. When she tried to thrust her hands into the tub, however, she was prevented from doing so and whisked away into the corridor. "At this level of precision even a single bubble is a veritable catastrophe," Lavoisier explained to his guests while checking the temperature registered by a thermometer. Condorcet could not help but notice that Lavoisier seemed to have a real affinity for water.

Lavoisier liked to describe this task, for which he had abandoned his other work, as a journey that required no travel. When he compared his activity with that of his colleagues Méchain and Delambre, he spoke as though reciting a proverb: "They deal with lengths and travel all over the place, whereas I deal with weights and never leave this bathroom."

The "bathroom" was actually a makeshift laboratory that Lavoisier had set up in his apartment on the Boulevard de la Madeleine. A few weeks earlier he had been obliged to leave the Arsenal for political reasons.

He explained his activities to Sophie: "Different substances are not equally dense. In a given volume, some contain more matter than others. To determine the unit of weight is to weigh the quantity of matter contained in a specified volume of a given substance. Which substance?"

"I was just about to ask you that," said Sophie, pretending to be naïve.

"It has to be liquid, easy to purify, and available everywhere."

"Universality again," Condorcet remarked.

"Yes, always. It was difficult enough to win the battle over the meter. We wouldn't want to lose the battle over the kilogram." Lavoisier, who had begun to enjoy this guessing game, continued: "So, a liquid that exists everywhere and is easy to purify."

"Water!" Sophie exclaimed.

"Yes, distilled water." He cupped some water in the palm of his hand. "This is river water filtered through sand. Now, what will we weigh it in? A container whose volume can be precisely measured."

"A sphere!"

"A terrible idea! Nothing is more difficult to construct than a sphere."

"A cube?"

"Just as bad. It has too many corners. Think!"

Sophie was about to give up when she saw her husband standing behind Lavoisier and making gestures with his hands. "A cylinder!" she exclaimed.

"Bravo!" said Lavoisier. Then, turning to face the philosopher, he added, "No hints! In any case, no matter how carefully this cylinder is constructed, it will never be perfect."

"And this one?" Sophie asked, pointing to the cylinder floating in the tub.

"It's not perfect, either," the chemist admitted with a contrite expression as he plunged his hands into the tub. "Our handiwork never precisely matches the ideals that we create in our minds: such is man's lot. Perfection is impossible," he said morosely. "Yet man is so resourceful," he resumed in a brighter tone, "that he can determine just how far from perfection his creation is!"

As he watched Lavoisier at work over the tub, manipulating his cylinder with his sleeves rolled up, it occurred to Condorcet that if you stuck a sail on the floating object what you would have would be an overgrown child playing with a boat in a pool. Science at work! he smiled with pleasure as he removed the bell jar that served to protect the analytical balance. This was a unique instrument, said to be the most precise scale in the world. To this instrument Lavoisier owed one of his most important discoveries, for without it he would never have been able to assert that "nothing in nature is either created or destroyed." Lavoisier went over to the scale, for which he felt an obvious affection, and continued his explanation, telling Sophie, as attentive as ever, that it was of course important to use an accurate scale but just as important to use accurate weights. And even that was not enough: the two arms of the scale had to be the same length. "But how can we know that they are?" he asked, interrupting his own explanation. Naïvely, Sophie was on the point of answering that the way to know this was by measuring them, but Lavoisier cut her short: "Measuring them can never yield the desired precision. We therefore use only one arm, which will enable us to determine the weight of the cylinder independent of the arm's length."

A boy of fifteen now opened the door, blowing on his fingers: "Citizen Haüy says that it's ready."

"I'm coming," the chemist replied. "Where was I? Oh, yes, I almost forget. But the water—"

"Why do you always begin your sentences with *but?*" Sophie asked.

"To say *but* is to raise an objection, and in science objections are necessary to—"

"So there's no presumption of innocence in science?"

"Correct," Condorcet confirmed. "Whenever a scientist makes a claim, his colleagues set themselves up as a tribunal—a friendly tribunal, to be sure. Well, more or less friendly. And that tribunal sets itself the task of demonstrating that the claim is false. If all attempts to demonstrate the falsity of the claim fail, then the affirmation is accepted as true. It's the exact opposite of what we want for society."

"But the water," resumed Lavoisier, who had not lost the thread of his argument, "the water expands with heat and contracts with cold like any other substance. This ruler, for example, which I might have used to measure the arm of the balance, is longer when its temperature is higher. Take a piece of ice-cold iron and measure it with a hot ruler."

"And you will burn your fingers," Condorcet interrupted.

They burst out laughing. "All right, I'll stop. I see that I'm beginning to bore you."

But Sophie grabbed his arm: "I beg you, continue!" Seeing that she was sincere, Lavoisier went on: "Take a piece of cold iron and measure it with a hot ruler. Then heat the piece of iron and measure it again with the same ruler, but after it has been cooled. You won't obtain the same result!"

"You mean that you can never be sure of the size of an object?"

"I didn't say that. I said that length depends on temperature. But as we saw earlier, we are able to determine how great that dependency is."

In the next room a man was dipping a thermometer into a pan at regular intervals. It was Abbé René-Just Haüy, who had been assigned to assist Lavoisier in determining the unit of weight. A mineralogist, Haüy had recently founded the new science of crystallography. His brother Valentin was even better known: a calligrapher, he had developed a method that made it possible for the blind to read. Delambre had taken a great interest in the subject. Knowing both brothers well, he was fond of saying that one dealt with *cristaux* (crystals), the other with *cristallins* (the lenses of the eye).

While the youth with the red hands smashed a block of ice with a sledgehammer, Eliza ground up the fragments and with a very serious expression passed them to the abbé, who filled the pan with them.

From the Boulevard de la Madeleine, Condorcet, Sophie, and Eliza went to the Tuileries. In the courtyard of the palace they passed gardeners hard at work in the recently turned flower beds. In place of the royal carnations and camellias, the Convention had ordered that vegetables be planted: carrots, cabbages, turnips, and the brand new Parmentier potatoes.

Eliza broke into a run, and Condorcet tried but failed to catch her. He ran after her shouting, "Come here, my little queen!" Making a great show of her fear, Sophie caught up with him. "Quiet!" she said, looking all around. "Someone might hear you."

The child had gotten as far as the young poplar that had been planted a few days before Delambre and Méchain's departure. Two women from the *faubourgs* were laying sheaves of hay around the trunk of this tree. Seeing the child's stare, one of them explained that this was to protect the tree from the cold. Eliza turned to her father and showed him her frozen hands. "Papa," she asked, "why don't they put hay around my fingers?"

❧

The temperature was much higher in the Salle des Manèges, where the Convention met. With more than seven hundred deputies in attendance, the galleries were packed and the corridors crowded. Condorcet held Eliza tight by the hand. A booming voice resounded through the building. Eliza surged ahead, and before the guard could stop her, she was in the hall. Standing at the rail with his hand on his heart and his chest thrust out, a man with a splendid tenor voice sang the song of the *fédérés* of Marseille. Everyone chimed in at the refrain. Eliza clapped her hands.

Rising above the applause, the tenor's voice filled the hall: "Singing as we make our revolution is one of the best ways to make sure that it does not end in song. I propose assigning four professional singers to each of our armies. Add *chansons* to our *canons!* Songs for our hamlets, cannon for the castles!"

He then left and was immediately followed by a group of villagers in wooden clogs, who came forward timidly. They carried heavy baskets whose contents they emptied onto a large wooden table: candelabras, crosses, plates, censers, silver caskets. These items constituted the patriotic offering of the parishioners of Dun in Berry. Overcome by emotion, one elderly peasant spilled some of the contents of her basket onto the floor. A deputy helped her gather up the rosary beads she had dropped.

On her way out, the disoriented old peasant bumped into a plump woman dressed in oriental robes who was making her way majestically to the rail. After saluting the deputies, she launched into a lengthy speech in Turkish, which was immediately translated by a diminutive man standing alongside her: "The Ottoman princess Leila, a refugee in the beautiful country of France, wishes to pay her respects to the Assembly by making a patriotic gift of ten livres, which owing to her long series of misfortunes is all she can afford." Drawing a handful of coins out of the folds of her garment, the princess laid them on the table alongside the rosaries and censers. From the galleries came shouts of "Long live the Turks! Down with Austria!"

As she made her way out followed by her diminutive aide, Princess Leila passed a giant of a fellow who all but charged the rail on the double. He made quite an impression, and the chamber immediately fell silent: "Legislators, we have come from the city of Nantes, having paid for our own arms and uniforms. With us we bring six artillery pieces captured from Brunswick's forces, two of which we will leave with our Parisian brothers. We have come to ask you which army you wish us to join."

The chairman granted the volunteers permission to march through the chamber. Proudly carrying a tattered old banner, they filed into the hall. "As a replacement for their battle-scarred banner," the chairman proclaimed, "I propose that that this battalion be awarded one of the flags that decorate the door of this hall."

The flag was immediately taken down and handed to the giant, who affixed it to the old flagstaff. Two hundred of the Nantes volunteers marched past the standing deputies, who applauded the troops and were applauded in return. The shredded banner wound up on the large table on top of the Ottoman coins, the plates, and the censers.

Even before the last of the Nantais had exited the hall, another man entered, carrying a suit of clothes on a coat hanger. "Citizen Roux, I am a tailor by trade. The suit you see here is one that I made specially for this occasion. I offer it to a volunteer who cannot afford to buy his own uniform. I pledge that he shall wear it for the good and glory of the Nation and of his own people."

He laid the uniform down next to the tattered flag but retrieved the hanger. Already the tailor had been replaced by another man in his forties wearing the blouse of an artisan and carrying a metal contraption in his arms.

"Citizen Legros, artist of Paris, residing on rue de Thionville. I have invented a set of mechanical limbs that move easily with the aid of springs and can in some ways be used as a replacement for natural limbs."

Slipping a prosthetic limb over his left arm, he showed how it worked. The deputies in the galleries strained to get a better view. One of them stood up. While writing his text out on a piece of paper he simultaneously read it to the audience: "I propose the following decree: 'The Assembly has decided to provide, at the expense of the Republic, a mechanical limb to any citizen who may lose his own limb in defense of the Nation.'"

Sophie pressed close to Condorcet. Eliza had fallen asleep in her father's arms. When she opened her eyes, she thought she was still dreaming. A small boy was standing at the rail. "My name is Etienne Sallembert," the boy said, straining to make his voice sound more impressive than it was. "I am ten and a half years old, and I have brought—" From his pocket he removed a small box, which he tried to open, but the catch was stuck. The child desperately searched the galleries with his eyes, no doubt looking for his parents. But he fumbled with the box some more, and finally it opened. With a relieved smile he exhibited a ring. "I have brought this ring to help out widows and orphans," he said, and then ran off. Eliza, now completely awake, frantically pulled at Sophie's ring, trying to remove it from her mother's finger. But all she got for her trouble was a scolding.

After young Sallembert came a woman, or rather a girl, who wore her hair down and marched across the hall with a military bearing. "Citizen Antoinette Leydier," she forthrightly declared. "I have five brothers, three of whom are with the Army of the North and the other two in the Vendée. I am seventeen and a half years old. I joined the Twenty-Fourth Regiment as a cavalryman but was discharged when an officer noticed that one of his men was a woman." A gale of laughter greeted this revelation. Citizen Leydier continued unperturbed. "I have sacrificed the fear that ordinarily goes with my sex. In the flower of my youth am I to be sent home to live with my parents? I ask no favor of the Convention but this: to be authorized to rejoin my regiment. And I shall prove to the Republic that a woman's arm, when guided by honor and moved by the certainty of exterminating aristocrats, can be just as strong as a man's."

When she left the rail, it was mainly the women in the galleries who cheered. The reception of the deputies was lukewarm in comparison. Condorcet had applauded as hard as he could, shaking Eliza, who had fallen asleep again but did not wake up. Sophie leaned toward him and whispered in his ear: "Man enjoys rights solely because he is a sentient being capable of acquiring moral ideas and reasoning with them. Hence women, who possess the same qualities, should enjoy equal rights. Either no individual of the human race has true rights, or all have the same rights."

"You remember," he said, proud and amazed at what he heard. "I wrote those words, and in listening to the speech we've just heard I was more convinced than ever. But look!" He pointed at some of his colleagues who were making faces: "The Convention is not yet ready to follow me in this regard."

He felt someone touch his shoulder and turned around. It was Llucia. They had known each other on the benches of the Legislative Assembly when the mayor of Perpignan had served as the representative of the Pyrénées-Orientales. The two men embraced warmly. Eliza was all but crushed between their two immense bodies. Llucia handed Condorcet the letter from Méchain, which he read at a glance. Condorcet then handed Eliza to her mother and rose to request permission to speak.

"Deputies, colleagues: Only yesterday you were asking for news about the measurement of the meridian. I have just received a message from Citizen Méchain, and the news is good! The series of triangles that he was to measure in Catalonia is now complete. Méchain informs us that he will be returning to France next spring. He will continue his observations as far north as Rodez, working his way toward a meeting with Citizen Delambre."

Another deputy interrupted. "On foreign soil, in royalist Spain, the measurement is proceeding without difficulty, whereas within the borders of the Republic Citizen Delambre has had to contend with the severest of impediments. He has been suspected of treason, arrested, and threatened."

"Rest assured that Delambre has now been issued a new safe-conduct pass that will allow him to travel without hindrance," Condorcet replied. "We have given instructions that he be shown every courtesy."

❖

Delambre had indeed received the new pass that Condorcet had mentioned but not immediately, and until it arrived he had had to fend for himself, without help from the Convention.

We left him in the midst of a hostile crowd at Saint-Denis explaining to a surveyor how to use the repeating circle. "Everything was going well," he wrote in his travel diary. "I was showing him what to do, and the surveyor was just about to look through the lens when for some reason the shouting resumed. When things got really dangerous for us, the mayor of Lagny tried to save us by pretending to treat us harshly. He ordered our instruments sealed and our carriage seized and held at the guardhouse. We left the square surrounded by gendarmes.

"Meanwhile, someone spoke to the Assembly on our behalf. In Saint-Denis, where I had been in hiding since my adventure, I soon received a decree from the chairman of the Assembly. The safe-conduct pass arrived later. As a result, the very notoriety of our arrest became extremely useful to us.

"December 17: it is very late in the season. It will soon be time to break off our observations, as before long it will be very difficult if not impossible to continue. In the meantime we will press on as far as La Chapelle–l'Egalité, formerly known as Chapelle-la-Reine. The belfry there, which is open on all sides, is a most unsuitable observatory: first the wind, then the rain, and finally the snow have conspired to make us miserable while we search for the turret atop the bell tower of Boiscommun, which is invisible all day long even when the horizon is perfectly clear."

For two weeks Delambre and Bellet had been trapped from dawn to dusk, forced to look out on a desolate landscape from their cramped vantage on a rudimentary scaffold perched in a steeple forty feet above the ground. Enveloped by silence, they had peered through their telescope for hours on end, searching for the brown spot that would indicate the target way off in Boiscommun.

Twenty leagues to the north along the meridian, in the Grande Salle du Manège, the trial of Louis XVI was just getting under way. Meeting in continuous session, the Convention as a whole sat in judgment over the former sovereign. The people's deputies, 745 in number, would act as judges. Of course people in the village talked of nothing else. Still a faithful reader of the *Chronique de Paris,* the astronomer eagerly awaited the paper's arrival. Each day Condorcet reported on the trial in long, impassioned articles.

"Finally," Delambre wrote in his journal, "on December 31, after observing the whole day without success, I spotted the tower just as the sun dropped below the horizon. It suddenly loomed up in the eyepiece of the telescope and for a moment remained fixed there like a slender piece of thread. We moved as fast as we could, but already it was too late. It was gone."

Red-faced, his hands frozen and his limbs stiff with the cold, the astronomer and his assistant kept up their vigil. When fatigue got the better of them, they would get up as if to leave their observation post only to return a short while later. If the tower should appear again, it would be unthinkable to let the opportunity slip through their fingers. Hence they were condemned to remain at their posts. At times they succumbed to a kind of rage: it was one thing to track an unpredictable star or a comet on an improbable course, but to wait for a fixed object! They spent another ten days, their eyes burning, searching for the turret atop the bell tower of Boiscommun.

Had it not been for the *Chronique de Paris* they would have died of boredom. The paper was brought to them in the late afternoon. Delambre, whose eyes were nearly frozen shut, asked Bellet to read from the paper out loud. Bellet picked it up but felt no urge to flip through its frosty pages. In a toneless voice he began reading. "The trial ended this morning. The Convention has 745 members. The result of the vote was as follows. Roll call: deceased, 1; ill, 6; absent on assignment, 13; not voting, 4. That left 721 ballots cast, requiring 361 for an absolute majority." Bellet stopped long enough to warm his fingers and thought about making special gloves that would not prevent him from reading the paper. Delambre, standing in front of the circle, idly peered through the telescope. Bellet resumed his reading: "Votes cast: 2, for irons; 319, for detention; 366 for—"

Delambre cried out. "Quick, Bellet, it's going to be like last time." Bellet dropped the paper and was on his feet in a flash.

In the distance, beneath the setting sun, the bell tower of Boiscommun stood out as it had on day one. The spire they had despaired of ever seeing again glowed in the aperture like a gold wire sticking up out of the horizon. On the floor the newspaper lay open with its headline clearly legible: "Louis condemned to death by a majority of 366 votes."

7

Paris.

"It is with extreme reluctance that I find myself obliged to go to the capital, but while there I must visit the Pantheon as soon as possible. The triangles linked to that station are joined to two targets that cannot survive much longer: the bell tower of Dammartin, as I indicated earlier, is soon to be demolished; and the chimney at Malvoisine will have to come down immediately."

Immediately upon arriving, Delambre went to the Pantheon to check on the condition of the target. Bellet had only one ambition in mind: to have a good time. So naturally he went to the Palais-Royal. Revolution or no revolution, its gardens, arcades, and cafés were filled with women, games, and amusements. Before he had gone a few steps into one of the arcades, a dignified old man handed him a handsome brochure: "Schedule of Charges for the Prostitutes of the Palais-Royal." Bellet paid for a copy, went over to a bench, sat down, and began to read.

> To our brothers from the provinces who have been drawn to the capital by patriotic celebrations and the love of liberty: we wish to warn you against certain abuses lest you become victims.
>
> At a time when so many citizens have distinguished themselves by the magnitude of their sacrifices and when individual interests must be subordinated to the general good, the owners of certain rooming houses have outraged the public by shamelessly charging exorbitant rents for the use of their premises, thereby exploiting the patriotism of our provincial brothers.
>
> Now the ladies of the night are following the precedent set by these landlords. These traffickers in the wares of Cythera have dared to charge unheard-of prices for favors that used to be available at far more affordable rates. Our wallets have fallen prey to their voracious appetites. In the

interest of preserving this useful commodity, we are therefore making available to the public a detailed schedule of the prices that the priestesses of Venus normally charge for their charms—prices that cannot and should not be increased. The list below contains the names and addresses of certain of these ladies. Please bear in mind that only the most reputable practitioners are listed here, and rest assured that their services can be purchased in absolute security for the fee indicated:

Irène, Palais-Royal, above the cellar: 6 livres.

Thérèse, la Bavaroise, rue Jacob, at the butcher shop: 3 livres.

Jousse, Galerie de l'Assemblée Nationale. Supper and the night, 6.6 livres.

La Baronne, rue de Rohan, opposite the brothers Inère, caterers: 5 livres.

Le Brue, rue Montmartre, opposite the sewer: 5 livres.

Sophie and her sister, rue Basse-du-Rempart. For a threesome for the night with supper, 100 livres.

Stainville (a.k.a. la Maréchale), rue Neuve-des-Bons-Enfants. With her six young charges, 24 livres.

Vanboo (dancer), bd de la Comédie, at the harquebus maker's, 30 livres.

Yes, we, too, were astonished to see nymphs who had previously charged the customary fee of 12 livres voluntarily reduce their prices to a modest écu. More incredible still, a few unselfish souls have, for love of their fellow man, taken it upon themselves to devote two days per week to men in need, making all their charms available free of charge from eight in the morning until midnight, mealtimes excepted.

Such behavior can only be ascribed to an excess of civic love. But such is the nature of women: never moderate in what they do.

It was too cold. Bellet got up and put the brochure in his pocket. He looked around for the old man and found him under the arcades being loudly berated by two women. Meanwhile, another woman had stood up on a bench nearby, proudly displaying her breasts to the crowd that gathered around her. In a soft voice more accustomed to whispering words of love than to making public speeches, she nevertheless managed to make herself heard:

Everybody knows how much we as individuals have contributed to the Revolution. We were the first democrats and proud of it, because we never made distinctions on the basis of order or rank. Unlike those who used to call themselves marquesses and countesses, we admitted the footman to our beds after the duke and the humble chaplain after the bloated bishop.

Lowering her voice, she then pretended to be confiding a secret to the crowd, a secret that everyone strained to hear: "And when our hearts tilted to one side rather than the other, it was always the well-endowed commoner we favored." Whereupon every man in the crowd stuck out his chest so far as to rock himself back on his heels. Bellet straightened up slightly and, posing as a well-endowed commoner, devoured the speaker with his eyes. She went on with her harangue:

> Freedom, which we cherish, has delivered us from tyranny, but since then a horde of common tarts and amateur streetwalkers has been trying to move in on our territory, much to the regret of our more discerning clients.
>
> Citizens, I hereby submit to you my petition on behalf of the thousand girls who work the Palais-Royal. Remember all those expatriate aristocrats: they used to be our most faithful customers. And one thing you can be sure of if there's honor among thieves: we'll give them a patriotic education they'll remember.

The crowd surged forward, carrying Bellet along with it. The prostitute had been seized and carried off. A band of women arrived from La Halle. The whores had the field to themselves. Bellet got away before the gendarmes arrived, although given his experience at Saint-Denis he now felt a certain sympathy for them.

◈

Before going to the Pantheon, Delambre stopped in at the Academy. The climate there was one of considerable agitation. Marat had just published one of the incendiary articles that were his specialty. In it he had denounced "the despotism of the academies, which are forever persecuting men of talent who offend them, thereby perpetuating errors, preventing new truths from seeing the light of day, and denying society the benefit of useful discoveries." Later in the article Lavoisier came in for his share of criticism: "The putative father of all these discoveries changes systems the way other men change shoes. In the blink of an eye I watched him switch from enthusiastic support for the idea of pure phlogiston to uncompromising denial of its validity. He changed the term acid to oxygen, phlogiston to nitrogen, nitric to nitrous. Such are his claims to immortality." Marat then went on to attack the small group of scientists who maintained an iron grip on everything done in the name of science in France: "modern charlatans," he called them.

"Men like d'Alembert, Condorcet, Lalande, Laplace, Monge, Lavoisier, and other potentates of the guild of scientific charlatans sought to ensure that they alone would be looked to as beacons of scientific wisdom. They therefore criticized my discoveries throughout Europe and—can you believe it?—turned the continent's scientific societies against me." Marat devoted a full page to the persecution he had suffered at the hands of the Royal Academy of Science—he emphasized the word *royal*—in connection with his discoveries about light, which had been dismissed as "contrary to the established truths of optics."

As Delambre was leaving the building, he remembered the title of the work of Marat's that the Academy had rejected: "Memoir on the True Causes of the Colors Exhibited by Shards of Glass, Soap Bubbles, and Other Extremely Thin Diaphanous Materials." As he walked toward the Pantheon, he thought of Marat in his cellar blowing soap bubbles toward the roof in order to study their colors.

When he reached the Pantheon, Delambre discovered that the turret atop the dome that had been chosen as an aiming point had been demolished. He was too late!

What had been the Church of Sainte-Geneviève had been turned into a tomb! Forty first-story windows had been filled in to make the building resemble an ancient temple. Now the only illumination came from above. The building had been chosen as a repository for the ashes of those to whom the nation owed a debt of gratitude, and since then it had been under constant renovation—sorely needed because of fundamental flaws in its construction. The primary supporting pillars had suffered from the poor design. Even in the dim light Delambre could see cracks in the corner columns. There was reason to fear that the whole structure might collapse. The remains of the nation's heroes might have to be exhumed a second time! Work to save the edifice was proceeding at a fever pitch.

When the Constituent Assembly, following the lead of the Greeks, decided to create a "Pantheon" for the "gods" of the moment, only one person had been deemed worthy of the honor. Who but Mirabeau possessed the requisite qualities? Not only was he a contemporary figure and a popular hero, he was also safely deceased.

As a crypt the empty church seemed vast and bare, cold and sonorous. Very little of the space had been put to use. Such an enormous temple was too much for a single corpse. In order to fill the void, it had been suggested that the dead of earlier periods be recruited. Only popular figures were eligible, however, and they had to have died relatively recently. Fortunately there were a number of individuals who filled the bill, and their remains had promptly been "pantheonized."

Delambre was well aware of all this. He cast his mind back to 1791 and the beautiful weeks of early summer. On two occasions, two weeks apart, crowds had filled the Latin Quarter from the Seine to the Observatory as if for a great holiday. Two processions had traversed the capital. One, the cortège of the soon-to-be-condemned, had ended at the gates of the Tuileries in terrifying silence punctuated by occasional cries of rage that had seemed almost a deliverance. The other, the cortège of the soon-to-be-consecrated, had triggered joy, enthusiasm, and cheering wherever it passed on its way across Paris, ending at the entrance of the Pantheon. At the center of each procession was a man who had sought to flee the capital. One had succeeded, and it was no doubt his success in doing so that had allowed him to live to the ripe old age of eighty-four. The other had failed, and it was in part because of this failure that he was in danger of not living nearly so long. Imprisoned as in a catafalque was the living king, Louis XVI, obliged to return to Paris after his abortive escape ended in Varennes. The other, slowly making its way through the crowd like a nuptial convoy, celebrated the marriage of a dead philosopher with the people who cheered his name: Voltaire.

◆

As quickly as he could, Delambre climbed the stairway that led to where the turret had been. He emerged into the cold air, relieved to be out of the sinister sanctuary. Again he was dumbfounded by what he saw: Paris in all its immensity!

Even when surveyed from such a height, flattened by altitude, Paris was a bustling city: this was the first thing that struck him. It was a city of multitudes, multiplicity, and toil. The urban spirit was evident throughout. One had only to surrender to the city's density and size to understand why it was here that French policy was made; why the rest of the country counted for so little compared to the capital; why all Europe trembled before it; and why even the most rabid of royalists had vowed to destroy this "infamous Babylon," as they called it.

Elsewhere, whenever Delambre had climbed up to one of his observation posts to survey the surrounding countryside, he had looked upon nature in all its immensity as far as the eye could see: orchards, fields, and forests. Far below him, clustered around the base of the tower or huddled against the church, were homes nuzzled together like kittens from the same litter. Humans lived huddled together on tiny islands amidst a vast sea of green. Paris was obviously something else: from atop the Pantheon he could see nothing but roofs, terraces, and courtyards and a tangle of streets, a confused but organized maze of solid, unified dwellings. Far off in the distance, nature was relegated to the background.

That day the view was incredibly clear. High in the sky a veil of clouds encircled the capital, so that the humidity in the air was low. It was as if anything that might interfere with the limpidity of the atmosphere had been barred: sun, fog, moisture. It was not dark. The air was clear but not bright, and gray was the dominant color: in the tiled roofs, in the paving stones of the streets, in the stone of building walls. There was nothing to blur the city's outlines: everything conspired to emphasize the rigor of its relief, the strict precision of its forms, the definition of its details. Delambre was sorry he had not brought his instruments. Observing conditions were at that moment ideal.

A short distance from where he stood he could see the impressive heft of what looked like a mountain, or rather a sheer cliff plunging straight down into the river: Notre-Dame. That morning there was little traffic along the curving loops of the Seine, just three or four barges at the Port de la Rapée. An impressive void not far from the bank held his eye: there, a demolition site was all that remained of the Bastille. The old prison had been smashed, battered, and pulverized until nothing but fragments remained. One sensed that in this emptiness work was proceeding, sapping the energies of the bustling *faubourg* Saint-Antoine, the anxious and menacing working-class quarter whose vital substance stood ready to fill the obscene hole where a piece had been cut out of the city's dense flesh.

Doing an about-face, Delambre looked down on the *faubourg* Saint-

Marcel, following the district's streets with his eyes. Around the Church of Saint-Marcel he saw where the tanners worked; around Saint-Paul were the masons, around Roule the ragpickers, and around Chaillot the blacksmiths. What an observatory! That morning, however, there were no processions. Paris remained sullenly idle.

With a dozen observation posts like this one, the entire city could be kept under surveillance. Then no one in Paris could make a move without drawing the attention of the police. But the city's towers had yet to be tapped for such a purpose. Delambre was glad that astronomers and policemen did not work side by side, the former keeping an eye on the stars, the latter on the people.

Farther off in the distance, coaches waited in endless lines at various points along the city's periphery: these marked the location of customs barriers. Even farther out a range of hills overlooked the capital. Out of professional habit Delambre spent some time studying the topography. Ménilmontant, Belleville, Montmartre, the hill of Chaillot, the forest of Sèvres. But to the south there was not a single usable site.

<hr>

In eight months Delambre had completed measurements for just fourteen stations, even though he had not voluntarily wasted a single moment. At the other end of the meridian, Méchain, despite having to contend with mountainous terrain, had finished up nine stations in just two months of work.

Delambre wanted to get started again as quickly as possible. But if he hoped to have any chance of completing his mission, he would first have to obtain a pile of documents, and these were not easy to come by.

The first sign of trouble came when the General Assembly of the Commune voted unanimously to deny him the passports he had been seeking for six weeks. But then, for no apparent reason, Chaumette, the communal prosecutor, intervened on his behalf. The passports were then approved as unanimously as they had been denied a few days earlier. Delambre and Bellet immediately set out for Dunkirk.

> The obligation to carry passports, which we must produce at every step of the way, is one of the greatest impediments to speeding up our work. It makes communication from station to station more difficult and forces us to be more cautious about travel, which we no longer dare to undertake unless absolutely necessary. It draws suspicion to us by forcing us to

submit to searches by armed guards and requires us to obtain the approval not only of the magistrates and citizens among whom we must do our work but also of everyone we encounter along the way. This time, in addition to my passports, I've brought a letter of recommendation to General Custine, the commander of the Army of the North, because the theater of war is not very far from my own theater of operations.

We have a small army based at the foot of Mont-Cassel. The enemy has outposts near the Montagne des Chats, where I have a station that I shall soon be forced to abandon.

"Mr. Astronomer! Mr. Astronomer!"

Delambre had heard himself addressed in this fashion while on a return trip from the Montagne des Chats.

"I am Etienne Charpy, the surveyor! You remember? Saint-Denis? I recognized the carriage. There's no other like it."

"No, you're wrong, there are two, but you're not likely to see the other one around here," Delambre replied.

Etienne was accompanied by his friend Gustave Lantier, an artilleryman. The two were inseparable. Gustave was the soldier who had handed Delambre his bayonet just as the astronomer was about to plunge into his lecture on geodesy. The two men were headed to Dunkirk with their battalion.

With difficulty the berlin threaded its way through groups of volunteers. Some marched barefoot, while others were lucky enough to wear shoes whose soles had been worn down to almost nothing. Compared to the unshod soldiers, those with shoes of any kind seemed well off indeed. Among them were many skilled craftsmen, including painters, who were recognizable by their attire, and weavers. It was said that initially there had been enough painters to fill an entire battalion by themselves. Uniforms had been in short supply, and most of the men still wore their working attire, which made the armies of the republic look like what they in fact were: ragtag armies of civilians. Later, in the wake of heavy losses at Verdun, Longwy, and especially Valmy, it had often been necessary to reassign troops from one battalion to another. Tragic events had thus reshaped the French army, depriving its units of whatever distinctive character they might have possessed at the outset.

A small woman, pretty but made up in a brazen way, gave Bellet the eye as she brushed past him. Among the troops he saw numerous women, whom the soldiers affectionately called "wives." A squad of cavalrymen galloped past, nearly knocking Bellet down. One of the soldiers shouted after the riders: "So much for equality. The cavalry are still on horseback, and we're still on foot!"

"If the cavalry were on foot, they'd be the infantry!" his neighbor shouted.

❧

Trapped by nightfall, the astronomer and his assistant were invited to make camp with the soldiers. Gathered around the fire, the troops ate in silence, their faces hard with anger and sadness. They had just heard the incredible news: Dumouriez, their general, the man who had led them to victory at Valmy, had gone over to the enemy.

The surveyor made the necessary introductions. In this unit volunteers and regulars had been mixed in equal proportions. While on guard at headquarters, Etienne told them, he had studied all the maps he could get his hands on and little by little had deduced the path of the meridian. "It passes through Berry, doesn't it? Because I'm from Dun-le-Roy." Gustave interrupted: "I'm from Valmy. Don't believe a word he says. It's all one village. He's from the next town over."

"Sure, I'm from Valmy. I didn't die there, so it's as though that's where I was born."

"Your Berry isn't the center of the world," one of the regulars put in. Bellet pointed out that even if Berry wasn't the center of the world, it was indeed the center of France. He also confirmed for Etienne that Dun was one of their stations.

Walking with Delambre back to the berlin, Etienne insisted on giving the astronomer his parents' address. "I've often thought about what you said about the triangles. It's damned interesting." Then he fell silent. All around them campfires gleamed in the night. Embarrassed, Etienne began a sentence, cut himself short, then began again: "Listen, when it comes time to measure the baseline, you wouldn't want to take me along, would you? When the war is over, I mean."

❧

Dunkirk was a proud city, which boasted of being the "beam in England's eye." By the time Delambre and Bellet's bright green berlin entered its gates, the city was in a frenzy. Lookouts on the parapets had spotted thirty British battleships escorted by four frigates arrayed for battle with guns trained on the city's fortifications. The English commodore had issued an ultimatum, to which the commander of the fortress of Dunkirk had responded, "Do me the honor of attacking, and it will be my privilege to parry."

The entire population was pressed into service. Unmarried men were enlisted as soldiers. Married men were set to work making arms and transporting supplies. Women sewed tents and uniforms, girls worked in hospitals, and children tore up old linen for bandages. Even the elderly played their part: responding to a request to "have themselves transported to public places in order to spur the courage of the troops," they waited for the moment when they might be needed. Everyone, soldiers and civilians alike, had been galvanized by the presence of Carnot, whom the Convention had sent to organize the resistance. The attack was repulsed.

Carnot, dressed for his mission as representative of the Convention, sported a short saber dangling from a black leather shoulder harness hung around his neck, a scarf for a belt, and a round hat topped by three feathers in the national colors, with red the highest. He was everywhere at once, giving orders and solving problems. Except for one, which defeated his best efforts: the prostitutes! The barracks and camps were full of them. There were more girls than soldiers. In Douai, for example, the garrison was down to 350 men, but more than 3,000 women remained in the city, ten for every soldier. How dare anyone say that the Republic had failed to supply its troops with what they needed! It was impossible to get rid of these women despite the law banning all females other than soldiers' wives from army camps everywhere. To hear the women tell it, they were all soldiers' wives. Carnot grabbed his pen and dashed off a missive to the Convention: "Get rid of all the camp followers and things will go well. They get the men all worked up, and the diseases they carry have cost us far more men than all the enemy's forces combined." The Committee of Public Safety ordered that all women traveling with the army, even those acknowledged as wives, should be sent home forthwith with the exception of laundresses and vivandières, whose role was to sell food and liquor to the troops. It seemed, however, that the number of vivandières was very large indeed.

Despite the prostitutes, the war, and the English blockade, the work continued. In Dunkirk, which stood at one end of the meridian to be measured, Delambre set out to measure the city's latitude, which was a very important parameter. While Bellet adjusted the level, Delambre was getting ready to focus the repeating circle's telescope on the star Polaris when someone arrived with a letter forwarded from his home on the rue de Paradis in Paris. It had been sent from Barcelona. At last, news from Méchain! His first letter!

◆

Montjouy, February 23, 1793

To Citizen Delambre,
Sir and dear colleague,

I have been meaning to write you for quite some time, but since I have been wandering for months in the mountains of Catalonia, it wasn't easy, and in any case I didn't know where to reach you. I've only just learned that you returned to Paris in January.

I read about your misadventures in *Le Moniteur* of September and was deeply affected. I was also greatly pleased to learn of your success in measuring angles. We, on the other hand, have been unable to complete our triangles with the degree of precision you have achieved. Apart from my lack of skill, there are difficulties in these mountains of a sort not commonly encountered in flatter country. Good moments here are rare and invariably brief.

It is impossible to remain on station as long as we would like and not easy to return once we have left, especially when we are not alone and not free to move about as we might wish. Nevertheless, we have benefited from enthusiastic support and have been given everything we need to do our work.

We are nearly done with our celestial observations. I have already sent our observations of Polaris to M. Borda. This week I was hoping to send off the results of my observations of Xi Ursae Majoris along with my preliminary calculations, but I have been obliged to defer this dispatch because in the present circumstances our Spanish colleagues are pressing us to see all our work, and they require several copies.

If people in Paris want us to make other observations of stars at the zenith, they had better let us know promptly, because we certainly cannot remain here much longer. Yesterday, our Spanish collaborator, M. Gonzales, had to leave us to chase a corsair that on the night of January 19 seized a Spanish warship just below the fort of Montjouy where I was making my latitude measurements. I had just arrived. . . .

❦

As he did every evening, during the part of the day known in these parts as *las tardes,* Méchain set up his instruments on the flat roof of the fortress, to which one gained access by climbing through a trapdoor. He had had a small hut built next to one corner of the tower in such a way that his instrument's plumb bob hung directly over a point on the wall of the building itself. The feet of the repeating circle rested on heavy blocks of stone, and when the windows of the hut were opened and the hatches raised it was possible to see the entire meridian from the sea's horizon to the mountains of the north coast.

The building stood at the top of a hill overlooking the port of Barcelona. To get there one had to pass through one of the city's most dangerous *barrios,* a maze of streets hard against the port. Unless you were a sailor, a soldier, or a thief you went there only at your own risk. The astronomer never would have attempted it had he not been accompanied by Gonzales, a captain in the Royal Navy.

Outcroppings of the fortress projected into the sea itself, and from the roof one looked down on the water as from the mast of a ship: the Mediterranean as far as the eye could see.

To the south, halfway to Africa but invisible, lay the Balearic Islands. Even farther off in the same direction was Algiers. Méchain stared at the endless sea for a good long while. If only he could do what he dreamed of doing: measure the meridian all the way to the Baleares! And then Africa, why not? The vastness of the sea is the stuff of dreams. All it would take was a little more progress in optics and technology, and of course peace with the bey of Algiers, and—What a grandiose idea: to measure the meridian from Dunkirk to Algiers! But the idea was so insane that he breathed not a word of it to anyone, allowing it to ripen in secret instead.

For the time being his business lay to the north. Every night, as he packed up his instrument and with his naked eye stared for the hundredth time at the pole star, Polaris, he could not stop himself from thinking that the Little Bear was on its way north with him, to Rodez. And Auriga, the Great Chariot, was Delambre's green berlin, headed south. Encircling the North Star and preventing any flight to the south was the Dragon with its threatening head and endless tail, which would imprison him until the end of time. Méchain shivered despite his heavy fur cloak. Barcelona's nights were chilly, and it was wintertime, even if it was almost possible to forget this during the day.

With one hand Tranchot held a small lantern to light the level while Méchain refined his measurement. From the base of the tower it was just barely possible to make out two active shadows bustling about in the dim light.

Far below, the barrio was enjoying another wild night. Its dives and taverns were crowded with sailors from the four corners of the earth: Levantines, Greeks, Englishmen, and Portuguese. Bursts of loud noise punctuated by hand clapping penetrated the darkness. Obscene songs, raucous shouts, and the sound of fighting reached Méchain's ears as if muffled, relieved of their freight of violence, and languorous sea ballads, so different from the chants he had heard on the summit of Montserrat, wafted over the roof as he worked. There were hundreds of stars to measure: Alpha Draconis, Beta Tauri, Beta Procyon, and so many others.

◈

The sun sank toward the horizon. Accompanied by Tranchot and Gonzales, Méchain had just arrived on the roof. The three men were busy setting up their equipment when the sound of detonations reached them from the direction of the sea. "Madre de Dios!" Gonzales exclaimed as he reached for a spyglass. A schooner flying a Spanish flag was under heavy attack by an apparently well-armed corsair, which slipped in and out of view with the ease of a dolphin. Gonzales turned his glass on the docks. Not a single ship was in port! In a helpless rage he left the Frenchmen without a farewell.

Like a flash of lightning before a thunderclap, the sea suddenly erupted in light, after which came a terrifying explosion. The schooner had sunk. Rumors were already making their rounds: the ship had just returned from America laden with gold coins and bars. Some claimed that the corsair was Moorish, while others insisted that it was French. Méchain and Tranchot quickly packed their instruments and vanished without calling undue attention to themselves.

Upon returning to the inn, Méchain decided to write to Delambre. He recounted what he had just witnessed and ended his letter thus:

It has been uncomfortable for Frenchmen here for some time now, and living conditions are difficult or at any rate ungracious. I was thinking of returning to France before the end of the month, but a new commanding general has been appointed and I eagerly await his arrival. Depending on what he says and what he is willing to let us do, we will make up our minds about how to proceed. Obviously, however, things are very much up in the air.

My dear colleague, I beg you to send details about how you build your targets and what shape you have chosen for them. I need this information in order to harmonize our methods.

Another time, just after leaving the fort at the end of a long day of observations, Méchain was slowly making his way through the port and back to the inn when something in the sky caught his eye. He squinted for a clearer look. The guards on watch that night at Fort Montjouy were startled to see the French astronomer climb back up to his observatory as quickly as he had climbed down a short while earlier.

How beautiful it was with its clearly defined head, narrow tail, and streaming "hair," which was no doubt beautiful to behold though impossible to see clearly through the surrounding nebula. The comet had just about passed Xi Draconis. For the first time in his life, purely by chance, Méchain had spotted one with his naked eye.

What strange planets comets are! They reveal themselves to us for a few moments only to vanish again for centuries. The next day the sky was clear and the hair on the comet easy to see. It passed north of Cepheus. Then it moved close to Beta Cassiopeiae. Three days later all that could be seen of the tail was a pale trace that seemed almost eaten away by azure, while the nucleus, like a metal marble, traced its path through the sky with a precision that seemed alarming to anyone who was not an astronomer. On the following day it disappeared into thick clouds, and it was two days before Méchain spotted it again in the neighborhood of Beta Arietis. Calm then returned to the sky, but the comet stuck so close to the moon that its light was dimmed. For a brief while the two celestial bodies seemed to move in concert, but as the comet moved away from the lunar orb it regained its colors, especially as it drew near Pi Piscium.

Night after night the moon grew brighter and the comet correspondingly dimmer. It soon became impossible for Méchain to gauge its appearance. It receded into the distance, passing first Kappa Ceti, then Sigma Orionis, then Mu Virginis. And then it was gone, swallowed up by the cosmic vastness.

His first love!

Once again Méchain felt like an astronomer. He had recorded the successive positions of the comet with the utmost precision. When it came to comets, was he not the best observer of all? He did, however, have one rival: Miss Caroline.

"Year 1786. On January 17 M. Méchain discovered a comet in Aquarius, while on August 1 Miss Caroline Herschel observed a small comet in Bootes and Hercules, a body not visible to the naked eye that would surely have escaped our notice had it not been for this new observer's steady and careful vigilance." From that moment on Pierre and Caroline had been rivals. In 1789 the Englishwoman had outdone the Frenchman: she discovered two comets, he only one. In 1790 the match was more even: Caroline detected a comet in Pegasus on January 7, while Méchain discovered his eighth comet in Pisces two days later. In 1792, on the eve of Méchain's departure on the present expedition, the two were tied: each discovered three comets. Some day, perhaps when the war was over, he would meet this Englishwoman. At Greenwich of course.

On the following day, February 25, Méchain left Barcelona in response to an invitation from Dr. Salva, an amateur astronomer who had taken a liking to him. Tranchot went with him. That night there was to be a lunar eclipse.

Dr. Salva lived on a large estate near Montserrat. He and his wife Maria welcomed the two travelers. Maria was a small, energetic brunette with simple manners who spoke impeccable French with virtually no accent. Méchain kissed her hand, much to her pleasure. "I see that in France good manners have not been forgotten. What is it you call each other now? *Citoillens?*"

"*Citoyens,*" Tranchot corrected.

"Citizen Tranchot, Citizen Méchain. I have to say I like the sound of it."

Salva could not wait to show his visitors his new acquisition: a water pump. "Ten *veltes* per hour. A minor miracle!" Maria talked him out of it, however.

Within a few hours instruments had been set up in the garden, and Maria took up a position at Méchain's side. In a specially prepared dovecote at the far end of his property, Salva made identical observations using his own equipment. Maria had many questions about astronomy. "Astronomy is precise, regular, and mathematical," Méchain explained. "It is the astronomer's task to detect patterns, deduce trajectories, and calculate the paths of the celestial bodies he observes."

"Hence to know the future," Maria interrupted.

He had never thought of his work that way. He pondered the lady's remark: "True," he reflected, "if no cataclysm disrupts the world's order, that is indeed what we are trying to do: divining the future of the universe."

The sky darkened: the eclipse had begun. Maria and the astronomer stood close together. As they talked in the dark, she imagined her companion's gestures, while he pictured her hanging on his every word.

"If the earth comes between the moon and the sun, it acts as a screen, and the moon becomes invisible. We call this a lunar eclipse. When it's the moon that comes between the earth and the sun, the sun disappears from view. Then you have a solar eclipse. Total eclipses of the sun are quite brief, never more than two minutes. And they're very rare. The last one was in 1724."

"When will the next one be?"

"That's the second time I've been asked that question!" Méchain exclaimed. "The first was in the Tuileries." He couldn't see Maria's eyes. Everything about France, and especially Paris, excited her.

"Everyone on the Commission was there that day, lined up in two rows. We had been waiting a quarter of an hour. Suddenly, in front of us, was the king. No one had heard him come in. I had never seen him before. He resembled the portrait in the great hall of the Academy, perhaps a little plumper and a little older. He spoke first to one of the scientists, Cassini, whom he knew personally: 'So, Mr. Cassini, they tell me that you're going to measure the meridian again, as your grandfather did before you. Do you think you can do a better job?' 'I certainly would not flatter myself that I could do a better job if I did not have a great advantage over him,' Cassini replied. 'The instruments that my grandfather used were capable of measuring angles only to within fifteen seconds of arc. This gentleman, Monsieur le Chevalier de Borda, has perfected a circle capable of measuring to within one second. My only merit, Sire, is to be in a position to use this new instrument.'

"Borda was standing next to Cassini. Louis XVI questioned him next: 'My sincere congratulations, Monsieur le Chevalier. I hope that you will explain to me how it works after I've returned to my workshop in Versailles.'

"Next to Borda was Condorcet, then Lavoisier, and then me. The king stopped in front of me. 'You've made a specialty of observing comets,' he said, 'and lunar eclipses. Do you know when the next one will be?' 'In a year and a half, if my calculations are correct, Sire, on February 25, 1793.' 'And the next eclipse of the sun?' 'In 2026, Sire.' 'We mustn't ask for the impossible. Let's settle for the eclipse of the moon. We shall watch it together. Your expedition will no doubt be finished by then, will it not?'"

When the moon returned, Méchain was once again able to see Maria. She was sitting on the grass. His eyes met hers, and he sat down beside her to finish his story. "An officer came in, all out of breath, and began speaking in a very low voice to the king, who all of a sudden seemed quite anxious. For a moment he said nothing and then made a brusque movement in our direction: 'I'm sorry, gentlemen. I am obliged to cut short our interview. Let us wish one another good luck, and may each of us complete his journey as quickly as possible.'"

Méchain rose: "Five hours later, Louis XVI left Paris on what has become known as the flight to Varennes."

"And on the night of the lunar eclipse, he was no longer around to keep his appointment," Maria observed.

"Lunar eclipses are not all that common, but the decapitation of a king is even less so," Méchain glumly responded.

At that point Salva returned from the dovecote. His voice boomed out through the night. He was speaking to Tranchot: "Do you know that yesterday in Barcelona I met one of your most eminent physicians, Dr. Thierry of the Faculty of Medicine in Paris? He was on his way back from Madrid, where he wrote a very long essay entitled 'There Are No Longer Any Pyrenees, My Son.' In it, he told me, he explains in detail how the colic in Madrid differs from the colic observed in various other places."

"Did he find any significant differences?" Méchain asked ingenuously, just as a bright skeletal crescent appeared in the sky. The eclipse had lasted two hours.

◈

It was late by the time they woke up. Salva immediately took them to see the water pump he had mentioned the previous night. The gleaming new machine had been installed next to a barn. Maria, who had no interest in such "novelties," which she thought dangerous, left them.

"Maria is for progress in politics but against it when it comes to technology," Salva complained.

"And my husband is just the opposite," she rejoined.

Ordinarily the pump was operated by a pair of horses, but that morning the animals were off plowing a neighbor's field. Salva was dying to show how the pump worked anyway, so he talked Tranchot into helping him and sent Méchain into the barn to signal when the water arrived via a pipe.

With each person at his assigned post, Méchain listened as his friends strained to operate the pump. Water spurted from the end of the pipe. Then he heard screams from outside and ran to see what was happening. The men had lost control of the machine: propelled by the pump's huge flywheel, Salva and Tranchot were in danger of being smashed against the wall of the well. The two men grabbed the huge lever and held on with all their might as the belt stretched. Méchain leaped up to grab the flywheel. But when he came level with it, the tension in the belt became too much for his companions, and they let go. Méchain had just enough time to see what looked like a tongue of flame aimed straight at him, the tail of a comet that was about to set him ablaze. He bore the full brunt of the shock and fell to the ground in a heap.

Unconscious, he lay in a strange position, his face and upper body covered with blood and his right arm dislocated. Salva offered the first diagnosis: the chance of survival was slim. Behind the body, in the unbearable silence, the lever continued to rotate.

8

"We hereby petition the National Convention to establish equality in weights and measures before the interminable task of measuring the meridian has been completed, for that measurement is intended to achieve a degree of precision beyond what is absolutely required." Who had dared to write a thing like that? None other than Condorcet in the *Chronique de Paris!* Upon opening his newspaper just outside the post office, Delambre had spotted the offending article at once, but before he could believe his eyes he had had to read it all the way through. *Interminable!* Condorcet had written *interminable!*

Instead of going to the church where Bellet was supposed to meet him, Delambre headed for the outskirts of town. What was the point of hurrying now? And then he thought, no, the thing to do was to return to Paris immediately to have it out with Condorcet, call a meeting of the Commission, and persuade his colleagues. The thing to do—But what was the point? Faced with the enormity of the undertaking, Delambre felt overwhelmed by a deep sense of fatigue. It was probably true that the Revolution no longer required perfection; efficiency alone was enough, he thought, as he dug his feet deeper into the light soil of the fields.

How could Condorcet have changed so much? Had he not been the orator who had proclaimed from the podium of the Legislative Assembly that "we should concern ourselves not so much with easy answers as with achieving perfection as nearly as possible"? Now the perfection that had been so much admired only yesterday was no longer deemed absolutely essential. Essential to whom? Essential for what?

Delambre knew that Condorcet was overworked, exhausted by his work on the many committees of which he was the heart and soul, especially the Committee on Instruction, where he had laid the groundwork for a really new program of education, a program that people everywhere were calling "revolutionary." But the basic problem lay elsewhere. The Convention had decided to bestow a new constitution on the Republic, and Condorcet had been responsible for drafting one of the texts under consideration, the other being the work of Robespierre and his friends. As a result the philosopher had come under harsh attack. And even that wasn't the whole story. Delambre had learned that the Commission on Weights and Measures had been dissolved and replaced by a "Temporary Agency for Weights and Measures." In short, everyone in Paris apparently agreed with what Condorcet had said. Delambre fumed. "Of course if you lock yourself up inside some miserable office in the capital, time must begin to drag, and you no doubt feel a desperate urge to speed things up!"

What would be the chief mission of this temporary agency? An exercise in long division! The plan was in fact to take Cassini's fifty-year-old result for the length of the meridian and divide it by forty million. Upon completing this immense task, the agency could then proudly announce that it had established the provisional length of the meter! "Why, I could do that calculation right now, sitting here on this rock," Delambre thought, "and save the agency all that hard work!"

But what about Lavoisier and Borda and Monge and Haüy and Lagrange? Would they let a thing like that happen? All of them had work of their own to do, and measuring the meridian was just one of their concerns. "The only people for whom this work is fundamental are the four of us: Bellet, Tranchot, Méchain, and myself." With growing bitterness Delambre felt that he had been cheated by his colleagues and by events. "They sent the four of us out to sea and then abandoned us. Back on land, life goes on as usual; the shipping magnates who dispatched us have forgotten us. Soon Méchain will come crashing down from his high mountaintops, and I from my belfries. We'll fall to the ground like forgotten fruit."

Rage soon gave way to resolution, however. No, he would not give up. On the contrary, he would be obliged to work faster, hasten things along, and complete his measurements so rapidly that it would be impossible to turn back. He decided to warn Méchain of the danger and urge him to redouble his efforts. They would beat Paris to the punch.

◆

He worked faster than ever. Fiefs, Gravelines, Béthune, Le Mesnil, Sauti, Beauquesne. To be sure, the region lent itself to the task: it had all the towers anyone would ever need, and all the churches anyone would want. Everything was proceeding according to plan.

The news came as a shock in the form of a short letter from the agency: "Our colleague has been injured in a tragic accident. . . . Deep coma. . . . Has probably died." Tranchot had relayed the news to Borda the day after the accident.

Crushed, Delambre stared blankly at the last letter Méchain had sent him and the copy of the letter he had just written. Then he thought about simple, material matters, as if by focusing on details he could avoid dwelling on the dreadful news. "The Academy must do something for the family: take up a collection, retrieve the body. . . . And Thérèse: they'll let her go on living in the apartment at the Observatory for a while, but eventually they'll ask her to give it up." What exactly had happened? Why not send someone to Catalonia?

◆

On the Catalonian coast spring promised to be splendid. In the countryside around Barcelona two sleepwalking horses turned round and round, attached by halters to Dr. Salva's tireless water pump. Water flowed through the countless furrows of Maria's vegetable garden. A great deal of it was needed. So densely were the vegetables planted that there were enough to supply the whole village.

Huddled in an armchair protected from the sun by a large oak and facing the garden, Méchain sat motionless, apparently asleep under a heavy wool blanket of many colors. The chirping of the birds mingled with sounds from the kitchen and a servant girl's song. Not far from the oak, Maria sat on a stool shelling beans, while Tranchot worked with tiny pincers to repair the capillary hygrometer.

Méchain was not actually asleep. With a vacant expression, his eyes half-closed, he slowly raised his head. The cover slipped off. Clumsily he tried to stop it, but failed. His face, marked by wounds that had yet to heal, betrayed a poignant sense of helplessness. The astronomer's head was wrapped in an enormous bandage, which ran from his forehead down to the back of his neck.

As the blanket fell away, it revealed that his whole right side—arm, shoulder, and clavicle—was held by a sort of a truss. None of this escaped Maria's notice. In an instant she was at his side, picking up the blanket and brushing the dust off before wrapping it again around Méchain's shoulders.

On the night of the accident they had given him up for dead. Salva, after administering first aid himself, had sent to Barcelona for his most distinguished colleagues. None had held out the slightest hope. The blow had been so severe that the doctors were surprised Méchain had not been killed instantly; his death was expected momentarily. But Salva was a true healer, besides feeling responsible for the accident, so he was willing to try the impossible.

Tranchot wandered about the estate in a daze. It had all happened so suddenly! As the days passed and Méchain did not die, however, Tranchot was rather surprised to discover his affection for the man. Along with Maria he kept vigil over the patient.

Silent and efficient, Maria had proved tireless. Her consistent good cheer dispelled the general gloom. Having conceived an affection for the dour Frenchman on the basis of a single evening's acquaintance, she swore now to save him. She confided this to her husband, who had built a terrible wall of silence around himself. For Salva the accident had been a tragic affair. It was bad enough for a guest in his home to suffer a fatal accident, but for a man to die because of his host's carelessness was to stain hospitality with blood. The fault was irreparable.

Then, one afternoon a few days after the accident, Méchain had opened his eyes. It was as though he had been given a new pair of eyes, eyes still unfamiliar with images, or, rather, still incapable of interpreting the images they perceived: in this case, three faces peering down at him. He stared in dumbfounded amazement until suddenly memory revived. For a fraction of a second a spark illuminated his pupils: the past had been resurrected. That moment was now two months in the past.

When Maria readjusted the blanket, she gently caressed Méchain's paralyzed arm: "You'll see, before long we'll have it working again." His lengthy convalescence had only just begun. Salva believed that the astronomer would never regain the use of his right arm; Maria clung to the belief that he would.

Méchain, convinced that he would remain paralyzed, sank into a deep depression. It took every ounce of Maria's persuasiveness, every bit of Tranchot's devotion, and every one of Salva's medical skills to keep the patient from regressing.

One day Maria asked Tranchot to set the repeating circle up in the garden. Tranchot immediately grasped her intention. On that day Méchain's true rehabilitation began. Every morning the servants carried the astronomer out to a spot near the oak tree opposite the garden. From there he could see the surrounding mountains. Propped up in his chair and steadied by a pile of cushions, he learned once again to manipulate the instrument. His right arm hung stiffly by his side, as heavy as lead, while with his left hand he worked the knurled knob, adjusted fittings, moved the telescope, and operated the mechanism of the alidade.

Tranchot was bent over the instrument when Méchain, unable to contain his sadness any longer, spoke. "You know, things were going really well for us, Tranchot. Twelve triangles! And how far ahead of Delambre were we?"

"Five triangles," Tranchot answered, awkwardly endeavoring to conceal his emotion.

"We would have reached Rodez this year, before Delambre no doubt. By the way, what do they know in Paris about what's happened?"

Embarrassed, Tranchot told Méchain what he had written in his first letter after the accident. "Have you at least corrected your mistake?" Méchain asked.

"I have, I have. Everyone knows that you're very much alive and by no means prepared to give up the expedition."

A few days later a visitor arrived late in the afternoon: a dashing captain came riding through the gates of Salva's estate. Méchain, who had spent the entire day in bed, had missed the captain's auspicious arrival, but when he saw Gonzales in the door of his room, his face, until then contorted with pain, brightened with genuine pleasure.

"You're in uniform again! Are you a sailor now rather than an astronomer?" Overcome by emotion, Gonzales did not answer. Méchain, feigning gaiety, filled the ensuing silence: "That reminds me of a story that Condorcet told me once. He was the head of a delegation that was supposed to be received at the Tuileries. Louis XVI kept them waiting quite a long time. Some young soldiers in the anteroom openly mocked the deputies' appearance. Condorcet went over to them. 'Is your problem with us, gentlemen, that we don't look very military? Well, you, if I may say so, don't look very civil.'" Gonzales burst out laughing.

"My dear captain, you'll have to find yourself another occupation until July."

"Why July?"

"Because in July the three of us will be heading back out into the field."

Gonzales did not tell Méchain that in July he would no longer be with them. The captain had just received his new assignment: war had been declared between France and Spain.

❧

Delambre received Tranchot's letter informing him not only of Méchain's "resurrection" but also of his intention to carry on with the expedition. Meanwhile, he learned that the temporary agency was at least saying that it had not given up on the idea of measuring the meridian. At last the horizon was free of clouds.

Delambre now raced from station to station all the more rapidly because these were places he knew well. He and Bellet were now in Picardy, whose capital was Delambre's native Amiens. The provincial capital liked to boast of three of its native sons. One was the artilleryman who had invented the hollow shell known on one side of the Rhine as a *Haubitze* and on the other as an *obus*. His name was Choderlos de Laclos, and he was said to cultivate a penchant for literature. The second was Lamarck, who, after serving as a soldier and botanist to the king, had lately developed a passion for "invertebrate animals."

The third was the son of a humble draper with a shop on the rue de Viesserie who had almost chosen the priesthood but had become an academician instead. This was of course Delambre, and to welcome him home his five siblings had planned quite a celebration. Dozens of people came to congratulate him. Fortunately he had just been paid. The method of payment had changed somewhat, however. He no longer exchanged a salary coupon for hard cash. Rather, he was paid in the form of *assignats,* paper currency issued by the revolutionary government.

The notes were beautiful and convenient because they didn't weigh much, but prices were rising.

At eight sous per pound, bread was becoming a luxury item. Bellet, who was furious about the situation, liked to say that the only people who could afford to buy so much as a slice of bread were those who weren't hungry. He knew full well that there was no shortage of grain because he had been traveling widely in Brie, the Beauce, and the Parisis.

Evenings at the inn became increasingly raucous. Many people were beginning to feel they had been had. One night, a young man climbed up on a table, and the room fell silent: "When there is no bread, there is no equality," he thundered, "not a dram or an ounce! When the law grinds people down, the people must rise up and crush the law."

Revolt erupted in nearby Péronne. Angry that after three years of revolution bread was in short supply, a mob had marched through the town fixing the price of grain, peas, and candles and beating any bourgeois who stood in their way. Was the country in for a new period of unrest? Delambre took the precaution of obtaining a "temporary" residence certificate. Two signatures appeared at the bottom of the document. No sooner had Delambre deciphered them than he burst out laughing: the president of the Directory called himself "Prophet," and the district president had chosen the name "Pretty Boy"!

At dawn, with his precious document in hand, he left. He spent a day in Mailli, where he had to climb 107 stairs to reach the belfry. The next day took him to Coivrel, where he made a remarkable discovery: a brand new bell tower. The old one, damaged by lightning down to its base, had been replaced. In Beauquesne he stumbled on something that warmed his heart: the remains of a scaffold built by Cassini. Delambre meditated briefly in front of these "relics." Would the structures he had erected last as long? That night he returned to his room. Things were calm and orderly and might have remained that way . . .

. . . had not the split that had developed in the Convention propagated throughout the country. Some thirty of the most illustrious deputies, "the fathers of the Republic," as they were known, including men like Rolland, Vergniaud, and Brissot—the so-called "Girondins"—had been impeached by the assembly. And Condorcet had followed hard on their heels. Amiens was split in two: how many quarrels erupted among Delambre's five brothers and sisters!

For most citizens, the choice until now had been simple: between a depleted, intolerable, indefensible past and a future that promised— why not?—prosperity at the end of the rainbow. For four years everyone had made the journey together: artisans, lawyers, peasants, workers, even priests. They had been against the aristocrats at first, then the king, and finally for the Republic, but now they were being asked to choose "for the Girondins against the Montagnards" or "for the Montagnards against the Girondins." This time it was the heart of the Republic that was being ripped in two. Some wanted the Revolution to continue, while others, only too happy with the gains they had already made, wanted it to stop. "Reach for the stars and miss the moon," said some, while others insisted that "you don't change horses in midstream."

Delambre carefully scanned every issue of the *Chronique*. For two days it inexplicably failed to arrive, but then, the next morning, it reappeared. Publication had halted because the print shop had been sacked. The front page contained an open letter from the printer:

> Seven minutes was all it took for a large number of armed men, most of them in uniform and all well dressed, to destroy my print shop. I was assured that they had nothing against me personally, or so they said as they poked at my chest with a pistol.
>
> You may be wondering what I was doing while these men were smashing my shop. I was trying to reason with them. I told them that a printer is no more responsible for what he prints than is the child who collects the rags used to make the paper he prints it on. Are you seeking vengeance against the authors? You've chosen the wrong target. My argument must have been a good one, because they stopped smashing things the minute I stopped talking. By then, of course, everything was in a shambles.

None of the articles bore Condorcet's byline. His name never again appeared in the paper.

◈

On his way back to Paris, Delambre decided to make a detour in order to check his setup in Saint-Martin-du-Tertre. A crowd awaited him. No sooner had he climbed down from the berlin than he was met with a question from Lakanal, a deputy and member of the Committee of Instruction. The Convention had directed him to conduct experiments with a new piece of equipment: the telegraph, an invention of the

Chappe brothers. He had therefore gone to Saint-Martin, while his colleague Daunou had gone to the park in Saint-Fargeau, eight and a half leagues away.

Lakanal's messages reached Daunou and vice versa. The experiment was a success. An enthusiastic Lakanal told an amazed Delambre that "we will set up telegraph stations throughout France. That's the best way to answer those who say that France is too large for a *single* Republic. This machine has the power to shrink distances. You might say that it brings an entire population together in one place. Just think of it: within an hour after the Convention promulgates a decree, it can be transmitted to every point in the Republic." At this point Lakanal's assistant joined the conversation to report that Chappe claimed to have used his machine to warn of an oncoming storm and that it was more famous than the wind. Soon it would be possible to transmit ideas by day as well as by night and almost at the speed of light.

Upon returning to his carriage, Delambre began to dream: within two hours, three at most, Méchain, way over on the other side of the Pyrenees, would be able to reply to questions submitted to him the very same day.

9

Méchain's berlin started off once again for the Pyrenees. The paint on the right door had begun to flake off, and in places the bare wood was visible. The astronomer, abandoning the beautiful Catalonian estate where he had nearly died, bade farewell to Maria and Dr. Salva and his tireless water pump. After six months of inactivity, he was burning to get back to work! The only way to cope with his continuing depression was to start making measurements once again. Would he have strength enough to complete the mission? It had become a matter of some urgency to prove to the members of the Commission that he would.

Therefore anyone traveling near the Spanish border in midsummer of 1793 might have witnessed a strange spectacle: a chair flanked by a couple of pack mules and wedged among the rocks, and on that chair, shaded by a large hat, a man with his arm in a sling bent over an instrument similarly wedged into the rocks. The man's eye was glued to a telescope, which another man manipulated according to his instructions.

Bucolic as this scene was, it was anything but silent, despite the lofty altitude. From the valley below came the din of exploding shells. The country was at war! The fighting centered on Bellegarde, which had come under heavy attack from Spanish troops commanded by Don Ricardos. Because Méchain maintained excellent relations with the Spanish commander, however, the astronomer and his assistant were free to travel where no one else was allowed.

Méchain had regained some of his strength, but his right arm remained paralyzed despite numerous immersions in the hot springs at nearby Caldas. The mountain peaks were extremely high, the slopes steep, and the trails treacherous. Tranchot could have done the necessary measurements without Méchain's help. He possessed all the necessary skills, and the astronomer could have delegated his jobs to his assistant. But as head of the expedition he bore full responsibility for its success, or so he believed. He therefore insisted that nothing be done without him, even if his presence slowed the entire operation. No ship puts out to sea without its captain on board. Gonzales, the sailor, would have understood. No doubt he was even now engaged in battle not far from where they stood. Although Méchain may have been right about Gonzales, Tranchot still found the astronomer's recalcitrance hard to swallow. It troubled him that Méchain didn't trust him to perform the measurements on his own.

Trust or no trust, there were some days when Méchain was forced to remain in camp. For all his courage—and pigheadedness—he was not always strong enough to climb onto a mule for the ride up to the observation post. Some days his migraines were so bad that his head felt as though caught in a vise, and he shut himself up in his room, his face white and distorted by the pain, which sapped all his energy. But the next day he was ready to go again.

Before long all that remained was to measure the last few segments between the stations on the Spanish side of the border and those on the French side. Although the work would take a few weeks at most, frequent border crossings would be required. One day, as Méchain and Tranchot were on their way to the mountain, a rider bearing a message overtook their coach: Ricardos had issued orders that they were not to be allowed to cross the border. The two Frenchmen found themselves trapped in Spain!

Méchain hurried to Ricardos's headquarters, where the general offered his personal assurance that the order would soon be lifted. Within a week Perpignan would be encircled and the Pyrenees would no longer be the border.

◈

Everything depended on Bellegarde. If the fortress fell, Perpignan was finished. Under direct fire from Spanish guns, the city would not be able to hold out. Ricardos was well aware of this, as were the French generals. The Spaniard dispatched troops to attack the fort, to which the French sent the only available reinforcements: the battalion of volunteers from Nantes who had been sent to Perpignan with the new flag given them by the Convention. Bellegarde became a symbol. Despite repeated assaults and constant shelling by Spanish batteries, the fortress held.

◆

One morning Méchain remained in camp with one of the migraines that frequently left him exhausted and helpless. Bitterly he watched as his assistant set out alone in the direction of the "unbreachable" border. Where exactly was the frontier located? It was hard to say, even for a geographer as knowledgeable as Tranchot. Particularly when he hoped to derive a certain benefit from pretending not to know. Lost in his measurements, forging ahead from peak to peak, he passed the symbolic line without noticing.

Despite the difficulty of the terrain, he progressed rapidly, stopping from time to time to study the summits, marking them on his map, making a few notes, and then moving on. He was working his way up a slope when someone behind him barked out an order. Armed men concealed at the edge of a tree line had him in their sights. He dropped his binoculars and bent down to pick them up, but a shout caused him to freeze. Spanish or French? There was no way to know. Wearing a mixture of military and civilian clothing and speaking Catalan, the men approached. Tranchot tried to explain what he was doing. With his first word, however, the jig was up: they had thought he was Spanish, but he turned out to be French. "Damn traitor! Lousy émigré!" they screamed as they fell upon him. Bound and gagged, he was rudely dragged away.

He had been captured by a squad of *miquelets,* sharpshooters recruited by Carnot during his tour of the region. They were all men from the area, experienced mountaineers as well as committed republicans, and they roamed the hills harassing the Spaniards and hunting for émigrés.

The cannon had not stopped firing all day long. Exploding shells echoed through the valleys, as nature magnified man's violence. It was as though a terrible storm raged in the distance, a looming menace that sent shivers down the spines of the *miquelets.* In the late afternoon the shelling intensified. Worried, the squad paused to take stock of the situation. One of them picked up Tranchot's binoculars and focused them on Bellegarde.

The ramparts had suffered considerable damage from the shelling, but in places they remained impregnable. Sappers had blown away the buttresses. Like a cornered animal attacked from the front and flanks, the fortress was in a difficult spot.

Only a handful of men remained inside the walls. An hour earlier Ricardos had offered these last defenders a chance to surrender with honor. The officers and men took a vote, however, and the offer was rejected.

Four volunteers had stationed themselves on a salient of one of the ramparts. With their backs literally to the wall, they hid in ambush behind debris left by the shelling. The Spanish artillery having done its work, silence reigned once more. From above it was impossible to see the assault force concealed behind rocks, but the defenders knew that the attackers had to be out there. Off in the distance lay the fort's cemetery. Suddenly the four volunteers began firing.

Over the din of the shooting, the corporal, a giant of a man, put a question to his troops. "Well, men, what would you say we need most right now?"

"Reinforcements!" one screamed

"Food and ammunition!" shouted another.

"Uh—" stammered the third.

"Come on, spit it out," said the corporal.

"Women!"

"None of you has it right yet. What we need is professional singers!" the corporal said with a laugh. The men stared at him in disbelief, but slowly smiles came to their lips and then they, too, burst out laughing. For an instant their four rifles seemed to dance above the parapet, as the weapons fell silent. One man's laughter merged into the beginning of a chorus, which the next man then took up. They sang at the top of their lungs. To anyone else they might have seemed possessed as they belted out a drinking song. A sort of tragic joy had taken hold of them. Each man tried out a different voice: one sang alto, another bass, a third baritone, while the corporal took tenor. Then came the attack. "We're done for!" shouted the man who had said that what they needed was women. "Shut up and sing!" screamed the corporal.

"If I shut up, boss, I can't sing."

"Shit! Sing, fire, sing!" thundered the corporal, who rose up above his men. Then came a flash, and he fell, his last word cut short by a bullet. The singing stopped. The three volunteers looked at their leader as he lay there on the rampart with his back to the sky. One of them, his voice quaking with emotion, slowly resumed singing. Then one of the others joined in, and finally the third added his voice to the chorus.

◈

The *miquelets* had not moved. The one who had been peering through the binoculars told the others what was happening. Tranchot, still tied up, sat on the ground and took it all in. A cloud of smoke rose from the fort, staining the azure sky. As if the smoke were a signal, a loud rumbling then spread like an avalanche through the valley below. Suddenly the shooting stopped. A thick veil settled over the mountain. The silence was even more terrifying than the previous furor. The *miquelets* bowed their heads. One of them relieved the tension by jamming the butt of his rifle into the back of the "traitor." Tranchot made as if to defend himself, received another blow, and decided that resistance was futile.

The group resumed its march. Beyond the mountain lay the Vallespir, a much-feared valley swarming with royalists and refractory priests who had proved impossible to dislodge from their positions. The leader of the *miquelets* ordered his men to remain silent, and their watchfulness increased. At last the lights of the city appeared.

◈

Gloom reigned in Perpignan. The entire population had assembled on its own in the central square. Before Llucia had opened his mouth, everyone knew what he was going to say: Bellegarde had fallen! After thirty-one days! The fort had held out longer than anyone had dared hope. Llucia sensed a new solidarity in the somber mass of citizens before him. Though unable to make out anyone's face, he knew that they were all out there. Even in the darkness he sensed the presence of the residents of Estagel, Corneillas, and Vernet.

People returned to their homes in silence. As the city hall emptied, a drowsy feeling settled over the huge building. Llucia returned to his office. Through the open window he could hear what sounded like the babbling of a stream. How beautiful was the Catalan night! Some men camped into the square, soldiers and civilians alike. Many slept, while others spoke in low voices. Before daybreak they would be heading for the banks of the Têt, where the fate of the city and of all Roussillon would be decided.

Never in all its days had the city been so silent. Only now did Llucia become aware that the mountain was once again mute, the guns of Bellegarde having been stifled. He thought of all those volunteers, mostly from Nantes, who had arrived in the city five weeks earlier. Now they were all either dead, wounded, or captured. He had welcomed them in the city hall square. What a great day that had been! Tears came to his eyes: tears of sadness and rebellion. The Republic was not yet a year old and already it was in its death throes: Nantes under siege; Saumur seized by the Vendéens; Angers and Toulon occupied by royalists. The English blockade was strangling the country by shutting down its ports. Traitors who called themselves Frenchmen had made a gift of Toulon to the British crown. Valenciennes had surrendered. The Calvados and Bordeaux regions were in rebellion against Paris. Most distressing of all was the civil war among republicans. Though close to the Girondins, Llucia had done all he could to keep this conflict out of his city. Sadly, he sat down and selected a sheet of paper bearing the letterhead of the city of Perpignan.

A new sense of solidarity had sprung up among the newly elected officials who were beginning to establish the authority of the Republic throughout France. District assemblies, regional and municipal officials, and bureaucrats in various departments of the government had begun to communicate with one another directly, bypassing Paris, which had its hands full. They exchanged information and when necessary helped each other out, but most of all they wrote to one another because they shared a desperate need for unity and a common goal.

❖

This was what Llucia wrote:

To the municipal officials of Nantes:

I congratulate the city of Nantes on having produced so many citizens worthy of the public's gratitude. We entrusted the key to the Pyrenees to them, and they defended it with every ounce of their strength. Bravely they faced the greatest of dangers, and many, rather than surrender, chose burial in the rubble.

Although we are separated by a distance of more than two hundred leagues, our souls are in contact and our hearts beat as one. In each of our homes your brave sons of Nantes will find mourners, friends, and avengers.

A loud noise came from the corridor as a group of prisoners was brought in. The shouts of one could be heard above the rest. A man was insisting that the soldiers were about to make a serious mistake and demanding to speak to the mayor. Llucia, in a rage, opened the door of his office. The prisoner struggled mightily to free himself from the grip of the two *miquelets* who had him by the arms. Llucia immediately recognized Tranchot. The next day the mayor did what he could to help Tranchot return to Spain, where he rejoined Méchain.

⬦

Perpignan did not fall, and Don Ricardos was deprived of the victory he had hoped for. The war dragged on.

The French scientists found themselves in an increasingly difficult situation. They were once again forbidden to return to France on the grounds that the topographical knowledge they had acquired in crossing the Pyrenees could be used against Spain. They were free to choose where they wished to stay, however. Méchain chose Barcelona so as to be close to the fortress of Montjouy, where he had measured the city's latitude the year before.

The fortress had become one of the most inaccessible and closely guarded places in all of Catalonia. For Méchain to enter was out of the question. "Bad luck follows me wherever I go," he complained to anyone willing to listen.

How were the men to fill their long days? Tranchot located a small inn in the center of town, the Fontana de Oro. Neither the beds nor the dining room were much to speak of, but it did have a terrace that offered an astonishingly unobstructed view. Méchain was quick to set up his instruments.

⬦

The summer of '93 was one of the hottest of the century. When we last left Delambre, it was June and the weather was mild. Now we rejoin him in the dog days of August. In those few months France had adopted a new Constitution and established a provisional standard for the meter.

Delambre was still working in the vicinity of Amiens, between the Somme and the Oise. Meetings were being held in every village in the area. At these sessions Delambre and Bellet were warmly received, especially when people learned that their efforts would bring glory to the Republic. In several places they were recognized: these were the same villages in which they had been arrested a few months earlier, often by the same people who now applauded their efforts. Onlookers waved to their carriage as it passed, though people were still puzzled by the strange trunk affixed to its rear.

Preparations were under way everywhere for the huge Festival of the Federation. A vast pyramid had been created. From Mailli to Bayonvillers, from Vignacourt to Sourdon, from the humblest village in the Oise to the capital of the *département,* assemblies were meeting to choose the people who would have the honor of representing them at the festival in Paris. But it was the high season, when every hand was needed in the fields and not a minute's labor could be spared. Still for such a joyous occasion, time would have to be found. Everyone hoped to be among those chosen to celebrate "the union—the unity and indivisibility of France."

The festival was held on August 10, the anniversary of the seizure of the Tuileries. Already a year! thought Delambre. We were in Dammartin then, twenty leagues from here, and our work had just begun! Neither he nor his assistant went to Paris, but they heard about everything that happened there. In the Vexin and Beauvaisis, tongues didn't stop wagging about the eighty-six delegates from the *départements* who marched off to the capital as a group carrying a bouquet consisting of ears of grain and fruit. How proud the peasants had been to discover that the procession was led by a simple oxcart carrying an old farmer and his wife! "A good thing for those of us who work the soil," said one harvest worker, his face browned by the August sun.

❖

A few days later, between Englemont and Mailli, Delambre received a letter from Lavoisier informing him that all the academies had been abolished. Delambre had expected this. How could institutions such as the academies survive when everything else was changing around them?

From the very first days of the Revolution Mirabeau had voiced doubts about the academicians' commitment to new ideas. "I grant that in this time of crisis the Academies have been models of patriotism, but such propitious circumstances cannot be expected to last, and some day we may see, within the Academy itself, repentant philosophers shamelessly attacking the Revolution in text or speech." Marat expressed still graver doubts: "For the good of science and literature it is important that there should no longer be academic bodies in France, yet somehow encouragement must still be offered to people who cultivate literature and science." And Abbé Grégoire, a member of the Committee of Instruction, did not mince words: "Overturn the armchairs of these parasitic institutions!" he proclaimed.

Since Delambre had been elected to the Academy of Sciences in 1792 and no one had been elected after him, it occurred to him that he would henceforth be known as "the last academician." He immediately responded to Lavoisier, stating that he found it impossible to believe that the Convention could wish to destroy an institution that had brought so much honor to France. "Surely the intention was only to revamp the academies, and scientists may well have reason to be pleased with the proposed changes. In any case, this news, far from slowing me down, will only cause me to redouble my efforts."

As he sealed his letter, Delambre suddenly remembered the face of the sansculotte in Lagny who had taunted him with the words, "'Cademy, 'Cademy, there is no more 'Cademy."

As Delambre suggested in his letter to Lavoisier, the reason for the abolition of the academies was not that scientists had been deemed subversive of the new order. Nor did the action spell an end to intellectual work. On the contrary, people were hungry for knowledge, and not just knowledge glazed with the patina of time. They were also avid for new discoveries such as the telegraph invented by the brothers Chappe, the balloons developed by the Montgolfiers, and Lavoisier's chemistry, to name a few prominent examples. And they snapped up the works of Rousseau and Voltaire, of Abbé Condillac and Hobbes, and of the ancient Greeks and Romans, the first philosophers of democracy.

The new fashion went beyond literary form and stylistic flourish. At no other time in history had the understanding of the past played so essential a role in the creation of the new. Although Frenchmen proudly claimed to have achieved what no one before them had attempted, they were equally proud of a long line of historical precedents. These founders acknowledged their fathers. To the men in charge of France, knowledge was a precious thing. Countless assembly meetings devoted to the elaboration of a new system of instruction attest to this. The French were in love with reason, the voice of progress.

The sciences especially were above suspicion. Among the deputies of the Convention were Fourcroy, a chemist; Monge, a geometer; and Romme, a mathematician. And there were lesser known men as well, such as Marcoz, a mathematics teacher from Chambéry who served as deputy from Mont-Blanc. Knowing that France suffered grievously from lack of technical know-how, many people called upon scientists to toil on the Republic's behalf.

When Carnot and Prieur of Côte-d'Or joined the Committee of Public Safety in mid-August, this tendency was reinforced. Both of these prominent Montagnards took a passionate interest in science. Prieur, like Carnot an officer in the corps of engineers, had taken an active interest in problems of measurement from the first days of the Revolution. So it was only natural for him to join the temporary commission that had been set up to deal with the issue.

As for the "provisional meter," the bill adopting it as the official unit of length had been passed so hastily that any number of errors had crept in, not only typographical errors but also—a more serious matter—errors of calculation. The authors of the document, novices in the use of the decimal system, had made mistakes in the placement of decimal points. Since the whole point was to establish a new unit of measurement that was supposed to be the ultimate in precision, this left a rather bad impression. Hundreds of copies of the document had been sent all over France, and these now had to be quickly recalled and destroyed. Not an auspicious beginning! History would remember that the first meter had been not just provisional but erroneous. When Delambre learned of the mistakes that all this ill-advised haste had caused, he silently gloated for a moment, but even he had to admit that such vengeful feelings were rather petty.

With the official pronouncements out of the way, it was time to deal in material objects. Once again Lavoisier's talents as an organizer were put to use. For months he had been collecting all the platinum he could lay his hands on. Whenever he received a tip concerning the whereabouts of a few ounces of the substance, he immediately dispatched one of his coworkers or even went himself to arrange to purchase it at the lowest possible price. With patience he had managed to amass a considerable quantity of this precious metal from the Americas. By now he had accumulated enough to cast the two primary standards, the meter and the kilogram.

Dozens of copies of these provisional units would have to be sent to the *départements* without delay. Men capable of fabricating these standards would have to be found: carpenters, machinists, and foundry men—skilled craftsmen all. The need could not have come at a worse time. Mass conscription, which had been instituted a few days earlier, was snapping up every able-bodied citizen and shipping them off to the frontiers—more than a million men! Lavoisier had to fight to hold on to the few skilled craftsmen he managed to locate: the army wanted them all.

Copper was needed, but just try and find any at a time when the arsenals were empty and gun makers needed all they could get their hands on. Cannons and standards were suddenly in competition—yet another unforeseen difficulty. Of course everyone insisted that both the weapons of war and the weapons of peace were necessary and deplored the conflict between the two. Defeat the enemies of freedom and perfect the tools to preserve that freedom: who could be opposed to either one? Everyone wanted to do *everything!*

Construction and destruction: both were all-consuming activities that left no time for rest. Astonishingly, the Convention rose to the challenge of doing battle on all fronts simultaneously. It was as though the deputies understood that these were unusual times, a deviation from the normal course of events; hence they felt the urgency of creating a new world. They also recognized the magnitude of the task. The Convention was caught in the jaws of a vise that would soon crush it unless it did everything in its power to pry those jaws apart. In the space thus wrested from the forces of vengeance, the mission of the Convention was to inaugurate, to institute, to invent. If they worked feverishly enough, the deputies must have felt, then no matter how zealous the forces of reaction might prove to be they would never be able to restore what had gone before. As new enemies arose, as new fronts opened up in the ongoing war, the Convention felt itself obliged to fashion new arms to smite the invader. The goal was to keep the enemy at bay, to buy time. *Liberty or death!*

The Convention had two faces: the Committee of Instruction and the Committee of War, both toiling away at a fever pitch, one shaping the present, the other elaborating the future. Together they addressed the craftsmen brought together to create the new standards of measurement:

> Even as courage bends iron and brass to the cause of victory, in your workshops metal and wood, docile in your hands, will learn new ways of contributing to the splendor of France.

Where was copper to be found, given that it constituted more than ninety percent of the alloy used in the manufacture of cannon barrels? And how was it to be obtained from England, Russia, and Sweden, two of which were enemies of France while the other was cut off by a blockade?

And what about saltpeter? Where was it to be found? In India! But the problem was soon solved. In rage people lifted their eyes unto the sky, and in despair they lowered them to the earth. And there they found the answers they were seeking. Copper up above in the belfries, saltpeter down below in basements.

Unfortunately bells were cast of an alloy of copper and tin in a proportion different from that used for cannon barrels. The chemist Fourcroy found a way to separate the two metals. One of his assistants, vaunting the master's technical prowess, remarked that "Fourcroy puts asunder what the Church has joined together."

One morning, Delambre, having set up operations in the bell tower of Bayonvillers, received an unexpected visit from two workmen carrying ropes who immediately began installing pulleys and erecting scaffolding. They had come for the bells. After securing their work area, one of them crawled under the bronze bell and unfastened the leather strip fastening the clapper to the ring. Once the bell was silenced, it was possible to rig ropes around it. One rope was run through the handles and hammer; a second was looped around the throat of the bell, holding it in place. The third, tied to the inner ring, ran along the sound bow and was attached to both handles. Delambre was impressed when the huge, silent mass was gently eased through the opening in the bell tower, swaying slightly back and forth as it was lowered.

A poster had been nailed to the door of the church: on it was printed the text of a decree of the National Convention ordering that "only a single bell shall be left in each parish." The removed bell was set alongside three others on a cart drawn by two pair of oxen. One of the workers told Bellet that bells from this district alone had already supplied thirty thousand pounds of metal. "Enough to equip two batteries of eighteens or one twenty-four and two fours." A woman asked one of the workmen, "Why are you taking our bells? You have no right!" The man answered that "if we don't take them today to make weapons, tomorrow they'll be sounding our death knell!" The cart shuddered into motion.

As for saltpeter, workmen in Bayonvilliers set to work scraping down damp walls and scrubbing barns, stables, and old farmhouses. Laundry water had been found to contain quantities of the stuff, so posters went up in washhouses everywhere calling upon washerwomen to do their patriotic duty: "Citizens, you too can contribute to the manufacture of saltpeter by making a gift of the ashes from your laundry soaps to the cause of freedom. Carefully collect your waste water and ship it to the patriotic workshops located in the capital of each district."

As Bellet was about to leave his laundry at one of the washhouses, a pretty washerwoman addressed him in these terms: "Leave your wash for me. As you see, I'm washing for the Republic!"

Silence had insidiously spread over the countryside. Delambre had been slow to notice. As the bells left their towers one by one—Cécile, Jézabel, Bernadette, and Maraine, each bell bearing a name inscribed in the surface of the metal itself—a peculiar void remained.

By dint of working continually between heaven and earth, Delambre had become keenly sensitive to the sounds of the countryside, the density of the air, and the purity of the atmosphere. Now, in this late autumn, the ancestral dialogue among the village bells in this part of the world had been broken off. As Delambre carried out his measurements, he felt on edge in spite of himself, not sure what if anything would break the silence now that the sound of bells no longer added to the lushness of the scenery. As one who had often cursed those very bells, he found that he missed them now that they were gone. One night he was almost relieved when the sole surviving bell sounded an alarm. He was not the only person that night who responded to the danger signal with a twinge of nostalgia.

The silence of the countryside stood in stark contrast to the tumultuous meetings of the Temporary Commission on Weights and Measures, which usually met at Lavoisier's home on the boulevard de la Madeleine. Pinned to the wall was a map of France on which a vertical line represented the Paris meridian. It resembled the map that Bellet had shown to the crowd in Saint-Denis. On it Delambre's progress toward Dunkirk to the north had been traced with pen marks as far as Montlhéry, while Méchain's progress toward Barcelona to the south had been marked off as far as Bellegarde. Since Prieur of Côte-d'Or had been appointed to the commission, its debates had become more animated. The discussion no longer dealt exclusively with meters and myriameters, ares and centiares. Politics had made a raucous entrance. Prieur was a fervent Montagnard; the other members of the commission were not. He was a mere captain of engineers, whereas they were among the leading scientists of the day. These men had known one another a long time. Some had developed genuine bonds of friendship through the incessant meetings of groups of "experts" named by the Academy to judge one discovery or another. They constituted an "aristocracy," from which Prieur immediately felt excluded. To make matters worse, no one made any effort to welcome him into the club, not least because he stood for Authority. As a member of the very powerful Committee of Public Safety who met daily with Robespierre, Saint-Just, Couthon, Carnot, and the rest, he was one of the ten men who governed France.

There were numerous clashes, primarily with Lavoisier, who adopted a somewhat haughty tone toward the interloper and took pleasure in needling him. Prieur, for his part, felt little affection for the chemist, who had been a powerful figure in the Ancien Régime. Despite these difficulties and the absence of several of its members, the commission did a great deal to ensure that the temporary standards would be implemented.

Cassini did not meet with the commission because he was suspected of royalism, nor did Condorcet, who was suspected of "Girondism." But why was Méchain absent? After the premature report of his death, the commission decided to wait until he had recovered before deciding the future of the expedition. Meanwhile, Delambre, having finished measuring all the triangles north of Paris, had just returned to La Chapelle–Egalité, where winter had interrupted his work the previous year.

❧

The region was thickly forested. Everyone of course believed that the somber forests abounded with mysteries. Submerged in fog and covered with snow, the woods were the breeding ground of dark conspiracies: of this the villagers were convinced, particularly the inhabitants of La Cour–Dieu, who had caused Delambre a bit of trouble as a result. He recounted the story in a letter to Lavoisier, who liked to hear about other people's adventures. "Our work in the forests had made us suspect," Delambre wrote. "We were denounced to the revolutionary committee of Boiscommun. Someone reported that three or four hundred brigands had been spotted in La Cour–Dieu building scaffolds and cutting holes in the bell tower. People were certain that these men had come to scout out the terrain in preparation for another counterrevolutionary uprising like the one in the Vendée. Therefore a request was submitted for five or six hundred men to put us down." In retelling his story, Delambre laughed at the memory of the troops' disappointment upon discovering who it was they had been sent to drive out. Lavoisier would appreciate the anecdote.

In the event, however, Lavoisier was unable to enjoy the tale. By the time Delambre's letter reached the boulevard de la Madeleine, the chemist had been in jail for five days at Port-Libre, formerly known as Port-Royal, a monastery that had been turned into a prison. A decision had been made to hold a mass trial of farmers-general, the men who had collected taxes for the monarchy. The authorities had wanted to try them all but managed to lay hands on just twenty-two. One of those twenty-two was Lavoisier.

Borda immediately sent messages to the members of the Commission. How could Lavoisier's release be arranged? The Convention was keen to have a unified system of measurement put in place as rapidly as possible. The commissioners would need to prove that Lavoisier's imprisonment threatened to delay their work for a considerable length of time. Borda proposed writing a neutral, objective, technical letter. Above all he advised against showing any political solidarity with the accused, because to do so would very likely produce the opposite of the desired effect.

"Owing to the need for numerous verifications of standards of weight and measure of all sorts," Borda wrote, "the presence of Citizen Lavoisier, a member [of the commission], has become necessary in view of his special talent in all matters requiring precision." Coulomb proposed adding a statement to the effect that when it came to measuring weights, Lavoisier was irreplaceable. Borda wrote: "His work on the measurement of weight has been interrupted by his absence, and a new commissioner would be obliged to redo all of it. We can state categorically that it would be very difficult to find a replacement for Citizen Lavoisier in this position." He ended by stating "how urgent it is for this citizen to return to the important work that has been interrupted by his absence."

Borda read the letter out loud and signed it. Before handing the quill to his colleagues, he reminded them of the risks that signing such a letter might entail. The quill was passed from hand to hand.

When the Committee of Public Safety received the letter from the commission, it bore six names: Borda, Brisson, Coulomb, Delambre, Haüy, and Laplace.

10

In the place known hereabouts as the Heights of Châtillon lies a small farm with a single plowed field. The remainder of the land is covered with very tall oak trees. The road from Pithiviers to Châteauneuf runs along the field. After a number of attempts I decided to build a target sixty feet high in the area between the road and the edge of the woods. The construction is very costly, and under present circumstances there is a danger that it may alarm the locals.

We use the fourth level of the structure as our observatory. Atop this stage stands a pyramid similar to our other targets. For protection from the wind and snow we have covered this structure with clapboard on four sides.

This makes it harder for the wind to get at us, but it also means that the target itself offers considerable resistance. We were unable to supervise the work of the carpenter, who did not fully honor the terms of his contract. In particular, he failed to take steps to ensure the solidity of the structure. The slightest breeze causes the whole thing to shake so badly that it not only interferes with our observations but also frightens us out of our wits. We therefore mount the structure only when the wind is calm and immediately abandon our positions if the wind picks up. We have to take the instrument down with us, however, and this takes a quarter of an hour. The days are also very short, and the cold very biting.

Snow has begun to fall.

Delambre and Bellet were at the inn in Châtillon for their second Christmas. Bellet, sitting in front of a cavernous fireplace, coughed and sneezed for the tenth time. An old man handed him a glass of whiskey and sat down beside him. "Here, drink, there's no better remedy for an ill wind." The man, who had been chosen to care for the liberty tree in the village square, was consequently known as "Père-la-Liberté," Father Liberty. He was part gardener, part watchman, responsible for both tending the tree and making sure that no one damaged it.

The door opened, sending a shiver down Bellet's spine. A snowman shook himself off in the vestibule: it was Delambre. Without even pausing to remove his overcoat, he hastened to his assistant's side. "I've just thought of another way to do what we have to do. Instead of taking turns making the same measurement, we'll work together." In lieu of an answer Bellet handed him a glass of whiskey. "You'll take one telescope, and I'll take the other," the astronomer continued. "We'll finish up twice as fast!" He emptied his glass. Père-la-Liberté stared at the two men in amazement. "So you're the scientists?" His face lit up. "Léonne! Another jug of whiskey and some glasses! This round is on me!" Delambre indicated that he didn't want anything to drink. "What's that? You don't want any? Today's a day for celebration. The mayor said that in Paris they've voted to make school compulsory—and free!"

A well-dressed man seated at a nearby table had been eavesdropping on this conversation. "I don't think school should be compulsory. How do you square compulsory education with the idea of freedom? School should be like the army. You go if you volunteer."

"But you ain't no volunteer, is you?" the old man replied and walked over to where the other man was sitting. "It wouldn't be because it's free that you're all worked up, would it, fella? You know how to read already, don't you?" The man nodded. "I knew it! Well, I don't," the old man continued.

The well-dressed man replied in a tone of contempt: "What good would it do you if you knew how to read?"

"It would help me, uh, uh—"

Léonne arrived just in time to prevent the old man from choking. After setting down the bottle and glasses, she whispered, "You know what would surprise me would be if your school was open to girls as well as boys." Delambre looked up, but she had already gone. They drank toasts to the school under the disapproving gaze of the well-dressed stranger, who dared not speak aloud thoughts that others had already written down on paper: "To me it seems essential that there should be ignorant beggars. It is not the manual laborer who needs education but the good bourgeois." The same writer had also expressed his doubts that "the common herd will ever have the time or ability to learn." That writer was Voltaire: the Voltaire of the Enlightenment! Nobody's perfect!

Everyone sat down to dinner. On Christmas Eve it was the custom for all the guests of the inn to dine together. A very long table stretched from one end of the dining room to the other. The innkeeper rubbed his hands together because the inn was full: the snowstorm had forced many travelers to interrupt their journeys.

The well-dressed guest was a merchant from Pithiviers who dealt in starch. A shipment he was accompanying had become stuck in a pothole. Next to him sat a charming young man accompanied by a somewhat older man with a remarkably alert expression. The younger of the two was a priest, Jean Chambraud; the older, his bishop, Torné, one of the first clergymen to take the oath of loyalty to the Republic.

At the end of the table, between Chambraud and the starch dealer, sat a beautiful woman who had arrived late in the day with two young children. As luck would have it, the children were asleep. Dinner consisted of a succulent turkey accompanied by an excellent wine from Mâcon. Léonne ran herself ragged serving all the guests.

The two clergymen were on their way to Culan, where the bishop was scheduled to preside over the priest's wedding to a young woman from the village. This would not be the first such wedding at which Torné had officiated. A few weeks earlier he had given his blessing when another priest, Nicolas Moulin, had married one of his parishioners in the parish of Verneuil.

To the beautiful woman the news of these priestly marriages came as an outrage. "What about the vow of chastity?" she asked in horror.

Chambraud, the handsome priest, glanced her way with angelic eyes but said nothing. With an even more angelic gaze Torné explained in very soothing tones that "no vow is legitimate if it goes against the vow of nature, dear citizen. My only regret is that because of my advanced age—I'm sixty-seven—I can't set an example for others now that this admirable reform has made it lawful for priests to marry."

Some time later, Delambre learned that within a month of this Christmas dinner Torné had married Thérèse Collet of Issoudun, whom he would divorce two years later.

Around the table groups of guests engaged in separate conversations, but at times, usually when a new dish arrived, everyone joined in general discussion. Through sheer perseverance Père-la-Liberté managed to

turn the conversation to the subject of education. Of the guests the best
informed on this topic was Chambraud. He seemed to know by heart
the text written by Condorcet that had served as the basis of the law
passed three days earlier. He quoted a passage about the need "to establish genuine equality among citizens . . . and achieve in reality the political equality acknowledged by the law." The words warmed him as he
spoke: "Education must not turn its backs on people the moment they
leave school. It must include people of all ages." The old man was delighted, but the starch dealer said, "Now they're promising us schools for
old folks!" These words were spoken over the shoulder of his beautiful
neighbor, who now turned to the priest with a question. "Excuse me, Father"—she insisted on addressing him in the customary manner—"but
if we spend all our lives in school, when will we find time to do any
work?" She then turned her attention back to her plate and continued
working on the large piece of thigh she had been served. Chambraud
brushed the question aside: "This adult education is all the more necessary because primary education has been neglected. Its purpose will be
to give everyone the means to satisfy their own needs, to secure their
prosperity, and to understand and exercise their rights." To which the
beautiful woman, her eyes agleam, responded, "Monsieur le Curé, that's
a regular sermon you've been giving us."

Léonne shuttled back and forth between the kitchen and the table
with huge platters that the guests promptly emptied. The innkeeper had
laid on a real feast, which everyone appreciated all the more because they
could hear the terrible blizzard raging outside. Someone said that if the
government took a hand in education, it might dictate the content of
the curriculum. Seated opposite Delambre was a small man who had
thus far remained silent, but now he exploded: "The people who say that
are the same ones who for centuries raised no objection when the
Church controlled the schools, but now they cluck like geese to insist
that 'education must be independent.'"

"Like turkeys," the merchant corrected.

"What do you mean, turkeys?" the small man asked.

"Who clucks like a goose?"

Père-la-Liberté leaped from his seat. "No, Citizen, no! You honk like
a goose, cackle like a chicken, and cluck like a turkey." After glancing
around the table with pride, he sat back down, his explanation having

met with a gale of laughter. At this point Chambraud returned with Condorcet's text and walked around the table reading it out loud: "Since the primary prerequisite of all education is that nothing shall be taught but the truth, the schools must be as independent as possible of all authority." In his blind perambulation the priest nearly ran into Léonne, provoking a horrified cry from the guests because she was carrying the dessert! Chambraud carried on with his reading, blithely unaware of his near mishap: "No power should be entrusted with the authority to prevent the discovery of new truth or the teaching of theories contrary to its policies or interests." He set the open book down on the table. Grease from the turkey stained its cover.

As sometimes happens at dinner parties, all the conversations stopped except one. The well-dressed man was still talking to his neighbor. In the silence a few minutes before midnight, this is what the other guests overheard: "In a barrel with a capacity of one *demi-queue* of Burgundy, I mix fifty pounds of rotten beans and lentils with fifteen pounds of spoiled rice, twelve pounds of potatoes, and five or six pounds of bryony scrapings." The beautiful woman listened with a rapt expression on her face. Before the man had finished giving her, and of course the other guests as well, the recipe for making starch, the old man interrupted him. "But it's all rotten!" he exclaimed with disgust. "So that's the stuff you use to stiffen the collars of ex-aristocrats!" But the other man, refusing to be silenced, rose with a solemn look on his face: "Not ex-aristocrats. I supply starch to the army and to the deputies of the Convention and to Robespierre himself, Citizen!" At that moment Léonne began banging on a large pot. It was midnight. Everyone exchanged kisses.

Within a short time almost everyone had gone to bed, leaving only two men in the dining room: Père-la-Liberté, still talking a blue streak, and Bellet, dozing in front of the fireplace. "The ones who stayed home have no heart," the old man was complaining. "The best men left in '92, and I bet you they don't all come back. As for the people selling supplies to the army, they're getting rich at the expense of our volunteers!" He reached over and affectionately touched Bellet's arm. "You see, friend, it's like this. The Revolution? It had no choice but to follow nature's example and hibernate, you understand? Take the winter off, then start up again when the good weather comes back, stronger and healthier than ever." Then he wrapped himself in a large cape and vanished from sight. "You two must have seen quite a bit of the country. Tell me, is France a really big place?" Though asleep, Bellet heard himself reply, "Big enough, big enough."

❦

Not far from Châtillon was a town called Marchecourt. A group there known as the Popular Society boasted twenty members under the leadership of Citizen Gasnier, formerly the parish priest. It enjoyed the distinction of being one of the most active political groups in the Loiret.

Alongside the road from Malesherbes to Pithiviers stood a small monument on which an inscription had been engraved. Designed to resemble a feudal marker, the monument reminded the villagers of the much-reviled toll stations where travelers had once been required to pay a toll to the local lord at every bridge, town gate, and crossroads.

At the December 17 meeting of the Popular Society, Gasnier spoke: "Citizens, brothers, an odious reminder of despotism still exists on our communal land. I am speaking of course of the stone pyramid known as 'the Meridian,' which the erstwhile lords of this place built in the days of their glory. I ask the society to vote tonight to dismantle this pyramid and bring its stones to Marchecourt for use in improving our streets." The members did as they were asked, and within a few days the streets of Marchecourt were in much better shape than they had been.

Père-la-Liberté mentioned this to Delambre, who hastened to Marchecourt. Where the pyramid had been he found only rubble, but a thorough search of the area turned up a marble plaque bearing the inscription, "Meridian of the Observatory, Constructed by Cassini in 1748." He took it with him.

❦

For a week the astronomer and his assistant were unable to leave the inn and watched in dispiriting idleness as the other guests left one by one. The starch dealer returned to Pithiviers after his wagon was pulled out of the pothole it had been stuck in. Then Torné and Chambraud left to keep their date with the latter's intended. Only the beautiful woman remained with her two babies, who unfortunately were not always asleep and soon made the inn unbearable. The episode only confirmed Delambre's determination to remain a bachelor.

◆

Although the storm had abated, the sky remained cloudy. Eventually a persistent east wind drove the last clouds away. A thick blanket of snow still covered the countryside. In the distance a dark mass rose out of the ice: it was the bell tower of Pithiviers, on which Bellet focused the lower telescope. Delambre, glued to the upper eyepiece, waited for his assistant to finish. It was the first time that both men had made simultaneous observations.

As the astronomer had predicted, the work now proceeded twice as fast. The cold was intense. Bellet was wearing the gloves whose fingertips he had cut off. Working without gloves, Delambre was obliged to pause from time to time to rub his hands together. The pauses were beginning to seem like an obsession, and an irritated Bellet called upon his colleague to "do as I do and wear gloves." "What good would that do? It's the tips of my fingers that are freezing." On hearing this Bellet reached into his pocket and solemnly withdrew ten small pieces of black wool, which he placed over the ends of each of his fingers. Only the left thumb remained to be covered when the two men heard a voice calling to them from below. At the base of the tower they could see a man who looked like Père-la-Liberté holding something out to them. Delambre grumbled as he climbed down the ladder.

"Seems to have come from Paris," the old man said as he handed the astronomer an envelope. Before he could decipher the name of the sender, the old man had pulled a poster out of his sack and unfolded it: "Could you read this for me? What a world—I have to hang up posters I can't read!"

The poster read:

Whereas in periods of famine the use of potatoes is limited to humans, the Committee of Public Safety decrees that:

Article I. No one is permitted to convert potatoes into starch.

Article II. Violators of Article I—

The old man's face lit up, and he laughed so hard that he could barely fold the poster back up again. "That starch man from Pithiviers will have a fit when he reads that!" he said as he wrapped himself in his cape and walked away.

Delambre broke the seal on the letter and started to read it. In a matter of moments the color had drained from his face: "In view of the importance of delegating functions and assigning missions only to men whose republican virtues and hatred of kings make them worthy of the public trust, The Committee of Public Safety hereby declares that Borda, Lavoisier, Laplace, Coulomb, and Delambre shall as of this day cease to be members of the Commission on Weights and Measures and shall deliver forthwith any instruments, calculations, notes, and reports in their possession." The letter was signed by Prieur of the Côte-d'Or, Barère, Robespierre, Couthon, Saint-Just, and Collot d'Herbois. Delambre stood transfixed at the base of the tower. From the platform above, Bellet was gesturing excitedly to him that he should come back up.

Old Borda was right to have warned them. Everyone who had signed the letter in support of Lavoisier had been dismissed, except for Haüy, who had no doubt been overlooked. Delambre was not sorry to have done what he had to do. He had of course expected to be punished but not so promptly or harshly. To be interrupted in the midst of his measurements, even before his winter campaign was finished, made him furious.

❖

On his way back past the tower, Père-la-Liberté saw two dark silhouettes wreathed in crimson. The astronomer and his assistant were sadly packing up their instruments.

Delambre turned toward Bellet so suddenly that he caused the frame of the structure to shake. "I have a proposition for you," he said. "You're not obliged to accept. We've done the bulk of the work. All the targets from here to Bourges are in place. It would be criminal and stupid to give up now. I won't force you to go with me, but I plan to carry on. I'm going to play dumb, as if I hadn't received any letter. I'll continue on to Bourges, and afterwards I'll hand everything over to them: instruments, calculations, notes, reports—everything!" Bellet remained silent. Delambre stuck his nose back into the instrument case and returned to his packing. Neither man said anything. Bellet sneezed. "Damn cold!" he complained. Then he started coughing. Finally, in the midst of a series of coughs, Delambre heard him say, "So, when do we start for Bourges?" The two men hastily embraced.

Bellet abruptly broke off the accolade and seized the letter, whose text he devoured. His face lit up. He planted himself in front of Delambre and read the text out loud, pausing between words: ". . . declares that Borda, Lavoisier, Laplace, Coulomb, and Delambre shall as of this day cease," etc. Then he thrust the letter under the nose of Delambre, who had no idea what was happening.

"Méchain is not mentioned!" Bellet matter-of-factly remarked.

"That's true," Delambre replied after taking another look to make sure. "So what?"

"If Méchain isn't mentioned, it must be that he hasn't been dismissed. And if he hasn't been dismissed, he'll be able to carry on with the work, since he's no longer dead!"

◆

In keeping with their decision, they continued their work in secret as far as the cathedral of Orléans before returning to Paris. The trip back was a sad one, during which the astronomer and his assistant did not exchange a single word. Bellet, distraught, wondered what he could do next. If his present situation was to be his only reward for all the effort he had devoted to the expedition, he would have done better to enlist in Dammartin when he had the chance. He remembered Delambre's brave declaration at the time: "If Dunkirk falls, we'll carry on! If Perpignan falls. . . ."

Delambre's thoughts were no more cheerful than his assistant's. Turning recent events over in his mind, he tried to understand how things had gone wrong so quickly. "When they asked me to undertake a mission as difficult as this in times as troubled as these, surely they didn't expect me to climb down from my towers and neglect my measurements in order to attend political meetings, and they didn't want me to hurry my calculations in order to parade my republican sentiments and hatred of kings. But now they've adopted a provisional meter, and then, on top of that, they've sent out a notice of dismissal on which the first signature is Prieur's!" From these reflections the astronomer drew a morose conclusion: "Obviously they intend either to change the mission radically or to put an end to it altogether."

At a way station Bellet left the berlin to wait for a stage coach that would take him to his family's village. After unloading his bags, he walked over to the door of the carriage he had just left. Delambre, who pretended to be rummaging through papers in a large briefcase, paused and looked up. Their eyes met. Bellet winked and gave the horse a good clap on its hindquarters, sending it on its way.

Rue de Paradis. Home at last! The astronomer ran up the stairs four at a time, only to find his door sealed shut. He ran to the headquarters of his section. What a relief to discover that the seals had been affixed in order to protect his property! The officials had worried about his prolonged absence. The move was not connected in any way with his dismissal, about which he was careful to say nothing. Instead he hastened to give proof of his mission by producing the authorizations that had been issued first by the Legislative Assembly and later by the Convention. Then he flabbergasted the sectional officials by handing over an enormous bundle of documents containing certificates from the local authorities in all the towns he had stayed in since leaving Paris.

By that evening the seals had been removed from his apartment. The next day Delambre let his friends know that he was back in Paris. Laplace was about to leave for Melun, where he had a house. Coulomb had already gone to Blois, where Borda was to join him shortly.

A year and a half after the two shiny coaches had rolled out of the courtyard of the Tuileries, this was how things stood: Lavoisier was in prison, Condorcet was on the run, Borda and Delambre had been dismissed from their posts, and Méchain, partially disabled, was detained in Spain.

Delambre inquired about Condorcet and was told that he had left Paris. This was not true. The new Montagnard government had not called for the heads of the Girondins. It had simply asked them to remain silent and discreetly exit the political scene. This did not happen, however. After the leaders of the Girondins returned home, they launched a rebellion against Paris, against the Montagnards and sansculottes. Condorcet, who had refused to muzzle himself for Louis XVI, was not about to muzzle himself for Robespierre. He took up his pen and wrote a broadside, which he then sent to his colleagues in the Convention: "Citizens, I have fled the tyranny under which you are moaning still. If the Convention had wished to question me, I would have answered. I want to know why those who fought to abolish monarchy in 1791 are today committed almost exclusively to persecution. I want to know why so much effort is being expended to get rid of men whose intelligence and implacable republicanism posed a stronger obstacle to the restoration of monarchy." Nor was the philosopher content simply to send this broadside to his colleagues; he also saw to it that it was circulated to the general public. Soon thereafter the Convention indicted him on charges of sedition.

Where could he hide? A small circle of friends gathered to ponder the question. Julie was joined by the renowned physician Cabanis and a young colleague by the name of Pinel. The latter, recently named physician-in-chief at the Bicêtre hospital, had caused a stir by ordering the chains to be removed from the lunatics incarcerated there, a measure that Condorcet had warmly applauded. After many sleepless nights, Condorcet's friends finally located a place right in the middle of Paris where they hoped he would be safe.

Between the Luxembourg Palace and Saint-Sulpice ran a narrow street that cut like a channel between blocks of houses: the rue des Fossoyeurs. On this street stood a four-story house, with a sign on its second-floor balcony advertising the Pension Vernet, a guest house. A man approached this house late one afternoon, just as one of the guests was climbing the staircase to the residential quarters. The arriving guest was Citizen Marcoz, a deputy of the Convention who sat on the Montagnard benches. A mathematics teacher at the lycée of Chambéry, he represented the *département* of Mont-Blanc.

No sooner had he closed the door behind him than a small woman stationed in the corridor called out to him, "Citizen Marcoz!"

"Yes, Citizen Vernet."

Her face clouded briefly as she seemed to think better of what she was about to do. But a moment later she decided to take the plunge and told Marcoz that someone was waiting for him in the salon. Marcoz went in. Standing in the middle of the room, bent slightly and staring at the floor in a deeply meditative pose, was Condorcet. The philosopher looked up. "I was expecting you," he told his colleague from the Assembly.

"Now you know that he is living here. If they arrest him, it will be on your head," Mme Vernet threatened. Then she made a move as if to leave. Condorcet signaled her to stop. "You know that I have nothing to hide from you. Stay." He then turned to Marcoz. "You seem surprised. Did you know that we've been living under the same roof for almost two months?"

"But this is insanely dangerous!"

"Do you mean, Marcoz, that it's insanely dangerous to live under the same roof as you?"

"This is no laughing matter. You're a wanted man. Why, just yesterday—"

"I know. I'm a scoundrel, a wretch, and an 'Academician,'" Condorcet laughed. "And it also seems that according to Robespierre, I believe it my duty to impose laws on the Republic just because I used to sit among learned men."

Marcoz was not laughing. "If they find you, you know what—"

"Death!" Condorcet interrupted. "I've taken precautions," he said calmly, holding out his hand. On his ring finger he wore a gold ring with a secret compartment that contained a small dose of poison.

"My God!" Mme Vernet exclaimed.

"Rolland committed suicide under an oak tree near Rouen," Condorcet continued. "Pétion killed himself in a quarry outside Bordeaux." He seemed to be speaking not so much to the others as to himself. "I ardently desired this Revolution, and I would allow the Revolution to guillotine me!" He paled at the thought. To die under a republican government, at the hands of the Republic! "But this government is not revolutionary!" he thundered. "Mark my words, Marcoz. 'Revolutionary' is a word that should apply only to movements that take liberty as their goal. Anything else usurps the name."

With effort Condorcet resumed a conversational tone. He walked over to a painting on the wall. "Aren't M. Vernet's seascapes magnificent? Did you know that our hostess can boast of more painters in her family than the Bourbons can boast of kings in theirs?"

Obviously Marcoz had no interest in M. Vernet's seascapes. He took a few steps toward Condorcet. "You can have total confidence in me. I will never reveal your hiding place."

"Thank you, Marcoz. You are an honorable man. You are taking a great risk. If I am found out, you will be accused of 'tenderheartedness' or arrested as a Girondin."

"Me a Girondin!" Marcoz burst out laughing.

"They have dared to accuse me of being a royalist!" Condorcet rejoined.

In the kitchen Mme Vernet neglected the meal she was preparing for her other guests in order to make something for Marcoz and Condorcet.

Returning to the salon platter in hand, she heard Marcoz say, "You know, Condorcet, there were only two ways to go. Either we continued the Revolution and extended its benefits to the poorest among us, or we held that the rich should be its only beneficiaries. A choice had to be made."

"A choice, yes, but to cut off heads!"

"I have consistently opposed these executions," a devastated Marcoz replied. "Every head cut off has done more to create enemies of the Revolution than all the battalions of priests and royalists combined. But how can we keep the oppressors from winning without curtailing freedom? You yourself had no answer to this question."

"We never resolved that conundrum. That is true," Condorcet quietly conceded. "We leave it to future generations. We must after all leave them some things to find out for themselves. But it won't be easy. Our enemies have an enormous advantage over us. For them, things are simple. They're against liberty, hence they eliminate those who wish to liberate themselves. It's only logical. But for us—" He left his sentence unfinished.

After searching his pockets for tobacco and coming up empty, Condorcet asked Marcoz if he had any. Marcoz handed him a leather pouch. Condorcet tried to give it back, but Marcoz refused. That very day he had decided to give up the vice for good. "The wine of Savoy is enough for me, but I no longer have time to drink it. And you?" he asked. "How do you spend your days?"

"I write. I write. I'm making up for lost time." The philosopher got up, walked over to another seascape, and stared at it for quite some time. It depicted the vast expanse of the sea, with a small brown spot in one corner: a tiny sail filled with wind. "And then I dream," he added.

In Burgundy and the Bordelais, on the Butte Montmartre, in Clamart-le-Vignoble, and in the Catalonian hills, the grape harvest was in full swing. When the sun rose it was October 5, 1793, and when it set it was 14 Vendémiaire, Year II.

The change had been effected within the walls of the Convention. A minor revolution, it was the work of a young mathematics teacher and Montagnard deputy named Gilbert Romme. He had walked slowly to the podium and as usual addressed his colleagues in a calm voice, but what he said left them almost speechless:

> You have taken an important step toward progress in the Arts and of the human spirit: eliminating diversity, incoherence, and inexactitude in weights and measures.
>
> In the Arts and History time is an essential element and necessary instrument. These disciplines therefore call upon you as well to provide new measures of duration that will be equally free of the errors of credulity, routine, and superstition.

With these few words the old way of measuring time on French soil came to an end.

From the same podium a few weeks earlier, another deputy, Barère, had proclaimed that "the National Convention should assume responsibility for the world's prosperity." Could the stages of this new era be marked out with the same signposts that had served in centuries of oppression? No. So the Convention, taking seriously the desire to begin the world anew, established a new commencement of Time. In so doing it indicated to people living on this earth at this moment that they were witnesses to a new beginning—to an enormous task of foundation. Everything would have to be reconsidered, reinterpreted, remeasured.

The Constituent Assembly had taken up the question of space; the Convention would deal with time. To Delambre and Méchain had fallen the task of measuring lengths and defining the meter, and it was left to Romme to measure time and devise a new calendar.

To be assigned to such an ambitious project was not displeasing to Delambre, for whom none of this came as a surprise. Romme and Lalande had called upon him to carry out long and arduous astronomical calculations in connection with the development of the new calendar.

Romme chose to base the calendar on two fundamental principles: the decimal system and Nature. Nature promised legitimacy, and the decimal system promised efficiency. The measurement of space was to be based on the earth itself, while the measurement of duration was to be rooted in the course of Nature. And the decimal system, which quantified distance, was also to be used for reckoning time. Just as there were one hundred centimeters in a meter, so too there ought to be one hundred minutes in an hour. But such a change would have required replacing the mechanism of every watch in the world and removing every clock from every tower and belfry. It was beyond the realm of possibility.

Much has been said about the clashes between royalists and republicans and between Girondins and Montagnards in these troubled times, but relatively little about the hidden war between the partisans of ten and the proponents of twelve, or, what comes to the same thing, between the adepts of one hundred and the champions of sixty. If one were to personify the two clans, one might propose Laplace as the ardent proponent of counting by hundreds and Condorcet as the zealous advocate of counting by sixties. So as not to tip the balance one way or the other, it was decided that hours should continue to consist of sixty minutes but that the length of the week would be increased to ten days.

It was proposed that the days of the week should be named for the great champions of liberty, but the proposition was rejected lest these men become idols. Delambre, who was present when the Convention voted on the measure, was enchanted by one exchange, which he remembered long afterward. When Romme, a confirmed bachelor, proposed to the Assembly that the first day of the year should be "husbands' day," one of the deputies, Albitte, had shouted out that "every day is husbands' day."

A way had to be found to give expression to the eternal round of the seasons, to nature's time. For this the deputies turned to a poet, and who better to name the months than Fabre-d'Eglantine, the author of the line "Il pleut, il pleut bergère"? For the months of autumn he chose names of grave tone and medium measure: Vendémiaire, Brumaire, and Frimaire. For winter, names heavier in tone and of longer measure: Nivôse, Pluviôse, Ventôse. For spring, names of light tone and short measure: Germinal, Floréal, Prairial. And for summer, names of sonorous tone and broad measure: Messidor, Thermidor, Fructidor.

❖

"Nonédi, 14 Nivôse, Year III of the Republic." Méchain's astonishment was complete when he saw this date printed at the head of the page of the newspaper that had just reached him after months of delay. What next? It was bad enough that Paris had sent him two repeating circles calibrated in different units, one in degrees, the other in *"grades,"* one *grade* being the angle subtended by an arc equal in length to one one-hundredth of a quadrant of the circle, thus forcing him to make constant conversions between the two units. Now he would have to travel about with a dictionary in order to translate old dates into new ones. To make matters worse, he would also be obliged to make retroactive changes in all his notebooks of observations.

"To say nothing of the elimination of Sundays," Tranchot whined, although he had not been to mass since his first communion. The last word on the subject was that of Salva, who remarked that whatever the names of the days might be, the fact was that henceforth there would be only one day of rest in every ten, or one fewer per month than before. "You have to say it's strange for a revolutionary government to make people work more than ever!"

❖

Sunday was no day of rest for Méchain and his assistant, who had recently embarked on an ambitious adventure. If they were prohibited from traveling north, they would go south instead. If they were prevented from measuring their triangles north of the Pyrenees, in French territory, they would do their work south of Barcelona, on Spanish soil. Méchain at last had all the leisure he needed to carry out his secret dream of extending his meridian measurements southward all the way to the Balearic Islands.

What was intriguing about this new project was that for the first time they would be measuring the meridian without the complications introduced by the features of the earth's surface, since the surface of the ocean was perfectly flat. This would be the most brilliant and novel achievement of the whole expedition—if Paris was willing to allow it.

The Spanish authorities fitted out a corvette. The ship was to take the Frenchmen from Cartagena to Majorca. After hastily completing preparations for the voyage, Méchain threw himself into the adventure. He chose the worst possible moment, however: the middle of the winter, which even in this region turned out not to be a propitious time for the kinds of observations he wanted to make. If a single snowflake fell anywhere in the area, it was sure to land on the highest summit in the precise location where the astronomer was setting up his targets. Méchain abandoned his project, and the corvette, assigned to other duties, sailed away from Cartagena.

Méchain returned to Barcelona, where the ban against travel to France remained in effect. He took advantage of this enforced vacation to make a fair copy of the observations he had accumulated since his departure. As his work proceeded, he imagined what effect these documents would have when the Commission at last had a look at them. His notebooks contained all of his measurements of triangles in Spain and all of his calculations. How many times had he rechecked each calculation? He had two reputations to uphold: that of a flawless observer and that of a punctilious and indefatigable calculator.

Writing was not easy for him because he was afflicted with synarthrosis, especially in the shoulder. The blow he had received had left it petrified, as useless as a frozen hinge. The stiffness radiated throughout his arm, affecting every joint.

When he had resumed his observations early that summer, his arm had felt like a block of marble from his shoulder down to his fingertips. "One and indivisible," Tranchot had said, making a jest of a republican slogan in order to cheer up his companion, but Méchain had not appreciated the joke. The summer sun and fresh air had done him some good, but the crucial thing was the constant effort to which he had subjected himself: by forcing himself to make continual small movements, he tried to save his arm from the fatal idleness of paralysis.

Once the notebooks were ready, Méchain made a pretty package and sealed the documents inside. The box was addressed to the Commission on Weights and Measures, Paris.

The next day the scientist was summoned to the citadel. He emerged in a state of bewilderment, rage, and anxiety. He had just been warned that if he attempted to communicate information of this sort again, his mail would be confiscated and he would be arrested. The numbers that filled his notebooks had been mistaken for secret military codes.

Package in hand, a depressed Méchain returned to his room at the Inn of the Fontana de Oro. He hastened to alert the Commission: "If we are granted permission to leave Spain during the month of March, and if we are allowed to enter France, we will reach Bourges in July, and this important effort will have been completed in two years despite the delays and the accidents." Seated at his rickety writing table, he imagined himself striding across the Pyrenees league after league, sweeping aside all difficulties, and following the meridian all the way back to Rodez. And then, energized by success, he would not stop there but continue on into Delambre's territory. All in four months! But he ended his missive on a darker note: "Alas, where am I? I speak as a man free to surrender to the ardor of his zeal."

He found employment for that unused zeal in a minor astronomical labor: measuring the inclination of the ecliptic, the angle that the great circle of the sun makes with the equator, which is responsible for the differences between one season and another. Working from the terrace of the Fontana de Oro, Méchain patiently recorded his findings. Tranchot had been right to choose this inn.

The work required knowledge of the latitude of Barcelona. Rather than save time by using the measurements made the previous year at the Fort of Montjouy, Méchain decided to start again from the beginning. No doubt he felt that this would be a good way to check his earlier work.

The results were dramatic, however: comparison of the two sets of measurements revealed an anomaly of three seconds of arc. Not a very large angle, but still enormous for someone who made a religion of exactitude and perfection. Those three seconds were impossible to explain.

❖

How sad that second winter in Barcelona was! The hordes of émigrés who had descended on the Catalonian capital made a point of spreading alarming rumors about orgies defiling that "infamous Babylon," revolutionary Paris. Méchain made every effort to obtain news of his family, but not one word arrived from Thérèse and not a single letter from the

Commission. This time the bridges had truly been cut. To add insult to injury, his funds were seized as enemy property—not just the official funds of the expedition but his personal funds as well. Before long he was short of cash.

Frequent visits by Salva and Maria were not enough to cheer him up. His friends suggested that he return to their estate, but he refused. He had too many bad memories of that place.

❧

When Tranchot returned from his strolls through the *barrio,* he often found Méchain poring over a sea of papers, scribbling and erasing. The astronomer would look up, make an imperceptible sign to his assistant, and run the tip of a finger over the scar marking the top of his forehead. Then he would turn back to his calculations, crumpling sheet after sheet and tossing the discarded pages onto the floor at his feet.

Late one night, as Tranchot sat reading quietly in his room, he heard hasty footsteps in the corridor. The door burst open, and Méchain entered. Taking up a position at the foot of the bed, he asked Tranchot point-blank if he had sent the Montjouy latitude measurements to the Commission. Surprised and irritated, Tranchot did not immediately grasp the implications of the question. Of course he had sent the results, and as always he had sent them immediately after receiving them from Méchain. "But that was a year ago!" Tranchot exclaimed. "If there's something wrong, if an error has crept in, we'll fix it tomorrow." Méchain stiffened. "Who said anything about an error? Who said anything about an error?" he screamed, as he danced nervously in front of the bed. "Excuse me, I'd like to go to bed," Tranchot curtly replied. Méchain's rage abruptly subsided. "Forgive me, I'm a bit tired. I need to rest," he whispered. Suddenly overcome with fatigue, he collapsed in a chair in Tranchot's room and fell asleep.

Since his accident, Méchain had been more prone to irritation than before. And after that night in the Fontana de Oro, he became more taciturn and anxious.

❧

Falling asleep on a chair! The same thing had happened to Delambre, when he had collapsed with exhaustion over his books in his frigid apartment on the rue de Paradis. In Barcelona Méchain had been unable to send his notebooks off to the Commission. In Paris Delambre had been summoned to turn his over "forthwith," or so it was stipulated in the order removing him from his post.

He threw himself into his work with stubborn rage, much as one might do if, compelled to leave a home to which one felt passionately attached, one made it a point of honor to get out as quickly as possible but not before making sure that the place was perfectly immaculate.

The thirty-five stations he had visited from Dunkirk to Orléans had yielded an enormous mass of information, measurements, and calculations. Delambre set to work with supreme diligence, including every detail, every iota of information, so that anyone who looked at his notebooks would have access to all the data he had gathered.

He scarcely left the rue de Paradis and nearly managed to forget what was happening in the capital. Only one thing troubled him: he had no news of Condorcet. Where was he? Was he still in Paris? Nobody knew anything. Perhaps the silence was a good thing, he thought to reassure himself. The notoriously inefficient police of the Committee of General Security managed to arrest suspects only when rumor revealed their hiding places. Thus there was hope that Condorcet might escape.

For Lavoisier there was no hope. Everyone knew that he was imprisoned at Fort-Libre. Delambre learned that even as the seals were being removed from his own house, they were also being removed from Lavoisier's house on the boulevard de la Madeleine so that the place could be searched for "papers, machines, and sums related to activities pertaining to weights and measures." Lavoisier had been present when the search was conducted. Rumor had it that Romme and Fourcroy had also been present as members of the Committee of Instruction.

It was reported that while searching the chemist's papers they had been dumbfounded to discover texts with such strange titles as "Report on a Stone Claimed to Have Fallen from the Sky during a Storm," "On a Chair for Use by the Sick," "On the Tobacco Grinder," "On the Sensation of Cold in the Mountains," "Report on a Method for Lighting Large Numbers of Lanterns Simultaneously," and, last but not least, one paper whose title took their breath away, "Report on the Divining Rod." Obviously none of this had anything to do with the metric system.

When the two men left the apartment, the small metal cylinder was still floating in the bathtub, which was still filled with river water filtered through sand.

❦

Each morning Lavoisier went to a room in the offices of the Committee on Paper Money and Coin accompanied by two gendarmes, who called for him at the prison. There he worked on the new five-*décime* coin. Think of it: a poor sansculotte buying a wretched loaf of bread that already cost too much for his taste and being obliged to pay for it with a coin bearing the image of a head that the guillotine had removed from the neck of its owner some time before! Such things were still commonplace a year after the king's death. Fortunately they were soon to end: the *louis* was to be replaced by the *franc.* A new currency was in the offing.

The decree that established the new units of length, weight, and volume also defined a new unit of currency: the franc. Just as the means of measurement were to be unified, so were the means of payment: the decimal system was to be used for both. New coins therefore had to be designed and minted.

The five-*décime* coin raised certain difficulties. It was so small that new weights had to be fabricated in order to weigh it, and this was a particularly delicate task. Lavoisier was of course the best "weigher" in the Republic.

As the days passed, Lavoisier went about his work of weighing, but still he was not freed. Delambre reassured himself with the thought that no one would dare touch a hair on Lavoisier's head. He was the greatest of all French scientists. All Europe envied France that he was one of hers. Before long he would be set free and resume work on the kilogram. And Delambre would return to his calculations.

❦

After a lengthy stint of work by dim candlelight, Delambre's eyes sometimes grew too weak to go on with his calculations, so he would go out into the city. Leaving the river near the Arsenal, he passed the place where the Bastille had once stood, passed the Hôpital Saint-Louis, continued until he reached the first fields beyond the customs barrier, and then turned around and retraced his footsteps, following the path of the future Saint-Martin Canal.

On the day he placed his notebooks in a small sack he felt a twinge in his heart. Two years of work. The figures he had recorded with his own hand—angles, azimuths, and so on—were far more than just numbers. They stood for flesh and blood, patience and passion. To gather all these data, how many ladders had he climbed, how many staircases had he hurried down, how many scaffolds had he erected? All that waiting, all that heat and cold, rain and frost, snow and fog, clouds and sudden, unexpected, joyful clearings! How his heart had leaped at the sight of a target gleaming as brilliantly as on the first day! It was hard for him to give up his notebooks, which he could not help thinking of as his own property.

This work had been a commission, however. He had been assigned to carry out a task, and he had completed his assignment. He was no longer deemed fit to continue in his post, and he had been sacked. He had been paid for his work; now it was time to hand in the results. Try as he might, he could not take such a cynical view of the matter. One thing was clear, however: these documents did not belong to him and never had, any more than a house belongs to the architect who draws up the plan or to the mason who builds the walls.

Delambre climbed into the shiny green berlin for the last time. He was headed for the headquarters of the Commission, where he was to hand over all his notebooks, instruments, calculations, notes, and memoranda.

A chapter closed! Pretending to be carefree as he made his way down the chilly streets of the capital, he forced himself to take his time, but one question consumed him: Who would replace him in the work of measuring the meridian? As he wandered the narrow streets of the Marais, he reviewed the list of possible candidates. Would it be an astronomer? Lalande perhaps? But no, he was too old and too fond of Paris. Bailly, a celebrated astronomer and former master of Paris, had been guillotined only a short time before. Cassini? Sacked from all his posts, the aristocratic astronomer had just been forced to move out of the Observatory. For the first time in more than a century no Cassini was in residence there! Might it be a mathematician? Legendre perhaps? Had he not taken part along with Méchain in a similar project to measure the distance from Greenwich to Paris? And Méchain of course! How could Delambre have forgotten him? He was the one. They would choose him to finish the project alone. They would ask him to continue his measurements all the way to Orléans instead of stopping at Rodez. That was the simplest solution! Would Méchain accept? Delambre could not predict his colleague's reaction. What did he know about him? About his personality and feelings? How many letters had they exchanged since the beginning of their mission? Two or three at most. Was Méchain even aware of his dismissal?

No, Méchain would not take his place. He had been weakened too much by his accident. Had they not been afraid that he wouldn't be able to finish the southern portion? And then there were the rumors that Méchain had emigrated. Delambre did not believe this. Méchain was too stubborn, he told himself over and over. He would never emigrate. At any rate not before reaching Rodez!

Thérèse had not hidden her anxiety from him, not because she believed the rumors but because the Committee of Surveillance seemed to believe them. Indeed, it had been so convinced of their veracity that she was now imprisoned at Port-Libre as the wife of an émigré.

By the time Delambre returned to the rue de Paradis he still had not settled upon the name of the individual likely to replace him. He carefully replaced a heavy folder among his files. It contained the copies he had scrupulously made of every page of the notebooks he had turned over to the Commission. Only then did he feel relieved of a great burden. He was done with the meter, the meridian, and the repeating circle. Now at last he was free to return to the astronomical work he had interrupted two years earlier. Once again he would be an astronomer and mathematician. There was only one thing left for him to do. He took out his travel diary and his pen and wrote, "Who knows when the expedition will resume? Or even if it will resume?"

The next day, Delambre went to the Committee of Instruction and asked to see Romme. He had discovered that according to the republican calendar the year 3600 was not supposed to be a leap year. Romme had immediately submitted a proposal to the committee to deal with the matter. But Abbé Grégoire, who opposed the new calendar, interrupted: "Are you asking us to establish eternity by fiat?" He then proposed that a vote on the bill be postponed until 3600. The postponement was immediately approved.

◆

Eternity! To Méchain, who had been held up in Spain for months, every week seemed like an eternity, which he was now convinced would not end until the war was over—no matter who won.

Perpignan still had not fallen. After the fall of Bellegarde, the Spanish had been on the verge of taking the city. But the Tech and the Têt, the two rivers of the Aspres, had decided otherwise. The villagers of the border region had mobilized. The residents of Corneillas had called upon the residents of Estagel for help: "The Spaniards are certain to come after us. If you back us up, we will do the same when you are in danger." The people of Estagel had come, with Arago in the van. Everyone had taken part, even the children, who fired stones with their slingshots.

Although Don Ricardos was a good professional soldier, he suffered the same fate that had already befallen his Austrian and Prussian comrades in the north. Brunswick, who had seen it all before, could have predicted the course of events. At first it would appear that the enemy would be defeated within a few days. A series of easy victories would seem to bear this out. But just as final victory seemed within reach, the invader would find himself bogged down on French soil, as if the enemy had with time firmed up his defenses without sacrificing his flexibility and ability to react quickly. Meanwhile, the invaders would begin to feel slow and dull-witted. This was exactly what Don Ricardos felt as his troops became bogged down in the eastern Pyrenees.

Despite his worries, the general continued to receive Méchain. After informing the Frenchman that his "shiny bronze" berlin was being held in a secure spot, the Spanish general said, "Let's discuss the situation, if you will. France is going to lose this war. My understanding is that the government of your country is not dear to your heart. You do not appear to be what you might call a raving sansculotte. Your Academy has been abolished for almost a year now. There is no longer any place for you in France. Stay in Spain! We need scientists of your talent."

"Emigrate? You're asking me to emigrate?" Oddly enough, Méchain had never give the idea a moment's thought. Indeed, the squawking flocks of émigrés he had met in Catalonia had disgusted him. Perhaps when the measurement of the meridian was complete and his family was safe, but not before. Keeping his thoughts to himself, he put a brusque question to the general: "Do you know a single French scientist who has emigrated?" Ricardos was unable to name one.

◆

The war dragged on. Méchain dispatched a series of letters to the Committee of Public Safety, the Temporary Commission, and Llucia, informing them that he was being held in Spain against his will. Llucia did not receive the letter addressed to him, however. Suspected of Girondism, he had been quietly relieved of his duties and replaced by Arago.

Suddenly the war took a new direction. The "French disease" had not been vanquished, and now Spanish defenses were breached by revolutionary soldiers, who braved the Pyrenees and retook Mont-Louis and Port-Vendres. Don Ricardos passed away, of sadness perhaps, or shame, or perhaps simply of heart failure. In Barcelona, "rear-echelon heroes" moved into action after the battle was over, as was their wont, courageously massacring any number of French civilians, not all of whom were republicans. Méchain and Tranchot miraculously escaped. Don Ricardos was replaced. The astronomer and his assistant were held in a "secure site" in part for their own protection but in part to make sure they did not escape.

◆

The citadel of Barcelona, a massive structure embedded right in the heart of the city, bristled with cannon and was well protected. From a window in Méchain's room one could peer out through the south façade of the fortress. His instrument cases were stacked up in one corner. In another corner was his personal baggage, arranged as if for an imminent departure, although the astronomer knew that he was not about to leave.

Leaning on the sill of the window, which overlooked the sea, Méchain stood deep in thought, his eyes fixed on the tower of Montjouy, which seemed to mock him from afar. Somehow this fortress seemed destined to remain forever off-limits to him.

The door opened. Méchain did not move. A guard entered and announced "El señor Gobernador!" The new governor walked into Méchain's room.

"Good day, Méchain. I hope you don't hold this against me. I had no choice. On the outside you would have risked your life. Just this morning two more of your compatriots were massacred. There was nothing we could do. The mob, as you know—"

Feeling gloomy, Méchain said nothing. Then, slowly, he turned around. "Your Excellency," he said, "the best way to make sure that I am not massacred is not to hold me prisoner."

"You are not a prisoner. I will allow no one to say that you are. You are simply being detained for your own good."

"As you wish. But as I was saying, the only way that I will not be massacred is if I am allowed to leave this country and return to France."

"Do you really believe that? Do you know what has happened to your colleague Lavoisier?"

Méchain looked at him and said nothing.

"Since you say nothing, I deduce that you suspect the truth. He was just guillotined, as they say in France."

Méchain took this news without flinching. He walked over to the window and stood with his face to the sea, without moving, stunned. The islands. Cabrera, Majorca. To travel. Far away. . . . The governor respected his silence.

"I must complete my triangles," Méchain said quietly, without turning around. "I simply must continue as far as Rodez. Please allow me to return to France. I beg of you."

"Your measurements along the border have put you in possession of military information. I cannot allow you to return to France."

"Since I am condemned to remain here, will you at least allow me to redo my latitude measurements at Montjouy?"

"That is impossible, as you know full well, Méchain. The fortress is a military installation, you are French, and we are at war with France. It will have to wait until the war is over."

"The war, the war!" Méchain screamed. "Let each man attend to his own work. Let me do mine. I have nothing to do with the war! I'm an astronomer."

"Let's not speak of it any longer," the governor curtly replied.

Méchain could restrain himself no longer: "It's as if you were in league against me, you and the French government! Since I am in Spain and not an émigré, I am in prison in Barcelona and therefore cannot return to France. And since I do not return to France, they think I'm an émigré. So my wife is imprisoned in Paris. Logical, no?"

The gendarme entered the house, his saber knocking against a stair. It was dawn, and most of the women were still asleep. As always, the guard opened the barred door so that it squeaked on its hinges. All the women sat up at once. The guard held up a piece of paper and cleared his throat before beginning to read the long list of names. Despite his heavy western accent, which made a hash of every syllable, Thérèse recognized her name when it was called. She froze: fire and ice, hope and fear. Choked up, she was unable to respond to the roll call. The gendarme became agitated, and Thérèse's neighbor squeezed her arm. The guard scrutinized the women's faces and repeated the name. Thérèse got hold of herself. In a firm voice she answered, "Yes, I'm here." The gendarme led her away.

❧

When Thérèse entered the room, the secretary of the Observatory section was finishing up his report. An order of the Committee of General Security was clearly visible on the table. After rereading his report and correcting occasional errors in spelling, the secretary glanced over at Thérèse, who was still on her feet, and motioned for her to sit down. She did, and he began to read:

> The Committee, having examined the letter that led to the arrest of Citizen Thérèse Méchain, residing at the Observatory:
>
> Whereas it emerges from these documents that Citizen Méchain, her husband, assigned by the Convention to conduct research wherever he deemed necessary for the purpose of perfecting weights and measures, traveled to the Pyrenees and thence to Spain in pursuit of his research;
>
> And whereas having completed these operations, he wished to return to the Republic but was prevented from doing so by the commanding general of the Spanish army, who required him to reside in Catalonia;

And whereas letters written since that time prove that he applied not only to the National Convention but also to the ministers of the Republic and the Court of Spain for permission to return to France;

And whereas the aforementioned Citizen Thérèse Méchain cannot on these grounds be deemed a suspect,

It is hereby ordered that she be released at once.

◈

Thérèse found herself standing in front of the section headquarters with a small package in her hand. Without thinking she hastened away from the spot in the direction of the Observatory. Things had moved so quickly! Only the day before she had still been at Port-Libre, and now she was free, strolling down a street she knew quite well. Her first thoughts were about her children and then about Méchain. So he was being held in Spain. "Prevented from returning": what did that mean? Was he in prison, as she had been, or had he simply given his word of honor that he would not attempt to flee in exchange for freedom of movement? Had the Spaniards charged him with anything?

After reclaiming her children, she planned to inquire at the Temporary Agency for further details. Then she would go to see Prieur, who seemed to be the man in charge. And Delambre: it would be a pleasure to let him know of her release, but he was probably no longer in Paris. Three days earlier he had come to see her in prison and told her that he was about to leave for Bruyères. But then she began to enjoy her walk down the boulevard so much that she forgot everything else, feasting her eyes on the trees in the Luxembourg Gardens, which glistened in the sun. It was such a beautiful day—rare for a March 24 in Paris. She knelt to tie her shoe. A man passed her. His step was rapid but somehow awkward, yet she paid no attention to him. He was an imposing fellow in a red cap, felt trousers, and striped vest under a threadbare jacket. How could she possibly have guessed that this was Condorcet? The philosopher was fleeing Paris in the uniform of the sansculottes.

Meanwhile, a short distance away, a sinister-looking tumbrel emerged from the Luxembourg Palace, which had been converted into a prison. In it was a prisoner, whose hands had been bound: the man known throughout Europe as the "Orator of the Human Race," Condorcet's friend Anacharsis Cloots.

Even before the philosopher passed through the customs barrier on the road to Maine, the former Prussian baron turned sansculotte had been guillotined for having loved Paris more than any other city, France more than any other nation, humanity more than France, and the Revolution more than life itself. Born on a twenty-fourth of March in faraway Prussia, he died on another twenty-fourth of March on a blood-stained square in his adopted country. Was it possible under the circumstances to hold on to even a glimmer of hope?

A few days earlier, Condorcet had tried to answer this question: "Our hopes for the future of the human race can be boiled down to three main points: the elimination of inequality among nations, the progress of equality within each people, and finally, the genuine perfection of man."

Why had the philosopher left his refuge on the rue des Fossoyeurs, where he had been coddled by the gentle Mme Vernet? All in all, his winter there had gone quite well, and the danger seemed to be diminishing. There, moreover, he had been able to enjoy delightful visits with Sophie and on occasion Eliza.

All day long he worked in his room, which overlooked a courtyard with five splendid lindens. Through the window above the door, which gave him a clear view of the sky, he could watch night fall. After dinner he was free to enjoy evenings in the salon, where the atmosphere ranged from calm to animated, quiet to impassioned. Some evenings Mme Vernet invited "outsiders" such as Drs. Cabanis and Pinel. Dr. Cabanis liked to talk about physical suffering, while Dr. Pinel spoke of his inability to alleviate the spiritual pain afflicting his patients at Bicêtre, a hospital for the insane. Usually, though, there were just the other boarders: Marcoz and Citizen Sarret, who was a friend of the hostess. Sarret set himself the task of making a fair copy of what Condorcet had written during the day, which he then read to the others, while the philosopher amplified his text with oral commentaries.

Condorcet, hungry for news, was always impatient for Marcoz to return with the latest from the Convention, whether good or not so good. On February 4, for instance, he learned that the Assembly had voted to abolish slavery. That night he was wild with joy, as happy as a child, and all his cares were forgotten in an instant: "Wondrous Convention, this redeems everything!" He went up to his room and returned with an old book from the bottom of one of his trunks. He read aloud from the text:

Admittedly there are profound politicians who insist that the twenty-two million white, or almost white, people of France cannot prosper unless three or four hundred thousand blacks expire under the lash two thousand leagues from French soil. They say that there is no other way for us to enjoy sugar, indigo, and other such commodities at reasonable prices. It was the same when Louis le Hutin freed the serfs on his estates, and people said that because those serfs were now free to do nothing rather than work, all our fields would go uncultivated. The same politicians also say that the slavery of the Negro is not as distressing as some people would have us believe, that it's in fact quite a pleasant thing for an African to be plucked from his country, loaded onto a crowded ship where he must be kept in chains lest he kill himself, sold at auction like a beast of burden, and condemned along with his posterity to hard labor, humiliation, and whippings. The truth, however, is that Whites have no right to do such favors for Blacks, and by itself this argument should suffice to put an end to the practice.

Marcoz and Sarret had not been able to stop laughing. Mme Vernet had served spirits, and everyone had gone to bed quite late. That night on the rue des Fossoyeurs, liberty had been ebony in color.

Cheered by such news, Condorcet had set to work on any number of articles on education, war, and other vast topics, and Marcoz had delivered them anonymously to the Committee of Public Safety. Thus Condorcet had been able to continue contributing to the Republic's success.

Later, when he learned of the execution of his friends, tears came to his eyes, and these words escaped his lips: "Alas, all human beings need clemency." Then he went to his room and in a rage wrote throughout the night at breakneck speed. "Any society that is not enlightened by philosophers is deceived by charlatans. They always follow the same course, seeking to win the favor of the people in order to reign as tyrants. . . . It is criminal to think that injustice can be dictated by the needs of public safety. . . . Only if we make it our principle to act with the people and through the people, by leading the people, can we preserve the law in a time of popular revolution." For two days he had remained in his room, avoiding the salon. The others had respected his solitude.

After being formally charged during the summer, he had sat down to write an indignant brief justifying his actions over the previous few months. Breaking with her custom, Sophie had tried to persuade him otherwise: "What do those few months matter compared with the centuries to come? How does this handful of accusers matter to you, or the shifting currents in this assembly? Forget about them! If you must write, let it be for all of us." She hesitated. "Let it be for the generations to come, for the human race, as our friend Cloots would say."

"Do you remember that he used to call you Young Venus?" Condorcet reminded her.

Sophie smiled. That night, Condorcet abandoned his brief and threw himself wholeheartedly into the writing of his most famous work, the *Esquisse d'un tableau historique des progrès de l'esprit humain*. Every day he worked on it in the tranquillity of his room.

One morning, Mme Vernet handed him a letter from his wife:

> Six months' absence will place you on the list of émigrés. Measures have just been passed to punish the wives of the missing: they will not be allowed to retain any property whatsoever. I will therefore lose control not only of our assets but also of what my mother left me.
>
> In order to ensure that our daughter does not lose what little she has, I must ask a favor. I cannot tell you how dearly this sacrifice will cost me. This apparent separation, when my attachment to you and to the bond between us is indissoluble, is for me the ultimate misery. I dare to believe that you have no need of my assurances to be certain that the remainder of my life will explain the meaning of my action and that when we are reunited nothing will change in our attitudes toward each other. I shall continue to bear a name that in my eyes is ever more dear and more honorable.

What was this action whose name Sophie could not bring herself to write? Suddenly Condorcet understood: she was going to file for divorce! It was impossible. It cut him to the quick. Sophie was leaving just when he needed her most, at a time when so many other important things had collapsed. Of course she was doing it to protect little Eliza's interests. Soon she would be known by her maiden name, Sophie Grouchy, as she had been known before he met her. Names! he laughed cynically. The rue le-Cul-de-Sac-Taitbout was now known as the impasse Brutus, yet nothing had changed. Would Eliza at least retain the name Condorcet?

What were Sophie's reasons for acting as she did? When the philosopher was banished, all his property had been immediately confiscated. His affairs had been placed under seal and his assets frozen. Sophie had had to go to work. Knowing how to paint, she had opened a studio on the mezzanine of a lingerie shop on the rue Saint-Honoré, a short distance from the bakery where Robespierre had his lodgings. She spent her days there from dawn to dusk, then began the long trek home to Auteuil. As the wife of a condemned man, she was not allowed to remain in the capital at night. In the morning, when the time came to pass through the city gates in the other direction, she mingled with crowds of people whose fondest wish was to see the guillotine in action. How could she go on this way?

A law had just been passed allowing the spouse of a condemned person to recover his or her property upon divorce. This offered Sophie a way out.

Mme Vernet tried to argue that divorce was a mere formality, that Sophie had been forced into it, that it was the only thing she could do to protect Eliza's interests, that the times alone were responsible, that the government would not last forever, and that once it fell, the divorce would be annulled and everything would be as before. She tried. But it was one thing to understand the world as a philosopher, another to embrace it. Condorcet tried to understand but failed. Or, rather, he understood Sophie's attitude but refused to accept it.

On certain nights the silhouette of a peasant woman could be seen creeping along the rue des Fossoyeurs after dark with a basket of provisions in her hand. Sophie, braving the cold, the dark, and the many dangers, was on her way to give her old philosopher a hug or deliver him a note: "I've brought you lentils and beans. This should last you for a month. I am making you a nice vest. Avoid the damp and keep yourself in good health for the sake of your child, who speaks of you constantly." She had not appeared for a week, but yesterday there had been a letter: "I beg you to remain calm. You're safe with Mme Vernet. I throw myself at your feet to urge you not to abandon your shelter." She alone had sensed what was about to happen. Neither Pinel nor Cabanis nor even good Mme Vernet had suspected a thing. That very day, the philosopher put the finishing touches on the *Esquisse*. At last the work was done. In his eyes it was the most important book he had written, his testament for future generations, as Sophie had wished. He was now free to do as he wished. So he made up his mind.

◈

Sophie's letter was still on the desk, along with the manuscript of the *Esquisse*. He put them away. The tile roofs sparkled in the early light, and the bedroom filled with brightness. He got up, removed his nightshirt, and hung it up. From a valise stowed away under the bed, he took his clothes: felt trousers and a striped vest. Then he put on his threadbare jacket and adjusted the big red cotton cap on his head. As big as it was, it was still too small for him. Without cracking a smile he looked at himself in the mirror. A handsome silver watch with gold hands indicating the hour, minute, second, week, and day hung next to the mirror. He took it down and slipped it into the watch pocket of his vest. From a drawer he took a pencil holder, a pair of scissors, a razor with an ivory handle, and a knife with a handle of horn. All of these items he placed in his pocket.

One last look: the room was in order, the papers were arranged, the bed was made. A portrait of Eliza stood prominently on the night table. His hawthorn cane hung from the door handle. He took it and grasped the steel knob, every ridge of which felt familiar to his palm. Then he selected a book from the shelf and slipped it into his pocket as well. Just as he was about to leave, he stopped, turned around, took out the tobacco pouch that Marcoz had given him, and placed it on the bed. He gently closed the door behind him.

◆

"Already up so early in the morning? What's come over you?" Usually Condorcet worked in bed until noon. Surprised by his unexpected appearance, Mme Vernet turned around to look at him.

"My God, what are you doing in that get-up?" She couldn't believe her eyes. In a reproachful tone she added, "And those clothes are too small for you!"

"My colleague Cassini, who didn't like me very much, never tired of saying that I had traded my academician's uniform for the uniform of leader of the sansculottes. I've decided to prove that he wasn't a liar." Condorcet looked out the window. The splendid lindens in the courtyard glistened in the bright morning sun. "According to the new calendar, this is the month of Germinal, no? It's the beginning of spring." He fell silent for a time. Mme Vernet went back to making breakfast. She was tense. It broke her heart to think of him standing there ill at ease behind her, made up like a bad actor. She was afraid of what he was going to say.

Condorcet spoke softly. "I've finished what I had to do. It's been a long time since I've walked in the country. To feel the earth beneath my feet! This is the season when nature is reborn." All the while he was thinking: "I cannot bear to be shut up in my room any longer, to jump at the slightest sound, to cringe like an animal in its burrow." But all he said was, "I'm going away."

"You're not comfortable here?" she asked naïvely. It was a childish ploy.

"If I stay any longer, I'll get you in trouble without doing myself any good. Don't you understand? The Convention has made me an outlaw."

"It has made you an outlaw, but it can't put you outside humanity. Stay, I beg you."

Condorcet sat down, apparently won over by the determination of his hostess. He took off his cap and drank slowly from the bowl she handed him. Then he reached into his pocket, as she had seen him do so many times before, and pretended to be surprised: "My tobacco! I must have left it in my room." He made as if to get up and go look for it. "Drink," she said. "I'll fetch your tobacco." She moved toward the door, hesitated, then glanced trustingly at Condorcet. He returned her smile.

Mme Vernet's footsteps echoed in the staircase. By the time she returned with the tobacco pouch, Condorcet was gone.

When Marcoz heard the news, he turned pale, knowing what fate lay in store if a banished person was captured. If Condorcet had been arrested, though, the Assembly would have been notified immediately. Therefore he must still be free. Sophie, meanwhile, decided not to leave Auteuil. If there were an arrest, the official notice would be sent to her there. There was nothing to do but wait.

After their meal, Marcoz, Mme Vernet, and Sarret came together in his room. Without saying a word, acting simply out of habit, one by one they had climbed the stairs and quietly opened the door. But now there were only three of them. Only now did they really feel his absence.

Sarret, the first to enter the room, had found the envelope addressed to Mme Vernet, attached to a manuscript addressed "to my child, Eliza Condorcet. Advice to my daughter when she reaches the age of fifteen."

Mme Vernet put on her glasses, but everything was a blur. Sarret took the testament from her hands. "If my daughter is destined to lose everything, I beg her second mother to heed these last wishes of an innocent and unfortunate father. I ask that she be spoken to often of us, that our memory be kept alive so that she may preserve it, and that she be urged in due course to read our instructions in the original."

When Mme Vernet heard the words "second mother," she collapsed. Sarret held her close. She allowed herself to sink into his arms. He kissed her. Through her tears she looked at Marcoz as if to beg his pardon and then said, "M. Sarret and I have been married for several months. I don't know why we decided to keep it secret." She tried to smile. Marcoz got up, kissed her, and affectionately shook Sarret's hand.

They spent the night putting the manuscripts in order. Mme Vernet fell asleep. When she looked up, she was surprised by the silence. Marcoz and Sarret had fallen asleep as well, one in the armchair, the other on the bed. She took off her glasses and looked up at the window over the door. It was daybreak.

At the same moment, several leagues from Paris, in a niche in the wall of a quarry, Condorcet slept with his cap pulled down over his eyes and his head resting on a book. Sleep came very late, as it does to serious insomniacs and anxious fugitives. It was not until that frigid March night was almost over that torpor finally overcame the philosopher's anxieties.

Condorcet awoke suddenly at the sound of voices coming from the road nearby. Dawn already, dawn at last. . . . The voices belonged to workmen on their way to work. Trying not to be seen, Condorcet made haste to move on. In his hurry he tripped over a rock and fell. A sharp pain radiated through his leg, and a red stain appeared on his trousers. He quickly fashioned a bandage and picked up his things, which had scattered up and down the slope. Luckily the watch was not damaged. He left the quarry without being spotted and made his way to the road, not without difficulty. Limping badly and leaning on his cane, he walked on. The sun had warmed the air, nature was ready to begin anew, and birds in the sky above described simple figures as they flew. Happiness! Everything would have been perfect, even the leg, had it not been for the terrible gnaw of hunger.

Just ahead lay the village of Clamart-le-Vignoble.

❧

At a tiny inn Condorcet ordered an omelet. "How many eggs?" asked the innkeeper.

"A dozen," answered the philosopher.

"A dozen! Can you pay for it?"

Condorcet showed his money. The innkeeper's exclamation had caused Nicolas Fleury, who was drinking with another man at a nearby table, to turn around.

The plate was soon empty. Condorcet, his stomach full, stared longingly at the tobacco on Nicolas's table. He took out his book and began to read. Nicolas questioned him. "I've never seen you around here. Are you not from these parts?" Condorcet was slow to answer. Nicolas was already on his feet next to his table. The philosopher carried no residence certificate, civic certificate, or section card. He wasn't even wearing the tricolor cockade. "Your passport?" Nicolas asked.

"I don't have it. I . . . lost it when I fell," he said, exhibiting his injured leg.

"Your name?"

"Pierre Simon, born in Ribemont, near Saint-Quentin. I am an unemployed servant."

"What are you doing here?"

"I'm scouring the countryside for work in the saltpeter industry, or whatever I can find."

"Saltpeter! Show your hands!"

Condorcet held out his hands. They were white and smooth, more accustomed to wielding a pen than a pickax. Nobody pulled the wool over Nicolas Fleury's eyes! He knew an ex-noble when he saw one. This one didn't look very fierce. Let him go? What if he were a spy? Injured as he was?

"Will you come with me . . . Citizen?" The question was not an idle one. Condorcet looked at Nicolas to make it clear that he'd seen the trap and responded in a firm voice, "Simon, Pierre Simon."

He got up with difficulty. While he sat, his leg had stiffened. The effort of rising revived the sharp pain. The man who had been drinking with Nicolas and who had thus far stayed out of things now asked his friend where he was going. Fleury said that he was taking the suspect to Bourg-l'Egalité. Condorcet could not suppress a smile: all these new names! He repeated to himself the new name of Bourg-la-Reine. It occurred to him that he might die under an assumed name: Simon was the name of his former servant. He remembered that his silver watch with gold hands showing the hour, minute, second, and date was engraved with his initials: a riddle for anyone who might find it. His smile was read as a grimace of pain.

"Leave him alone, Nicolas," the man said. "Obviously the poor fellow is hurt. He doesn't look very dangerous."

"If he isn't dangerous, they'll release him tomorrow. No harm done," Nicolas replied as he offered his arm to Condorcet.

One limping, the other marching as proudly as he knew how, they left the inn. A piece of bread remained on the table, along with a drop of wine in the bottom of a glass and a few bits of omelet stuck to the plate, which the innkeeper removed. On the bench was an open copy of a collection of poems by Lucretius. When the man leafed through it, he saw that it was not written in French. Some of the words resembled words he remembered from his childhood prayers. Latin! Poetry! The man was lost in thought when the sound of wagon wheels caught his attention.

A cart filled with the crates and baskets used by grape growers was passing in front of the inn. Condorcet was seated in the rear, his leg resting on a crate.

The man hastened outside and ran after the cart. He caught up with it. "Citizen Simon, your book!" Surprised, Condorcet took the book in the hand that wore the fatal ring and gripped its pages, in which the poet almost two thousand years earlier had written that man must "try to live" in spite of everything. The cart continued to move forward. The man was left standing in the middle of the road. He made up his mind to run after the cart, caught up with it once again, and without saying a word handed Condorcet his tobacco pouch.

— *13* —

Now here was a man, a learned man, a former academician once believed to be an émigré, who when held against his will in a foreign country had insisted on returning to republican soil. Imagine how proud the
Committee of Public Safety had felt when it learned of Méchain's efforts
to return to France. But whereas they were thinking "France," Méchain
was thinking "meridian."

Thérèse, upon being released from prison, did several things. First,
she went to the Temporary Agency but found few people there: the place
was in the doldrums. Then she managed to obtain an interview with
Prieur, who had played such an active role in having Delambre removed
from his position. Despite this, he now agreed to play just as active a role
in seeking Méchain's release.

The authorities allocated sixty thousand livres—a tidy sum in these
hard times—for the purpose of bringing the astronomer home. The
Army of the Eastern Pyrenees was ordered to get him back. General
Dugommier, the army's commander, thought of exchanging Méchain
and Tranchot for his many Spanish prisoners. But this proved to be un-
necessary, because the defeated Spanish forces were no longer in a position to dictate terms. Having retreated beyond the Pyrenees, they now
held only one strong point on French soil, Bellegarde. Nevertheless, the
fortress withstood every attempt by republican forces to recapture it.

Arago, who now presided over his departmental directorate, had appealed to the Spaniards to return the astronomer and his assistant and
believed that their release was imminent. But he waited in vain. In fact,
Méchain and Tranchot were no longer in Spain. They had set sail for
Italy. For reasons that were not clear, the Spanish authorities had chosen
not to send the two men back to France. Instead, they had placed them
aboard a ship bound for Livorno, which was in the hands of the English.

Méchain and Tranchot thus found themselves in the middle of the Mediterranean. Although under constant threat from corsairs, their ship, superbly sailed, had thus far managed to elude capture. But now a ship had been pursuing them for the past two days. Méchain thought he recognized it as the corsair that two years earlier had sunk the galleon laden with American gold in the waters below Montjouy. Each time dark sails loomed on the horizon, Méchain would scurry below decks, where, safe from prying eyes, he would check his crates and make sure that everything was in order. From one of the trunks he would then take a folder containing a manuscript and bind it around his torso with a length of ribbon. Having done this, he would button his shirt, straighten his clothes, and climb back up on deck. From a position in the stern he would then focus his binoculars on the corsair, whose course he would carefully follow until night had hidden the pursuer's brown sails and mahogany hull in its dusky folds.

At that point things would begin to move very quickly. The captain, taking control of the helm, would change course repeatedly at brief, unpredictable intervals. Woe unto anyone who dared shout an order or light a candle: silent and blind, the ship would sail on into the night, free of the pursuing Barbary pirates. Méchain often fell asleep on deck, where Tranchot would find him at dawn the next morning. He would then throw a cloak over his comrade and wait until he awoke to tell him, always in the same words, that once again they had cheated fate: he, Tranchot, would not end his days as a eunuch of the sultan, nor would Méchain wind up as the caliph's official astronomer.

After arriving in Italy, Méchain and Tranchot took up residence first in Livorno, then in Genoa. Having tried Catalan, they now sampled Tuscan. For two months they remained out of touch. Neither Thérèse in Paris nor Delambre in Bruyères-le-Châtel, where he had gone after leaving the capital, had any news of their whereabouts.

◆

Delambre's protector, the estimable M. d'Assy, had set up a small observatory in a house in Bruyères. The house was simple but comfortable, and compared to the wretched inns he had lived in for the past two years, Delambre thought it a veritable palace. Managing the household was left to an old servant, a woman named Julie, as garrulous as she was energetic, and the more she worked, the more she talked. At times the astronomer had to order her to stop work just to shut her up. He would then put aside his pen, glasses, and writing desk and busy himself with household chores under the reproachful eye of Julie, who, though she burned with impatience, was silent at last.

The house stood one league from Arpajon and ten leagues from Paris. Despite this proximity to the capital, the village, a short distance away on the Vaugrigneuse road, seemed remote from everything. Isolated from the main highways and regional power centers, it had been spared by the whirlwind that had sucked everything toward the capital. This isolation had not, however, prevented the villagers from sprucing up the name of the place by substituting "Liberté" for "Châtel." No matter what the village was called, one felt forgotten there, and that was exactly what Delambre wanted.

After a time communing with the stars, mathematics, and Julie, Delambre felt the urge to get moving again. As luck would have it, Bruyères lay between Blois, where Coulomb and Borda lived in retirement, and Melun, where Laplace had gone after being removed from office. Since Melun was closer, Delambre decided to go see Laplace.

Upon reaching the outskirts of Melun, his carriage was forced to slow down because the road was clogged by people from surrounding villages on their way into town. Delambre asked his traveling companions what was happening. The man sitting next to him repeated the allegations that were on everyone's lips: "They're starving the people. Wheat is in short supply, the flour is wretched, and the bread is not even edible." According to this man, the object of the crowd's wrath was the dealers who had supposedly been hoarding grain; bakers were also suspect. Just now people were flocking to the Hôtel de Ville, where a jury of women were to deliver their verdict.

The man who said all this had a thick black beard and smallpox scars on his forehead. "Bread is the poor man's gold!" he grumbled. He took a piece of paper from his briefcase and handed it to Delambre: "I represent the People's Society," he proudly proclaimed.

Unity, Indivisibility of the Republic
Liberty, Equality, Fraternity, or death.
Society of Sansculottes Jacobins.
The presidents and secretaries of the Society of Sansculottes Jacobins

sitting in Melun hereby certify to their brothers and friends in all the people's societies of the Republic, that Citizen Jacques Clareau, aged thirty-six. . . .

Et cetera, et cetera. This was followed by a description ending with "black beard, low forehead marked by smallpox." Rather stupidly, Delambre raised his eyes to verify that the description was accurate. "Before the Revolution," the document stated, "Citizen Clareau was a weaver. He still is." Delambre handed back the piece of paper, the first of its kind that he had been able to examine.

When the carriage turned into a broad street, the man pointed to a house: "Rue Neuve: this is where they arrested Bailly." One of the passengers looked at him with surprise. "Yes, indeed, Bailly, the astronomer, who ordered the troops to fire on the people on the Champ-de-Mars."

Without omitting a single detail, Clareau told the story of how Bailly had been recognized by passing *fédérés* and taken to the communal headquarters under arrest, and then from there to the former Visitandine monastery before being sent to the capital, where he was executed.

Citizen Clareau also told them what the executioner had said on the scaffold: "You're shivering, Bailly?" And the condemned man had replied, "Yes, my friend, from the cold." Delambre recalled that Bailly had been arrested after leaving Nantes, where he had been safe in hiding for many months. Why did he leave a place in which he had been safe, like Condorcet?

The rumor was that he had left to visit Laplace in Melun. Laplace, when asked about this, did not confirm the rumor. Bailly was one of the greatest astronomers of his day. When the Revolution came, he had abandoned everything to throw himself into action. One day someone asked him, "What are you doing these days about the stars, the planets, and the comets?" Bailly stared at his interlocutor and absently replied, "A thunderbolt has struck my head and knocked all my ideas about science clear out of it. To tell the truth, I can barely remember having been an astronomer." Whenever Delambre recalled these words, he felt a profound unease and a sort of affection for his colleague, whom he had never counted among his friends. Delambre admitted to himself that he had never felt the passion for the Revolution that had overcome Bailly and driven Condorcet into battle. No lightning or thunder for him: just benevolent interest. But no passion. None at all.

Upon drawing near the Hôtel de Ville, the carriage was obliged to halt. Delambre climbed down, as did Citizen Claireau, who accompanied him into the square. The women delegated by the crowd to witness the making of bread had just arrived from the various bakeries in which they had spent the night. Perched on a crate, a young mother, a calm, energetic woman wearing a white cap, gave a report of the mission. Accompanied by municipal officials, the women had visited one bakery after another, observing the work of the bakers and their assistants. Some of the wheat had been of rather poor quality: probably washed previously and poorly dried, rough in texture but soft to the tooth, yet still edible. Other portions had been full of dark grains and signs of blight and rust and had to be thrown out. But most of the wheat was healthy, yielding a mediocre but acceptable flour; the yeast tasted sufficiently bitter, and the proper cooking time had been respected.

The woman took two loaves out of a sack and held them up to the crowd. Someone handed her a knife. The loaves were sliced and distributed to the people in the crowd. They ate, and as they did a murmur ran through the square. The bread was good! Several bakers standing in front of a bakeshop breathed a sigh of relief.

Delambre had tarried longer than he should have, and by the time he arrived at Laplace's house, the mathematician had gone out. A letter awaited him: "I am at the apothecary's. While you're waiting, would you kindly have a look at this manuscript." The manuscript, which had been placed on a small table next to a vase of roses, bore the title *Système du monde*. His friend had spoken to him previously about this project, the most ambitious attempt ever to describe all known celestial phenomena in terms of Mr. Newton's general theory of gravitation.

In this work Laplace had written that

> if on a clear night you pay close attention to the spectacle of the heavens, you will see that they are in constant flux. Stars rise and set. Some appear in the east, while others disappear in the west. Some, such as Polaris and the stars of the Big Dipper, never sink below the horizon at our latitudes.
>
> The curvature of the earth is perceptible to sailors at sea. When they approach a coast, what they see first are the highest points on land; only later do lower-lying areas initially hidden by the convexity of the earth loom into view. The curvature of the earth also explains why the sun, on first rising, gilds mountaintops before it illuminates the plains beneath.

Leafing through the manuscript, Delambre was surprised not to find any mathematical formulas. There were pages and pages without diagrams or calculations. How difficult it must have been to eliminate every trace of mathematics. And it was particularly astonishing that this should have been done by Laplace, whose previous work had been devoted entirely to reducing mechanics and astronomy to pure algebra. Using mathematical analysis to give a rigorous treatment of the world system was an idea that had appealed to Delambre immediately.

In April 1787, he recalled, he had gone regularly to lectures at the Collège de France. One day he arrived shortly after the lecture began. Simon Laplace was explaining his brand-new theory of the substantial differences between Saturn and Jupiter. On the blackboard he had written down the secular equations and calculated the period with the utmost precision: 877 years. The purity of the equations and the rigor of the results came as a revelation. Everything seemed more certain, more uniform, and easier to do. With mathematics alone it was possible to explain things that had hitherto baffled the finest minds. It was while sitting in that amphitheater that a dazzled Delambre had decided to become an astronomer. When the lecture was over he hastened to his room. With a blank sheet of paper and the most recent observational tables, he sat down to respond to the challenge he had just set himself: to recalculate all the known observations of the two planets. This was a considerable task, and it became his first work, the one that had established his reputation as an astronomer.

After that he had been gripped by a sort of hunger for work. He had checked the solar tables and then observed his first eclipse. After that he had worked on the tables for Uranus, the sun, Saturn, and Jupiter and its satellites. Ultimately he was without peer when it came to deducing astronomical results from analytical formulas, regardless of their complexity.

He heard voices in the garden. Laplace had returned with his young wife and two children. The elder boy gamboled ahead of his parents, while the younger one, barely two years old, delighted in slowing the family's progress. With them was the apothecary, who had insisted on seeing them home.

"A spoonful of soup every five hours," the apothecary reminded the mathematician as he prepared to leave.

"But we're not about to wake him in the middle of the night to give him this potion, which is theoretically supposed to put him to sleep!"

"Perhaps you know some other way to treat a cough? . . . One final question: I've given careful thought to all your explanations. If you were asked to explain the world system without invoking Providence, what would you say?"

For a while Laplace remained silent. Then Delambre, who unintentionally overheard the conversation, heard him say, "I would answer that I had no need of that hypothesis." Then, with a hearty laugh, he added, "And as Newton said, anything that is not necessary is superfluous."

"But Newton also said that just as the blind man has no idea of color, so too are we without ideas about the ways in which God in His wisdom feels and understands."

"Still you must grant that today we are less blind than we used to be."

Delambre nearly knocked over the table with the vase of roses. Some water spilled, and while Delambre was wiping it up with the mat, he heard the apothecary ask another question: "You wouldn't be an atheist, would you, Citizen Laplace?"

"I scarcely have the time."

"Robespierre himself believes in a Supreme Being," the apothecary managed to gasp.

"But Robespierre is not a mathematician."

◈

After the apothecary had left, Delambre found himself alone with his friends. He hadn't had such an evening in a long time. The two children had been perfect, nothing like the ones who had made him flee the inn in Châtillon. Dinner was delicious, and there was no shortage of bread: a marvelous white loaf.

The two men had not seen each other for months and had a thousand things to discuss, ranging from gossip to news of Borda and Coulomb. Both gently poked fun at Lalande, who had presided over the Festival of Reason. They also talked about the new institutions that the Convention was busily creating. "Before long they'll be short of teachers. You'll see, Delambre: they'll be obliged to call on us."

Then they went back to discussing the *Système du monde.* How could they have done otherwise, when one of them spent all his time working on the book and the other knew that it contained answers to his most basic questions?

"It is clear that the present state of the universe is the effect of its past and the cause of its future," Laplace calmly asserted.

"So you hold that everything is predetermined?"

"Not predetermined, determined. With differential equations we wield a weapon of unrivaled power. For the first time in the history of knowledge, we are capable of knowing the present and future states of the world system."

It was a revolution! The two men lapsed into silence. Laplace went over and picked up the bottle of potion. It had been five hours since his child had taken his last dose. Delambre, left alone, noticed that the damp spot on the mat had dried. Laplace looked pleased when he returned. "He drank it all without waking up."

"Still, this discussion we're having is very strange," Delambre blurted out. "We're talking about reducing the 'inequalities of the planets,' about proving the stability of the world, about knowing the future of the universe, and yet here we are, both of us, out of work and incapable of predicting what tomorrow will bring. Five years ago, who would have predicted what has now happened? Then there was a king, now we live in a republic. Then people adulated Lafayette, Mirabeau, and Bailly, but now Lafayette has gone over to the Austrians, Mirabeau sold himself to the king, and Bailly was guillotined by the people of Paris. After them came Marat and Danton. Marat was murdered and Danton condemned to death. Now there is Robespierre. Who can say how long he'll remain in office, or even what will happen between now and next summer?"

"And in six years, the end of the century!" Laplace concluded.

◆

The next day they went off to scout out a site for the "baseline." Between Melun and Lieusaint they found an ideal location: approximately six thousand *toises* in a straight line across the forest in relatively flat terrain. A few humps to flatten out, a few trees to cut down, and they could begin work. When? It began to rain.

◆

With the bad weather the atmosphere in the Bruyères house turned gloomy. In the kitchen Delambre curled up in a chair close to the fireplace and read. Julie, sitting on a stool, knitted by his side. At the end of each row she gave a sharp pull on her yarn, causing the ball to jump in its basket. They could hear the sound of rain outside.

For the past few weeks Delambre had taken a keen interest in a series of articles that Parmentier had published in *La Feuille du cultivateur.* The endlessly eclectic "father of the potato" was now interested in "ducks and their upbringing." Julie asked Delambre what he was reading. He closed the newsletter, laid it on the table, and began to lecture:

> Among the many types of ducks found around the world, basically only two live on our farms: the dabbling or domestic duck and the Barbary or Muscovy duck. The dabbling duck is so called because it apparently likes to swim in shallow water, into which it dips its beak in search of food. It mingles mainly with other ducks of the same species. By contrast, the Muscovy drake will mate readily with females of other varieties, giving rise to mixed breeds. One drake can service ten females. An Indian drake doesn't need as many females, and the young are more difficult to raise though no less voracious. M. Dambourney, a respected scholar, believes that ducklings from the same brood will not mix on either water or land unless virtually crossbred. Each one keeps to itself, remains apart from the others, and there is no fighting or enmity among them.

"What a memory," Julie exclaimed, "and at your age!"

"What do you mean, at my age? Do you know why my memory is so good, Julie?" Delambre, who disliked talking about himself, cut himself off abruptly.

"No," Julie protested. "Now that you've started, you must continue."

"When I was young, I nearly went blind," Delambre confessed. "I was told that by the time I was twenty I would no longer be able to see. So I made an effort to memorize everything I read or saw. In order to impress things on my memory, I tried to learn them by heart. It was almost frightening. I wanted to acquaint myself with everything, to store it all up and make provision for the future."

He shivered at this memory of childhood.

"So that's why you became an astronomer: to see the heavens!" In making this remark Julie turned serious, as peasant women do when a matter of fundamental importance is broached.

"My God, no! At the time I couldn't even bear the light of day." But Julie's observation was right on target. Delambre had never made the connection between his impending blindness and his passion for astronomy.

"Your collar is worn. Your sleeves are coming apart. There are holes in the elbows!" Julie exclaimed as she took hold of Delambre's sleeve to check its condition. "It needs mending there and there and there." Then, as if suddenly remembering an old grievance, she said, "Why didn't you do your expedition among the savages? It must be hot down there at the ecator. I wouldn't have had to wear my eyes out mending your things."

"I've already told you a hundred times, Julie. There are lots of meridians but only one equator."

"Exactly." With a visible effort at thought, she grumbled, "But I still don't understand why. If it's a ball, it's round all over. So there must be ecators everywhere too."

Delambre was beginning to lose patience, but to end the discussion he said, "It's a ball that isn't really round." That did it!

"A ball that isn't round isn't a ball! Do you think I was born yesterday?"

"How stubborn you are!"

"Now, don't shout!" The ball of yarn jumped so sharply that it nearly leaped out of the basket. Delambre picked it up and flattened it between his hands. Julie shot him a funny look. "That's just what I was saying. It's not a ball any more."

Ostentatiously ignoring her remark, he stuck a knitting needle through the ball of yarn and rotated the whole thing: "These are the poles, see. There are two of them. This is the equator. There's only one, like a belt around the waist. Here, here, and here are meridians, there are plenty of them. Now you should be able to understand why I didn't go off to live among savages!" He pulled the knitting needle out so violently that a whole row of knitting came undone.

"Now he's destroying my knitting," Julie complained, as she grabbed the needle from him just as forcefully. The ball of yarn fell to the ground and rolled across the tile floor, leaving a long, twisting thread of wool behind it.

"My poor Julie, when will you stop clucking like a goose?"

"Clucking like a goose?" she asked ironically.

"I know, honk like a goose and puck like a chicken and cluck like a turkey. And since you're so smart when it comes to the barnyard, tell me what the difference is between a dabbling duck and a Muscovy?"

She looked at him as one might look at a seriously ill patient and beat a hasty retreat, taking her knitting with her.

◆

It was hot that morning. At dawn Delambre had already taken his place in the observatory attached to his Bruyères house. He'd rather have been in the basement than up in the attic, but just try observing the stars from a cellar. The glass cupola acted as a greenhouse. As the sun moved higher in the sky, Delambre felt as though he was a young plant happily growing in the warmth of its rays. He stripped to the waist, then tried to keep his sweat from dripping onto the ocular of his telescope. The only thing covering his skin now was a pair of long underwear, which Julie shortened a bit each day. The room was like a steam bath. Thermidor: the month deserved its name.

He heard sounds at the front door. So much for his peace and quiet. Julie's voice reached his ears from below. Now she was even talking to herself! The sound got louder though, and other voices mingled with Julie's. So she wasn't alone after all, Delambre mused as he got up to ask them all to pipe down. What a chatterbox! He ought to go right down and give her hair a good pull. But dressed as he was, how could he? He leaned over the opening for the ladder. "Julie!" No answer. Was she deaf? "Julie! Julie! What's all that noise?"

"Monsieur, Monsieur, it's—"

"It's what?"

"It's Robespierre—"

Stunned, Delambre cast about for his breeches. "What?"

"He's been guillotined!"

Delambre dropped his breeches.

◆

The changes that had taken place in France had no effect on Méchain. He seemed intent on holing up in Italy. What was the point of returning to France as long as war was still raging in the Pyrenees?

If he had read the issue of *Le Moniteur universel* dated 3 Vendémiaire, he would have learned the following: "Bellegarde Is Returned to the Republic! No Enemies Remain on French Soil!" It was Fourcroy, speaking on behalf of the Committee of Public Safety, who announced the news to the Convention's seven hundred joyful deputies. The fortress of Belle-garde had been the last enemy stronghold in France, so millions of French citizens could now be told that not a single square inch of French soil remained in enemy hands. The Republic had triumphed over the coalition of all the European powers. So much for Brunswick's boastful threats.

Fourcroy, holding a letter from the Convention's representative-on-mission to the Pyrénées-Orientales in his hand, read the final sentence: "You have bestowed the name 'Nord-Libre' on the fortress of Condé, and we have bestowed the name 'Midi-Libre' on Bellegarde pending of course your final approval of this new name." The deputies and specta-tors greeted these words with a standing ovation. Then Fourcroy re-sumed his speech: "The fortress of Bellegarde shall henceforth be known as Sud-Libre. The news of its surrender shall be transmitted to all the armies. The telegraph will convey it instantaneously to the Army of the North." No one ever found out why the Assembly had chosen the name "Sud" rather than "Midi." Perhaps the emendation was not so much lin-guistic as political: its purpose may have been to let the representatives-on-mission know that only the Convention had the power to make decisions, including what names should be given to things.

Fourcroy's statement also brings up another point. Why was the news of the surrender "instantaneously" transmitted only to the Army of the North? The answer is simple. There was as yet only one line implement-ing M. Chappe's telegraph in all of France: the one that linked Paris to Lille, where the Army of the North had its headquarters.

Méchain knew nothing of all this and therefore saw no reason to re-turn to France. By contrast, Delambre had a thousand reasons to leave Bruyères and return to Paris.

But before leaving Bruyères he felt he must take every precaution. Now that Robespierre was dead, some émigrés were attempting to re-turn home. In order to avoid trouble later on in Paris, Delambre was careful to obtain any number of documents proving that he had never emigrated or been imprisoned for counterrevolutionary activities.

It was the period of certificates. For a very brief time people in every one of France's thirty-six thousand communes had been obliged to go to their town halls and consult their mayors. In Bruyères the mayor was Ernest Briard.

On the morning when Delambre sought him out, the mayor happened to be at the town hall. Briard prided himself on his fine handwriting, which many in the village envied. Seated behind a makeshift desk, he wrote carefully: "I, Ernest Briard, mayor of Bruyères, hereby certify that Citizen Jean-Baptiste Delambre, a resident of my commune for the past year, neither emigrated nor was held on suspicion of counterrevolutionary activity. His description follows." He looked up at the citizen standing before him and scrutinized him with a practiced eye.

"Hair and eyebrows?" He muttered: "Brown." Then he wrote: brown. "Eyes? Blue." He wrote blue. "Nose? Large." Delambre scowled. The mayor wrote: large. "Mouth?" Delambre pressed his lips together; his mouth thinned. Briard wrote: medium. "Chin? Round." He wrote: round. "Height?" He mumbled: "Five feet three inches." Delambre straightened himself and said, "Five feet five inches!" Briard wrote: Five feet four inches.

◆

"How can this be! Three years after the fall of the monarchy, republicans are still reporting their height and measuring their fields in the king's yards, feet, and inches, when they have vowed to root out every last vestige of tyranny," shouted Prieur of the Côte-d'Or, who had taken up a combative posture on the podium of the Assembly.

"The tyranny of the sansculottes," screamed a voice from the gallery, and a dozen others immediately took up the cry.

Prieur continued undaunted. After two years everyone had grown used to such shouts and insults on the floor of the Convention. Since the beginning of summer—since Thermidor—things had been changing, however: it was no longer the same people shouting insults as before. Their clothing was different, they came from different parts of the city, and even physically they were different. The eastern precincts of Paris had given way to the western precincts. The *faubourgs* of the poor had been replaced by the posh quarters of the rich. Where there had been workingmen in smocks, now there were rich young men in starched collars.

These young men were known as *muscadins*. Unlike those who had shouted insults before them, they were well scrubbed and had fine manners. With carefully manicured hands they skillfully brandished elegant canes whose handles were artfully embossed. And they had it in for Prieur, who, along with Carnot, was the only remaining member of the

Year II committees: of Public Safety, Surveillance, and so on. All the others had been arrested.

"Death to the sansculottes!"

Undeterred by the tempest of invective, Prieur continued with his speech: "Citizens, the introduction of the decimal system is going to revolutionize calculation. Things will be simplified to the point where everyone will want to learn arithmetic."

"Woe unto those who wear out our peaceful and hardworking citizens with pointless changes!" objected a deputy on the right side of the chamber.

"And woe unto those who take advantage of the people's weariness to reject needed improvements!" another deputy on the left immediately replied. Prieur thought he recognized the voice of Romme.

Prieur waited for the exchange to end before resuming. "The new measures will be called 'republican.'" Cheers broke out, immediately followed by jeers from the gallery. But most of the deputies in the chamber applauded. Buoyed by this approval, Prieur went on: "The names of the units should suggest the principle of universality that governed their definition."

He paused for a moment, and the silence stunned everyone. Then, in a solemn voice, he proclaimed: "The unit of length shall be called the Meter, from the Greek *metron,* measure. The other units shall be the Liter, the Gram, the Are, and the Franc. The subdivisions shall be Latin: deci, centi. Multiples shall be Greek: deca, hecto, kilo."

As the new names were announced, a buzz filled the hall. In the galleries two old men in spectacles squared off like cocks about to fight.

"Kilo! No, no! Not *ki, chi!* It's a chi that's needed," said the younger one.

"*Ki,*" the other insisted. "Not *chi!* What's needed is a kappa."

A short distance away another man sputtered: "The people will never take to obscure technical terms like those."

"The people! The people! What do you know about the people?" challenged an artisan from the *faubourgs.*

"And 'aristocrat?' Before the revolution the people had never heard the word. But it wasn't so hard to get used to, now, was it?" he said to his companion. And then he sang the revolutionary song: *"Ah, ça ira, ça ira, les aristocrates. . . ."*

Below, on the floor of the Assembly, Prieur continued: "Among the new measuring instruments, the most common will probably be the double decimeter, which can be carried on the person without a hinge and without needing protection at the ends and which can be manufactured at low cost." Then, gesturing with his hands to reinforce his words, he said, "And last but not least, the meter will serve as a most agreeable unit of measurement for those of our citizens who like to carry canes, provided they choose canes a meter in length."

In the galleries *muscadins* raised their canes and brought them down on the heads of the men from the *faubourgs,* whose smocks turned red with blood. The chief participants in this unequal battle now left the hall to continue their fight outside. The legislative session was adjourned.

The hall quickly emptied. Only the two old men remained in the deserted gallery, isolated inside a linguistic bubble.

"The Latins represented Greek chi with the letters "ch" and already pronounced it as a guttural."

"But how can you say such a thing, Alexander? You weren't there."

"I wasn't at Marignan either, Alfred, and yet I know—"

"You know what, Alexander? That kilometer and kilogram should be pronounced like *chiromancie* and *chiropraxie?*"

"What do I know, Alfred? That you want to pronounce chilometer and chilogram like *chirurgie* and *chimie?*"

In the street oaths turned to cries of pain. Here the battle was not over philology or phonetics. It was not only the system of measurement that had changed; people had begun to express themselves in new ways. Well-scrubbed *muscadins* liked to take what they termed "civic strolls," in the course of which they took delight in savaging any filthy sansculottes they happened upon. The use of the familiar *tu* form of address became suspect, as did the wearing of the Phrygian cap, and as for the Carmagnole. . . . The novel terror of the past two years gave way to another terror, which some deemed less repellent because more traditional. Its victims were drawn as in the past from the "lower orders." This was far more compatible with the status quo.

Words that began with chi were often misused in vulgar ways, and it was to prevent this that the Gallic *kilo* was preferred to the Hellenic *chilio.* The decision was not an ignorant choice of uneducated republicans but a wise and deliberate one. It was better to be reproached for barbarism than for vulgarity. And wasn't the art of governing always to choose the lesser of two evils?

Delambre approved of this choice. An accomplished Hellenist, he cited Homer—*Iliad,* book 5, line 860—to the delight of his colleagues when the new commission met for the first time. For there was indeed a new commission. Still qualified as "temporary"—one could never be sure—it had been appointed at Prieur's behest. Still, it was strange to have this adjective connoting ephemerality attached to a commission whose job was to establish a system of measurement destined to endure for all eternity.

❖

As he entered the hall, Delambre was radiant. The warmth of earlier meetings came back to him. After a year of solitude in Bruyères, it felt good to see so many familiar faces: Berthollet, Monge, Vandermonde, Abbé Haüy, Legendre, Prony, and all the men who had been "sacked," including Coulomb, Brisson, and Borda. The Convention had done things properly. No one had been left out. But what about Méchain? Where was their long-lost colleague? In Italy. Still! everyone exclaimed. What is he waiting for? Was it his accident, perhaps? No, that had been taken care of.

Delambre did not hide his disappointment at Méchain's absence. He looked forward to seeing him again. He had so much to tell him, and so many questions to ask.

"Everyone is here. The meeting can begin," the chair announced, signaling to Prieur that he should begin reading the report that was to be submitted to the Convention for a vote two days hence. Delambre took in none of what was said. His joy had evaporated. "Everyone is here": only after those words were uttered was it truly borne in on him that Condorcet and Lavoisier were gone.

Prieur raised the issue of what metal would be used for the standard units. The prototypes were to be "as precise, durable, and unalterable as it is within the power of man to make them," and for this the metal to be used was platinum. What other substance had qualities to rival platinum's? The precious metal was very expensive and very rare, but fortunately Lavoisier had stockpiled a sufficient reserve, and this could be pressed into service.

The standards to be kept in the capital of each *département* were to be made of copper. "Of course," Prieur conceded, "this metal lacks many of the advantages of platinum. It is susceptible initially to certain alterations upon contact with the air, but," he reassured his audience, "it fairly quickly achieves a state of permanence."

Unfortunately, copper too was in short supply. Therefore the standards to be kept in district capitals would have to be made of soft cast iron or sheet metal. "A hierarchy of towns and a hierarchy of metals," thought Delambre, who had begun to pay attention.

Exchanging the saltpeter and cannon of Year II for the platinum and standards of Year III, a trio of celebrated "metallurgists"—Berthollet, Monge, and Vandermonde—was assigned to oversee the production of these various standards.

When the question of a standard of weight arose, all eyes turned to Haüy. The abbé rose, and a hush came over the hall: "We had almost completed our task. All that remained was to determine how water's volume and weight varied with temperature. . . . But we didn't have time to finish the work. . . . A few days later he was arrested." The documents had remained in Lavoisier's apartment on the boulevard de la Madeleine at the time of his arrest, but when he, Haüy, had scoured the premises for them after his death, they were gone. "Today we can say with confidence that they are lost." The abbé sat down. Thus nothing would remain of Lavoisier's last work—not one page.

The commission proposed that Haüy begin the work anew. In a halting voice he said, "I already have too much to do with crystals and rhombohedrons."

Standards, platinum, baselines—these were all well and good. But Delambre was interested in one thing only: what would they decide on the subject of the meridian? Would they resume the expedition or not?

Prieur announced that all operations pertaining to the determination of units of measurement would be continued until completed. What about the meridian? Delambre was impatient to hear. Finally the speaker came to the subject that interested him: "Citizen Delambre will leave as soon as possible and work his way southward. Citizen Méchain will start from the Pyrenees and perform the same measurements until he meets up with Citizen Delambre." Delambre's heart leaped. "However," Prieur continued, "Citizen Méchain shall go first to Paris, and only after conferring with him will the Assembly make a final decision as to the probable duration of the operation and the steps needed to ensure the most accurate measurement possible."

◈

Upon leaving the meeting, Delambre was caught up in the waves of a procession coming from Saint-Marceau. It was a peaceful but tense procession consisting mainly of women and children. The marchers repeated the same words over and over: "Bread and the Constitution! Bread and the Constitution!" Delambre headed toward the Assembly.

As he took his place in the gallery, he heard someone say, "You must guarantee the property of the rich." The speaker at the podium was a deputy named Boissy d'Anglas. Things had changed a good deal, Delambre thought. "We must be governed by the best people among us," the deputy continued. "The best people are the best educated and most interested in upholding the laws. With few exceptions, you will find such men only among those who, because they own property, are attached to the country in which that property is located. A country governed by the owners of property enjoys social order, whereas a country in which those who do not own property govern is in a state of nature."

These words were greeted with howls from the left side of the chamber, as if to demonstrate that those who responded in this way were indeed in a state of nature. The howls had come from a small group of deputies known as "the Crest of the Mountain," men who had refused to go along with the excesses of the Terror but who wished to continue the Revolution without the murderous abuses that had tarnished its reputation.

Another deputy rose to respond, and Delambre saw that it was a frightfully thinner Gilbert Romme. "Our institutions must seek to provide at the very least what is necessary. Only then can the superfluous be tolerated."

"The man without property depends entirely upon virtue to maintain his interest in an order that preserves nothing of his own," Boissy d'Anglas calmly replied.

"Having been blessed with life, all men are endowed with an equal right to preserve that life."

"Absolute equality is nothing but a chimera!" boomed Boissy in fine, vibrant tones.

What Romme had said in the Assembly chamber was also being whispered in the *faubourgs*. Eventually people began to voice similar sentiments out loud, and then they began to scream. For a while "the superfluous" had remained discreet, but now it was back in all its splendor, and in a time of famine this seemed almost obscene. To those who suffered it made misery that much more unbearable.

Fine carriages transported groups of young bourgeois living in high style. Well-dressed fops—the *merveilleuses*—were a colorful presence in the streets, where their fancy clothes made a rustling sound as they passed. How much more elegant their outfits looked than the crude clothing of the sansculottes, and how much softer their fabrics felt to the touch. And wasn't the clacking of carriage wheels over cobblestone more pleasing to the ear than the sound of the guillotine chopping off the heads of the condemned? These young people were happy, handsome, and rich; equality was a chimera. Now that "liberty" had been rediscovered, the price of bread was once again free to rise.

Once again the people of Paris flocked to the Assembly. Was the whole cycle about to begin again? Troops were mobilized against the processions. Women siphoned water from the gutters to squirt at the soldiers.

The Convention was invaded while Boissy d'Anglas was presiding. The mob attacked one deputy, and a few hotheads cut off his head on the spot. Other deputies left the hall unmolested. A handful remained inside, including, of course, the Crest of the Mountain. Not only did they support the people of the *faubourgs;* they also hoped that their presence, by maintaining a semblance of legality, would help prevent the revolt from turning into an insurrection.

"Bread and the Constitution!" One of the deputies rose to speak. Perhaps it was Romme, or else his friend Goujon, or Soubrany. "A government must be considered bad to the utmost degree when, on the same earth, under the shadow of the same laws, we see some people in want of the most elementary necessities and others whose tables and houses can barely hold up beneath the weight of excess."

The National Guard was dispatched with orders to fire on the demonstrators. But the detachments had been drawn from the city's poorer sections, especially Saint-Marceau. The artillerymen made common cause with the demonstrators and refused to fire on them. It was a fine day in Prairial, in the pleasant month of May. The trees in the Tuileries were green and the sky in Paris was blue, but prosperity was no longer the watchword of the hour. No one believed in it any more. Justice was enough: the demonstrators demanded the release of patriots left moldering in the prisons since Thermidor. Orders were issued that everyone should eat the same bread. Pastry makers were forbidden to make pastries. Only bread was allowed.

Carried away with enthusiasm, a deputy belonging to the Crest rose to speak: "Citizens, I propose to end this day in an unforgettable way by abolishing the death penalty once and for all."

"No, no!" yelled the crowd. The proposal was rejected.

Once again the National Guard was sent in, but this time the troops were drawn from the wealthier neighborhoods. The artillerymen from the western sections of Paris had no compunctions about firing on the mob of people from the *faubourgs*. The insurrection was over.

A few days later Delambre returned to the Assembly and was jostled by an elegantly dressed woman who was leaving the chamber in a huff. The reason for her anger was a poster displayed in the vestibule: "The National Convention decrees that until calm has been restored in the streets of Paris, no woman shall be admitted to the galleries during legislative sessions. It further decrees that in the future no woman shall be admitted unless accompanied by a male citizen, who will be required to show his card."

Not so long ago Robespierre had banned foreigners from the assembly chamber itself. Now his enemies were banning women from the galleries. What had changed?

The artillerymen from Saint-Marceau were guillotined. The front page of *Le Moniteur universel* for 30 Prairial contained this item:

> This morning the Military Commission completed the trial of several deputies that began several days ago. It sentenced the following to death: Goujon, Romme, Duroy, Duquesnoy, Bourbotte, and Soubrany. After the verdict was announced, the six condemned men stabbed themselves with knives they had concealed on their persons.

Delambre tried to find out more about what had happened. After the verdict, Goujon had rushed to the stairs and taken out his knife, which he then plunged into his breast. Bourbotte had shouted, "Now you will see how men of courage choose to die!"

Romme, seeing that Goujon was still breathing, took him in his arms and laid his body down on one of the stairs. Then he took the knife from the dying man's hands and stabbed himself twice. He collapsed on the same stair. At the bottom of the staircase, Duquesnoy and Bourbotte watched their two friends die and then stabbed themselves, one with a pair of scissors, the other with a knife. Duquesnoy fell in a heap, while Bourbotte staggered on his last legs. Soubrany rushed over to Bourbotte and helped him lie down. Bourbotte then offered him his knife, and Soubrany stabbed himself. Duroy, the sixth man, managed only to wound himself before the gendarmes disarmed him. The whole thing lasted no more than a few seconds. In the courtroom on the second floor, the military judges were still congratulating themselves on their exemplary sentence. Meanwhile, on the stairs, three men lay dead: Romme, Goujon, and Duquesnoy. Soubrany was dying. And two others were gravely wounded.

The three men still living were carted away from the scene to the scaffold. Soubrany was dead by the time they arrived, so the executioner was left that day to finish off just two seriously wounded men.

This collective suicide made an impression on Delambre. He was not alone. People were already murmuring that the "Martyrs of Prairial" were not dead and would soon be back to rekindle the torch of the Revolution.

In the green berlin, which had been returned to him, Delambre recalled the words of Abbé Grégoire: "Romme, you're asking us to establish eternity by fiat."

14

"18 Messidor, Year III. After a hiatus of seventeen and a half months, I am leaving for Bourges in order to take advantage of the good weather for azimuth observations." Sitting on the platform of the cathedral turret, Delambre wrote in his old logbook. What a pleasure it was to leaf through its pages! There he found notes about Saint-Denis, Dunkirk, and Boiscommun. Then his eyes fell upon the final sentence, written, he recalled, one dark winter afternoon on the rue de Paradis: "Who knows when the expedition will resume? Or even if it will?"

He returned to his writing. "The area between the Loire and Bourges is very difficult, especially since the fire in the belfry of Salbris, whose steeple once rose to a considerable height above the church. All that remains today is one damaged tower. What can possibly take its place?"

The ladder clattered against the masonry. Delambre closed his notebook. A moment later his assistant emerged from the dark hole through which the top of the ladder protruded. He was out of breath, dazzled by the light, and disoriented, like a diver breaking the surface. Delambre as usual waited for the climber to catch his breath before speaking to him.

Bellet—for it was none other than he—was quick to say that he had found a supply of wood beams at an affordable price. The astronomer remembered how glad he had been to be reunited with his old assistant. No sooner did he learn that the expedition would resume than he had dashed off an express letter, afraid that Bellet would already have found other work. But a reply arrived by return mail: "Like an old globetrotting sailor, I am free to embark with you once again on the great journey." The man himself had arrived that evening.

How lucky Méchain was to have Tranchot, and Delambre to have Bellet. For all their disappointments, at least the two astronomers had had the good fortune to find collaborators of such quality. Or so Delambre mused as he sat on a low wall a few steps away from the iron pelican that served as a weather vane on the cathedral turret, which he had used as a target. Wide open spaces! All he could see was the sky and the birds. With the squeaking pelican as his lullaby, the astronomer might have believed he was on the deck of a ship.

❧

A few hundred leagues away, Méchain really was on the deck of a ship. He was on his way back to France after more than a year in Italy. Tranchot was with him.

Irritated by the constant chafing of the rigging and apprehensive about his return, which he had delayed as long as possible, Méchain had finally yielded to the repeated entreaties of the Commission, whose last letter had looked like nothing less than a summons: "Citizen Méchain shall first return to Paris, and only after consulting with him will the Assembly come to a final decision." There was no way to ignore such a clear injunction.

Upon landing in Marseilles, Méchain and Tranchot immediately began making preparations to leave for Paris. Tranchot went off to find a carriage, but no one was willing to part with one for such a long journey. After scouring taverns where freelance carriage men gathered, he finally found one willing to make the trip. Meanwhile, Méchain, glad to be back on dry land and safe from the rolling sea, seized the opportunity to catch up on his correspondence.

Marseilles, 8 Thermidor, Year III.
Citizen Delambre,

I am pleased to learn that you will be extending the chain of triangles that you have already so brilliantly mapped out from Dunkirk to Orléans, but my pleasure is clouded by my regret at having been unable to meet up with you.

May I presume on our friendship to ask for your help? Please tell me something about your resources and methods, and let me know how you keep your records, so that I may bring my practices in line with yours.

Did you know that I no longer have a carriage? What is more, the Commission is determined to deprive me of Tranchot. We got on well together and collaborated very effectively. He has been a wonderful assistant. And did you know that we now have only one circle. I was forced to sell the other to some Italian scientists but got a good price for it.

I embrace you warmly, my dear colleague. May your health prosper and no obstacles impede your work. Please remain my friend, and count upon the sincerity of my feelings for you and upon my continuing devotion.

N.B. When you have a few free moments, you will oblige me greatly if you let me know how you recorded the receipts and expenditures incurred in the course of your work.

Salut et fraternité,
Méchain

Where should he send this letter? By now Delambre was surely out in the country somewhere. "He's already ahead of me," Méchain mused. "And now I have to go all the way to Paris before I can get back to work. What a waste of time! And Tranchot isn't back yet. I hope nothing has happened to him." Méchain had never liked big cities, Paris least of all. And weren't people saying that as recently as the beginning of Prairial the city was still in a state of insurrection?

Méchain got up abruptly.

❧

Five livres per day. In the tavern, the carter, having sniffed out an opportunity to make some money, refused to lower his price. Tranchot made a sign as if to accept the man's terms and gave him the address of their inn together with Méchain's name and information about who he was. Then he changed his mind. In the end, after drinking a few more pints, they agreed to split the difference: the price would be four livres per day, and they would start out the next morning.

Meanwhile, however, Méchain had come to a different decision. At the end of his letter to Delambre he added this sentence: "Please send your reply to me in care of General Delivery, Perpignan." That night the astronomer and his assistant set sail on a small vessel for Port-Vendres. As they were disembarking, Tranchot suddenly remembered that he had forgotten to notify the carter. "Never mind," Méchain reassured him. "He'll find other clients, and in any case he charged far too much." Without further ado they headed straight for the mountain.

❧

Soon they were in serious trouble. Bugarach was a terrifying peak known to be quite dangerous to climbers. Thousands were said to have perished there. The small caravan nevertheless continued. In the lead was a young native of the region by the name of Agoustenc, who knew the mountain well. Behind him came four porters, all sturdy climbers, who bent under the weight of the instruments and wooden beams they carried. And then came Méchain, who used a cane to help maintain his footing. In places the trail vanished, obliterated by rock. Here the climbers halted while Agoustenc went ahead to reconnoiter. When he located the place where the trail resumed a little farther on or higher up, he would wave to the others, who would then proceed.

The wind began to blow, the passage narrowed, and the drop from the trail became so precipitous that the climbers were forced to crawl on all fours. In places they needed to hold on to scrub vegetation or the tops of boulders to steady themselves. The ground, gullied by rain, gave way beneath their feet, triggering terrifying landslides. The second porter tripped, began to slide, tried to grab on to something, but was carried away by his load. The accident happened too quickly for Méchain to react. The man who had been climbing in front of him simply disappeared. Through the whistling wind the sound of his fall could be heard, magnified by the echo.

The man lay in a heap at the bottom of a ravine. The crate he had been carrying lay smashed. The repeating circle was a twisted wreck. Its telescopes were opaque, their lenses pulverized. The alidades were in pieces, the precision mechanisms shattered. Méchain, who stood petrified at the edge of the precipice, imagined the scene in a flash. Then all was silence. The astronomer leaned over and scanned the abyss. A short distance below him he caught sight of a patch of color. As if lying on a cot the porter lay stretched out on a bed of branches. Amazed to be alive, he stared at Méchain, who stared right back. It would have been difficult to say which man was more surprised; both burst out laughing. A little bit lower down they located the crate containing the repeating circle. Its fall, too, had been broken by a shrub. Had Méchain been a believer, he might have—But he wasn't: surely it was his lucky star. Nothing but his lucky star.

Neither the man nor the instrument had suffered the slightest damage. Before resuming his climb, however, the porter who had been saved by a miracle turned and crossed himself. Then the men continued up the mountain, but not before swearing an oath that no power on earth would ever force them to make such a climb again.

It was quite late by the time the caravan reached the summit. Two surprises were in store for Méchain, one good, the other bad. The good news was the extent of the panorama, which stretched over dozens of leagues as far as the eye could see. To the west lay the Pyrenees, which seemed endless; to the east lay the Corbières range and Black Mountain; and to the south lay the sea. The bad news was that there was very little flat area on top. Not enough for a tent and just barely enough for the target.

It was time to start back down. None of the porters was willing to remain at the summit. They used the canvas tent to cover the crates and weighed it down with heavy rocks. Méchain felt terrible. He was leaving his only repeating circle, without which he was helpless, on a mountaintop, unguarded. He had never attempted anything quite so reckless before. But what choice did he have? Carry the crates back down that evening and carry them back up again the next morning? The porters would have refused. Spend the night at the summit? He thought about it. Alone, without a tent, in the cold and wind at an altitude of five thousand feet: it was pure madness. He would not survive. A sea captain forced to abandon ship in a storm could not have looked more distressed than Méchain did that night when he decided to abandon the mountaintop. Noticing the astronomer's anxiety, Agoustenc sought to reassure him: "A fellow'd have to be pretty crazy to climb the mountain in the middle of the night to steal that thing!" The porters burst out laughing: "Sure enough, you'd have to be pretty crazy." Then they began the descent, which was no less perilous than the climb.

At no time did anyone suggest spending the night at the summit. No one even wanted to be up there alone during the day. Every evening the two men on watch entrusted the instruments to the grace of God, as they liked to say, and climbed back down to the valley below.

Méchain and his assistants set up headquarters at the Pâtres farm at the base of the mountain. Although this was one of the highest farms in the area, it still took two full hours to climb back up to the target. But that was nothing compared to Mount Canigou, which took nine hours to climb, as Tranchot exhausted himself finding out.

Tranchot! Hadn't he gone back to Paris? The Commission had recalled him for the simple reason that he was overqualified to serve as Méchain's assistant. A geographer of his competence could more usefully be assigned to other tasks, particularly since people in Paris did not look kindly on Méchain's insubordination in resuming his measurements without conferring with the Commission.

But the astronomer had insisted on keeping his assistant, and Borda had intervened on his behalf. The incident had been forgotten, and Tranchot had remained. He had only recently set out to reconnoiter the stations in the mountains over by Bellegarde.

"Don't you know who I am, Citizen?" Taken by surprise, Tranchot looked all around. Directly ahead he saw a man walking toward him out of the brush. "You really don't recognize me?" said the man, stopping in front of Tranchot. "That's because you're not one to hold a grudge. I remember you, with your binoculars. I'm one of the fellows who nabbed you in the mountains. You remember me now?"

Tranchot recognized him as one of the *miquelets* who had grabbed him not far from where they were now and had taken him to Perpignan. With his hand he made a sweeping gesture that took in the entire countryside. In a rather melancholy voice he said, "Quieter now than it was then, eh? I owe you a drink." And he led Tranchot to his house, which stood apart from the rest of the hamlet. Tranchot stayed for two days, long enough to survey the target at Camellas, a measurement he had not been able to complete two years earlier because of what his host had done to prevent him.

The man spoke virtually nonstop throughout the meal, as mountain people sometimes will when their solitude is interrupted. He talked about his animals, his mountain, and, last but not least, his war. He said nothing about the fighting, but at one point he got up, went over to an old trunk, took out a carefully folded poster, and laid it on the table. It was the text of an order issued by Don Ricardos during the Spanish occupation of the region. "Disputes between sovereigns are settled by troops," it read, "but private individuals were never authorized to use weapons in this conflict. Any resident claiming to serve as a *miquelet* and caught with a weapon will be arrested and hanged on the spot."

"I escaped them twice!" As he said this, the former *miquelet* unwittingly rubbed his neck. "After that I laid low until the attack was launched on Bellegarde—I mean Midi-Libre. I'll never get used to it. After the fort was recaptured, I was given the mission of taking the prisoners to Perpignan. One of them was a *soumaten:* not a Spaniard or an émigré but a fellow who lived on the other side of the mountain. Three leagues from here and it's another country. We became friendly. One day he told me what happened when they took the fort from the French. It seems that their leader, Don Ricardos, the fellow who wanted to hang us *miquelets,* had assembled his troops. He told them that misfortune deserves respect: 'I forbid anyone to insult or hit a prisoner. Anyone who disobeys this order will be beaten: a minimum of six strokes of the baton.' And then he said that if honor wasn't reason enough, the troops should remember that the fortunes of war are unpredictable and that they, too, could wind up prisoners some day."

The gate was banging outside, so the former *miquelet* threw a cover over his shoulders and went out, muttering, "It's true: misfortune deserves respect."

◆

Ninety-eight percent! *Assignats,* paper notes issued by the Revolution, were being discounted at a rate of ninety-eight percent, and even so no one would accept them. Even if they had gone lower, people still would have turned up their noses. All of the salary and expedition funds sent to Méchain and Tranchot as well as to Delambre and Bellet were in the form of "scrap paper," as the *assignats* were known in the mountains. Without hard cash they could not purchase food or lodging. Either they came up with coins or went without so much as a glass of water. Fortunately, the astronomer had held on to some metal currency from the funds that Prieur had made available to win his release when he was being held prisoner in Spain. But this reserve was soon exhausted.

Each guard was paid a hundred francs per day, and still the astronomer had to order them to work. It was the same for the animals and wagons. No one wanted to rent to him. He had to requisition what he needed. People began to mutter: the army was bad enough, but now we have feed these scientists who are measuring God knows what. As time went by, Méchain began to carry less and less baggage: the repeating circle, a few tools, a reflector, a tent—just the absolute essentials. The experience at Bugarach had been useful. Méchain had had two small crates constructed, and the various parts of the circle were distributed among them. These were lugged up and down the steepest trails leading to the most inaccessible peaks, sometimes on the backs of mules but more often than not on the backs of men.

And when they got up there, what did they find? Clouds! Clouds enveloping one of the stations, clinging to it all day long. And when the weather finally cleared in one direction, another station off in another direction disappeared from view, leaving Méchain fit to be tied.

One night, as he lay sleeping in the farm at the base of the mountain, he suddenly awoke. He felt as though the roof was about to fly off and the walls were about to collapse. "My God, a storm!" Lashed by the gale, the barn seemed on the point of giving way even though it stood in a hollow sheltered from the winds. What would it be like on top of the mountain? Méchain remained awake, waiting for dawn.

"What I was afraid of has come to pass: the target has been carried off by the wind. It is impossible not to feel discouraged," he wrote to Delambre the next day.

"What is more, I have no idea why most of my wife's letters are not reaching me. This worries me greatly. For the past four years, I have lived every day in a state of anxiety deeper than if I had been in the midst of the horrors that have been committed in our country. My state of mind is indescribable. My jeremiads are inadequate. I don't see any way out of this mess."

Having begun his letter to Delambre at the Pâtres farm on the day after the storm, Méchain returned to it at the home of his friend Arago in Estagel. While there he received a short note from Delambre: "My dear colleague, Rest assured that I shall always be pleased to keep you abreast of all my doings, but allow me to ask as well for your advice and for any lessons you may have learned from your work." Méchain eagerly unfolded the accompanying manuscripts. Everything was there: tables of observations, records of calculations, and so on, all perfectly clear and explained in detail with the aid of sketches.

"If only I had asked sooner," Méchain lamented. "I'm going to have to redo everything. The information you have given me has been most instructive, and I shall do my best to put it to good use," he responded to his colleague. "To be sure, I deeply regret that, owing to circumstances and want of intelligence, I was unable to plan my work as well as you have done. Now, however, with your guidance, I shall attempt to follow a more certain course."

The door opened. A child entered, carrying a bowl of milk. It was a boy of about ten, brisk in his movements and with his hair disheveled. "What is your name?" asked Méchain.

"François-Augustin." Méchain gave a start. Augustin! Like his younger son. It had been four years since he'd last seen the boy. Could he even imagine him? It isn't easy to imagine a child becoming an adolescent. Surely he had grown up to be a handsome youth, as Thérèse had written in the only letter he'd received from her. "Reserved and timid," she had added. Not like this boy, who on the pretext of clearing the table to make room for the bowl of milk was already rummaging among his things.

Thinking to get rid of him more quickly, Méchain opened the crate containing the circle. A mistake! Amazed, the boy stared at all the pieces. He was burning with desire to touch them but didn't lift a finger. His desire was so obvious, though, that Méchain, touched by his interest, took the pieces out of the case and explained what each one was for before setting it down on the bed. He even operated a few of the mechanisms to illustrate his lecture. Before long, all the pieces of the repeating circle were laid out on the bedspread. The boy stared at Méchain in the hope that he might assemble the instrument. But this Méchain refused to do. "I didn't ask for anything," the boy replied. "Tsk, tsk, tsk—did you think I didn't see what you wanted?" Suddenly François pointed at the bedspread. There was his revenge: stains had formed in two places where grease had dripped from the instrument. "I won't say anything to Mother." After giving Méchain a conspiratorial wink, he began to ask questions. The astronomer was all but swept away by the flood. Each question opened the door to a series of others. So insistent was the child that the astronomer answered his questions as carefully as he could. Woe unto him if he had done otherwise!

The next day, the boy returned. When he was still at the bottom of the stairs, Méchain heard him reciting a sort of counting rhyme, which he was still reciting as he entered the room. But he was talking so fast that it was impossible to make out a single word. When he slowed down, however, Méchain recognized the list of the eighty-six *départements* of France and their capitals—a list that every student had to learn by heart. When he finished, he thrust an incomprehensible colored drawing under the astronomer's nose. Méchain pushed the piece of paper away, and as sometimes happens when one moves away from a stained-glass window, suddenly the drawing made sense. Each color represented a *département*. At the bottom of the page, written in aquamarine crayon in a childish hand were the words: "The Republic: One and Indivisible."

Méchain gave the paper back to the boy, who continued with his litany. How irritating he was!

They became good friends. After school every day François paid a visit to the astronomer. He had two favorite objects: the quill, which he handled with ease, and the slingshot, which he wielded with dexterity. He had nearly clobbered a *soumaten* with it at the time of the Spanish invasion. The Spaniards had attacked repeatedly during the war. When a few soldiers became separated from their comrades, some of the village youths spotted them. Without alerting anyone, the boys had attacked and wounded two soldiers. Upon returning to the village they were first severely reprimanded but then hailed as heroes.

So much for the slingshot. The quill may have been a less heroic instrument but it was more durable. François loved school. Reading and writing were his passions.

School! What the Legislative Assembly and the Convention had achieved before Thermidor, the authorities were now slowly undoing. The law establishing free and compulsory education was coming under increasing attack. Every commune in France was supposed to establish a "primary school" for young children, but in fact only one out of every three or four communes had yet created such a school. The state was supposed to pay the teachers, but it had ceased to do so. And the schools, which were supposed to be free and conveniently located, were turning out to be difficult to get to or afford. There weren't enough classrooms to accommodate all the children, especially the girls.

When one of his friends was not admitted to the school in Estagel, François decided to teach the boy to read and write himself. For an hour each day he conscientiously transformed himself into a schoolmaster, whose lessons were not only listened to but also effective.

Old Arago was constantly denouncing the authorities' shilly-shallying. He had been more of a Montagnard than a Girondin but had shed no tears over the end of the Committee of Public Safety and its Terror. But now he was all the more outraged by the increasing boldness of the reactionaries. One night he returned home calmer than usual carrying a heavy tome: Condorcet's *Esquisse d'un tableau historique des progrès de l'esprit humain.* Over dinner he explained to Méchain how the book had reached him. It was Romme whom he had to thank. A few weeks before being expelled from the Convention and sentenced to death, Romme had won approval of a measure to send several copies of Condorcet's last work to every one of the country's *départements*. All factions had applauded the proposal. Three thousand copies had been sent out to mayors, schoolmasters, magistrates, and battalion commanders.

That evening perhaps, gathered around the fireplace because it was freezing everywhere, men and women from Dunkirk to Marseilles, from Brest to Rodez, had listened as sentences of the text were read out in the accents of Brittany or the Nord, Marseilles or Auvergne: "Such is the purpose of the work I have set out to write, whose result will be to prove, by reasoning and by facts, that Nature has set no limits to the perfection of the human faculties; that the perfectibility of man is truly infinite; and that progress toward perfection, henceforth unfettered by any power on earth, has no limit other than the duration of the globe upon which Nature has placed us."

In the Aragos' large kitchen in Estagel, all the children were asleep except for François, the eldest, who struggled to stay awake so that he might listen to sentences whose meaning he did not fully grasp but that he gathered from the way his father read them were of the utmost importance. Of course Arago's way of pronouncing the words lent them a particular flavor that made them seem a promise of happy days to come.

Méchain was overwhelmed by the strength of conviction in this text, by the intransigent hope that animated it, by the quality of the voice announcing the unlimited perfectibility of man. He was all the more impressed because of his past doubts about Condorcet, who had thrown himself into the affairs of his time body and soul—a choice that had rather shocked the astronomer, who believed that scientists have a duty to remain aloof from political debate.

It was bedtime. Méchain felt very much at home in this family's warmth. As he drifted off to sleep, he felt a desperate need to be with his own family.

As he was preparing to leave Estagel to rejoin Tranchot in the mountains, François came into his room for one last visit. Much to the boy's surprise and delight, he found the repeating circle all assembled in the middle of the room, ready for use.

❧

To end the long letter he had begun writing on Mount Bugarach several days earlier, Méchain chose these words: "Please forgive the chaotic composition of this letter. It is far too long to contain anything of interest. My main purpose was to resume my correspondence with you, dear colleague. All the benefit will be mine. I hope you find it pleasant as well. I sincerely hope that you will be willing to spend some time on it."

This letter inaugurated a sustained correspondence between the two astronomers, who exchanged more than a hundred letters. How difficult it was, nevertheless, for those missives to reach their intended recipients. It was as if two blind men were searching for each other in the dark. One letter reached Evaux after its recipient had left for Dun, and when forwarded to Dun arrived just after he had left there as well. Another was returned to its sender months after being dispatched. Where should letters be sent? That depended: "You can write to me in Paris, rue de Paradis, or in Bruyères by way of Arpajon, in the Seine-et-Oise *département,* or care of General Delivery in Bourges, which would be the most direct and reliable route." It would hardly be surprising to learn that such a letter was lost forever. Or that another continued to follow its intended recipient about without ever reaching him. Or that yet another reached its destination long before its addressee, so that by the time it came into his possession, all it had to offer was old news.

With a shivering quill dipped in almost frozen ink Méchain wrote: "Back again is your importunate astronomer, whose letters and requests for favors are more frequent than the apparitions of comets. On Sunday we had several feet of snow. If the weather does not improve, I shall soon surrender the territory to ice, frost, and the ever more numerous wolves, to say nothing of the bears, one of which ate four or five sheep not far from here."

Delambre, with his feet soaking in a bowl of hot water and an escritoire resting on his knees, answered: "Your mountains are too high; ours are not high enough. But I must say that our situation has always been rather grim compared to yours." He then launched into a description of the last station he'd visited: "I had six hours of work to do, but it would take me ten days. I therefore decided to set up camp in a nearby cowshed. By 'nearby' I mean an hour and a half away. For those ten days I was unable to change my clothes. I slept on a couple of sheaves of hay and ate whatever I could find. I was first seared by the sun, then chilled by the wind, and finally drenched by the rain. By the way, do you feel any aftereffects of your cruel accident?"

A month later Méchain answered: "News of my arm? It's much improved. The head has yet to heal, but I'm working on it. Yes, my dear colleague: if I seem to suffer from Rousseau's misanthropy, your impression may be correct. Unfortunately that is the only way in which I resemble him. It is a malady from which I shall try to extricate myself."

"He needs a change at all cost," Delambre thought. "He needs to spend some time with his family." He immediately took up a sheet of writing paper: "After an absence of four and a half years, it seems to me that it might be more pleasant for you to do your observing in Paris, where you can be with your family, rather than in that small and unpleasant town." When Méchain refused to go to Paris, Delambre insisted: "I am alone. Your family situation is different. You deserve every preference for all sorts of reasons, leaving aside your seniority and your lengthy labors." A brief note at the bottom of the page stirred Méchain once again: "Do you hope to reach Rodez this year? What are your plans? I am very keen to learn the answers to these questions."

They were far from done with their work, but like children they played. You could do this, and I could do that. You could come as far as one of the two bell towers just before Rodez, while I could go. . . . This is the plan I'm proposing. Change it as you see fit. Méchain would then make his changes, and Delambre. . . .

Before long the correspondence expanded to become triangular. One side of the triangle was always the same, though perpetually in motion: its two vertices were Delambre-Méchain. A third vertex was in Paris, occupied by a changing cast of characters: Borda, Thérèse, Lalande. In other words, the staff at Paris headquarters had changed: Condorcet and Lavoisier had been replaced by Lalande and Thérèse. Indeed, Thérèse served increasingly as the link between her husband and the Commission.

Méchain had regained his old enthusiasm. He went off for several days and returned exhausted with his team of porters. The woman was waiting for them. Before the men had removed their coats, she was pouring soup into large bowls carved right into the wood of the table. They ate in silence. With a damp cloth she wiped the wood clean. The bowls were then ready for the next meal.

Once the table was dry, Méchain sat down. The porters stood like statues around the fireplace. The woman hung the wash from a line above their heads, then paused to glance around the room, taking in both the men and the things in it. Satisfied with what she saw, she went over to the astronomer, pushing a lamp toward the sheet of paper on which he had already begun to write: "My dear Delambre, I am ashamed at having put off sending you my Barcelona measurements until now. My only excuse is that for so long now they have been a source of sorrow and consuming anxiety. Farewell, my dear colleague, and continue to grant me your friendship."

◈

The green berlin moved through the forest. The color was something one guessed rather than recognized. Bellet was driving. Inside, Delambre reread the letter from Méchain. It worried him. "I regard your Barcelona measurements as the most precise and accurate one can hope for. I would never even think of trying to do better or even as well." This was the answer he proposed to make that very evening.

The carriage stopped in the middle of a meadow. Delambre made a fire. The horse grazed quietly. With its snowy-gray robe and mahogany mane and extremities, it might have seemed decked out in evening dress had it been combed and brushed. It was a sturdy animal, not too high-strung and never capricious: a horse for the long haul. Bellet lifted one of the animal's hooves and seemed preoccupied with the condition of its shoe.

Delambre sat down to write. "My dear colleague, May I make so bold as to reassure you about the quality of your observations. I am not saying this to you alone. On my last trip to Paris, I made the same point several times to the Commission and the Bureau of Longitudes." Aware of his colleague's endless quest for absolute perfection, Delambre tried to reassure him: "Anyone who has any idea of the difficulties we faced will give us due credit for the degree of exactitude we have achieved and will not complain about the few small errors that could not have been avoided under the circumstances." The horse neighed quietly. Delambre looked up. His eyes came to rest on the berlin. "Our carriage surely won't hold up as far as Rodez. It seems to be on its last legs. We have erected targets from Dunkirk to Morlac. When will we be able to link them up with yours? That will be a red-letter day for both of us."

◈

In Dun, Bellet led the horse to the blacksmith's shop. The blacksmith was a tall, taciturn fellow with a bushy, red-tipped mustache and a wool cap over hair that hung down the back of his neck. The man's nickname was "L'Amourette," or Sweetheart, which came from the unusual way he had of talking to horses. As he laid out his tools, he addressed a few words to the animal as if to make its acquaintance. After putting the horseshoes in the fire, he started to explain things to the horse: "These are pincers, this is a rasp, and this a mallet. I'm going to groove your hooves with this. They're bothering you, those hooves, aren't they? Now I'm going to shoe you. Don't be afraid, Sweetheart, it's only hoof, you won't feel a thing." When the time came to take the red-hot metal from the fire with a pair of long tongs, he began to talk even faster. His voice became gentler and more cajoling. The fire was hot and had a distinct smell, and Sweetheart hammered the iron shoe with its carefully punched nail-holes until it fit. He quieted down only briefly, while nailing the shoe to the hoof, and then only because his mouth was full of nails. When the last nail was in, he patted the horse. "So, Sweetheart, that wasn't so bad, was it? A little? But you were brave, and who's going to go off galloping now like a wild little colt?" he chanted, as he popped a piece of sugar into the horse's mouth.

When they left Dun the weather was superb. The measurements had proceeded without difficulty. With its shoe fixed, the gray horse was now trotting. A little too fast, thought Delambre, who was sitting on the front seat next to Bellet. The two men were singing the Visitandines' song at the top of their lungs:

> Miserable bachelor
> Who prefers emptiness
> To the happy state of husband and father,
> Charms of society,
> When decline comes with old age,
> When beset with infirmities
> The fruit of excess and lust . . .

Suddenly there was an alarming crack, and the berlin veered off the road. A few moments later, the astronomer and his assistant found themselves sadly looking at their carriage, now upside down in a ditch.

15

"So now we're not equal anymore," Bellet exclaimed. "Too bad. I was just getting used to it." Delambre soon learned the cause of his assistant's irritation: the first article of the Declaration of the Rights of Man was not included in the new Constitution.

Like a woman dying in childbirth, the Convention had mustered the strength to bring forth a constitution before passing away. In its last session it offered the country two gifts: it renamed the "Place de la Révolution" the "Place de la Concorde," and it created the Institute, not by passing a mere law that could be revoked as a result of petty political maneuvering but by including an article in the Constitution establishing the new learned body. This article stipulated that the Institute must report to the legislature annually on the progress of science and the work of each of its sections.

"If you allow the scientists who used to be members of the now-defunct Academy time to retire to the country, take up other positions in society, and engage in lucrative occupations, you will destroy the organization of the sciences, and half a century will not be enough to train a new generation of scientists," Lavoisier had warned. Apparently his warning had been heeded.

As the last member to be nominated to the erstwhile Academy, Delambre had participated in no more than three or four meetings. "To all intents and purposes I was never an academician, but I shall be a full-fledged member of the Institute," he promised himself. He was swallowed up by the crowd that had gathered to witness the inauguration of the new Institute. The event was intended as a symbol. It was the first of this size since the beginning of the Revolution, and it marked a change from the vulgar popular festivals that had been so common over the past few years. The women in attendance now were beautiful, and beautifully dressed. Milliners, seamstresses, plumers, trimmers, lacemakers, and hairdressers had all found new employment. In the fashion business, things were going very well indeed.

The ceremony began. Except for two or three clouds, the skies were clear. Someone of dark disposition pointed out that Bailly's death had opened up three seats, the late astronomer having been the only person other than Fontenelle ever to have held a seat simultaneously in all three academies. Among the new members inducted into the moral sciences section were several powerful men of the hour—men who had not been powerful a short time earlier. In the science section, however, continuity triumphed. All of the former academicians retained their seats. A few new names were added to an already long list, which included Lamarck and Jussieu in botany, Daubenton, Cuvier, and Lacépède in anatomy, Haüy in mineralogy, Monge and Prony in arts and crafts, Berthollet, Guyton de Mourveau, and Fourcroy in chemistry, Coulomb in physics, Parmentier in rural economics, and of course Cabanis and Pinel in medicine.

And what about Méchain? He was not forgotten. He was awarded a seat alongside Cassini and Lalande in astronomy. Meanwhile, Delambre took his place in the mathematics section alongside Lagrange, Laplace, Legendre, Borda, and Bossut.

Delambre was intensely proud of the fact that he was considered a mathematician, since no one could deny that he was also an astronomer. Mathematics, after all, was the queen of sciences.

When he was asked about the expedition, the question was always the same: "When will it be over?" This was the only thing anyone seemed to care about. Irritated, Delambre replied that "it is now four years since this work began. I have devoted myself to it wholeheartedly, interrupting the work that means the most to me. No one wants to see an end to this project more than I. If not for the revolutionary tempest it would certainly have been finished long ago. On the other hand, had it not been for the Revolution, the project might never have gotten off the ground." Invariably a pinched expression greeted this last remark. Apparently tiring of the subject, the questioner would then observe that Méchain was once again not present. Whether comatose in Catalonia, imprisoned in Spain, banished to Italy, or stuck on a mountaintop in Languedoc, there had always been a good reason for his absence. The two astronomers were inextricably associated in everyone's eyes by their joint work. There was nothing they could do about it. How often were the names Méchain-Delambre and Delambre-Méchain pronounced that night as though they designated a single individual?

Before leaving Paris, Delambre had a promise to keep. He crossed the Pont-Neuf to the Left Bank, climbed the Montagne Sainte-Geneviève, passed the Pantheon, then turned around and craned his neck to see if the tower for which he had drawn up plans two years earlier had been built. From the ground it was impossible to see anything. He therefore went inside and once there could not refrain from checking on the condition of the pillars, which he found deplorable. Would they last until the end of the century? The question was especially urgent in light of the fact that there was much traffic in and out of the building: it had become common to remove the remains of anyone no longer in favor with whoever happened to be in power.

He then left the building and started down the small street that leads away from its south façade. After walking a short distance, he stopped in front of a building with a pediment bearing a brand new plaque: Ecole Normale Supérieure. A strange name, he thought, but one that had the benefit of candor: since the Republic One and Indivisible intended to sanction one and only one way of teaching, it was within these walls that the "norm" would be defined. An entire generation was to be bound by a single set of principles and a common purpose.

Every village in France was to have its *petite école,* but in Paris would flourish a quartet of *grandes écoles:* "Such instruction as can be dispensed to all must be dispensed to all equally, but no segment of the citizenry shall be denied the right to the higher education that cannot be shared by the masses," Condorcet had written. "Education of the first kind is necessary because it is useful to those who receive it, while education of the second kind is necessary because it is useful even to those who do not receive it." Delambre remembered the Christmas dinner at the inn in Châtillon where the young curé—what was his name? Chambraud, Jean Chambraud—had spoken at such length about philosophy. The memory made him want to stop in Châtillon on his way south.

"To translate a problem into algebraic language is to write equations. The art of expressing a problem in the form of equations and of choosing appropriate unknowns in order to arrive at the most elegant possible solution is a matter of the mathematician's skill. How are unknown quantities designated? By letters of the alphabet such as *a, b, x,* or *y.*" The lecture had begun. In the pit of the amphitheater Laplace stood in front of the blackboard addressing a crowd of silent pupils.

The students were not adolescents but adults. Some seemed passionate, others earnest; some naïve, others severe, and still others prepared to be dazzled. Delambre guessed that most of them were authentic autodidacts from every corner of France, men representing every possible trade, from artisan to priest, clerk to artist. They had been chosen by their fellow citizens as the most apt to teach their children and thereby establish genuine equality, beyond the merely political equality recognized by law. Achieving real equality was all the more important now that the law no longer did much to guarantee it.

"One of the most fruitful things that has been done in science is the application of algebra to the theory of curves. From this came infinitesimal analysis," Laplace continued. Sweat moistened the students' brows as quills scratched and pages were turned, and Delambre smelled a familiar smell, "the smell of learning." In a flash it all came back to him—Delambre, the perpetual student, who had not finished his last lecture course until he was well past thirty. The pleasure of learning, of knowing, of teaching! He had always wanted to be a teacher. At twenty he had believed that, because he was likely to go blind, teaching would be the only work he would be able to do—a marriage of convenience. But by the time he was twenty-five he had become convinced that there was no finer occupation—a marriage of love. At thirty he still believed this. To be sure, he would have loved to teach in one of the prestigious new institutions, but no one had offered him a position. He reassured himself with the thought that this was probably because of the expedition. It was impossible to be on the road and in the classroom at the same time. Either one stayed put and taught within four walls, or one traveled in wide-open spaces and endured the elements: one or the other. Still, he was jealous of Lagrange and Laplace, Haüy and Berthollet, Vandermonde and Daubenton and Monge, who staggered beneath their teaching loads.

On his way out of the building he was again overcome by curiosity and opened another door. The teacher was gesticulating impressively, and Delambre recognized him at once: it was Monge. Didn't people often say that he owed his success in geometry to his incredible skill at representing the most complex surfaces and objects with subtle movements of his hands?

"Other men are better speakers, but no one is a better teacher." Not everyone shared this opinion, however. Monge had been under attack in the press for some time. He remained a Montagnard at a time when it was better to forget that one had ever been associated with that group. What is more, he persisted in using radical teaching methods. He broke his classes up into small groups and organized debates between students and teachers "so that teaching will be the result not of a single mind at work but of the simultaneous effort of twelve to fifteen hundred men." Such audacity: a course whose teachings were open to debate—and in mathematics, of all subjects! And at a time when the authorities were striving to reinstitute discipline and obedience in the barracks!

◈

On his way back to his station, Delambre stopped in Châtillon. He decided to spend the night at the inn. Léonne the servant was still there, still slaving away, while Père-la-Liberté sat as still as a statue in his chair, apparently asleep. But he recognized Delambre at once.

When the astronomer asked what had become of the liberty tree, the old man's face took on a few additional wrinkles. "They chopped it down, the bastards!" he roared. "I warned the gendarmes that it was going to happen. One morning I found a king of diamonds." Delambre looked puzzled. "A card, a playing card. They'd stuck it to the trunk with a butcher's hook. The next day there was nothing: no trunk, no tree."

Léonne served a bottle of whiskey. "Tell him about Marchecourt!" she said.

"Oh, yes," replied the old man. "The pyramid. You remember? The one for your meridian that the fellows from the popular society tore down to repair a road? Well, this summer, the departmental directorate sentenced them to rebuild the thing. It cost them three thousand livres! Go to Marchecourt and you'll see the monument. It's like new. But the road is full of holes. Isn't that right, Léonne?" By then, however, she had already moved on to other chores.

The next day Delambre continued on his way. He was supposed to meet up with Bellet in the Creuse. He was tempted to continue his journey just to visit Méchain. Why not? But one thing held him back:

Rodez. If he went beyond Rodez, it would be as if he were trespassing on somebody else's territory. France divided.

◈

Méchain was at home one day when he learned that his berlin was waiting for him in Perpignan. His old berlin—still alive, he almost said. Unbelievable! When he set sail for Italy, he had been forced, much to his regret, to leave the carriage with the Spanish. But the local authorities had managed to get it back, and now they had just informed Méchain that it was ready. He rushed off to Perpignan.

But it wasn't where it had been, nor was it where he had been told it soon would be. In fact, the berlin was nowhere to be found. Where could it be? Obviously at the church of Saint-Jacques. A berlin in a church? In these times anything was possible.

Upon opening the door, Méchain literally ran into a wall, or, rather, a rampart composed of bales of hay piled every which way to the very tops of the buttresses. The nave was filled with hay, the church having been transformed only recently into a fodder depot for the Army of the Eastern Pyrenees. Standing in the entry, Méchain was jostled by a group of soldiers. Seeing his expression of astonishment, one of the soldiers said, "Hey, what? You don't like the manger? We already had the cow and the baby Jesus. All we needed was the ass!" He walked off to the laughter of his comrades. The astronomer felt as though he was being pursued by hay. It was bad enough that he had had to sleep on the stuff while staying at remote farms, but now here it was again, in the heart of the city.

Méchain finally found his berlin not "in" but "near" the church, covered with a tarpaulin in a nearby shed and waiting for someone to come and put it back into service. And given its perfect condition, it was entitled to such an ambition. Wheels, doors, axles—everything seemed to be in perfect working order. Even the paint had withstood the test of time, although the color had turned a bit pastel, not unlike the colors in the paintings of his compatriot Latour. The Spanish authorities deserved credit.

Méchain climbed into the passenger compartment and began an affectionate inspection. He detached the removable table and clamped it to the floor and ran his hand over the velvet upholstery. He made as if to dust the fabric. Perhaps he had left something in the niches. He searched them one after another: the one for the thermometer, then the one for the clock and the one for the capillary hygrometer. They were empty.

Then, remembering the document compartment, he raised his hand, felt around in the cavity in the ceiling, and was dumbfounded to find a map of Montserrat that still bore his own annotations. He settled into his favorite spot: the right rear seat.

"It might be a good idea to have a place of one's own, even in a berlin, the way children have their playhouses," he thought to himself. "If life should ever become difficult, I could go there for refuge." To be constantly on the move—never the same inn, never the same people, never the same bed—in the end such a life can drive a person mad. Everyone needs continuity, permanence: Méchain believed that the berlin might be able to offer him these things. He thought of keeping it.

But add to the—exorbitant—price of a horse the cost of keeping it in hay, not to mention the difficulty of obtaining feed and the time spent caring for the animal. Sadly, Méchain persuaded himself that it was more reasonable to let the carriage go.

He found Arago in the great hall of the Hôtel de Ville. He told him the whole story, unable to suppress his astonishment that, given all the upheavals in the region, the berlin had been returned in perfect condition.

"That's bureaucracy for you," Arago responded. "Steady and persevering. And since for the bureaucracy everything is abstract, all things are equally important in its eyes. Governments may change, but bureaucracy lives on. Are deputy undersecretaries likely to be beheaded? Leaves may fall, branches may break, but the roots remain." Then he started in on the story of the royal lottery. In the time of Robespierre, the Commission on the Arts had wasted a huge amount of energy on a difficult question involving the lottery. Louis XVI had been a lucky gambler. Before being imprisoned, he had bought a lottery ticket issued by a charitable institution. In due course the winning numbers were drawn, and the king's was among them. His prizes were ready to be claimed, but he was no longer around to claim them. The Commission on the Arts was assigned to deal with the problem. They duly labeled and catalogued each item but could not decide whom to give them to, so they held on to them in case—"

"In case the monarchy was restored," Méchain quipped.

◆

Arago proposed that in the meantime the berlin be kept in Estagel. Only Borda could decide what should be done with it. Méchain wrote to him about the matter and took the opportunity to raise other issues as well. What should be done with the instruments he no longer needed? And what about the Italian money? By Italian money, he meant the money earned from selling the repeating circle to Italian astronomers during his stay in Genoa.

Two weeks later to the day—exactly the time it took for a round-trip to Paris—Borda's reply reached him. "I feel it is my duty to apprise you of the current state of thinking within the Commission," it began. "In the past, as you know, we dealt with problems reasonably promptly. Things are different now. We act with circumspection, if I may put it that way. Or, to put it more bluntly, we are hopelessly indecisive. Hence you had best not wait for decisions from us. You and Delambre have no choice but to do as you think best. Rest assured of our support, whatever you may decide."

"As for the berlin, sell it or turn it over to the *département,* as you wish. You complain that I offer you no advice, so I shall give you some: think it over for an hour or a day, and whatever you think best is precisely what I advise you to do. If you would be so kind as to inform me of your decision afterward, I shall know what advice I have given you on the matter."

"Second request: Where to send the instruments you no longer need? Answer: I think it would be best to leave them all in a safe place, because it would cost money to ship them. When the instruments are needed, we will know where to find them."

"Third request: To whom should you send the proceeds from your sale of instruments to the Italians? My answer is that you should hold on to the money for now. We shall have to look into whether it might be possible to let you have it and at the same time have the government pay for the instrument so as to diminish by that amount the sums of money we shall need to send you in the future."

"I turn now to what you have told me about Delambre's work. Now I shall really be angry with you. Where did you come up with the idea that his observations, whether astronomical or terrestrial, are better than yours? And why denigrate your work—or, rather, the work of the commission that approved it—when everyone thinks your observations are fine?"

"To continue with my scolding, I do not understand why you don't want to work with Delambre on the observations at Evaux."

"Now my anger has subsided. I embrace you tenderly and assure you that my elderly heart, though chilled by age and infirmity and scarred by all that I have seen these past six years, is sincerely devoted to you. To conclude, please accept my apologies for leaving some of your letters unanswered. As you know, my dear friend, I suffer from being unable to write. As you probably also know, I am old, much older than I was when you left Paris, so this is a flaw I cannot hope to correct."

Méchain read the letter and concluded that "apparently they have as many problems in Paris as I have here." This pleased him. A moment later, Arago entered, accompanied by a Spanish officer. It was Gonzales.

"Dios!" Gonzales exclaimed, as he hastened toward Méchain.

"Deu!" Méchain corrected, as he shook the captain's hand. That very afternoon they rode off on horseback for Mount Mazamet.

Now that a peace treaty had been signed between France and Spain, the Spanish government had sent Gonzales to study the conditions under which cooperation between the two countries might resume. The two men spoke of this as they rode away from town.

Once they reached the country, Méchain set his horse to a gallop. Gonzales could not conceal his surprise at finding the astronomer so at ease in the saddle. It amazed him that not a single trace remained of the accident, except for a scar over one eye. His last image of Méchain was of an invalid confined to an armchair in Salva's garden.

The men slowed their horses as they began the climb. Méchain listened eagerly to what Gonzales told him about his accident. It was the first time he'd discussed it with anyone. He learned, for example, that while he lay in a coma, Don Ricardos had authorized a French doctor among the prisoners to visit him, and that in order to prevent a blood clot from obstructing circulation to his brain, this doctor had bled him to the maximum extent possible. After that, there had been a frightening effusion of blood through the right ear. It was this, they said, that had saved him. Méchain remembered none of this. As he listened to Gonzales's story, which included details that no one else had mentioned, he felt a chill at the back of his neck. "Just after the accident," Gonzales told him, "everyone was so sure you wouldn't make it that they just wrapped you in the skin of a freshly slaughtered sheep to keep you warm."

Méchain felt as though he might throw up. He brought his horse up short. The thought of himself naked, his mangled body wrapped in the skin of a sheep, his blood mingled with the blood of the animal, himself lying for days in the dead beast's hide—it was too much for him. He tried hard not to vomit. Gonzales, worried, asked him if he was totally healed. Méchain was slow to respond. At last, in a quiet voice, he answered, "As you see, time is a better healer than the doctors." Then he spurred his horse forward and set off at a trot despite the slope.

At the summit they erected a small pyramid of stones as a sort of target and identified various sites before starting back down. Midway down they heard someone shouting at them. Some soldiers signaled for them to stop. Their intention was clearly hostile. Méchain made a sign to Gonzales, and the two spurred their horses to a gallop. Did Méchain choose to flee because he remembered the *miquelets* who had bound and gagged Tranchot or because it would obviously be difficult to explain the presence of a Spanish captain such a long way from the border? The soldiers briefly gave chase and fired a few shots in their direction, but Méchain and Gonzales managed to escape. For the captain, the experience was a revelation. Like Méchain four years earlier, he decided that he would rather wait until "things calmed down." Méchain smiled.

As a result of this incident, Mount Mazamet sadly forfeited the honor of being included among the stations of the meridian, and Franco-Spanish cooperation in establishing the standard meter was interrupted. The matter did not end there, however. The soldiers, having spotted the pyramid of stones, concluded that it was a signal of some sort. A signal to whom and of what? These were troubling questions. And there were abundant grounds for worry. In nearby Vallespir, émigrés were continuing to make trouble, and royalists throughout the south of France were attempting to stir up new Vendées. Reports of the incident made it all the way to the top of the chain of command. Military intelligence became involved, and when local villagers were interrogated, they mentioned a Spanish officer. Perpignan was alerted, and the whole episode was on the verge of being blown up into a major incident, when Arago at last let the air out of the bubble.

The news also reached a corporal whose unit happened to be camped at the base of the mountain. After conducting his own investigation, this corporal became convinced that he knew what the signal was all about and asked for a leave. His request was granted.

◆

Méchain and Tranchot had taken rooms at the inn of Tuchan in Corbières. It was mealtime, and the dining room was full. That night a game of lotto was to be played. Accompanied by a soldier, the corporal pushed open the door of the inn and strolled among the tables in the dining hall, examining the faces of the customers as he went. Two men sitting next to a pillar had to be the ones he was looking for. Removing his garrison cap, he introduced himself: "Etienne Charpy, corporal of the third battalion. And you're Citizen Méchain, are you not? And you, Citizen Tranchot?" It was the surveyor, accompanied by his constant companion Gustave, the artilleryman. Etienne explained how he had found them. He also recounted in detail the story of his having met Delambre in Saint-Denis and of the astronomer's lesson on geodesy, the repeating circle, and the surveyor's chain. Méchain interrupted him: "Geodesy grew out of the methods of surveying. It was only natural that you two should meet. Aren't surveyors in a sense our forerunners?"

Etienne was grateful to this man who said what no man had ever said to him before. Méchain begged him to continue, and Etienne repeated all the ideas that had been running through his head on the subject of the triangles. Then he talked about battles, Valmy above all. Gustave now piped up for the first time: "As I told your colleague, me, I was born at Valmy." Etienne signaled for him to keep quiet, however, and Gustave cut himself off in midsentence. Then the surveyor sprang his surprise: their having come upon Delambre's berlin on the road to Dunkirk. "You're the fellow who has the other one, aren't you?" Etienne asked.

"I had it, but it's been sold. Mine was bronze," Méchain answered.

The astronomer was excited by the fact that this stranger wanted to converse with him about things so dear to his heart. He asked a thousand questions about Delambre. This soldier was the only man to have seen both of them since their departure: a corporal surveyor, the only living connection between two civilian astronomers. Méchain smiled. Etienne asked whether the Melun baseline had been measured. "Neither of the two baselines has been measured yet," Méchain answered. He was touched by the expression of joy that spread over Etienne's face: "The thing is, I promised Citizen Delambre to do the Melun measurement with him."

"Well, if you like, you can come along with us and do the Perpignan measurement as well. Isn't that right, Tranchot?" Tranchot made no objection. The surveyor asked where Delambre was, and Méchain wrote the address for him on a piece of newspaper. The tables were cleared so that the game of lotto could begin.

Each man bought a lotto card. A superb hat occupied a place of prominence on a table in the middle of the room. The master of ceremonies thrust his hand into the hat and stirred its contents vigorously with his arm, as if feeling about in the entrails of a chicken. Then he withdrew a handful of small bone markers, chose one, and began to bellow at the top of his lungs: "What number is it? What number? Who can say what number?" Then he tossed the marker into the air, where it spun oddly until he snatched it on the fly and with a loud smack brought it down on the palm of his other hand. At a glance he read the number engraved on the marker, and then his hand snapped shut like a valve, instantly bringing silence to the room. His mouth then slowly formed itself into a circle until it resembled a hen's bottom, whereupon he abruptly spit out the words, "Nigh-yun teen! Nigh-yun teen!"

A wave of *ahs* rolled over the room, accompanied by a wave of *ohs*. Any player who had the winning number on his card placed a bean on the nineteen. Eventually, the noise in the room subsided, and everyone looked attentive once again. The emcee then whirled around, danced a few steps, and finally came to rest in front of a pair of silent ducks, which he indicated to the crowd. Next to the ducks were several rabbits, and next to them a cage full of pigeons, a demijohn of wine, and a host of other lesser prizes. These things represented the lap of luxury, a veritable feast in a time of famine.

The game proceeded like a well-oiled machine. With each repetition of the ritual, only the number changed: "Sixty-five! Eighteen!" Tranchot, Gustave, Etienne, and Méchain sat off to one side. They had bought lotto cards and followed the game, but in the meantime they continued their discussion.

The fighting in the east had come right at the beginning, in 1792. Then the focus had shifted to the north, around Dunkirk, and after that to the west, in the Vendée, where rebels known as *chouans* had taken up arms against the Revolution. Now the main front was in the south and the Pyrenees. "We've seen it all," Etienne said to Tranchot. "And you've also been around. In a way you passed straight through France, whereas we've done a tour around the edges." He stopped short, and a smile spread across his face as he hit on just the words to say what he had in mind: "You've done the diameter, we've done the circumference." Gustave stared admiringly at his friend, but Etienne wasn't finished yet:

"And now, you know, they want to send us to Italy! That will complete the circle. Why Italy? The Italians haven't done anything to us. I don't like it. I volunteered to defend the Republic, not to conquer anybody!"

"There wasn't no Republic yet when we volunteered," Gustave reminded him.

"Makes no difference. Anyway, not to conquer anybody." In making his point, Etienne could barely contain his rage. Then he pointed to a corporal seated at a nearby table: "You see that fellow over there. He was at Bellegarde." He was interrupted by the emcee: "Forty-two!" One of his numbers. He smashed a bean down on his card.

"Forty-two! Seventeen! Twenty!" Méchain was no longer listening to the conversation. Lost in thought, he had wandered a long way from the inn, the numbers shouted out at regular intervals, and the alternating clamor and silence in the room. He imagined himself on the platform of the fortress at Montjouy, high above the invisible sea and the sound of waves. Overhead the sky was dreamlike: all the stars and constellations were visible, as beautiful as in a children's book of the heavens. Just above him Polaris and the Little Chariot stood out clearly, steadfastly pointing the way north and indicating the enveloping Dragon. The emcee's voice merged with his own announcing the result of a measurement: 42 degrees, 17 minutes, 20 seconds. Suddenly he remembered the Homa-Morta and the legend that Gonzales had told him about. Entire sentences from Gonzales's account came back to him: Homa-Morta, the man who died of holding his tongue . . . one of the peaks symbolized error, the other truth, but no one knew which one. Which one! Which one! All around him people were screaming. Some were pounding on the tables with their hands, others with wine goblets. The emcee had dropped one of his little markers, and most of the lotto players were insisting that the round should be canceled, especially since this was the last one. A new game was begun.

❖

The emcee packed up his baskets as the hall slowly emptied. Gustave got up to go. "The night's not over yet. Got to get back, Etienne. Tomorrow we strike camp. You haven't forgotten that we're leaving?"

"What the hell are you going to Italy for? Me, I'm not going. I'm not! It's not the same anymore. It's not the same war. You understand?" The corporal at the nearby table had turned to look at them. Some of the patrons thought that a few of the soldiers might have had a little too much to drink and that there might be trouble.

"Understand?" Gustave replied. "What I understand is that while we were off fighting, other people bought up the land. You know they did. We had nothing, and we still have nothing. Go home if you want. What are you going to do when you get there? Play lotto? As for me, I've been gone so long, I have no place to go back to. I've got no home. Not even Valmy," he added, trying hard to smile. He showed his burned hands. "And anyway, gunner is a fine trade. I don't see why . . . And I've developed a taste for travel. And you know . . . shit!" he concluded, and walked off.

Méchain heard what Gustave said and left the inn just behind him. "As different as that gunner and I are," he thought, "we're also alike. We left our families behind, and now we don't want to go home. We can't go home. What is there for us to do at home?"

Back at the inn, the corporal rose from his seat. He was a giant of a man, and he seemed in no hurry to leave. In one hand he held the pair of ducks he had won at lotto: the grand prize. With the other he supported himself with the help of a crutch, because one leg had been cut off at the groin.

◆

A few weeks later, Tranchot was reading the *Echo des Pyrénées,* as he always did, when he came upon a declaration made by the commanding general of the Army of Italy, which was reproduced in full on the front page:

> Soldiers, you are ill clothed and ill fed. The government owes you a great deal, but it can give you nothing. The patience and courage that you have demonstrated in these mountains have been admirable, but they have brought you no glory and no splendor. I will lead you into the world's most fertile plains. Rich provinces and great cities will be in our power. There you will find honor, glory, and riches.

The text was signed, "Bonaparte. Headquarters. Nice. 7 Germinal, Year IV."

Tranchot thought of Gustave.

16

"This letter is from the Institute," the awed postmaster announced. Instantly the crowd fell silent, as necks craned to see the name of the person to whom it was addressed. My God! It was for "the beadle." *Beadle* was the nickname the villagers had bestowed on Delambre because he spent most of his time in the church.

The letter was an invitation to participate in an election to "fill the post left vacant by Citizen Lazare Carnot."

"He didn't resign!" Delambre exclaimed. Carnot, until recently one of the five "directors" who collectively headed the French government, had just been sentenced to deportation.

Fate is ironic: Carnot was not being deported to Cayenne because he had been one of the most influential members of the Committee of Public Safety throughout the Terror, nor because he had signed arrest warrants for Danton, Camille Desmoulins, and so many others. Instead, he had been found guilty of taking part in a royalist "conspiracy"! Carnot a royalist! Not really, of course. But because he had been a fanatical Jacobin and never a royalist, his later anti-Jacobinism was even more fanatical than his antiroyalism.

"So, there you have it: overnight your colleague has become a bad mathematician!" Bellet commented. Even back in 1792, at the height of the turmoil, the former Academy had always stubbornly refused to accede to pressure that it expel members suspected of "royalism." Compared to such independence, the Institute's obedience to the powers-that-be seemed abject, or so Bellet believed.

On his way to Paris, Delambre stopped in Melun, where he and Laplace had gone together to check the baseline. Delambre naturally congratulated Laplace on the publication of his *Système du monde*, which had been a stunning success. Then he made a surprise visit to

Bruyères. Julie was surprised, but not as surprised as Delambre at the sight of his elderly servant struck speechless with shock and delight at finding him standing there in her kitchen.

Paris. In the chamber of the Commission on Weights and Measures a map was pinned to the wall. On it, a line representing the progress of the meridian measurement approached Rodez from the north, but little progress appeared to have been made in the south. Borda gave Delambre the news that Lenoir was a candidate for Carnot's post. He was a good friend, and it was good to see his work rewarded at last, his art honored. It was hard to imagine what state physics and astronomy would be in without artists of his quality. What would we know of the heavens without Galileo's lens? Where would Lavoisier's new chemistry be without precision balances? And where would the measurement of the meridian be without the repeating circle?

Never mind the arias of the theorists: without instruments there is no science. Thinking, reasoning, writing are one thing, but weighing and measuring are another. Delambre now felt he had an additional reason not to miss the vote.

Just as Delambre was handing Borda a letter from Méchain, the arrival of the minister of foreign relations was announced. Talleyrand—for it was none other than he—leaned on his cane. He had come to speak with Borda about his latest project: the convocation of an International Commission. Made up of the world's leading scientists, it would be given the mission of announcing the results of the meridian measurement.

The bishop—Talleyrand—had opportunely vanished from the political scene at a time when to play a prominent role in politics meant to risk one's life. When the storm subsided he made a surprising comeback. Having spent the revolutionary years abroad, he was well equipped to run the Ministry of Foreign Relations. Talleyrand had always taken an interest in the standardization of weights and measures. Had he not been the first to submit a bill for that purpose to the Constituent Assembly in 1790? It was then that Borda made his acquaintance. "To ensure one's place in history," Delambre mused, "it makes excellent sense to be in at the beginning of things and at the end."

"Vendémiaire! That's impossible. The standards will never be ready by Vendémiaire," Borda fumed. "How do you expect us to present them to the legislature by then?"

"The faster you move, the farther you go," was Talleyrand's parting shot.

Borda, who still held Méchain's letter in his hand, began to read it. After a few seconds he asked in an irritated voice, "But where is this damn Pradelles anyway?"

"According to my information," Delambre said, "it's in the Black Mountains." Meanwhile, Borda walked over to Cassini's great map of France and tried to locate the village in which Méchain had spent the past several months.

"It's nearly ten months now that he hasn't budged from that hole. What in the world can he be up to there?"

Borda was concerned. Only yesterday the Directory had asked him to speed things up. How could he move the operation along without frightening Méchain? He knew how easily the astronomer could take offense and how sensitive he was to any perceived slight. To go to him would be best, but travel was impossible: "I've just received the proofs of my decimal trigonometric tables. The proofreading will take days." He went on talking as if to convince himself that travel was out of the question: "A mistaken number in a table like this would render the whole thing useless!" Then he went back to reading the letter: "Barcelona! Barcelona! Why does he want to go back there?"

"A woman, perhaps," Delambre suggested ironically. Both men burst out laughing.

Two weeks later, Méchain, still stuck in Pradelles, received the following brief note from Borda:

I do not think it advisable for you to repeat any of your work in Barcelona. The observations you made there are excellent, and I defy you or anyone else to do them better, or to choose the sites more carefully, or to achieve equally conclusive results. I'm even planning to use your results in my work on refraction, which they corroborate quite nicely. There is only one thing with which you need to concern yourself, my dear friend: completing your triangles all the way to Rodez. In the meantime, Delambre will measure the baseline in Melun, and then we shall see if it makes sense for him to join you for the one in Perpignan, which you could do together.

In any case, whatever you do will be well done. I urge you not to worry about anything. If by chance some of your results do not agree with Cassini's, so be it. You weren't sent out to obtain the same results as your predecessors but to determine the truth, and that is surely what you have done, because you are more scrupulous in your observations. Farewell, my dear friend, be well, and reserve a portion of your friendship for me.

To Méchain this letter came as both a relief and a curse. Borda was a true friend. "But what is this ridiculous idea of sending Delambre down to Perpignan? And why measure the baseline together, when that task was assigned to me alone? Have they lost confidence in me in Paris?" He hastened to banish that dread thought. But none of this was encouragement to leave Pradelles.

He wanted to remain there with his few friends: Citizen Fabre, the old man from the Tour-Saint-Vincent, and Agoustenc, who was now always with him. Unlike Delambre, Méchain would not go to Paris to vote on a replacement for Carnot.

On his way to the Institute, Delambre stopped at the Luxembourg Palace. What did ordinary people know about the new units of measurement? The Commission had decided to teach them about the meter by exhibiting specimens in public. These had to be visible enough to attract the attention of passersby but substantial enough to withstand the elements and the inevitable assaults of vandals. Marble was therefore chosen for the models. Carrara marble from Italy would have been preferable, but none was available, so French stone was used instead: an enormous chunk of marble from Marly was cut up into some twenty pieces, which were then placed in some of the busiest spots in the capital: in the Tuileries Garden, at the entrance to the Palais-Egalité, in the courtyard of the Palais de Justice, at several of the city's gates (Antoine, Martin, and Denis), at the Bibliothèque Nationale, at the entrance to the Galerie des Tableaux, at the post office, on the Pont-Neuf, on Place Maubert, in the Place de Grève, on the Boulevard des Italiens, and at the Luxembourg Palace.

One of the marble samples of the meter had been installed about head high in a wall of the Petit Luxembourg. Despite the late December chill, a small crowd had gathered by the time Delambre arrived. On observing the sample each person instinctively spread his or her hands to gauge its length, then turned around in a single motion, shoulders rigid and neck stiff with hands fixed in position. Some grumbled, while others smiled. Those not satisfied with a single rough estimate would spread their fingers and try to gauge the length of the sample in terms of spans from thumb to little finger. For most people the meter was about four hands wide, but those with massive paws could make do with three, while one little lady who had to stand on her tiptoes to reach it took five. Some people said it was a good length and seemed pleased, while others felt that a worse choice could not possibly have been made.

A boy perched on his father's shoulders cried about not being able to remove his mittens. Delambre helped the child out, and as soon as his hands were free, he began imitating the adults. Running his little hand over the cold marble, he laughed and kicked his father's side with his heels as they moved quickly from one end of the meter to the other. Delambre continued on his way.

Leaving the rue de Vaugirard, he headed for the Seine along the rue des Fossoyeurs. He noticed a sign attached to a building: Pension Vernet, Guest Rooms. Delambre pushed the door open. In the middle of the tiny courtyard, five lindens shivered in the winter wind. A curtain was drawn over an upper-story window. A clock struck six: the time for voting would soon be over. Delambre broke into a run without pausing to check whether the trace of the Meridian of 1743 was still visible on the grounds of the former Saint-Sulpice church, now transformed into a Temple of Philosophy.

"For the post left vacant": such a pleasant circumlocution, Delambre thought. "For the post left vacant in the Mathematics Section, Citizen Lenoir has received 191 votes, Citizen Bonaparte, Napoleon, 411 votes. Citizen Bonaparte is elected."

The general, already well on his way to becoming the toast of Paris, came forward to thank his new colleagues. He presented himself with studied diffidence. "Yet another battle won without firing a shot!" trumpeted an elderly member of the Arts Section. "First the Alma Bridge, then the podium of the Institute!" someone from the Letters Section chimed in.

The general had loaded the dice in advance of the vote. Upon his return to Paris, still basking in the glory of his Apennine victories, he had remained out of sight, which made people want to see him all the more. Rather than swagger his way through the Left Bank's raucous salons, he had used his rare outings to attend dry lectures at the Institute, where he pretended to be interested in what was being said.

Was that enough to claim a seat in the Mathematics Section? The Letters Section was one thing, but Mathematics! A place among the six best mathematicians in France!

Bonaparte could boast of several claims to the honor. Had he not returned from Italy with a string of scientists at his side? Had not Berthollet and Monge become his friends? Had he not chosen Monge to deliver the triumphal Treaty of Campo-Formio to Paris? Along with the treaty, Monge had delivered a manuscript by Bonaparte that had played a significant part in his election. What was it? A battle plan? A political manifesto? No: a *theorem!*

It was a new theorem by Lorenzo Mascheroni, one of Italy's leading mathematicians, with whom the general had become friendly in his spare moments between battles and raids. The theorem itself was something of a surprise, a minor revolution in mathematics. Ancient mathematics had banished from its proofs all figures other than those that could be constructed with the two primary instruments of geometry: the straightedge and the compass. For two thousand years mathematicians had worked within the small universe of objects born of the exclusive love of these two devices. But the Italian Mascheroni proved to be even more stringent than the Greek Euclid: he showed that any figure constructed with straightedge and compass could be constructed with the compass alone.

The general also deserved credit for his interest in astronomy. But a man can love the stars without having the skill to discover one, just as he can love women without winning their love in return. Publicizing someone else's results does not make a man their author. And befriending numerous scientists, no matter how great, does not prove that a man is himself a scientist.

An artilleryman is necessarily to some extent both a geometer and a physicist. Isn't the trajectory of a cannonball described by an equation? Of course. But what exactly were Bonaparte's scientific accomplishments? None comes immediately to mind.

But wait! At a meeting opportunely scheduled for just before the election, the general had added an unforgettable page to the great book of mathematics. In the presence of his assembled colleagues, he had located the center of a circle using only a compass. This feat earned him abundant praise and compliments. Even Simon Laplace had rushed forward to shake Napoleon's hand, still white with chalk: "From you, general, we expected everything but lessons in geometry!" In the face of such an exploit, what chance did poor Lenoir have of winning the open seat in the Mathematics Section?

◆

Méchain was a long way from Paris and the excitement of the Institute. Still on Mount Bugarach. Why that accursed peak? Stupid question! Had there been any other choice? Méchain knew full well that there was no substitute for Bugarach, to which he was condemned to return as if in a nightmare. For weeks the target had been left unguarded. There were not enough men for the mission, nor was there enough money to persuade them to run the risk.

The climb was neither more nor less arduous than usual. Still, Méchain had to stop midway because of a nasty pain in his arm and head. Although Agoustenc insisted on remaining with him, Méchain ordered him to continue onward. With great misgivings the young man left the astronomer, who had become a kind of teacher to him. Méchain fell asleep. Soon he was aware of being awakened. He thought he had been asleep only a short time. To be sure, Agoustenc had returned sooner than planned. Despite the fresh air and exercise he looked pale. He told his story without wasted words, in the curt style of mountain people. Méchain had already grabbed his cane and started toward the summit. Of course he knew that there was no point. Agoustenc told him so. He climbed anyway, spurred on by a perverse desire to see with his own eyes what he was afraid to behold.

"It wasn't a storm this time!" he roared when the extent of the disaster became clear. "No, obviously it wasn't," was all that Agoustenc could think to answer. The hurricane had left signs of its passage, leftovers from its awe-inspiring repast. This time it was different. Apart from the base of the target, which lay buried beneath the surface of the ground, nothing remained on the minuscule plateau. It had been picked clean, like the bones of the animals eaten by those Amazon fish that Jussieu had described in his book. "Not even the nails! They took everything," Méchain exclaimed. "It's malevolence, pure malevolence."

"No, it's pilferage!" Agoustenc objected.

"And aren't you the one who said that anybody would have to be crazy to climb up here to steal this?"

"Things have changed. When people are desperate enough, you know, thieves. . . . And then it was good wood. It will make a fine fire." Agoustenc uttered those last words calmly, in the tone of a man who knows what he is talking about, but Méchain, had he been listening, might have taken them as an impudent provocation. "Still, we can't have gendarmes standing guard over all our targets!"

After returning to the Pâtres farm, Méchain did not set foot outside. Each day he seemed a little more withdrawn than the day before. Rebuild the target? What for? It would just be destroyed again.

Disheveled and unshaven, he was standing one morning in the big room, lost in thought. The woman whom everyone called "Mother" was watching him out of the corner of an eye. Eventually she came over and gently took the knife from his hands.

"You're not moving very quickly. Give it here, then, if you want to eat tonight."

Méchain got up and went out without saying a word. A fine drizzle had left everything damp. He sat down on a rock near the entry to the sheepfold. Mother watched him for a few minutes and saw that he remained as still as a statue. She threw a scarf over her shoulders, walked over to where he was sitting, and sat down next to him. She had been quiet about it, so he hadn't heard her coming. It was as if she just materialized out of the rain. "Go back inside! You'll catch your death of cold." He didn't move. "Look at me!" Out of politeness, though not without effort, he looked up. His face was dripping wet. Shaking her head as she did when one of her animals was sick, she reached out and handed him his cap, which he had left inside. "You're not well," she said. "Go home until you feel better. You're not alone. You have a wife and kids. When things are better, you'll come back."

"Go back to Paris? Now? Before I've finished?" He shook his head as if to dismiss the idea out of hand.

"Tranchot can replace you. He's a sturdy fellow."

Méchain started. "Tranchot! I've been entrusted with a mission. Me, not my assistant. Nobody will make these measurements for me. No one will go to Paris and tell them Méchain hasn't finished his job, Méchain has given up. No one!"

Mother gave him a hard look. She had no idea what was eating him, but she sensed that it would be best to stop his rant then and there. With a stern face she said, "I don't give a damn about your measurements, my boy. I'm telling you this for your own good."

"Excuse me, Mother. I'm turning into a real savage."

"Stop!"

He went with her into the sheepfold, and then they returned to the house together.

❖

That night, after Mother had cleared the table, he sat down next to the fireplace, put his bag on the table, and took out a sheet of paper. He raised his quill as if to write, then hesitated. . . . Lalande. If he could confide in anyone, it had to be Lalande. "Yes, my friend," he began, "my heart sank when I saw my targets destroyed and all our arduous labor reduced to naught. My courage abandoned me. What can I tell you about this apathy that comes over me and chills me to the bone as soon as I lie down or find myself alone? It paralyzes what little will I have. Discouragement and disgust have sapped my strength. The task, I confess, called for greater strength than I possessed and no doubt greater skill as well." Then he looked up, and his eye's met Mother's; he drew new courage from her quiet energy. "Nevertheless, I shall recover if I am asked to carry on. As soon as the order arrives, I will go and rebuild the targets on Black Mountain and the three Bridges. We should progress rapidly enough to meet Citizen Delambre in the fall if he continues to move toward us with the swiftness of an eagle." Just writing these words replenished his reserves of courage. Suddenly he felt warm and alive within. It was a good feeling. He felt himself coming back to life; things began to make sense as before. It was high time he got going. He must finish the letter quickly and get ready, for tomorrow at dawn the work would begin anew.

If anyone had ventured onto the mountaintop a few days later, he would have seen a strange sight: the target had been rebuilt and stood once more upright, solid, as good as new. Nearby, two men sat next to a small fire, warming themselves as best they could. Amid the jumble of rags protecting them from the cold a uniform could be glimpsed. Both men were gendarmes, one a private, the other a sergeant, sent by the district authorities. The private spoke. "Well, doesn't this beat all? Guarding four pieces of wood in the middle of a mountain range."

To which the sergeant replied, "Bah, if not one thing, it's another." He sat up straight. "That's how it is in the service."

17

Their clothing worn, their shoes down at the heels, Delambre and Bellet protected themselves as best they could from the cold. With their long beards and wool caps they looked like convicts as they bounced along in a crude cart up the steep road to their next station.

"We have just enough to pay for a horse and buggy to take us from station to station," Delambre had written in his travel diary,

us and the things we absolutely must have with us. In Soesme people refused to give us lodging, but that was because they knew us and knew that all we had for cash was *assignats*. If the local government hadn't promised to give grain to anyone who would provide us with bread, we wouldn't have been able to buy any. Even with the government's guarantee, people refused to sell us bread on several occasions.

More than once our unhealthy appearance cost us, as in Philopoemen. The people most favorably disposed toward us took us for prisoners of war being transported from one hospital to another. Others noticed the crates in which we store our repeating circles and mistook us for itinerant players without the means to pay for lodging, so we were turned away. This happened in Vouzon.

There's nothing quite like traveling in the middle of a revolution, and if we hadn't made up our minds once and for all to push on, we would have called the whole thing off.

"His collar is worn, his sleeves are unraveling, his elbows are full of holes," Delambre hummed as he drove, holding the reins in his ungloved hands. The carriage nearly bogged down for good in a pothole deeper than the rest. As the horse strained to pull it out, Delambre grumbled: "A hundred livres in *assignats* for a piece of barley sugar!"

Sitting in the back of the cart on the crates containing the parts of the circle, Bellet calmly counted a stack of paper notes. He was wearing the gloves with the fingertips cut off. "If we combine our two salaries," he said, "this month we should be able to afford"—he made a rapid calculation—"thirteen and a half pieces of barley sugar."

When they reached the village, Delambre made himself scarce, leaving Bellet to deal with the curious onlookers who gathered around the cart.

"You fellas selling something?" asked one of the peasants.

Bellet found himself at a loss for words. "You stupid or what?" asked the peasant. Turning to the others, he said, "He don't even know if he's selling anything. Come on, let's get out of here." And with that he grabbed his wife by the sleeve.

But she freed herself from his grip, planted herself directly in front of Bellet, and looked him in the eye. "You weren't over by Sermur the other day with some other fella, were you?" Without waiting for an answer, she turned to her husband and said, "They were holed up in the bell tower for quite a while. Who knows what they were sticking their noses into? Supposed to be scientists from Paris." The peasant screwed up his nose in disgust. Then he pointed at Bellet: "If that's what education leads to, I'm pulling the kid out of school today."

Meanwhile, Delambre was visiting his fourth barn. The man he was looking for—Antoine, the mayor—was sitting on a block of wood and milking a skinny cow with a distended udder. Delambre showed him his mission orders along with a requisition. Gruffly, the mayor grabbed the papers. With maddening slowness he deciphered the text, then returned to his milking, but not before wiping his hands. Eventually he asked, "So where is this Citizen Delambre?"

"I am Delambre!"

Like a horse trader scrutinizing an animal, the mayor inspected this bum who claimed to be an astronomer. Delambre did not flinch under his stare. "I'll be lucky if he doesn't look at my teeth," he thought.

"There are so many charlatans in these parts. We don't have much use for requisitions around here. The last time they came and took the eighth pig from every litter. Requisition, they said. Next season, every sow dropped a litter of seven. Guess why. So, what is it you want?"

"Something to eat and a place for two to sleep. I'm traveling with my assistant. And some hay for the horse, wood for the scaffold, a carpenter, and some workmen."

The mayor's jaw dropped. "That all?" he said.

"That's all—for now," Delambre explained.

"So folks up in Paris make up their minds to have you measure"—he searched for the word but couldn't come up with it—"decide to have you measure, and down here in Herment we have to care for you the way a mother takes care of her children."

Warm vapors rose from the pail between the mayor's legs. It was half full of milk. The mayor saw the look of thirst in Delambre's eyes. "Go on, drink up!" The liquid felt warm and smooth in the astronomer's mouth. A white mustache appeared above his black beard. Delambre wiped his lips. "We can pay, you know. But nobody will take our *assignats*."

"Damn it all," said the mayor. "You know how much it costs—"

"Yes, I know," Delambre cut him off. "A piece of barley sugar costs a hundred livres."

"You know that? You're eating barley sugar?"

"Every day. That's all we eat now. We can't afford anything else."

A few days later, Delambre and Bellet found themselves passing through a hamlet not far from Herment, one of those pretty little villages in which mud, manure, and garbage cover the ground in a layer so soft that your feet sink right in. Bellet hastened his step in order to get himself out of the sticky mess as quickly as possible. But when he turned around to see how his fellow traveler was doing, he was surprised to find him far behind, standing still in the middle of the road and staring at something Bellet could not make out. He retraced his steps back to Delambre's side. The astronomer was muttering to himself: "Six, seven." He pointed at several little bundles of pink moving slowly through the muck: a sow and her offspring wallowed in their sty.

"So now you're interested in pigs?"

"What did you say?" Delambre asked. He hadn't been paying attention.

"I said that the bell tower in Herment does not stand out clearly enough," replied an irritated Bellet. "The best thing would be to work at night with a reflector."

"No!" came Delambre's sharp reply. "Don't you think we've had enough trouble already? I'll say it again: Don't alarm the population, get them to accept us, pass unnoticed. Remember that I still hold you responsible for the burning of the Tuileries."

"The statute of limitations has run on that one!" Bellet chortled. But seeing that the sow was headed straight for them with a hungry look in her eyes, he beat a hasty retreat.

❖

Back in Herment, the long white sheet unrolled itself majestically down the length of the bell tower. Leaning out over the void, Delambre and Bellet attached the ends of the sheet to the beams of the scaffolding. Clearly satisfied with their work, they took their time gathering up their tools. After a while Bellet went over to the opening. Looking down at the square below, he saw a group of villagers. When Bellet's head appeared, they began shouting. Cheers or insults? When Delambre poked his head out alongside his assistant's, the shouts grew louder. Fists were brandished in their direction. "It looks like they're angry with us," Delambre naïvely mumbled.

Moments later, Antoine the mayor, breathing like a bull, burst onto the platform, which shook beneath his weight. "What the hell are you doing with that flag? I don't know where they stand in Paris, but here, goddamn it, we still have a Republic. You take down that royalist flag at once, or else."

"Royalist flag?" Delambre sputtered. Bellet, quicker on the uptake, laughed uproariously. The white sheet had been mistaken for an emblem of monarchy. "Don't alarm the population! Good job!" he jibed sarcastically before disappearing down the stairs. "I'll be back."

Delambre explained to the mayor that his damned belfry was dark, as were the mountains behind it, so that it was impossible to see it from Meymac. "That's why we put a white sheet in front of it. We would have chosen a black sheet if the background had been light. In that case you'd probably have thought we were pirates."

The crowd in the square below was getting restless. Pitchforks and muskets were brandished in the direction of the bell tower. Tempers were rising.

"The landlords are coming back!"

"This time we won't take it lying down. The land is ours. Let them come and try to take it!"

"What are we waiting for? Let's go and throw them out."

"Antoine has gone up to talk to them."

"Anybody know who it is?"

"It's those scientists," Mariette reported. She was the woman who had confronted Bellet on his arrival.

Her husband, calling her to witness, said, "I knew there was something funny about those two. I told you so, didn't I, Mariette? That dumb one who said he wasn't selling anything. What he wants, I'll bet, is to sell us his king!"

People were shouting, and everyone was trying to look determined, but the tension in some of the faces suggested that fear was also a factor. Off to one side, tucked away under a portico, a respectably dressed elderly couple stood with their eyes glued to the belfry. There wasn't a doubt in their minds that the lords were back: those two up in the tower were the advance guard.

"What's going to happen to them?" the old lady asked, lowering her voice so as not to be overheard.

"Don't worry," her husband reassured her, giving her hand a tender squeeze. "If they did what they did in broad daylight, there must be others with them."

By now the square was in an uproar. It was like a holiday: spirits were running high, and people were clapping their hands. All heads were tilted upward, all eyes glued to the church. Suddenly, two additional lengths of cloth were simultaneously unfurled. They hung down on either side of the white sheet to form a rather odd tricolor flag majestically embellishing the belfry.

The old man let go of the old woman's hand. He looked down and motioned for her to follow. "Let's go home," he said.

The heads of the two "republicans" now appeared just above the flag. Antoine peered out between them. Cheers went up from the crowd for all three and continued for some time. Mariette waved her apron at them and proudly proclaimed to one and all, "They're friends! Scientists from Paris!"

❖

"Since I'm not sure how long they will continue to respect my tricolor target, given the predominance of the color white, I have asked the administration of the Puy-de-Dôme *département* to place this installation under the protection of the authorities," Delambre noted in his diary. Such an adventure, he mused, could happen only to a draper's son like himself.

Bellet persisted in his refusal to say where he had come up with the red and blue cloth. Obliged to guess, Delambre could think of only one possibility: his assistant was known to have an "acquaintance" who lived in a small house just behind the church.

❧

They were so close to their goal now that they could smell it. They worked steadily, without pausing for Sundays off or "tenth days of rest." Tirelessly the astronomer and his assistant made their way toward Rodez in their new wagon, which, though considerably less magnificent than their berlin, held the road well. On the eleventh they were in Meymac, where local people led them to a mountain said to be the highest in the area, but rain blocked their view. On the twelfth they returned to the same peak. On the thirteenth they went to Bort-les-Orgues. On the fourteenth it rained all day. On the fifteenth they climbed to the top of the cliff overlooking the village. On the sixteenth, in Mauriac, it rained all day. On the seventeenth Bellet signaled from Mauriac to Peaux.

"On the nineteenth," he wrote,

> I immediately spot Puy Violent, on which snow is falling even as Bellet is on his way there. On the twentieth I call on the departmental authorities, who give me a letter for the mayor of Montasalvy. On the twenty-first we arrive in Montasalvy. On the twenty-second, a visit to the chapel of Saint-Pierre. The door is gone and the belfry half in ruins. It's nothing more than a sort of niche open on two sides. All the way there we travel in clouds. I hope to meet up with Méchain in Montasalvy. The itinerant lives we both lead make our correspondence very slow. On the twenty-third we return to Montasalvy. Méchain is not there.
>
> In Aubassin Dr. de Fontange informs me that the peak on which I set up my target is not Puy Violent, as I wrote, but rather Violan. Incidentally, a few words about the target in Bort: it was the object of frequent vandalism, and if not for the vigilance of the local authorities it would not have survived for long.

On the day Delambre and Bellet finished erecting that target, a terrible storm devastated the region. Tons of earth, mud, and stones from the mountain inundated the streets of the village to a depth of three feet. There were fears that the bridge over the Dordogne might be swept away. In the downpour the astronomer and his assistant clung to each other near the edge of the cliff, holding on for dear life against the gusts that threatened to hurl them into the abyss.

Behind them, on the crest of the mountain, stood the target. Lashed by rain, it seemed frozen in a series of strange postures by the lurid illumination of the lightning. It began to resemble a monstrous, broken body, a wooden Christ martyred by the elements. The two men fled the scene as soon as they were able to. At the gates of the village a hostile crowd awaited them. Someone had to be held responsible for the unusual violence of the storm. The villagers believed that somehow the target had caused the disaster. It was blamed for the continuous rains that for the past two months had hampered farming in the mountains. "Kill the sorcerers!" the crowd screamed. Except for the altitude and the rain the scene was reminiscent of the incident in Saint-Denis. And once again it was the mayor who saved the two men by taking them into his own home.

Soaking wet and chilled to the bone, the two "sorcerers" were a pitiful sight. For once Bellet apparently hadn't caught a cold, but Delambre couldn't stop sneezing and could barely breathe. No sooner did he manage to get some air into his lungs than he began to shout: "Spies, aristocrats, Vendéens, charlatans, émigrés, and now sorcerers! I've had just about enough. Enough!" Just as Delambre collapsed onto the bed, Bellet impishly extracted the cure for all ills from beneath his shirt: a lovely bottle of hooch.

An hour later, through windows still rattled by the wind, the mayor caught a glimpse of Delambre with a napkin tied around his neck and long johns to warm his legs. He was singing at the top of his lungs:

> Unhappy bachelor
> When you grow oooold
> And stiff in the joints
> After years of revelry . . .

"What revelry, I'd like to know," he interjected, his voice cracking.

> . . . What will you have to show?

❖

At last he fell asleep and did not wake until the next afternoon, still groggy and queasy. "What's the good of filling my diary with such details," he reflected hypocritically. "If any historian wants to write about this work in the future, would he find this sort of information useful? Other facts would be far more beneficial." And he began to write: "6 Fructidor, in La Gaste, I spot Méchain's target. On the seventh, on the road from Rieupeyroux to Rodez, I run into Tranchot by pure chance. He has just finished the mission Méchain had sent him to accomplish."

◆

Tranchot lowered himself gently into the tub. The water was hot, just the way he liked it, and the tub large enough to hold his entire body. He languished there for a full hour. As he began to shave, he heard a sound. Méchain was back. Tranchot rushed out to tell him the news. Delambre was about to reach Rodez! He might already be there. Méchain did not flinch. What he had feared had come to pass. Delambre had been assigned a more substantial piece of the operation than himself, and still Delambre had finished first.

Méchain walked away, downcast. Tranchot, who knew what this news signified for him, caught up with him: "I've thought about it. Delambre will arrive ahead of us. There's nothing we can do about it. But if we continue at the rate we've been going, we won't even finish before winter, and we'll have to make another foray. I see only one way to speed things up: let's do the measurements together."

Méchain turned on him angrily. "Why don't you just come right out and say I can't do it alone anymore?"

"No, that's not what I'm saying at all. I'm just saying that if we worked together, we'd at least have a chance of finishing this year. You'd take the upper telescope, and I'd take the lower, and we'd progress twice as quickly."

"It's out of the question."

Tranchot looked at him as if he didn't understand what Méchain had just said. "We've been working together for the past six years. For the past six years I've gone with you everywhere. I stayed with you when you had your accident. I've taken you up mountains. I held the telescope for you when you were crippled, and I followed you to Italy. I didn't go home, not once."

"Neither did I."

"You refused to go back to Paris. Delambre suggested several times that you return, but you always refused. I stayed because it never occurred to me to leave before the mission was accomplished."

"I didn't ask you to stay."

"But you did ask the Commission to allow me to stay with you."

"Didn't you want to?"

"I didn't say that. But you've changed since then, changed a great deal. And there's something else, something I'm no longer willing to put up with. You have yet to allow me to measure a single angle. Never once did you allow me to use the circle."

"What's wrong with that? The responsibility for measuring angles is mine alone. No one but me is allowed to use the circle for that purpose."

With that Tranchot could restrain himself no longer. After wiping the shaving cream from his face, he convulsively cleaned his hand on his shirt. "You've used me as an errand boy, just good enough to set up targets, scout out summits, spend a few days alone in the mountains. But the scientific work you've always reserved for yourself. I wasn't hired for that. Let me remind you that I'm a geographer, a geographical engineer. I'm fed up, do you hear, Méchain! I've had enough of your tyranny! And what's more, you're doing these things to slow the work down. As if you were afraid for it to be over."

Méchain froze, petrified. The two men faced each other. There were still traces of soap on Tranchot's face.

"What did you say?" Méchain mumbled, like a man walking in his sleep.

"I said that we've been going nowhere for months, making no progress. I said that I no longer have the slightest idea what you're up to. You don't want to get to Rodez."

"Go to Rodez if you want. Don't let me hold you back. Go and join Delambre, go and measure the baseline with him. You're dying to do it. Go, go, go!"

◆

A wagon slowly made its way across the naked plateau of the Causses, which lay baking in the African heat. The wagon's seat was protected from the sun by a cloth canopy stretched over a makeshift frame. Only the gray stallion seemed to be awake.

The two humans being pulled along by the animal had for some time been in no condition to react to the many bumps in the road. Stripped to the waist and dripping with sweat, they seemed either dead or asleep. Their trousers, cut off at the knees, made it possible to see the streaks of sweat in the gray dust covering their legs. The fabric above their heads colored their faces with strange patches of red and blue.

An hour later, everything had changed. Tall trees lined the road, giving the travelers and their horse welcome shade. Best of all, from the depths of the trees' shadows they could see a high tower rising from a hilltop: Rodez!

Delambre and Bellet laughed and laughed. They hugged each other like a couple of schoolboys and mimicked a wild Huron dance, much to the perplexity of their horse. Six years from Dunkirk to Rodez!

"When will we link our targets up with yours?" Delambre had written to Méchain. "That will be a red-letter day in both our lives." A desperate wish. Perhaps Méchain had already arrived. Instinctively, in a kind of reflex reaction, Delambre aimed his telescope. Except for the statue of the Virgin that dominated the city, the plateau was deserted.

Trying to hide his disappointment, Delambre patted the gray horse. "Tonight, oats for this fellow, Monsieur Bellet, the best oats that money can buy, and a double ration!" The horse neighed with pleasure. "There's Henri IV's white horse," Bellet said excitedly, "and now there the gray horse of the meridian. As a souvenir they can build the Mètre Etalon."[1]

Delambre began his diary entry with these words: "Tower of Rodez, 397 steps. At the zenith of the stone Virgin that served as our aiming point."

◈

Delambre lost little time in informing the Commission of his arrival in Rodez. That very night a letter was dispatched to Borda. "One of them has arrived!" Borda congratulated himself. "Now for the other." The greater difficulty, he knew, still remained. He had done all he could to hasten Méchain on his way. Now he was helpless. There was nothing to do but wait.

It was at this point that Thérèse decided to intervene. On several occasions, Borda, Lalande, and other members of the Commission had

---

1. An untranslatable play on words: Standard Meter or Master Stallion. *Trans.*

suggested that she try to improve her husband's attitude toward his work. She had always refused; this, she felt, was not her role. Time passed. The children grew older; Isaac, the eldest and an astronomer like his father, had left with General Bonaparte for Egypt.

She felt herself growing older too. She had become accustomed to life without her husband, as if she were married to a sailor. It was almost like being a widow. And still there was no sign of Méchain's return. Had it taken Columbus this long to discover America? Had it taken Magellan this long to circumnavigate the globe, or Vasco da Gama to sail to India? She felt lost and extremely unhappy. "He's stuck in the mountains of southern France. I must do something to set him free," she thought.

The decision came to her in a flash. She summoned her children: her daughter, who was so discreet, and Augustin, who was old enough to understand. Both approved of their mother's plan. The next day Thérèse was ready. She went to the Commission, where she was lucky enough to run into Borda.

"I've come to inform you that I'm about to go join my husband."

"No! You mustn't even think about it. It would be dangerous for you to go, and much too arduous," Borda managed to reply a moment later.

Brushing his warning aside, she said, "I've just sent him word that I'm on my way. I've booked the journey without waiting for his reply, so that he cannot talk me out of it again as he has done in the past. I will go directly to the Black Mountains."

"What if he's no longer there?"

"I'll look for him."

Borda smiled. He was beaten. But he worried about the journey: Thérèse was no longer young. He made one final attempt to dissuade her: "Madame Méchain, have you thought—"

"That I'm going to cost him even more time?" She was indignant. "Is that what you want to say? My purpose is quite the opposite: it is to speed up the measurement of the triangles. Nobody wants this expedition over with more than I do."

Worried that this speech might not have been convincing enough, she added an even more passionate coda: "I wrote and told him that he'd better not be foolish enough to return to the city to find me comfortable quarters. I don't want to take up even a quarter of an hour of his time. I will go and find him in the mountains, and I will sleep in his tent or in a farmhouse, and I will live on cheese and milk. If I'm with him, I can be comfortable anywhere. During the day we'll work together, and at night there will be plenty of time for talk." Thérèse blushed at having spoken so frankly and revealing so much of her passion. She quickly lowered her eyes. With a sharp pull she straightened her dress, but her hands were still shaking.

"Yes, I think I can help him, but please don't think that he's doing nothing right now. My husband tells me that after observing the North Star, he calculated its declination to within 0″17 of what Citizen Delambre calculated in Evaux. He also tells me that he made more than two hundred observations to determine the inclination of one side of one of his triangles to within one second of arc. But as he wrote me in his last letter, he doesn't have enough free time to put the finishing touches on the results and send them to you. He also sent me the results for the eclipse of 6 Messidor."

She blurted all this in one breath. Borda, stunned, asked if she had learned all this information by heart or if it had just sunk in after reading her husband's letter countless times. Quietly, she began to explain. "You see, Citizen Borda—" Then she hesitated. "Are you a bachelor?"

Taken off guard, he stammered. "Yes, I am indeed. Does that prevent my understanding certain things?"

She blushed again and refused to say more. But Borda urged her to go on. "I didn't mean to be indiscreet," she stammered. "I am his wife, and wives have some power. I put my hope in his esteem for me and in the fact that he trusts me implicitly. I'm confident that I can dispel the dark thoughts that are gnawing at him and distracting him from his goal in spite of himself. Maybe the three of us—you, Citizen Delambre, and myself— can rekindle his spirit. That, unfortunately, is all that is within my power."

A melancholy smile, almost a child's pout, formed on her lips. Suddenly she seemed tired. She felt like departing at once. In any case the stagecoach would be leaving soon. She had already opened the door but stopped and turned around. "I beg you to keep this conversation strictly to yourself. As far as anyone else knows, I'm going to the country. No one must know the reason for my trip, lest they say, 'She was obliged to go and fetch her husband home.'"

Before Borda could answer, Thérèse was already gone.

◈

While Thérèse was on her way to the mountains of the south, Delambre, having secured the station in Rodez, was hurrying northward, toward Melun, where Laplace awaited him. Measuring the baseline would be the next step. From that they could calculate the sides of the triangles, which would yield the length of the meridian. This was really the beginning of the end of the whole project. Little work had been done since the last inspection, however. Workers would have to be hired immediately: woodcutters, laborers, and carpenters. Bellet scoured the region for them. Like a recruiting sergeant, he visited inns everywhere in search of workers to hire. Nearly enough turned up at the site to fill out a battalion. They arrived with little slips of paper bearing Bellet's stamp and were greeted by Etienne, the surveyor. He himself had come one morning from his village, Dun, carrying a sack over his shoulder. As promised, Delambre had hired him on the spot.

Melun stood at one end of the baseline, Lieusaint at the other. In theory the endpoints determined the line. All that remained was to construct it. But the terrain was heavily forested: all those trees complicated the task.

The woodcutters went to work. Any tree in the designated path was to be cut down. While the woodcutters cut, sawed, toppled, and pruned, the laborers came along behind them and smoothed the surface, eliminating hillocks and mounds, filling in gullies, ravines, and holes. Earth removed in one place was used as fill in another. The goal was to create a level surface, and the surveyor, equipped with a level, checked regularly to ensure that the work surface was horizontal. Dozens of carts and wheelbarrows filled with dirt made constant trips to and fro, raising clouds of dust as they went.

With each passing day one could see a little farther along the path. What had been a crude trail blazed through the forest was little by little transformed into an impeccable avenue, tailored in the French style. Meanwhile, the carpenters were busy on a major project of their own: a wooden structure, a sort of chassis, built on pilings. The sounds of planes, hammers, mallets, and saws filled the air. Temporary workbenches mounted on sawhorses had been placed at intervals along the route. Felled trees lay on the ground waiting to be sectioned, sawed into boards, hewed into pilings, or carved into pegs. As with the dirt, a tree trunk that posed an obstacle in one place could be pressed into service in

another. To keep costs down, the work relied on a closed-circuit econ-
omy, a veritable autarky of building materials.

The structure had to be solid enough not to bend under load or flex
because of its length. As parts of the framework were completed, they
were hoisted onto pilings, fitted in place, and then adjusted. And the
work progressed.

Quickly the construction began to take shape. It stood about head
high and looked like a vast bridge spanning the countryside. The starting point, well marked, was embedded in the Melun target; the end-
point was yet to come. Peasants who came to view the work in progress
always asked the same questions. Was it to be used for transporting tim-
ber? Was it an aqueduct? By the time they left, they were shrugging their
shoulders. And the work, interrupted for a moment, resumed.

In the distance, when the wind direction was right, one could occasionally hear the sound of a large tree crashing to the ground and feel the
vibration of the ground. From not so far away came the muffled sound
of shoveling. Other sounds filled the air as well: constant shouts of men
calling to one another and whistles indicating that it was time for a break
or a meal. Occasionally a fight might break out—nothing serious. And
the men sang. At night the crackle of campfires mingled with the bark-
ing of dogs, which appeared out of nowhere.

Delambre was everywhere at once. His opinion was sought constantly, and he never had a moment's rest. The first day he had felt disoriented. This work was so different from what had gone before. Indeed,
it was quite the opposite. The transition from measuring angles to cal-
culating sides was a difficult one. No more ladders, no more staircases,
no more churches, no more towers. Every day his feet remained firmly
planted on the ground, his nose in the dirt. Gone were the summits and
the clear air of the heights, the silence, the wide-open spaces. In the forest, unless he stood squarely in the middle of the cleared path, he was
constantly surrounded by things. He felt nostalgic for the silence, for the
quiet moments when he could feel in control of time itself. How vast the
difference between those virtual lines hurled across the sky, swallowing
up the distance between two belfries, and this eminently palpable
wooden track riveted to the earth, the building of which required effort
every step of the way.

While inspecting this vast construction site, Delambre could easily
have thought of himself as a master builder, a Vauban of the forest. If

not for his pacifist leanings, he might easily have imagined himself a general in the field. The woodcutters followed on the heels of the laborers. Then came the carpenters and finally the "measurement men." Who were they? Laplace, Delambre, Bellet, the surveyor, and a young fellow by the name of Leblanc-Pommard, who had come with Delambre. It was a good team, but apparently it needed another member, because on the day before the measurement was to begin, the Commission sent a reinforcement: Tranchot. After receiving a warm welcome, he immediately went to work. Bellet quietly looked over his counterpart and found him robust, reliable, and a hard worker. So Delambre would have two assistants. When the surveyor realized that Tranchot was at the site, he hurried over to ask a series of questions about Méchain, but Tranchot's answers were evasive.

Following his dispute with Méchain, Tranchot had returned to Paris. The Commission, heeding a suggestion by Delambre, had proposed that he join in the work on the baseline, and he had accepted immediately.

The same carriage that brought Tranchot to the site also brought the measuring bars. These were made of platinum and numbered one to four. Borda and Lenoir had come up with an interesting temperature compensation mechanism. Embedded in the end of each bar was a small strip of brass, which served as a highly sensitive metallic thermometer. With the aid of this device, it would be possible to calculate the expansion or contraction of the metal due to fluctuations in temperature. The ideal, of course, would be to use a stable measuring instrument, but failing that it was essential to know how much the instrument itself changed in the course of measurement. Everything was now ready to go.

Laplace was given the honor of setting the first measuring bar in place. With Bellet's help he set it down squarely on the wooden support and adjusted the graduations with a microscope. Then the ballet began. Delambre placed the second bar. Then it was Tranchot's turn, followed by Leblanc-Pommard. And so on. In a single day the bars were placed in position more than ninety times, and marks were made to record the progress.

Etienne noted the countless precautions that had been built into the procedure. The bars were not laid down end to end, in contact with one another. If they had been, an accidental tap on one bar would have been transmitted to the next, shifting the whole assembly, and the whole measurement would have been ruined. In order to prevent this, it was decided to leave a space between consecutive bars, which could then be measured with a feeler gauge.

Another precaution was to cover the structure with a small roof to protect the bars from the sun and the rain. At night the bars were left in place, under guard, to make sure that no one moved them.

The next day the whole routine resumed. The work was endless and monotonous. Eventually they passed the midpoint of the run: they were closer to Lieusaint than to Melun. The overriding concern was always the same: keep it straight and keep it flat. For this they used levels and visual sighting aids, small metal points embedded in the roof of the support one after the other. The string used on previous expeditions was no longer state of the art: it was a physical straight line and as such subject to all sorts of distortions. Instead they now checked the straightness of the line visually, a method thought to be beyond reproach.

One day the wind was so strong that there were doubts about the accuracy of the tally. They next day they repeated the measurement and came up with exactly the same result. This unplanned check on their work pleased the members of the team and dispelled their anxiety. Now they could be sure of the quality of their work.

It rained for three days in a row. It was impossible to do anything until the sun returned and dried out the soil, the tents, and the men in them.

At first, when Lieusaint was still far off, their only thought had been to get away from Melun, but now they forgot Melun and thought only of reaching Lieusaint. Whenever they finished with one bar and were about to begin setting the next one in place, either Bellet or Tranchot or Leblanc-Pommard would repeat the established ritual of announcing in a loud voice the number of bars laid down since the morning. Every seven or eight minutes, a voice rang out, punctuating the day. It was like a human clock, marking the work completed and the distance nibbled away. After a while, anyone on the team could have told you the time of day from the number announced. If ten minutes passed without the announcement of a number, everyone would look up, puzzled and worried. When the count resumed, people would return to their work. The problem had been solved.

One day, when Tranchot and the surveyor were working together, they suddenly stopped and looked at each other. Both had thought of the same thing at the same time: the lotto game at the inn in Tuchan and the master of ceremonies who had shouted out the numbers. It all came back to them: the giant corporal with one leg, Méchain, Gustave. Tranchot asked about him. After Italy, Gustave had visited the village just two days before embarking for the Middle East: Egypt. Since then, there had been no news.

❖

It was the thirty-eighth day. Everyone was there: carpenters, woodcutters, laborers, Etienne, Tranchot, Laplace, and young Leblanc-Pommard and his mother, who had come just for the occasion. A hush came over the crowd. Delambre stepped forward and placed a measuring bar on the supports. It was the 3,038th. They had reached Lieusaint! Dozens of caps were tossed into the air, and bottles of wine were brought out to toast the event, but Delambre—haunted by the possibility of error, eager to check the results, obsessed with precision—was already thinking about starting again in the opposite direction.

It was a particularly pleasant day, and the astronomer conversed at length with Mme Leblanc-Pommard.

The structure was disassembled, the wood was sold, and the workers were dismissed. Soon no trace of their presence would remain. The grass would grow back. The forest would reclaim the thin strip of land from which it had briefly been banished. Unless, of course, the strip attracted travelers and was turned into a trail or bridle path.

❖

Delambre made the journey with Leblanc-Pommard. He developed a genuine affection for the young man, who became not just an aide or friend but almost an adopted son. Delambre thought about Méchain. It was strange: both men were in their fifties, one a bachelor, the other separated from his family for years, and at almost the same moment each felt the need to "adopt" a kind of son.

For Méchain it was Agoustenc, a reliable, sincere, straightforward young peasant from Corbières. For Delambre, it was Leblanc-Pommard, a likable, affectionate, energetic young townsman.

Mme Leblanc-Pommard, whom Delambre had met several times, was quite a beautiful woman: exquisite without being overrefined, elegant without being flirtatious, reserved without being affected, not too young, and wonderfully cultivated. There was never any question of taking her as a mistress: neither she nor he would have stood for such a thing. But a wife? To marry, she would have had to be a widow, and, alas, she was not. Was that a reason not to love her, not to wait for her, not to hope? Was it possible for the astronomer, like a young pup, to force the issue, to force himself upon the lady? In the belfries he had learned patience. Thick as the clouds may have seemed, eventually they would always dissipate, and there in the clear skies would be the target he had been waiting for.

18

The low barn seemed almost to disappear into the landscape. Its walls were made of the same stone that one saw everywhere—in fields and fences and along roadways—and it was so well hidden by a clump of skinny trees that, unless you stumbled onto it, it was impossible to see. The furnishing was rudimentary. A board stretched between stout blocks of stone served as a table. No bed or mattress, just a pile of straw. From outside came the sound of footsteps, then of boots knocked against the doorstep. The door opened, and Méchain walked in. The woman, who had been putting away her things in the gloomy half-light, turned around, still holding a shirt in her hand. "Thérèse!" She dropped the shirt and was swept up in his arms. He yearned to hold her close but at the same time wanted to push her away. First he hugged her, then he pushed her from him, and after that he began to pace the room, as if unable to find words to express all that was on his mind. "Why didn't you tell me?" he wondered. "I might not have been here. I might have been off in the mountains for weeks."

"But you are here! Didn't you receive my letter?" she asked ingenuously. "The mail, really! You're letting your beard grow?" She reached out and felt his whiskers with her hand. "It's not bad."

His hair and beard were completely unkempt. By now Méchain resembled the hermit he had encountered while climbing Montserrat.

Coquettishly she adjusted her scarf, which Méchain recognized as the one he had sent her years before from Catalonia. "You still have it? Perpignan. . . . That was so long ago. We'd just begun the expedition. Everything still seemed possible then." Changing the subject abruptly, he asked, "How did you find me? How did you get here?"

"By stagecoach, like everyone else."

"Yes, but here?"

"Everybody around here knows who you are, my dear Pierre. All I had to do was ask. A fellow by the name of Albert. You know who I mean? A very handsome man—"

"A poor devil, you mean. A hopeless alcoholic."

"I thought he was charming, and in any case he brought me here."

Méchain stared hard at her. "You haven't changed," he finally blurted out. How dearly she would have like to say the same to him, but it would most definitely have been a lie. "You've gotten thinner," she said in a deliberately jaunty tone. With the tip of her finger she caressed the scar on his forehead. For a brief instant she thought that he was going to allow her to continue, but suddenly he pulled away.

"Why did you come?" he asked, almost aggressively.

"How can you ask that? Have you forgotten, M. Méchain, that we're married? And since you've never deigned to come to Paris—" Leaving her sentence unfinished, she absentmindedly picked up the shirt and began to arrange the bed of straw. Méchain seemed startled. "What are you doing?"

"As you can see, I'm making the bed."

"You're crazy! You can't stay here. You must leave."

The color drained from her face. She turned around and faced him squarely. Making an effort to smile, she said calmly, "You don't think that I've come all this way just to turn around and go home again? Or to spend the night who knows where, in some inn two leagues away?" Abruptly, she changed her tone. "I've brought you some new clothes." She handed him the shirt: it was white, elegant, and made of silk.

"A silk shirt! What good will this do me? What I need is flannel, or burlap," he said, suddenly feeling in a lighter mood.

"All right, this one will be for Sunday, then."

"It is beautiful. You're quite right."

She patted the bed of straw as one might pat a mattress, releasing a cloud of straw and dust that made them both cough. He opened the door, then closed it again. She slipped down onto the bed. "I will sleep here. I'll go with you on your hikes. I've brought good shoes. I'll drink milk and eat cheese."

"But you've never liked milk and cheese."

"One changes in six years."

"You won't be comfortable."

"With you I'm comfortable everywhere."

He moved toward her and took her in his arms. This time, vanquished and willing, he let her do as she pleased.

The door opened. Imagine Agoustenc's surprise at discovering the dour Méchain in the arms of a woman—a woman whose clothes were flecked with straw! The young man managed to stammer out a few incomprehensible words of excuse before closing the door and walking off, nodding as if to say, "I'd never have believed that he was capable of such a thing!" Méchain ran after him. "Agoustenc, come back! It's my wife, Mme Méchain." Then he turned to Thérèse and said, "This is Agoustenc. He's been helping me with my work."

Agoustenc made himself scarce. Surprised to find Tranchot gone, Thérèse asked where he was. Méchain's only response was a mute stare.

A few days later Thérèse, increasingly puzzled by Tranchot's absence, brought the subject up again. Méchain turned pale. "Please, don't mention that scoundrel's name. He has nothing good to say about me. He's been telling people right and left that I'm all washed up." Unable to restrain himself any longer, Méchain poured out all his troubles. He told Thérèse about his dispute with Tranchot and his assistant's subsequent departure for Paris. "It's bad enough that he left me," Méchain shouted, "but he had to go to Melun to be with Delambre, to help him out, as if Bellet weren't enough. And now, to add insult to injury, here's the latest news." He drew a crumpled letter from his pocket. "Tranchot is to participate in the measurement of the Perpignan baseline. *My* baseline! I'm the one who single-handedly established its location and mapped its route. Now they're taking it away from me. Not officially, of course. Oh, no! And not only that: they've taken my assistant as well! As if it weren't enough to deprive me of my share of the work. As if everything from now on were to be done without me. I've become a troublemaker, the one thing standing in the way of finishing the work of the expedition." He stopped abruptly. The sentence had escaped his lips and now hung there in the silence. He was stunned: the meaning of his words had suddenly come home to him. He could read Thérèse's thoughts in her face: "It's true, you are the one who's standing in the way."

Crushed, he sat down. She moved toward him and caressed his head.

She heard him mutter under his breath. "Hard as it would have been for me, I was prepared to go to Perpignan, to work with Delambre, but that is no longer possible." How could she fault him? If her purpose had been to send him into a rage, she thought to herself, she couldn't have chosen a better way to do it. Méchain interpreted what had happened as a double betrayal: first his assistant had betrayed him, and then his colleague and the Commission had turned on him as well. Thérèse saw it all quite clearly.

"No one can take your achievements away from you," she assured him as gently as she could. "Other people may be able to measure that baseline, but nobody will believe that a man like Tranchot was chosen over a man like Méchain. Only a chambermaid could believe that sort of tittle-tattle."

He looked up, his eyes shining with gratitude. "So, then, you agree with me?" he asked, begging for her approval. "If I have even one ounce of dignity left, I can't possibly go to Perpignan now. If I went, no matter what I did, people would think that I was taking orders from Delambre, or at the very least working under his supervision. No one would think of the baseline measurement as mine. They'll credit Delambre with measuring two baselines, and me with none. And the worst of it is that I have to hold my tongue. I can't say a word about any of this, and I can't complain to Delambre or the Institute."

❦

Soon it was dark, and dinner was over. Thérèse and Méchain went to bed immediately afterward. Lying still with her eyes wide open, Thérèse turned over in her mind everything her husband had said and everything he hadn't. Agoustenc returned from the village singing. His voice carried in the silence of the night, and she strained to hear. The tune was the same as *La Marseillaise,* but the words were different:

C'est ainsi qu'un peuple d'abeilles,
Las de voir d'insolents frelons
Dévorer le fruit de ses veilles
Les expulse de ses rayons.
[And so a nation of bees, tired of watching insolent hornets devour its stored-up fruits, drives them from its cupboards.]

Agoustenc repeated this verse twice before Thérèse stopped listening. Méchain had just placed his hand on her breast. "Are you asleep?"

"No," she answered.

In a calm voice he said, "Tomorrow you will take the stagecoach. You must."

He felt her stiffen. She had thought. . . . She said nothing. He waited. The trembling in his body diminished. Then he asked her a question, but it wasn't really a question: "It was the Commission that sent you, wasn't it? They think I'm washed up, don't they?" She wept, without flinching, without movement of any kind: without a sound tears flowed from her, and nothing else. It was the first time he'd seen her cry, and he was devastated. "They're right. I've broken down. I don't have the strength to go on, or even the will. I'm giving up."

Thérèse sat up. "Pierre, what has happened to you?" She desperately hoped for an answer, but he offered none. She sat up. "You, give up? Impossible! After so many years of work? I've come to help you. I will take care of you. Your arm?" Without thinking, he moved his arm, involuntarily responding to her request. "You will get better, and everything will be as it was. Pierre, look at me. This job is one of many. There are many things left for you to do. And what about your astronomy? You don't think about that anymore?" After a long silence, she heard him murmur, as in a dream: "I have three stations left to do."

The next morning Thérèse left the barn. With the energy of despair Méchain threw himself into his work. He had lost none of his skills. Was he not one of the best observers of the age, if not *the* best? If Tranchot had been there, he would have admired, as he had done six years earlier in the Sierra of Montseny, the astronomer's flawless mastery, his precision, efficiency, and speed. Though heartbroken at Tranchot's absence, Méchain proceeded about his work with Agoustenc, who proved to be highly skilled. Would Méchain allow him to measure some of the angles?

◆

When Thérèse reached Paris, she went immediately to see Borda and was surprised to find Delambre at Commission headquarters. He had come to say goodbye before leaving for Perpignan. Still hanging in the same place on the wall was the map of the meridian. An almost continuous line now linked Dunkirk to Barcelona. Immediately to the south of Rodez a small gap remained: Méchain's three stations.

When Thérèse arrived, Delambre was telling Borda about his adventures at Bort-les-Orgues. "I spent some time there after your departure," Thérèse added. "They were still saying you were sorcerers. Such childishness! But what do you think of this story, which I heard from my husband? One of the men assigned to place targets for him went around telling the peasants that the targets were actually a new type of guillotine. The fool thought he was making a good joke!"

"At least we never had to deal with that!" Delambre exclaimed.

Taking a different tone, Thérèse now broached the subject she had come to discuss. "My trip was a total failure," she declared straightaway. "I had wanted to spur him on by telling him that I wouldn't leave until he had completed his triangles and joined up with you." She lowered her eyes. "He ordered me to leave." Anticipating the question they were burning to ask, she said, "No, he will not go to Perpignan." In saying this she could barely contain her anger. "Why did you send Citizen Tranchot to work on the baseline there? You knew of his quarrel with Pierre. You made a mistake."

Recognizing their error, they tried to make amends. "What if we wrote to him?"

She cut them off. "He was adamant. He said he would never play the role of assistant. He would rather die."

"Whose assistant?" Delambre exploded.

"Yours!"

There was a silence. Quietly, Thérèse resumed. "I wasn't strong enough to get him started again. And forgive me, but I haven't the heart to continue this painful discussion either."

"You'll see, everything will be all right," Delambre tried to reassure her. "When it's all over and the standard meter is presented to the Legislative Body, all will be forgotten. It will be the proudest moment of our lives. Tell me, how is he doing?"

"Physically, he's not bad. Better than I expected. But something is getting him down, I'm not sure what. His abilities are by no means diminished, of that I can assure you. They're as keen as ever. Believe me, he's feeling more unhappy than guilty. His heart is deeply wounded, but that is his only infirmity. I imagined him basking in glory: I'm afraid that what ought to be the proudest moment of his life—as you so eloquently put it, Citizen—may instead be the end of it."

◈

Two weeks later, the final phase of the project began: the measurement of the second baseline in Perpignan. It ran along the coast from Le Vernet to Salses. Here there was no problem of leveling the ground: the terrain was as flat and deserted as could be. But these advantages came with problems of their own. There was too much of everything: sun by day, humidity by night, sand all the time. And not a single tree for protection! The men were by now battle hardened, though. Except for Laplace, the whole Melun team had made the journey: Bellet, Etienne the surveyor, and young Leblanc-Pommard. Tranchot also took part, as planned. When Etienne learned that Méchain would not be participating, he felt a twinge of sadness. Méchain himself had invited him to come to Perpignan, and now it was Méchain who hadn't made it.

The alignment alone took seven days and the measuring forty-one, not counting three days of a dreadful sandstorm that proved hard on men and instruments alike. When at last the wind died down and the seas calmed, the surveyor, by now one of the leading specialists in "baseline measurement," hunted down the tiniest grains of sand in the most hidden recesses of the instruments, whose delicate mechanisms would have been jammed by even a small amount of grit.

Each night, while some members of the team crated the instruments for safe storage, others marked the spot where the measurement had been interrupted on the ground itself.

Fishermen out at sea spotted the interminable structure and approached the coast for a better look. Thus, throughout the operation, team members were able to dine on succulent fish three times a week.

The region was swampy, and there were always insects buzzing around. One morning, Bellet woke up all swollen, red, and pockmarked, as if he had caught some horrible disease, but it was only the result of a night's work by a family of mosquitoes. When Delambre placed the 3,038th bar to complete the measurement, Bellet was the most demonstrative in expressing his joy. Astonishingly enough, the number of bars was exactly the same as in Melun! Was this a coincidence? A mark of incredible precision? Separated by 160 leagues, nearly half the "length" of France, the two baselines differed by less than eleven inches!

To mark the ends of the baseline, two small granite pyramids were erected. These would serve as a record of the expedition. On leaving the site, Delambre mused that in science a "base" is usually the starting point of a structure, but here the "base" marked the end.

In Carcassonne, Delambre found a good inn, where he waited for forty days. One morning, Méchain arrived, unshaven. His hair was long, his pants were spattered and full of holes, and the beautiful silk shirt that Thérèse had given him had been reduced to tatters.

The two men stared at each other in disbelief. Méchain had grown terribly thin and had aged badly. Suffering had left deep marks on his face. He was a very different man from the one Delambre had last seen in the courtyard of the Tuileries one fine June morning in 1792. Delambre took a step forward and held out his hand; Méchain timidly reached out as well. They quickly embraced.

Méchain then blurted out a single sentence, as if he had to get something off his chest before doing anything else: "I've decided not to return to Paris." And then he fell silent.

"Do you know that I've been waiting for you here for forty days?" Delambre replied. "And it will all have been for naught."

"I've already cost you far too much time."

"We left together, we shall return together. And in any case people are expecting us."

"Expecting you. Why would I subject myself to this final humiliation? In Paris I can expect nothing but criticism, disdain, and contempt. Put yourself in my place for a moment, as horrible as that may be. Tell me honestly if you would have the temerity to return to the Institute, rejoin the Commission, and meet with foreign scientists. No, you wouldn't! I need a few months alone. I shall return in the spring. I will write to you frequently, ask your advice, and do as you tell me. My shame is already a matter of public record in Perpignan, as it is in Paris."

"But what are you talking about? What shame? What disdain? What contempt? Great gods, who would insult you that way?"

Méchain wanted to speak, but it was as if a powerful force had sealed his lips. In a workshop nearby, a barrel maker hammered a crosspiece into place with powerful blows of his mallet. Forced to raise his voice in order to make himself heard above the din, Méchain began shouting that he wanted to return to Spain. "I must, Delambre. I must. I need to go. It might give me back my confidence." Then he tried persuasion. "I know now what has to be done to eliminate every possible source of error. Don't worry: I won't ask for any new funds. I shall make do with what I have and use the opportunity to continue my measurements all the way to Majorca." But then, suddenly, he turned sad, and added, as if talking to himself, "What's the good of dreaming? The Commission will never approve this trip."

"Your proposal is a good one, and I'm sure that you'll be able to make a good case for it before the Commission, but first let's finish what we began together."

"Together? You've done virtually all the work alone. You've measured two-thirds of the triangles, and as for the baselines, I've had nothing to do with them. Don't you see, Delambre, that a man in my position had best learn to stay out of sight?"

Both men stared at the raindrops running down the window. Silent and distant, they had become strangers. After a while Méchain turned and faced his colleague. "I beg you not to take any of this personally." As he spoke, he grabbed Delambre's arm but then, afraid that he had crossed some boundary, abruptly withdrew his hand. "If you could read my heart, if you knew me better, you would find that my only feelings are of the most profound gratitude toward you and bitter regret that I was not of greater assistance."

These words were not spoken out of mere politeness. Méchain's sincerity was heart wrenching. Delambre, touched and embarrassed by such an open display of emotion, tried to smile. The rain kept falling. "My friend," Méchain confided, "if you only knew how much time I spent in anxious worry." As he said this, he stared vacantly at his mountains. "I allowed disgust to overwhelm me. What little ability I had was destroyed. I wavered constantly between hope of getting things back under control and fear of succumbing entirely. I could no longer concentrate on any of the things I was supposed to be doing. Since the present had become unbearable, I subjected everything I had done to endless criticism and trembled in fear for what might become of me."

Delambre now removed two letters from his pocket and handed them to Méchain, who, seeing that one was from Borda and the other from the Commission, hastened to read them. He learned that the authorities in Paris were keen for him to resume his work in astronomy and wished to offer him a new post—no, it was impossible, he had to read the words a second time!—as director of the Observatory. "So they still have confidence in me!" That was his first thought, but slowly incredulity contaminated his joy. He studied his colleague's face for a sign of confirmation. Delambre nodded slightly. So it was true! It was the first good news, the first bit of pleasure, he had had in years.

The coachman adjusted his cape. A sign announced that the mail coach to Paris was full, but a rear seat next to the window was empty. Delambre grew increasingly anxious as departure time drew near. Just as he was about to ask that the departure be delayed, Méchain came running into the station courtyard.

He had spent most of the day saying farewell to Agoustenc and Fabre. Then he had climbed up the Saint-Vincent tower to look for the old man who wound the clock. The target was still mounted on its platform. As a parting gesture, Méchain made his friend a gift of all the wood in the structure. In that frigid winter it was worth a fortune!

The coach started on its way and soon the city's high walls receded into the distance. The two astronomers had five full days to discuss the past six years. And so it came to pass that in that winter of 1798, a dozen French citizens, passengers in the postal coach from Carcassonne to Paris, enjoyed the distinct privilege of learning almost everything there was to know about the measurement of the meridian from the men primarily responsible for this feat.

As their carriage wended its way through the heart of the Massif Central, Delambre was discussing the shape of the earth using the results of various measurements they had made. Méchain, adopting an affectedly learned tone, interrupted him: "Don't you see, my dear colleague, that the earth is apparently refusing to adapt its shape to the analytic forms devised by our geometers, who insisted that it had to be a spheroid of revolution of homogeneous density. Unfortunately, your observations, and mine, have shown that the curvature of the globe is almost circular as far as Paris, then elliptical to Evaux, still more elliptical to Carcassonne and all the way to Barcelona. One question plagues me: why didn't

the fellow who had the fun of kneading our globe between his fingers re-
alize that he was working with soft earth from Dunkirk to Paris, then a
little stone as far south as Evaux, and then enormous masses of rock all
the way down to Barcelona?" Delambre listened with rapt attention.

"Now this is what comes of not understanding what you're up to,"
Méchain continued, encouraged by his colleague's reaction. "Given the
laws of motion, gravity, and conservation of mass—laws that the Cre-
ator may have made before all the rest—it follows that if the Earth was
indeed poorly constructed as I've described, it was inevitably forced to
assume an irregular shape. And now there is nothing to be done about it,
other than start over."

Méchain stood up to illustrate with his hands the fate of this
wretchedly confected Earth. It was as if God Himself, standing between
the coach's two seats and in danger of losing His balance with each
bump in the road, had decided to amuse His fellow passengers by complaining about what a poor job He had done. Delambre wept with
laughter. At the sight of these two scientists abandoning the serious
business that had occupied them since the beginning of the journey and
whooping like a couple of schoolboys, the other travelers could not keep
from laughing as well. For several minutes the coach was filled with
chortling, knee-slapping, coughing, and good cheer. Envious, the
coachman pounded on the window in a rage, and the laughing became
louder still.

First came the reunion with Thérèse, then the "discovery" of his daughter and his son Augustin. His elder son Isaac was still in Egypt with
Bonaparte. Then he donned a loose-fitting nightgown and had to get
used to sleeping on a soft mattress and soft sheets. Plus all the hot water
anyone could want, a well-honed razor, and perfumed soap.

From the moment he arrived Méchain was overwhelmed with honors. As promised, he was named director of the Observatory, where he
had previously served as "captain-concierge." What a fine gift! Day and
night he had at his disposal one of the day's technical marvels, Bird's
great quarter-circle, which Paris had added to its treasures during his absence.

A dinner had been planned for the Luxembourg to honor various foreign scientists, who were beginning to grow impatient. The fact that the reception had been postponed until the two astronomers returned shows how eagerly their arrival was awaited. Everyone particularly wanted to see Méchain, who remained a figure of mystery. For here was an émigré who had not emigrated, a member of the Institute who had not attended a single meeting of that august assembly, an astronomer who had not published anything for the past seven years other than his observation of a comet in Barcelona.

Méchain was suspicious of this curiosity about his person and even more reluctant to face such a crowd and answer everyone's questions and be obliged to talk about who knows what. Was he still a member of their community? During the past seven years had he shared anything of importance with any of them?

Like a soldier home from the front and unable to recount what he had seen, Méchain said nothing. Part of him was still in the mountains of the south with Agoustenc, with the old guardian of the tower in Carcassonne, with Mother and Fabre, to whom he suddenly felt an urgent need to write:

> Dear Friend, How much I miss you! Here I am, back in Paris. Will I be able to bear the honors that people wish to bestow on me and, as I hope and pray, carry out the duties that have been assigned to me? In my heart I know, my friend, that the first few days are the finest, like holidays. The empty days follow. I want to invite you here for a visit. You have all winter to prepare. I beg you to come look at Mercury with me under the May sun. Your devoted friend, Méchain.

The noise and pointless conversation that awaited him at the banquet would be impossible to bear, he confided to Thérèse, as she led him to a large wardrobe in which his clothes had been stored since his departure for protection against moths. This annoyed her. He disappeared into a shirt that had become too big for him, catching his head in one of the sleeves. Thérèse, half inside the wardrobe, was searching for a pair of shoes. The astronomer adjusted his breeches, and, as his wife handed him his jacket, she said, "A banquet for the cream of Paris society and Monsieur wants me to miss it on the pretext that he's become a savage—" He turned toward her. Her sentence remained unfinished. Thérèse burst out laughing: everything—the cut of the outfit, the style, the color, the shape of the shoes—was so out of date that Méchain looked as though he had just stepped out of a prerevolutionary engraving. A maid entered: "A gentleman is asking for Monsieur."

"Show him in!" Méchain replied jauntily.

Pretending not to notice Méchain's getup, a man wearing a coachman's frock stood in the doorway and in a strong southern accent stated flatly that he had come for his money. "A nice round sum, two livres per day for forty days, that comes to—" It was the coachman from Marseilles, whom Tranchot had forgotten to dismiss when they had left for Italy. A compromise was struck over the amount of the debt.

◆

Thérèse entrusted her husband to a tailor on the boulevard Saint-Germain. When Méchain arrived, the shop was crowded. A deputy had come specially for a final fitting of the new uniform to be worn by members of the Legislative Body. With pins in his armholes, the deputy showed off his new outfit to a host of couturiers. A trio of journalists had come to cover the event. The first made hasty color sketches, while the second dictated a description of the scene to the third. "As a special favor, we have been allowed to witness the finishing touches. Over a dark blue redingote we see a belt in three colors trimmed with gold fringe and piping eight or nine inches in height. Over that we have a full-length scarlet mantle with dark blue trim. It is fastened with a gold button over the right shoulder in such a way that the right arm is completely free. The head is covered with a hat of purple velvet embellished with a band of flaming red taffeta holding a tricolor plume curved to the rear."

Backing up a bit, the journalist blinked as if in bright sunlight: "It has to be said that the huge amount of red tires the eyes."

"To dazzle is not to blind," said the deputy, proud of his repartee.

"Why did you want a distinct costume, unlike the clothes worn by ordinary citizens?" the journalist asked.

"Beauty consists in regularity," replied the deputy. "Since the essence of the legislator is to inspire respect, we have chosen a costume that will cloak us in the dignity and nobility essential to that purpose."

Méchain, standing in the adjacent fitting room, heard everything and saw nothing.

◆

When Méchain appeared in the entry to the grand salon, the past forced its way into the Luxembourg Palace. Conversations faltered. It was not even ten years since anyone had last seen him, but that was before the Republic had been proclaimed, before the Tuileries had been burned. Louis still had his head, Robespierre was only a deputy, and the words "public safety" had yet to be uttered. The Prussians and Austrians were the great powers that threatened to exterminate Paris, whose People were busy printing the Law. The army was composed of civilians. How long ago all that seemed. The Revolution seemed as distant as the Monarchy. To the assembled guests, both seemed to belong to a vanished world. At the end of the year, those old clothes would be cast off and a new century would begin, a century that was at last MODERN. Yes, Méchain was a ghost, or perhaps a meteorite made up of minerals that no longer existed on earth.

He sensed all of this and imagined that in the next moment he would be struck dumb. He wanted to flee.

Advancing in her stately way along the thick carpet, Thérèse gave her arm to her husband. Because she understood what was going on in his mind and had an almost physical awareness of the conflicts he was experiencing, she clamped his arm firmly under hers, so firmly that it hurt both of them. The pressure forced Méchain's elbow sharply against her waist. No one saw her grimace. There was no question of turning back.

It was Borda who saved them. As the last sounds in the room died down, the old sailor hastened over to his friend. With him he brought a small group of people whom the astronomer did not know. They surrounded him, and conversation resumed.

Borda was said to be ill, but on this night he was spirited and elegant as always. If one looked closely, however, it was possible to see that the old sailor was making an effort to conceal the disease that was killing him. Delambre caught sight of Thérèse. Borda saw them exchange glances. Their former complicity was rekindled, and all three formed an ephemeral triangle around Méchain, who was beginning to relax.

He was enveloped in an aura of mystery and secrecy. He attracted people, and he worried them. What had he been doing all those years in those faraway mountains? People wanted to know every detail. He was even more secretive than usual. Since he was mute about his past, they questioned him about his future projects, but he refused to say anything about these either. An elderly member of the Institute, a man used to giving after-dinner speeches, whispered in his ear that he hoped to see him take his place "in the short list of observers whose fate it is to tell the world what condition it is in." Méchain gave his word.

◈

Talleyrand had scored a resounding success. No fewer than seven nations had sent their best scientists to Paris: Spaniards, Tuscans, Ligurians, Helvetians, Batavians, Sardinians, and Danes. Not one Englishman was in evidence, however, nor was there a single representative of the United States. The States were of course allies of France, while the British prided themselves on being her most persistent enemy. Still, the Greenwich Observatory was located on British soil, and that alone should have settled the matter, in Méchain's opinion. Delambre hoped that the absence of the British and the Americans would not have unfortunate consequences and that those two nations would ultimately choose not to forgo the benefits of the metric system.

The new units of measurement were to be universal, so it was only natural for an international commission to take charge of them. After checking the methods used and verifying the computations, the International Commission was to announce the results to the world, thereby consecrating the fundamental unit of the new system of measurement.

After the reception at the Luxembourg came the meetings at the Louvre. On the day after the gala banquet, the Commission held its first working session. At this meeting, the function of each instrument was demonstrated. In fact, some of the experiments to which the standard bars had been subjected were repeated in the hall, and there were demonstrations of how the baselines and angles had been measured. Then the commissioners broke up into small groups to study each observation in minute detail and recheck every calculation. They began by checking the latitude of Dunkirk and then started working their way through Delambre's records. When the time came to examine Méchain's records, however, the difficulties began. He seemed to be deliberately delaying disclosure of his results, because he stayed away from first one meeting, then another, and finally a third. Talleyrand grew impatient, and the president of the Legislative Body sent an emissary to hasten things along. Finally, the Commission decided to convene in Méchain's apartment at the Observatory. There everything was found to be in perfect order. His work drew praise above all for the precision of his measurements and computations; all his figures tallied perfectly. His slowness and delays were forgotten.

The checking continued. Delambre summed up the work in his log: "All the calculations were done separately by four different individuals: Messrs Tralles, Van Swinden, Legendre, and myself. Each one brought in his results, and we compared notes. During this work, Méchain and I determined the altitude of the pole, each of us using eighteen hundred observations. All the latitudes agreed to within a sixtieth of a second of arc!"

The work was minute, monotonous, and tiring, and Delambre's eyes were sorely tried. Mme Leblanc-Pommard was able to demonstrate her devotion by urging him to go easy on himself. Touched by her concern, the astronomer would answer, "Later, later," and gently squeeze her hand.

"Never before has such a project been subject to such close scrutiny," proudly proclaimed Van Swinden, the Batavian president of the International Commission, to the dozens of scientists assembled in the hall of the Institute. "The Commission considers it a duty and a pleasure to inform the Institute that Citizens Méchain and Delambre, anticipating the commissioners' desires in every respect, have been kind enough to submit every detail of their original registers to our scrutiny. They have done so with the noble candor characteristic of precise observers, who, far from fearing strict oversight, desire it because they know that it is the best way to bring to light the truth in all its splendor." All eyes now turned toward the two astronomers. Delambre looked humble, while Méchain turned pale.

"It took nothing less than men of this caliber to complete the greatest geodesic operation of all time," Van Swinden continued. By this point Méchain was listening only sporadically. "They were happy if, after a long day of toil, worry, and fatigue, a good observation was the result." Delambre was lost in a daydream and no longer paying attention. . . . "Patience without limit. And besides patience, they needed dexterity, and besides dexterity, sagacity." Delambre and Méchain looked at each other, smiled, and turned their attention back to the speaker. "When France was attacked from without and agitated within, they were prudent enough to anticipate and circumvent the dangers and stalwart enough to endure calmly those that could not be avoided." All eyes now turned toward the two astronomers. Again Delambre looked humble,

Méchain pale. But humility could no longer conceal Delambre's joy, and a new tranquillity was evident beneath his colleague's pallor.

◈

Things now began to move quickly. The next day, the two astronomers went to the hall where the ceremony had been held. They had expected to find it empty, and it was, except for a deputy standing at the rail and a few others scattered among the deserted benches. The Assembly was in session.

With his left arm in a sling and his right raised in a vengeful gesture, the deputy who had the floor seemed furious. Méchain understood his subject to be the cabriolets that could be seen everywhere rushing about the streets of Paris. "Think of it! They've knocked down the wretched stalls and humble abodes of poor family men yet done nothing to curb even the potential for harm in the gleaming chariots favored by our young upstarts! I ask you, is it acceptable that, in a state in which equality is supposed to reign, carriages are permitted other than those essential to serve the public?" The audience had no reaction. The deputy continued: "I propose that the Assembly decree that no carriage be allowed to travel through the streets of Paris faster than a man can walk." Méchain saw the wisdom in this proposal when, upon leaving the building with Delambre, he was nearly run over by a cabriolet.

They were still wiping their spattered clothing when a man emerged from the hall to join them. "Descombérousse, deputy from Isère to the Council of Ancients," he introduced himself, and added that he was a fervent admirer of the metric system. Nevertheless, he told the two astronomers that the new system faced fierce opposition in his own *département,* among other places. "People cling to the old measures as they cling to the old rituals of religious fanaticism. A new religion is in its birth throes, the religion of mercantilism. Most retail merchants belong to a sort of sect, which has given its blessing to the existing units of measure. Some of them defend their yards and bushels as tenaciously as others stand by their crucifixes and holy water." This entire speech was delivered without pausing for breath. "Rest assured, Citizens, that I shall stand beside you in this battle," the man added as he saluted the two astronomers.

◈

Van Swinden and Aeneae, the two Batavians, led the procession, followed by Balbo the Sardinian, Bugge the Dane, Ciscar and Pédrayes, both Spaniards, Fabbroni the Tuscan, Franchini the Roman, Mascheroni the Cisalpine, Multédo the Ligurian, and finally Tralles, the Helvetian. Then came the French: Laplace, Legendre, Lagrange, and Lefevre-Gineau, and all the other commissioners from the Institute. Monge and Berthollet, still virtually joined at the hip to Bonaparte, were in Egypt. Bellet and Tranchot brought up the rear. Borda was not among the dignitaries, however: death had claimed him just before the consecration of an expedition that, but for his efforts, would never have come to pass. Of the three men who had watched the two berlins leave the court of the Tuileries on June 25, 1792, none had lived to see the end of the mission: not Condorcet, not Lavoisier, not Borda.

The Assembly hall was sumptuously decorated; all the members of the Legislative Body were present; the galleries were full, as they always were on important occasions. The decree of Prairial prohibiting unaccompanied women from entering the hall was relaxed for the day. Thérèse and her daughter were accompanied by Augustin, who was almost old enough to vote. The widows of Lavoisier and Condorcet came with their new husbands. The young lady with curly hair was Eliza. Mme Vernet came on the arm of M. Sarret. Mme Leblanc-Pommard came with her son. Etienne the surveyor was also there. In talking to his neighbor, he could be seen making large gestures to explain how the repeating circle was operated.

When the procession reached the rail, the commissioners lined up in two rows. An usher announced in a loud voice, "Citizens Delambre and Méchain of the Institute!" They were moved by what they saw on entering the hall, still somewhat awkward, and of course dazzled, as one might well be at the sight of so much red in the brand-new uniforms of the seven hundred deputies. Méchain wore the outfit that the Saint-Germain tailor had made for him.

Somewhat off to the side, Talleyrand looked pleased as he surveyed the scene. When the band struck up, a huge bass caused the walls of the chamber to vibrate. The deputies rose. The piercing sound of the brass accentuated the sacred character of the moment. People in the audience had been so intent on the musicians that they had failed to notice the entrance of two men, but soon all eyes turned to watch them. With arms stretched out in front, one carried a cushion of purple velvet, the other a cushion covered with mauve lace. Gleaming on the first cushion was the latter-day grail, a bar of platinum. On the other rested a cylinder of the same metal, dense and shiny.

The two officiants advanced at a solemn pace along a deep carpet, which led them to a podium draped with tricolor bunting. Then both men came to a halt and together turned to face the audience. Total silence engulfed the room. Slowly, very slowly, the first man raised the cushion and, moving it along the arc of the amphitheater, showed it to the people in the hall. "Citizens representing the people, this is the true meter, the standard meter!" proclaimed the president of the Legislative Body. An ovation came from the crowd. People craned their necks, jostled one another, and stood on their tiptoes for a better view. Delambre recognized Deputy Descombérousse in the front row, applauding as hard as he could. Then silence returned, and as if in a perfectly choreographed ballet, the second man raised the lace-covered cushion and presented the cylinder to the crowd: "Citizens representing the people, this is nature's own kilogram, the standard kilogram!"

High up in the galleries, two old men, the philologists Alfred and Alexandre, who had spared no effort to be present for this occasion, continued their interminable dispute.

"Guttural or not, *chi*logram, with a 'chi,' is a linguistic abomination!" argued Alfred.

"Stop your kenannigans, my dear Alfred, what you say is kocking." Alfred's cry of outrage was immediately swallowed up by an avalanche of "shh's." At the bar of the chamber a man was making an announcement: "Citizens, I am authorized to announce that the meter is 3 feet, 11 lines, 296/1000 of the *toise* of Peru."

Upon hearing the exact value of the meter officially proclaimed, Delambre could not stop himself from saying, "Five years to gain only 145/1000 of a line over the provisional meter! A speck of dust!"

In the galleries a young boy parted his blind grandfather's hands to give him an idea of the size of the bar. Standing next to Etienne, a large, grumpy fellow railed against the new units: "They're all for the meter! And how much does a kilo weigh? They're not telling us!" The surveyor leaned over and whispered in his ear, as if confiding a secret: "It weighs 2 livres, 5 gros, 35 grains." The other man stared at him in amazement. Etienne leaned toward him again: "Or, if you prefer, 18,827 old grains in the *poids de marc*." The ceremony continued. A deputy holding a piece of paper advanced toward the bar: "Here it is at last: a unit of measurement based on the largest, most stable object that man can measure—the terrestrial globe itself." Then he folded his paper, broke into a smile, and continued in a confidential tone: "How delightful it will be from now on for a family man to be able to say that the field that provides food for my children is such-and-such a fraction of the globe. I am to that extent a co-owner of the world!"

The last sentence resounded through the silent hall. The ceremony was now indeed over. The new units of measurement, conceived by the men of 1789 in the name of Universality, Unity, and Eternity, had now been placed in the service of Property. Ten years already gone by! From "Master and Possessor of Nature" in the eighteenth century to "Co-Owner of the World" in the nineteenth: what a difference!

❦

The ravages of time? It was to resist those ravages that the standards had been fashioned from platinum. Kept in a locked, velvet-lined case, the two standards were to bear witness for centuries to come and serve as an ultimate reference for all measurement.

The true meter and the natural kilogram were entrusted to the Archives of the Republic for safekeeping. Méchain and Delambre were granted the honor of closing the doors of the double-walled iron safe in which the two standards were to be stored.

As they turned the four keys in the complex locks, each man had a different thought. "What is stored here," thought Méchain, "is a piece of the meridian." Whereas Delambre reflected that "if these two standards were to disappear and only the name remained, they would still be able to reconstruct them to the same degree of precision." Unwittingly he uttered these words out loud, and Laplace, who happened to be standing behind him, said, "Even if the elements were to contaminate the standards or an earthquake were to swallow them up or a terrible bolt of lightning were to melt the platinum, still there would be no—"

A little off to one side, Méchain read the official record of the occasion over the shoulder of the secretary, who wrote in a sprightly hand: "Year VII of the French Republic, One and Indivisible, Four Messidor, at three o'clock in the afternoon. . . ."

❦

To commemorate the event a medal was struck. On one side were engraved the words of Condorcet: "For all times, for all peoples." On the other was an image of the globe with a compass stretching from the equator to the north pole, topped by the stars of Ursa Minor. "The north, always the north!" thought Méchain upon seeing the first samples. One morning in Brumaire, even before the medal was cast, General Bonaparte, accompanied by a small number of soldiers, Gustave the gunner among them, turned up at the Assembly. The fine uniforms of the deputies did not inspire respect in the general, however. The deputies were driven from the hall, and two or three hundred men in red fled through the gardens, chased by handfuls of men in blue under the command of a general who was also a member of the Institute. The medal would never be cast: the Republic was done for.

Fabre never came to Paris to see Mercury under the May sun. On August 7, however, after a long, watchful night in "his" observatory, Méchain discovered history's eightieth comet. It was small and had no tail but was still clearly visible. Then, at 5:30 in the morning, on the day after Christmas, he saw another in Ophiceus.

A final comet: five days later, the year 1800 arrived. At the close of an interminable century of unprecedented events, France, having shed her royal finery, founded a Republic, and proclaimed certain inalienable rights of individuals everywhere, discovered that in her womb she carried a consul who would soon become an emperor.

Strange to say, a century in which the light of reason had shone more brightly than usual now found itself framed by an omnipotent king and a general who dreamed only of becoming omnipotent in his turn. The king had died on his throne in 1715. A hundred years later, what would become of the power of the general?

19

When Méchain left Paris on April 26, 1803, in the company of Augustin, his second son, he was pleased to have overcome the forces that had opposed his departure for so long and certain that it would take no more than a year to extend the meridian. Indeed, as he was only too glad to tell anyone who would listen, no one in Paris would have time to notice that he was gone. When he arrived in Spain, however, nothing was ready.

A ship had been designated to take him to the islands. When he reached the port of Cartagena, he discovered that it was the same vessel that Don Ricardos had made available to him ten years earlier. The captain was new, however, and unusually cautious: he refused to allow Méchain on board until he received an explicit order from the court. Everything had to be put on hold until the order arrived.

Once at sea, an epidemic of yellow fever broke out. Members of the crew were afflicted one after another; some twenty of them succumbed. Miraculously, neither Méchain nor Augustin fell ill. Upon reaching Minorca, the unfortunate vessel was required to remain at anchor under strict quarantine. Finally, when the quarantine was lifted, the astronomer and his team were authorized to leave the ship and transfer to a brigantine. A storm suddenly arose, and the new ship was driven onto reefs. At first the shipwrecked travelers thought that the coast on which they had landed was deserted, but it turned out not to be. Natives massed along the beach, and armed men advanced and ordered everyone to remain on board. Somehow the natives of the island had learned about the epidemic and feared that it might spread to them. They even refused to supply the ship with food and water for fear of coming into contact with the passengers and crew.

Méchain proposed that a message be sent to the governor, but this request was also denied on the grounds that the letter might be contaminated. The natives did agree, however, to send a runner to the governor with an oral message. The next day the messenger returned and shouted out the governor's answer: Méchain was authorized to write a letter. After a second trip, the messenger returned with authorization for Méchain to disembark, but alone and without instruments.

In order to reach the palace, he crossed the island on mule back, following a primitive trail along which steep, slippery slopes gave way to sheer rock cliffs. When the governor expressed curiosity about his mission and pretended to be distressed about the accident, Méchain's only reply was, "Fate has not smiled on this expedition."

The journey back to the ship was even more difficult than the journey out. The mule slipped, and Méchain nearly broke his neck but escaped with nothing more serious than a broken wrist and some bruises to the face. This time only fate was to blame: neither Salva nor a hydraulic pump had anything to do with it. Although the accident was not as serious as the previous one, Méchain was greatly shaken by it. Once again his right arm had been injured, and he had the dreadful feeling that he was reliving a nightmare.

Upon reaching the coast after enduring two days of torture on a swaying mule, he found nothing: the brigantine was nowhere in sight! The natives told the astronomer that a new storm had arisen after his departure, forcing the ship to make for open water so as not to be driven onto the reefs once again. It had sailed off in the direction of Majorca, where Méchain eventually rejoined his companions.

By now it was the height of summer, and the heat was suffocating. Méchain was nearly sixty years old and found the hikes across arid landscapes exhausting. Fortunately, Augustin was able to relieve his father of the most arduous tasks, but still the work was too much for him.

At last they came to a broad expanse of land flat enough and extensive enough to lay out a baseline. A river cut the plateau in two, and Méchain attempted to ford it at a place suggested by his guide. Advancing slowly into the water, he suddenly lost his footing and was carried away. The guide had made a mistake: the ford was actually some distance away. A young Majorcan who was assisting the team dived in and rescued the half-drowned astronomer. As soon as he was dry, Méchain started off once more.

He should have taken this incredible series of incidents as a warning, but the more harshly fate treated him, the more stubborn Méchain became; the more events conspired to force his surrender, the more he persevered. Augustin assisted his father every step of the way. Just as Thérèse had earlier been unable to prod Méchain on toward Rodez, so too was Augustin now incapable of stopping him from pressing on with this new expedition.

The astronomer had been warned that in late summer a nasty fever often infected the coast where he was working. The disease struck three members of his crew. A servant died within a few days, and two Spanish officers who shared a tent with the man were also afflicted, though less gravely. The others begged Méchain to postpone the remaining measurements until cold weather returned, but he refused. Determined to do everything himself—measuring both angles and baseline—he often remained awake all night, looking for the flickering light from the reflectors marking his stations. This time, nothing—not fever, not weather, not assistants—would stop him from completing his mission.

He was exhausted. One morning, he woke up shivering and burning with fever. He held on for a day, two days, three days. He was all alone. If only Augustin had been with him. But his son had gone off on a scouting mission. The next day, he was unable to get up.

Before being halted by fever, he had succeeded in extending the measurement of the meridian by ninety thousand *toises* and had added five new triangles, some of which mocked distance by proudly leaping nearly half the width of the Mediterranean.

Like an old wall suddenly deprived of support, Méchain collapsed. By the time he was brought, burning with fever, to the inn at Castellon de la Plana, he was only semiconscious. A bed was prepared. Neither quinine extract nor any other medicine yielded the slightest remission. In his mind he was still out in the field. Repeatedly he asked for his papers, urgently shouting his requests, sitting up in bed, only to exhaust himself with the effort and collapse again into a coma. No one could locate his papers. An urgent message was dispatched to Augustin.

Spain being a Catholic country, the innkeeper sent for a priest, who came and offered to hear Méchain's confession, but the astronomer refused, claiming that he was not that sick. "Do I have time to loll about in bed? In a few days I'll be back on my feet."

He regained consciousness after two days of delirium. Augustin sat by his bedside. Once again the astronomer asked for his papers. Augustin finally found them hidden in a knapsack at the bottom of a trunk.

Méchain grabbed the manuscript and clasped it to his breast, as if he wanted to bury the papers within his body. Eventually he fell asleep. The malady marked time.

❖

It was almost midnight when the door opened. Two people arrived, both covered with dust from their journey. The man sat down next to the patient. Méchain opened his eyes, and a childlike smile lit up his face. He tried to sit up. "Ah, Salva, my friend, you've come! Do you remember how you saved me so many years ago? I'm afraid that this time it may not be so easy. I'm not going to make it to the end of the journey." He paused to catch his breath before uttering this lament: "I'll never be done with this confounded measurement." And then he repeated what he had said to the governor: "Fate has not smiled on this expedition." Then he stopped and stared at the door.

Although the sound of footsteps was barely audible, he knew whose they were, and his eyes glistened. Having listened to the same sound so often during his convalescence, he had immediately recognized that almost silent step: it was Maria's! Despite his fever, she seemed to him radiant and calm, and illuminated like the Black Virgin of Montserrat. She looked peaceful, but also sad.

"Sad, Maria?"

"Yes, because you didn't come see us when you returned to Spain. You forgot about us."

As if to excuse himself, he raised his right arm and moved it slightly to show that it was working normally. "So you see, your lessons were not without effect." Then he fell silent and looked out the window. Despite the frost he could make out the iridescent circle of the full moon through the glass. "A beautiful night. The night of the eclipse was like this. Do you remember? I won't be watching the next one. . . . It will take place on—" He collapsed in exhaustion. Salva could not stop himself from finishing the sentence: "It will take place on January 5." Maria shot him a look of disapproval. Méchain, no longer strong enough even to open his eyes, nevertheless moved his hand in a gesture of gratitude: solidarity among astronomers.

He slept. Then suddenly, a few minutes before dawn, he seemed once again to come to his senses. He sat up. His manuscript! He wanted his manuscript! Remembering that he had put it down alongside him, he felt around the bed for the papers. His hand found what he was looking for, but he could barely lift it. He handed the manuscript to Augustin. "Give this to Delambre and no one else! Tell him—" No, it was too difficult to explain. He no longer had the strength. Then he made a strange gesture with his hand to signify that the matter was no longer under his control. Softly, he slid beneath the covers.

⬭

Together with Thérèse, Augustin turned his father's manuscript over to Delambre. Thérèse and Delambre had not seen each other since the presentation of the meter to the Legislative Body. She wore discreet mourning clothes, but her emotion was profound. The interview was brief, solemn, and restrained.

After seeing his visitors out, Delambre immediately ordered his secretary to cancel all his appointments. The manuscript lay on the table. It included all of his colleague's records, diaries, and notes. Delambre dived in as he might dive into a cold stream, both eager for and fearful of the contact, but before long the current had carried him away. He was with Méchain in the hermitage of San Geronimo at Montserrat. He was with him when he climbed Bugarach, reaching the summit just as the storm blew the target away. He could see the bales of hay piled high in the church of Saint-Vincent. He observed the comet of '93 and the eclipse of the moon and the sunspot Méchain had noted in the month of Pluviôse, Year VI. With his pen he traced the hexagonal base of one of Méchain's targets, and he reveled in the detailed description of the Matagall station and its strange twin peak with the depressing name Homa-Morta. And on a wrinkled sheet of paper he recorded his 104 observations of Polaris: it was the back of an old notice that had been sent out to the directorate of the *département* of the Pyrénées-Orientales. He smiled as he deciphered the content: "Arrest anyone leaving the kingdom. Prevent any exit of belongings, weapons, munitions, currency, gold and silver, horses, carriages. . . ." The document was much the worse for wear, and the ink had faded.

Suddenly everything turned topsy-turvy, as when a ship goes down. It was late, and Delambre was reading one of Méchain's earliest notebooks, from the winter of '93, when his eyes fell upon a passage that had him staring in disbelief. Impossible! What he was reading was impossible to believe, yet it was indeed in Méchain's handwriting. Here was proof, indubitable proof, that an error had been made.

What had happened was this: Méchain had measured the latitude of Barcelona on two separate occasions, a year apart. The results did not agree. Indeed, they were contradictory: Méchain, in his own handwriting, had noted a difference of three seconds! Having already published the first measurement, the one from the fort of Montjouy, he had kept the second, made from the terrace of the Fontana de Oro inn, secret. He had not told anyone about the inexplicable discrepancy. By now this secret was more than ten years old, and Méchain had kept it until his death. No one else had known about the error until now.

At least one of the two measurements was incorrect. But which?

Every calculation, every result, had been based on the Montjouy measurements. The entire edifice hung together; a single weak link, and the whole thing could collapse. Delambre was staggered, as if he had been struck by a blow from within. The ground opened up beneath his feet. The consequences of this one error were dragging him down into the abyss. Try as he might to dismiss the frightening thought that had just flashed through his mind, rid himself of it, draw its sting, deny its validity, he could not. For an instant he managed to silence his doubts, but then he found the evidence staring him in the face yet again, formulated with stark and tragic clarity: if the Montjouy observations were wrong, the standard meter stored in the Archives of the Republic was inaccurate!

Everything, absolutely everything, was inaccurate. To be sure, it was just a trifle, a hair's breadth: three seconds of arc over more than 1,100 kilometers, from Paris to Barcelona. He noticed that he had used the term "kilometer," but of course he had no right to use it if the measurement was wrong, any more than he had a right to use "kilogram" or "are." Like a cathedral demolished by a single, miraculously well placed explosive charge, the entire edifice crumbled.

Seven wasted years!

What was the good of selecting two dozen of Europe's most eminent scientists, inviting them to Paris to participate in months of meetings, to pore over records, to read and reread reports, to verify every computation, only to end up with nothing? What was the good of endless precautions in the field, innumerable checks and balances, systematic comparison of results, rejection of dubious measurements, and insisting on two signatures on every page of the records? It had all been for naught.

"Never before has such a project been subject to such close scrutiny," the International Commission had said. "The Commission considers it a duty and a pleasure to inform the Institute that Citizens Méchain and Delambre, anticipating the commissioners' desires in every respect, have been kind enough to submit every detail of their original registers to our scrutiny. They have done so with the noble candor characteristic of precise observers, who, far from fearing strict oversight, desire it because they know that it is the best way to bring to light the truth in all its splendor." In the face of this avalanche of praise from the Commission, Méchain had maintained his silence. Never had any text been as explicit about precautions and verifications. For the first time an International Commission had taken it upon itself to guarantee the results of scientific research—and had allowed a disastrous error to go unnoticed! To make matters worse, it had bestowed its seal of approval on that error. With this grotesque outcome: an expedition that had prided itself on being the most important geodesic measurement ever undertaken had yielded a false result!

It was all so unthinkable. The error was so enormous, and the consequences were so dreadful, that Delambre tried to persuade himself that it couldn't have happened. A small voice within said that it was impossible. But it was soon drowned out by another, more insistent voice, which said, There has to be a first time for everything. Delambre had never been so angry or bitter. The realization hit him hard. The fact that his reputation was at stake hardly bothered him, nor did the thought of the scandal that was likely to ensue. The metric system's many opponents could be counted on to make sure of that. For Delambre, the scandal was primarily personal. Having participated in the measurements, checked the computations, and bestowed his blessing on the results, he had a duty to accept responsibility for the fact that they were erroneous. "I am an accomplice to a falsification," he concluded. "I must submit my resignation effective tomorrow."

All of this was Méchain's fault. Anyone else would have admitted his mistake, but he had chosen to keep quiet. Why? "Who the devil cares why?" Delambre ranted, "the only thing that matters is that he did." Things began to fall into place. Now it was clear why Méchain had for so many years refused to return to Paris. The Terror had nothing to do with it; it hadn't touched him at all. And it was also clear why he had avoided all the meetings of the Commission, and why he had remained cloistered away in the Black Mountains, rejecting every effort to make contact with him. And his equivocations, refusals, retreats, embarrassment, terror, shame, and panic at the idea of appearing before his colleagues—"his judges," he had written. And the whole business with Tranchot? An alibi for not measuring the baseline. Now of course it was clear why Méchain himself had referred to "my unfortunate measurements in Barcelona."

Remembering that phrase gave Delambre pause, however. Indeed, it was difficult for him to deny that Méchain had several times mentioned the Barcelona measurements and his dissatisfaction with them. Actually, he had brought the subject up so often that it had become irritating. Had Méchain been trying to warn him? No! Delambre refused to believe it. Could such ambiguous comments be construed as warnings? And yet . . . once again Delambre hesitated. Had he truly wanted to hear what his colleague had been telling him, in veiled words, to be sure, but eloquent enough for anyone who cared to listen? How many similar messages of distress had Méchain sent to Delambre, Borda, and Lalande? Had he not insisted and begged that he be sent back to Spain to redo his "unfortunate measurements"?

Delambre dismissed this objection, unwilling to ask himself why all three of them had regularly insisted to Méchain that everything was going well, ignoring his pleas, obstinately refusing to listen to his "warnings," preferring to interpret them as the obsessions of a tired mind traumatized by a terrible accident. The words of a madman! Yet his letters had been so full of distress. How could he, Delambre, have missed it? Why had he noticed nothing?

To have heeded Méchain's tiresome pleas would have meant sending him back to Spain, thereby losing long months when the project was already well behind schedule, and largely because of Méchain's own delays. Thus there was every reason not to pay attention to his camouflaged confessions.

In any case, Méchain was known for the precision, not to say fanaticism, of his calculations. He was also reputed to be one of the best observers of the day and admired for his concern with accuracy. But at a time when the chain of triangles was not yet complete and the measurement process was dragging on, was it wise to take so many precautions? His scrupulousness had been seen as a luxury, an unwarranted caprice, the hobbyhorse of a doddering old scientist.

For Delambre, the crux of the matter was simple: it would have been more honest, more in keeping with scientific ethics, and, in a word, healthier to have admitted the mistake rather than cover it up. Undeniably, an error had been committed. On top of that, he felt betrayed, and that feeling of betrayal gnawed at his heart. He was outraged.

Delambre experienced this tempest of emotions without moving, while seated at his work table. He did not get up, pace about the room, or utter a single word. The crisis was so deep within him that it barely manifested itself on the surface. Suddenly he realized that he had assumed the worst: in his mind he had extrapolated all the possible consequences of Méchain's mistake. But this assumption might not be warranted. Nothing had yet been proven.

Enough of conjectures, probabilities, and possibilities. He absolutely had to know how things stood. Which of the two measurements was correct? He had to know before the sun rose again.

With demonic energy Delambre launched into his calculations. He used all the numbers at his disposal: the latitudes of Dunkirk, Evaux, and Carcassonne, the azimuths, the angles, and all the other results of the expedition.

When dawn finally arrived, an exhausted, bleary-eyed Delambre laid down his pen. The last numerical witnesses had been heard, and the verdict was beyond doubt. All suspicion had been dispelled: the figures for Montjouy were correct! What an insane night!

But Delambre felt no joy whatsoever. The improbable had been ruled out, the impossible rejected. Everything was as it had been before, early the previous evening when he had confidently sat down to read Méchain's manuscript. He had come full circle, but was he really back where he had started? In the meantime he had suffered doubt, anguish, and the pain of denial. He had imagined the unimaginable and believed that it might be real. Like a medieval knight subjected to "the Lord's trial," the platinum bar had been subjected to trial by doubt and verification and emerged from this night of passion as good as new. By dawn the meter-grail was truer still in Delambre's eyes than it had been before sunset.

But he knew full well that Méchain, who had not had all the results in his possession, could not have known the truth. Now that the accuracy of the meter was safe, Delambre, his mind at rest, was free to think of the man Pierre Méchain, whose name would inevitably be linked to his own for centuries to come. "Now at last he has faced the trial he had feared for so long, and I, his colleague, have been his sole judge."

Posthumous dishonor. Just as the point of a dagger balanced on a child's cheek will leave an imperceptible mark, so too would posterity preserve an image of Méchain as a stubborn man saved by death, an astronomer who falsified his results and in the end was spared the ultimate shame only by chance. What a hideous memory! Delambre made up his mind that it should not survive.

❖

A strange emotion took hold of him. Tears welled up from within. His vision clouded. "Please God," he thought, "spare me any relapse into the blindness of my youth." He remembered a line from a posthumous text of Condorcet's: "Alas, all humans are in need of clemency." Méchain, what a waste! It was heartbreaking that such a trivial mistake, which everyone would have excused if avowed in time, should have poisoned his final years and hastened his end.

All at once he saw the past with stark clarity. A whole series of events passed before his eyes, events that only moments before had stirred him to fury but that he now saw with a new eye. He recalled Méchain's panic whenever the subject of returning to Paris came up; his terror at having to present his results to his peers; his loss of confidence in his abilities; his constant demands for reassurance. All of his complaints now became evidence for the defense, and what had been incomprehensible now seemed blatantly obvious.

Then and only then did Delambre understand his colleague's tragic passion. One day in 1793, Méchain, until that moment ethically above reproach, had suffered an incomprehensible moral lapse. It would have taken him no more than a week to correct his mistake. But he said nothing, and as the months passed his lapse hardened into a crime. From that point on, one thing led inevitably to another until in the end Méchain collapsed under the pressure. What he had been unable to confess on the spur of the moment became forever unsayable. As time passed, words took on unbearable weight. Silence called for still more silence, still deeper concealment, until there was no way he could muster the strength necessary to own up to what he had done. His loneliness must have been terrifying. In whom could he confide? Who would have understood? His secret stood between him and the world. Three seconds of arc! Some decisions are irreversible.

His unanswered pleas were like the cries of a mute directed at the ears of the deaf. And the deaf in this case—Borda, Lalande, and Delambre himself—incurred no guilt for not answering, since they, having only the *correct* Montjouy measurements in their possession, *had no way of knowing* what Méchain was crying in the wilderness. This, at any rate, was what Delambre, in his own as well as his colleagues' defense, tried to persuade himself had happened.

Only Thérèse had guessed, if not the error itself, then at least what was going on in the depths of Méchain's soul: "He is more unhappy than guilty," she had confided upon returning from her melancholy journey. Perhaps she would have said that the dreadful mistake at Montjouy was not the only reason for her husband's collapse. For she might well have added that Pierre Méchain was a man had seen his world collapse with the walls of the Bastille—and not only his world but with it a settled worldview and comfortable way of life. He had been devoted to the old society as a farmer is devoted to his land: not by choice but indisputably attached nonetheless. He would have mourned its passing quietly, in discreet silence, but stubbornly, deeply, and instinctively.

Méchain had not been a brilliant man, like Cassini. Nor had he founded a vast discipline, like Lavoisier. Neither was he a universal intelligence like Condorcet, an admirable analyst like Laplace, a great organizer like Borda, a young prodigy like Lalande, a well-rounded individual like Bailly, or a Hellenist, Anglicist, and mathematician like the affable and universally well-liked Delambre. In a very real and very deep sense he was nothing but an astronomer. He was a solitary man who disliked the limelight, a man happy only when exercising the skills embodied in his eyes and fingers: observation and computation—these were his gifts, gifts of patience and detail. He lived for the infinity of the heavens and the columns of tiny figures that brought order to that infinity and cloaked it in the beauty of mathematics. And he was also a discoverer of comets.

With a quick motion of his hand, Delambre pushed the manuscript away. Still in front of him was the page that had triggered all these reflections. Gently he placed his hand on that page, as a person might close the eyelids of someone who has just passed away. Then he got up, went over to the window, and opened the curtain. Just barely visible through the thick January fog was the rising sun.

Delambre then walked over to a desk, from which he removed his travel diary. He opened it to the last page, in which he had placed a mark, set it down on his work table, and, drawing a deep breath as a diver might do in preparation for a final dive, sat down to write. Although his hand was tired, his pen seemed to move of its own accord.

The epidemic fever and extreme fatigue that Méchain endured with a steadfastness that one cannot help but deplore as well as admire put an end to his mission and took him from us on the third complementary day of Year XII in Castellon de la Plana in the kingdom of Valencia.

It is impossible to raise the slightest doubt about the great result of the operation in which Méchain and I had a hand. The proofs of these assertions will be preserved at the Observatory, together with all of his manuscripts. I certify that Méchain's error had no effect on the ultimate result of the measurement: *the meter is correct.*

Méchain, a man concerned above all else with exactness but at the same time careful of his reputation, unfortunately convinced himself that the repeating circle would be able to achieve a degree of precision and agreement among his observations that in reality were impossible to obtain.

When certain observations revealed disparities that, though inevitable, he had never before encountered, he did not alter his view as he should have done but instead began to doubt his own skill. He came to believe that he was no longer capable of making acceptable measurements.

Because he had formed this unjust opinion of himself, he was afraid that he might outlive his reputation. This fear was the reason for his lapses of judgment, with all their doubtless deplorable consequences. Nevertheless, I can attest to the fact that he was and will forever remain nothing less than an astronomer of the highest caliber.

The measurement of the meridian, cut short by Méchain's death, resumed some time later. Méchain's work was completed by a young man named François Arago.

Having satisfied himself that the meter was indeed correct, Delambre was now free to accept two further honors. Mme Leblanc-Pommard and the Institute concurred in their choice: he became the husband of the former and the perpetual secretary of the latter. Meanwhile, France acceded to the idea that the man who had been leading it under the title "First Consul" should continue to lead it under the new title of "Emperor." This put an end to the Republic, and with it to the "republican measures." The meter was relegated to oblivion. Eventually the Emperor too disappeared, as did one king and then, after a small revolution, another. Finally, on January 1, 1840, the meter was once again adopted as an official—and compulsory—standard.

◆

One hundred and forty years later . . .

The scene is a building known as the Pavillon de Breteuil on the edge of the Parc de Sèvres, which overlooks Paris.

Two men and a woman slowly descend a long staircase, which leads down into a vault nine meters below ground. At the bottom of the staircase is a double armored door. Each of the three individuals is holding a key, and when all three keys are simultaneously inserted into their corresponding locks, the door opens. It is five o'clock in the afternoon.

Record of Visit to the Repository of Metric Prototypes

The president of the International Committee of Weights and Measures, the director of the International Bureau of Weights and Measures, and the con-

servator of the Archives of France undertook to visit the repository of international metric prototypes.

The three keys needed to open the repository were assembled: one in the possession of the director of the Bureau, one kept in the National Archives, and one in the safekeeping of the president of the International Committee.

When the two steel doors of the vault were opened, the safe within was found to contain prototypes of the meter and the kilogram. The following indications were noted on the measuring instruments placed inside the safe:

Present temperature: 20.56° C.

Maximum temperature: 23° C.

Minimum temperature: 19° C.

Humidity: 57 percent.

Using mops, brooms, and sponges, two women wearing smocks quickly clean the place up. Air, dust, and humidity: like frescoes buried in the catacombs of Rome, the two prototype standards can be harmed by contact with these elements. At 5:45 the double armored doors are once again closed. The visit to the vault has lasted no more than three-quarters of an hour. The doors will not be reopened for another year, on the last Friday in September.

Appendices

A UNIVERSAL MEASUREMENT

For all times, for all men.
—Condorcet

When the appetite for knowledge is joined to what is admirable and marvelous, pleasure, which is the philter of science, is increased.

—Strabo

The *history* of science is full of *stories* about science, in which truth is not opposed to fiction but feeds it, and rigor is not opposed to narrative but underlies it. At a time when the influence of science on society is so profound, there is astonishingly little about science in films, plays, and novels. Science is seen as an effective tool or a part of a curriculum but rarely as the subject of a narrative.

Since ancient times all societies have had their storytellers, who serve an important social as well as private function. In telling their stories they rely on knowledge as well as imagination.

The realm of knowledge, scientific knowledge in particular, can also be a theater of powerful drama.

True Fiction

The historian of science has a duty to be rigorous in his retelling of the past. He must be careful not to fill in gaps in the evidence, whether that evidence comes from archives or eyewitness accounts. He must assert no more than the evidence permits. Only then is the authenticity of what he says guaranteed by the sources. But others can also make use of the same sources: novelists, for instance.

The historian thus provides the novelist with useful material. But that material carries with it certain obligations. The novelist is free to fill in gaps, to invent episodes, and to draw a continuous line between documented facts: this is where his creativity comes in. He creates in the interstices of the evidence, as it were, and because he does what is expected of him—namely, invents a world—people want to read him. But in inventing his world, the novelist works in full awareness of what the evidence says, and he is careful not to contradict it.

True fiction is fiction because it is the author's imagination that makes it worth reading, and it is true because it respects the scientific and historical truth.

The Unavoidable Truth

The author of a fictional narrative about science has to confront a number of issues. To speak of science is to speak of truth. But what can we say about truth? Can scientific truths be treated in the same way as other historical truths? How can a writer portray the character of a scientist seeking a truth that has yet to be discovered in a world whose possibilities remain open? What freedom does such a character have vis-à-vis the truth? And what are the implications of representing scientific concepts in a fictional context?

And what about the emotions? What part do they play in science? How do they manifest themselves? By what signs are they revealed? In other words, what is the relation between truth and emotion?

Measurement in the Enlightenment

What did the people of 1789 want? Standardized weights and measures. That was all. But that was a lot. If that had been the only criterion, and if the authorities had adopted, say, the *toise* of Peru as their standard, the course of events would have been very different. But in the 1790s French scientists and political leaders did not want simply to establish a "good" system of weights and measures for France. They had other ambitions as well.

Some wanted a new system based on scientific principles, while others wanted a system justified by the philosophical and political principles of the Enlightenment. To a surprising degree the desires of the two camps converged. For different reasons, both scientists and politicians wanted universality.

Such total convergence of the interests of the scientific community and the world of politics is rare. Seldom has history been so inextricably intertwined with the history of science.

The Longest Geodesic Measurement Ever Attempted

In order to carry out their measurements, our two astronomers had to climb to the highest points available to them in each locality. Their expedition through the heart of France actually involves us in two journeys, one along the ground, the other across the heights. The silence of the mountains and the peace and quiet of church belfries alternate with the roiling passions of the day. An astonishing distance separates the steeple, from whose vantage the village below seems minuscule indeed, from the village square engulfed in a historical conflict unprecedented in its scale.

The journey across France is therefore also a journey through history. The measurement of the meridian, which began in the last days of the monarchy, ended at the dawn of the Consulate. It coincided in time with the First Republic: seven years to "measure" 551,584 *toises*. The meter and the kilogram justly bear the name bestowed on them by France's National Assembly: *les mesures de la République*.

Well after writing this book, I asked myself a strange question: How many steps did Delambre climb during the seven years of the expedition? From the cupola of the dome of the Pantheon to the pelican of the church of Saint-Etienne in Bourges, from the steeple of Sainte-Croix in Orléans to that of Notre-Dame in Amiens, from the clock tower in Dun to the bell tower of the abbey of Evaux? Tens of thousands! This was one astronomer who must have been in awfully good shape!

The Masters of the Meter

Delambre, a man of energy and enthusiasm, and Méchain, reserved, distant, and tormented: two men, two worldviews, two journeys in opposite directions, two diametrically opposed sets of experiences. The turmoil of the period can be seen in the contrasts and contradictions of the two itineraries. One man found honor and fulfillment in this effort, while the other was overwhelmed by it and sacrificed his life. The contrasts between the two men and their accomplishments seemed ideal for a novel.

Méchain's Passion

The drama of the period was paralleled by the drama of an individual. Why did Méchain persist in wanting to return to Barcelona to redo measurements that all his colleagues judged to be excellent? Something in the numbers haunted him. An error, perhaps? Or was it simply the overwhelming immensity of the task: to give the world one set of measures for everyone. "For all times, for all men," Condorcet had proclaimed to the Assembly. Seven years for a gain of three minutes of arc: an impossible degree of perfection.

One Could Say . . .

One could say that the drama revolves around six elements: a time, a place, two men, a scientific method, and an instrument of measurement. The Revolution, the territory of the Republic, Méchain and Delambre, the method of triangulation, and the repeating circle. Out of the conjunction of these six elements came the *meter*, the universal standard of length.

Intervention de Prieur de la Côte d'Or
à l'Assemblée nationale

9 février 1790

« ... appelés près d'un roi, qui ne connaît de grandeur que la félicité de ses peuples, les représentants de la Nation ont brisé les fers qu'avait forgés le despotisme. La féodalité est détruite, le grand œuvre de notre génération est commencé et s'avance de jour en jour.

Les provinces vont s'oublier et se confondre dans la division plus régulière des départements et des districts.

La variété des coutumes, sources immenses d'abus, sera désormais remplacée dans toute la France par l'uniformité la plus exacte dans les lois d'administration de la justice.

Avec un ordre si beau, laissera-t-on subsister l'ancien chaos dû à la diversité de nos mesures ? »

Speech by Prieur of the Côte-d'Or
to the National Assembly

9 February 1970

. . . called by a king whose only grandeur lies in the felicity of his peoples, the representatives of the Nation have smashed the chains forged by despotism. Feudalism is destroyed, the great work of our generation has begun and progresses day by day.

The provinces shall be forgotten and confound themselves in the more regular division of *départements* and *districts*.

The variety of customary laws, a source of innumerable abuses, shall henceforth be replaced throughout France by the most scrupulous uniformity in the laws of administration of justice.

With an order so beautiful, shall the ancient chaos due to the diversity of our measures be allowed to persist?

RAPPORT

FAIT A L'ACADEMIE DES SCIENCES,

Sur le choix d'une unité de Mesures.

PAR MM. BORDA, LAGRANGE, LAPLACE, MONGE & CONDORCET.

19 mars 1791

L'IDÉE de rapporter toutes les mesures à une unité de longueur prise dans la nature s'est présentée aux mathématiciens dès l'instant où ils ont connu l'existence d'une telle unité & la possibilité de la déterminer. Ils ont vu que c'était le seul moyen d'exclure tout arbitraire du système des mesures, & d'être sûr de conserver toujours le même, sans qu'aucun autre événement, qu'aucune révolution dans l'ordre du monde pût y jeter de l'incertitude ; ils ont senti qu'un tel système n'appartenant exclusivement à aucune nation, on pouvait se flatter de le voir adopter par toutes.

En effet, si on prenait pour unité une mesure déjà usitée dans un pays, il serait difficile d'offrir aux autres des motifs de préférence capables de balancer l'espèce de répugnance, sinon philosophique, du moins très naturelle, qu'ont les peuples pour une imitation qui paraît toujours l'aveu d'une sorte d'infériorité : il y aurait donc au moins autant de mesures que de grandes nations. D'ailleurs,

quand même presque toutes auraient adopté une de ces bases arbitraires, mille événements faciles à prévoir pourraient faire naître des incertitudes sur la véritable grandeur de cette base ; & comme il n'existerait point de moyen rigoureux de vérification, il s'établirait à la longue des différences entre les mesures. La diversité qui existe aujourd'hui entre celles qui sont en usage dans les divers pays a moins pour cause une diversité originaire qui remonte à l'époque de leur établissement que des altérations produites par le temps. Enfin, on gagnerait peu, même dans une seule nation, à conserver une des unités de longueur qui y sont usitées ; il n'en faudrait pas moins corriger les autres vices du système des mesures, & l'opération entraînerait une incommodité presque égale pour le plus grand nombre.

On peut réduire à trois les unités qui paraissent les plus propres à servir de base ; la longueur du pendule, un quart du cercle de l'équateur, enfin un quart du méridien terrestre.

Report to the Academy of Sciences
on the Choice of a Unit of Measurement
by Messrs Borda, Lagrange, Laplace, Monge,
and Condorcet

19 March 1791

The idea of relating all measurement to a unit of length found in nature occurred to mathematicians the moment they conceived the existence of such a unit and the possibility of determining its length. They recognized that this was the only way of eliminating all arbitrariness from the system of measurement and of ensuring that it would always remain the same, regardless of the uncertainties attendant upon other events and revolutions in the world order. They felt that since such a system would not be the exclusive property of any nation, one might hope to see it adopted by all.

Indeed, if one were to adopt a unit of measurement already in use in a country, it would be difficult to present other countries with reasons for adopting it sufficient to counterbalance the natural if not philosophical reluctance of nations to accept imitations, which are inevitably seen as admissions of a kind of inferiority. Hence there would always be at least as many measures as there are great nations. Even if almost all nations were to adopt one of these arbitrary bases, any number of easily foreseeable events could give rise to uncertainties as to the true magnitude of that base; and since no rigorous means of verification would exist, differences among these measures would eventually come to exist. The diversity that exists today among the measures in use in various countries is due not so much to a diversity that existed at the time of their establishment as to changes induced by the passage of time. Finally, little is to be gained, even within a single nation, by maintaining one of the units of length already in use there. It would still be necessary to correct the other deficiencies of the system of measurement, and that effort would inconvenience the majority almost as much.

The units most suitable to serve as a base can be reduced in number to just three: the length of the pendulum, a quarter of the circle of the equator, and finally, a quarter of the earth's meridian.

Discours de Condorcet à l'Assemblée le 26 mars 1791

« L'Académie des sciences m'a chargé d'avoir l'honneur de vous présenter un rapport sur le choix d'une unité de longueur. Nous n'avons pas cru qu'il fût nécessaire d'attendre le concours des autres nations ni pour se décider sur le choix de l'unité de mesure ni pour commencer les opérations. En effet, nous avons exclu de ce choix toute détermination arbitraire ; nous n'avons admis que des éléments qui appartiennent également à toutes les nations.

Il est possible d'avoir une unité de longueur qui ne dépende d'aucune autre quantité. Cette unité de longueur sera prise sur la Terre même. Le quart du méridien terrestre deviendra l'unité réelle de mesure, et la dix millionième partie de cette longueur en sera l'unité usuelle.

Nous proposons donc de mesurer immédiatement un arc de méridien depuis Dunkerque jusqu'à Barcelone. Cet arc serait d'une étendue très suffisante ; il y aurait environ 6 degrés au nord et 3,5 au midi du parallèle moyen. A ces avantages se joint celui d'avoir les deux points extrêmes au niveau de la mer. Il ne se présente donc rien qui puisse donner prétexte au reproche d'avoir voulu affecter une sorte de prééminence.

En un mot, si la mémoire de ces travaux venait à s'effacer, si les résultats seuls étaient conservés, ils n'offriraient rien qui pût servir à faire connaître quelle nation en a conçu l'idée, en a suivi l'exécution. »

Condorcet's Speech to the Assembly on March 26, 1791

The Academy of Sciences has honored me with the mission of presenting to you its report on the selection of a unit of length. There is no need, in our judgment, to await the concurrence of other nations either to choose a unit of measurement or to begin our operations. Indeed, we have eliminated all arbitrariness from the determination and rely only on information equally accessible to all nations.

It is possible to have a unit of length that does not depend on any other quantity. That unit of length will be based on the earth itself. The quarter of the terrestrial meridian will become the real unit of measurement, and the ten-millionth part of that length will become the unit in common use.

We therefore propose to proceed forthwith to the measurement of a segment of the meridian from Dunkirk to Barcelona. This segment should be more than sufficient in length. It will extend roughly 6 degrees to the north and 3.5 to the south of the mean parallel. There is also the further advantage that both endpoints lie at sea level. Hence there are no grounds whatsoever for the reproach that we wish to establish some sort of preeminence.

In short, if the memory of our efforts were to be erased and only the results were preserved, they would contain no evidence to reveal which nation conceived the idea or put it into practice.

The new unit of measurement was to be universal and not arbitrary. The Academy's report listed three possible choices. Until the report was issued, the preferred unit had been the length of the pendulum, but within a week this had changed. The National Assembly voted in favor of the quarter of the terrestrial meridian. The text emphasizes the distinction between the real *unit, which is a segment of the earth's surface, and the* common *unit, which is one ten-millionth of the quarter-meridian.*

Proclamation du roi

10 juin 1792, l'An IV de la liberté

« Le Roi a donné et donne son approbation au choix fait par
l'Académie des sciences, de MM. Méchain et Delambre pour
s'occuper de la mesure du méridien depuis Dunkerque jusqu'à Barcelone. Le Roi recommande MM. Méchain et
Delambre à tous les corps administratifs et aux municipali-
tés [...] et principalement celles du Nord, du Pas-de-Calais,
de l'Oise, de la Seine et Oise, de Paris, du Loiret, du Cher,
de la Creuse, du Puy de Dôme, de l'Aude et des Pyrénées-
Orientales, de faciliter, autant qu'il sera en eux, lesdits
sieurs commissaires [...] et de leur procurer les moyens
d'établir en tels lieux qu'ils jugeront nécessaires les signaux,
les mâts, les réverbères et les échafauds, même sur le faîte
et à l'extérieur des clochers, tours et châteaux ; [de leur pro-
curer] les chevaux et les voitures dont ils pourront avoir
besoin pour le transport de leurs instruments, ainsi que les
bois et matériaux nécessaires pour la construction des échafauds, et de pourvoir à ce que lesdits commissaires ne soient
point troublés dans leurs observations, et à ce que les
signaux, échafauds et autres ouvrages qu'ils auront fait
construire ne soient ni endommagés ni détruits... »

Signé : Louis
Contresigné : Rolland

Royal Proclamation

10 June 1792, Year IV of Liberty

The king has given and hereby gives his approval to the Academy of Sciences' choice of Messrs Méchain and Delambre to measure the meridian from Dunkirk to Barcelona. The king recommends Messrs Méchain and Delambre to all administrative bodies and municipalities . . . and primarily those of the Nord, Pas-de-Calais, Oise, Seine-et-Oise, Paris, Loiret, Cher, Creuse, Puy-de-Dôme, Aude, and Pyrénées-Orientales, [and urges them] to facilitate to the maximum extent possible the work of the aforementioned commissioners . . . and to procure the means of establishing in such places as they may deem necessary targets, masts, reflectors, and scaffolds, even upon the tops or exteriors of belfries, towers, and chateaux; [to procure] such horses and carriages as they may need to transport their instruments, as well as wood and building materials for the construction of scaffolds; and to see to it that the aforementioned commissioners are not disturbed in their observations and that such targets, scaffolds, and other structures as they may erect are neither damaged nor destroyed. . . .

Signed: Louis
Countersigned: Rolland

Circulaire de recommandation

Messieurs les Administrateurs
du département du Puy de Dôme,

Paris, le 16 juin 1792, l'An IV de la Liberté

« [...] Le Comité d'instruction publique ne croit pas entreprendre sur les fonctions administratives en recommandant particulièrement M. Méchain à votre ardeur connue pour la gloire nationale, pour le progrès des Sciences et pour celui de la liberté, dont vous connaissez le prix et la nature. La liberté doit tout aux lumières de la philosophie, comme le despotisme tire sa force des ténèbres de l'ignorance. Des hommes doivent donc prendre un vif intérêt à l'accroissement des connaissances. [...] La protection qu'un gouvernement tyrannique avait donnée aux astronomes chargés de tracer la fameuse méridienne de l'Observatoire n'est pas le trait le moins saillant qu'aient fait valoir les panégyristes d'un Roi qui, en favorisant les sciences et les lettres, s'acquit une gloire ternie par l'asservissement de la Nation, par l'intolérance religieuse et par les conquêtes.

[...] Nous attendons de vous qu'après avoir procuré directement à M. Méchain tous les secours dont il aura besoin, vous voudrez bien encore les réclamer pour lui auprès de la commune de Herment, dans laquelle il doit se rendre. »

Les Présidents et Membres
du Comité de l'instruction publique.
C.-A. Prieur, L. Carnot, G. Romme...

Letter of Recommendation

Messieurs les Administrateurs
of the *département* of Puy-de-Dôme,

                              Paris, 16 June 1792, Year IV of Liberty
... The Committee of Public Instruction does not feel that it is en-
croaching upon the prerogatives of the administration in warmly recom-
mending M. Méchain to your well-known ardor for national glory and
for the progress of Science and liberty, of whose value and nature you are
well aware. Liberty owes everything to the enlightenment of philosophy,
just as despotism draws its strength from the darkness of ignorance. Men
must therefore take an active interest in the growth of knowledge. ...
The protection that a tyrannical government gave to the astronomers
charged with tracing the famous meridian of the Observatory was not
the least salient of the traits singled out by the panegyrists of a King who,
through the favor he bestowed upon science and letters, acquired for
himself a glory tarnished by his subjugation of the Nation, by his religious intolerance, and by his conquests.

... We hope that after you have accorded to M. Méchain such assistance as he may require, you will submit claims on his behalf to the commune of Herment, where he is to go.

                    The Presidents and Members
              of the Committee of Public Instruction.
              C.-A. Prieur, L. Carnot, G. Romme, ...

*Summer of 1792. In this turbulent period, Delambre and Méchain were obliged to
travel through much of France. On June 10, Louis signed safe-conduct passes that
would soon become evidence against the men to whom they had been issued.*

BASE

DU SYSTÈME MÈTRIQUE DÉCIMAL,

OU

MESURE DE L'ARC DU MÉRIDIEN

COMPRIS ENTRE LES PARALLÈLES

DE DUNKERQUE ET BARCELONE,

EXÉCUTÉE EN 1792 ET ANNÉES SUIVANTES,

PAR MM. MÉCHAIN ET DELAMBRE.

Rédigée par M. Delambre, secrétaire perpétuel de l'Institut pour les sciences mathématiques, membre du bureau des longitudes, des sociétés royales de Londres, d'Upsal et de Copenhague, des académies de Berlin et de Suède, de la société Italienne et de celle de Gottingue, et membre de la Légion d'honneur.

SUITE DES MÉMOIRES DE L'INSTITUT.

1652

TOME PREMIER.

1652

PARIS.

BAUDOUIN, IMPRIMEUR DE L'INSTITUT NATIONAL.

JANVIER 1806.

Observatoire de Paris

BASE

OF THE DECIMAL METRIC SYSTEM,

OR

MEASUREMENT OF THE ARC OF THE MERIDIAN

INCLUDED BETWEEN THE PARALLELS

OF DUNKIRK AND BARCELONA,

EXECUTED IN 1792 AND SUBSEQUENT YEARS,

BY MESSRS MÉCHAIN AND DELAMBRE.

Drafted by Mr. Delambre, perpetual secretary of the Institute for the Mathematical Sciences, member of the Bureau of Longitudes, the Royal Societies of London, Upsala, and Copenhagen, the Academies of Berlin and Sweden, the Italian Society and the Göttingen Society, and member of the Legion of Honor.

SERIES OF MEMOIRS OF THE INSTITUTE.

VOLUME ONE.

PARIS.

BAUDOUIN, PRINTER OF THE INSTITUT NATIONAL.

JANUARY 1806.

Observatory of Paris

Triangulation

Triangulation is a method of determining a rectilinear distance by measuring a series of angles together with the length of a single straight line. The method requires that one do the following:

1. Construct a series of triangles that span the path one wishes to measure. Elevated targets are then erected on either side of the path. Each target must be visible from the two previous targets and the two succeeding ones. Then determine the angles from target to target using an appropriate instrument, such as the repeating circle.

2. On the ground itself, measure one side of one of the triangles, referred to as the *baseline* of the triangulation, which establishes its *scale*. This measurement is carried out by means of flat measuring rules.

3. Measure the angles that the sides of the triangles form with the meridian. This is called measuring the *azimuths*.

The method relies on the trigonometric fact that "if one knows two angles and one side of a triangle, one knows all three sides."

One then has to determine the magnitude of the arc by measuring the latitude at each end. These astronomical measurements are also carried out with the repeating circle.

Next, all the measurements have to be referred to a single horizontal plane. The vertices of the triangles, physically marked by targets, are not all at the same height, so the triangles are tilted. In order to project them onto the horizontal plane, the *zenith* angle, which is the angle that each side makes with the vertical, has to be measured.

Because the earth is round, the sides of the triangles are not straight lines but (approximate) arcs of circles. Using mathematical formulas all the measurements are referred to sea level.

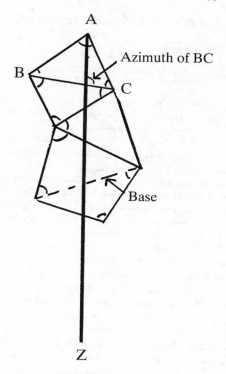

Media Collection in the History of Science, Cité des sciences

Letter from Delambre to Méchain

Observatory of Paris

The correspondence between Méchain and Delambre covers a period of seven years. It consists of more than a hundred letters, most of them from Méchain to Delambre.

After a hiatus of eighteen months, measurement of the meridian has resumed. Delambre is finding it difficult to make progress south of Bourges. Many of his targets have been destroyed either by storms or by the demolition of church belfries "by hammer-wielding Hébertistes." Paying for the work has also become more difficult, because the two astronomers, as official employees of the Republic, were paid in the paper currency known as assignats, whose value kept declining.

Letter from Méchain to Delambre

Observatory of Paris

Several dozen of Méchain's letters to his colleague make for poignant reading, because they tell of the slow deterioration of his psychological state. After leaving Spain in 1794, Méchain repeatedly expressed his desire to return to Barcelona to repeat certain measurements. He even proposed paying for the trip out of his own pocket. His pleas went unheeded, however. In this letter he speaks "of the chagrin and all-consuming anxiety that torment" him in connection with what he calls in another letter "his unfortunate Barcelona measurements."

Les Signaux de Montredon et de Montalet

Aux commissaires
près la commune de Lacaune et Montredon

29 Thermidor An VI

« Je demeure informé, citoyen, qu'on a construit depuis quelque temps sur l'endroit le plus élevé du château de Montredon et à Lacaune, au lieu appelé Montalet, une espèce de machine peinte en blanc, qui ressemble beaucoup à un pavillon, et que c'est un étranger soi-disant venant de Paris qui a donné le plan de cette machine et qui en a dirigé la construction.

Je vous invite, citoyen, à vous transporter sur-le-champ au château de Montredon, tant pour vous assurer que cette machine existe que pour vous informer avec les propriétaires du château à quel dessein elle a été construite et pour vous assurer si elle peut être utile aux projets des ennemis de la République. Vous voudrez bien m'en faire la description, et me faire part de tous les renseignements que vous vous serez procurés, en les joignant à ceux que j'ai déjà écrits. Il me sera facile alors de découvrir la vérité.

Dans la crise où nous sommes, rien ne doit paraître indifférent à un fonctionnaire relié à un agent de gouvernement. Les choses qui paraissent les plus simples peuvent couvrir des desseins pervers. Vous mettrez donc en cette circonstance tout le zèle, l'exactitude, la célérité dont vous pouvez être susceptible. »

Salut.

Archives départementales d'Albi, cote: L201, Folio 66

The Targets at Montredon and Montalet

To the Commissioners
Near the commune of Lacaune and Montredon

29 Thermidor Year VI

I am informed, citizen, that someone has recently erected a structure atop the highest point of the chateau of Montredon and in Lacaune, at the place known as Montalet, a sort of machine, painted white, which looks a good deal like a tent. I am told, moreover, that the plans for this machine were provided by a stranger claiming to come from Paris, and this same person directed the construction.

I urge you, citizen, to go immediately to the chateau of Montredon to ascertain whether this machine exists and to inquire of the owners of the chateau as to the purpose for which it was constructed, and, further, to determine whether it might be of use to the enemies of the republic. You will kindly describe the structure to me and pass on any information you may obtain, attached to this letter. It will then be easy for me to determine the truth.

In the present crisis no functionary serving as an agent of the government may take anything for granted. Even the simplest-seeming objects may conceal perverse intentions. You will therefore discharge this commission with all the zeal, scrupulousness, and speed of which you are capable.

Departmental archives of Albi, Cote L210, folio 66

During the summer of 1798, Méchain supervised the construction of a target at the Montredon station. In this letter that target is described as a "sort of machine, painted white." The fact that the color is mentioned is of special significance: white was still the color of royalty. As for the other target, in nearby Montalet, force had to be used to protect it from vandals. Rumors about it had so incensed the local hotheads that they destroyed the target several times despite a notice posted by the authorities explaining its purpose. "Guards also had to be stationed at several other targets," Méchain wrote Delambre.

À la commune de Lacaune

Alby, le 17 Fructidor An VI

« L'adjoint général qui commande la force armée dans le département n'ayant pu fournir les sept hommes d'infanterie que' nous lui avions demandés pour protéger le signal de Montalet, nous n'avons pas cru devoir les remplacer comme nous le proposait le général par un pareil nombre de hussards, attendu la difficulté qu'il y aurait eu peut-être à les faire vivre dans ces montagnes ; mais on ne doit jamais perdre de vue l'importance des opérations du citoyen Méchain. Vous voudrez bien mettre en réquisition deux ou trois hommes de la colonne mobile tant pour garder le signal que pour donner au citoyen Méchain les facilités et secours dont il aura besoin, vous ferez donner l'Étape à ces hommes conformément aux indications de notre lettre du 11 de ce mois, cet astronome ayant besoin de ce signal pour des observations qu'il doit faire dans le canton. Vous laisserez les gardes au signal jusqu'à ce que nous vous écrivions de les ôter.

Vous pourrez, si vous le jugez à-propos, faire relever ces hommes. Faites tous vos efforts pour que nous n'ayons pas encore le désagrément d'apprendre que les opérations de ce commissaire du gouvernement sont suspendues par le défaut de signal à Montalet. »

Salut.

Archives départementales d'Albi, cote: L266, Folio 123-N° 720

To the commune of Lacaune

Alby, 17 Fructidor Year VI

The adjutant general who commands the armed forces in the *département* was unable to provide the seven infantrymen we requested to protect the target in Montalet. We therefore did not feel obliged to replace them by a similar number of hussards, as the general suggested, in view of the likely difficulty of keeping the men supplied in these mountains. The importance of Citizen Méchain's operations should be kept in mind at all times, however. You will kindly requisition two or three men from the mobile column both to guard the target and to provide Citizen Méchain with whatever facilities and help he may require. You will billet these men as specified in our letter of the eleventh of this month, because the aforementioned astronomer requires this target for observations he is to make in the canton. You will leave the guards at the target until we authorize you in writing to remove them.

If you deem it necessary, you may relieve these men with others. Do everything within your power to ensure that we are not again disobliged by the news that the operations of this commissioner of the government have been suspended owing to difficulties with the target in Montalet.

Departmental archives of Albi, Cote L266, folio 123, no. 720

In the Base du système métrique *(1808), which is in a sense the bible of the expedition, Delambre recounted all aspects of the operation. For each station, he described the target and gave its exact location, the number of measurements made, the meteorological conditions, and the results of the measurements, along with notes of other events. The target of Nore formed a triangle with the targets of Montredon and Montalet. It was one of the most "dreadful" of the entire operation.*

SIGNAL DE NORE.

LXXVIII.

LA partie du sommet de la *Montagne-Noire* que l'on nomme *Nore*, en est la plus haute. C'est une espèce de butte ou proéminence assez étendue, et qui de loin se distingue bien du reste du sommet. On a trouvé sur Nore plusieurs enfoncemens qui rendoient incertain sur le véritable emplacement du signal de 1740 ; mais quelques indications données par un habitant de *Pradelles*, village situé dans la même montagne, à demi-lieue dans le sud-ouest de Nore, et 220 toises plus bas, ont fait présumer cet emplacement. On y a érigé le nouveau signal ; il étoit de même forme que les précédens, et sa hauteur au-dessus du piquet enfoncé au centre de sa base étoit de $2^t 4445$.

En quittant cette station on a rempli l'intérieur du signal d'un amas considérable de pierres, pour conserver le piquet et servir par la suite à le retrouver.

Les mauvais temps dont j'ai été accueilli à Nore, et sur-tout la destruction de presque tous les autres signaux correspondans, m'ont obligé d'y faire vingt-un voyages. Mon séjour dans un climat si âpre, et presque aussi sauvage que celui de Montalet, a été bien long, et il eût été assez pénible, si le citoyen Lavalette-Fabas, qui voulut bien me donner l'hospitalité chez lui à Pradelles, n'en eût adouci la rigueur et l'ennui par son aménité et l'intérêt dont il me donna des marques très-affectueuses.

OBSERVATIONS GÉODÉSIQUES. 349

DISTANCES AU ZÉNIT.

$$dH = 1^s8056.$$

Signal de Montrédon. (Le premier, hauteur 3^{t}2708.)

10 1012^{s}72875 1012272875 = 91° 8′ 44″12 (en terre.)
M. 18 vendémiaire an 6, vers midi. Signal éclairé ; mais il y a des vapeurs
et de l'ondulation.

La même.

10 1012^{s}7310 1012273100 = 91° 8′ 44″84
1 brumaire, à 3^h ¼. On voit bien l'objet.

Moyenne	91° 8′ 44″48	
pour la réduction à l'horison.		
Demi-épaisseur du fil	+ 3″00	
$dH' = 2^s6319$	+ 28″99	
pour la différence de niveau et la réfraction.	91° 9′ 16″47	

Extrémité de la tour du château de Montrédon.

8 809^{s}9915 1012489375 = 91° 7′ 26″56
pour la réduction à l'horison. M. 14 frimaire. Therm. 11⁴. Soleil ; un
peu de vapeurs.

Demi-épaisseur du fil	+ 3″00
$dH' = -0^s6389$	— 7″04
pour la différence de niveau et la réfraction.	91° 7′ 22″52

Montalet (bord du roc, le signal étant abattu).

10 1000^{s}7615 1000076150 = 90° 4′ 6″73 (dans le ciel.)
pour la réduction à l'horison. M. 18 vendémiaire, à midi ¼. Soleil ; un
peu d'ondulation.

Pour le fil	0″00
$dH' = -0^s6389$	— 7″03
pour différence de niveau et la réfraction.	90° 3′ 59″70

Méchain's Logs

Angles observés aux différentes Stations de la chaine de triangles de la Méridienne depuis le Mont-jouy près de Barcelone jusqu'aux environs de Perpignan.

1re Station au Mont-jouy.

Sur la plate-forme de la grande Tour des Signaux.
hauteur du cercle audessus du Niveau de la Mer 165 toi. pir. ½.

Observatory of Paris

All the angle and azimuth measurements were recorded and duly examined and verified by members of the International Commission, which convened in Paris for a period of several months. These records formed the basis of the series of calculations that led to the establishment of the meter.

Observatory of Paris

Pages 1 and 5 of the records in which Méchain reported on the measurements made at Montjouy, the southernmost point of the expedition.

Interruption de l'opération

Partie sud:

« 26 Floréal An I. Le Comité de salut public informe que le citoyen Méchain, astronome chargé de voyager pour prendre la mesure exacte de l'arc de méridien, est détenu à Barcelone, avec les deux citoyens qui l'accompagnent et partagent ses mesures, par ordre du général espagnol ; il manque des secours qui lui sont nécessaires ; charge les commissaires de la Trésorerie nationale de lui faire parvenir la somme de six mille francs en numéraires. »

R. Lindet, Prieur, Carnot.

« Le général en chef de l'armée des Pyrénées-Orientales a profité de la capitulation de Collioure pour forcer les Espagnols à nous renvoyer Méchain. »

Partie nord:

23 décembre 1793

« Le Comité de salut public, considérant combien il importe à l'amélioration de l'esprit public que ceux qui sont chargés du gouvernement ne délèguent de fonctions ni ne donnent de missions qu'à des hommes dignes de confiance par leurs vertus républicaines et leur haine pour les rois, après s'en être concerté avec les membres du Comité d'instruction publique occupés spécialement de l'opération des poids et mesures, arrête que Borda, Lavoisier, Laplace, Coulomb, Brisson et Delambre cesseront, à compter de ce jour, d'être membres de la Commission des poids et mesures, et remettront de suite, avec inventaire, aux membres restants, les instruments, calculs, notes, mémoires, et généralement tout ce qui est entre leurs mains de relatif à l'opération des mesures [...]. »

C.A. Prieur, B. Barrère, Carnot,
R. Lindet, Billaud-Varenne.

Archives nationales: AF ii.67, de la main de C. A. Prieur.

Interruption of Operations

Southern Part

---

26 Floréal, Year I. The Committee of Public Safety hereby informs you that Citizen Méchain, an astronomer to whom has been assigned the mission of traveling for the purpose of making an exact measurement of the meridian arc, is being held in Barcelona with the two citizens who are accompanying him and participating in his measurements, on orders of the Spanish general. He lacks needed assistance. The Committee hereby orders the commissioners of the National Treasury to send him the sum of six thousand francs in cash.

R. Lindet, Prieur, Carnot

The commanding general of the Army of the Eastern Pyrenees has seized the occasion of the surrender of Collioure to force the Spanish to send Méchain back to us.

But Méchain was unable to return to France and embarked for Italy instead. He returned from there in September 1795.

Northern Part

Delambre was sacked for signing a letter written by Borda in support of Lavoisier:

---

23 December 1793

The Committee of Public Safety, cognizant of how important it is for improving public morale that those who are charged to govern delegate duties and assign missions only to men worthy of confidence owing to their republican virtues and hatred of kings, and after consultation with the members of the Committee of Public Instruction especially concerned with matters of weights and measures, hereby decrees that Borda, Lavoisier, Laplace, Coulomb, Brisson, and Delambre shall as of this day cease to be members of the Commission on Weights and Measures and shall forthwith remit, with inventory, to the remaining members all instruments, calculations, notes, memoranda, and any other material in their possession that may pertain to the measurement venture. . . .

C. A. Prieur, B. Barrère, Carnot,
R. Lindet, Billaud-Varenne

Archives Nationales, AF 11.67, in the hand of C. A. Prieur.

Chain of Triangles from Dunkirk to Barcelona Measured by Messrs Delambre and Méchain

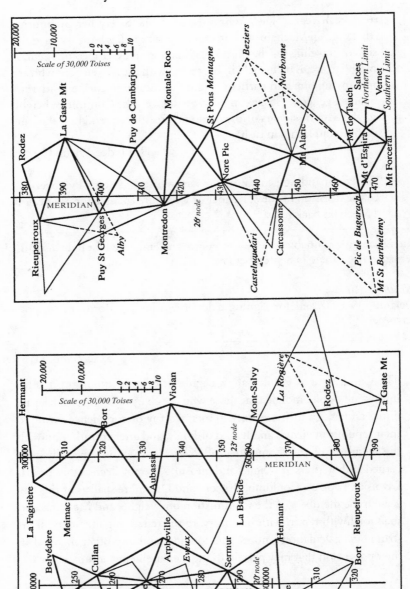

Drawings from Delambre's *Base du système métrique*

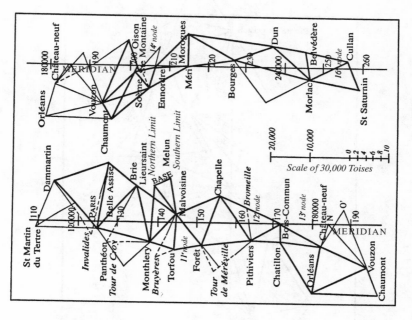

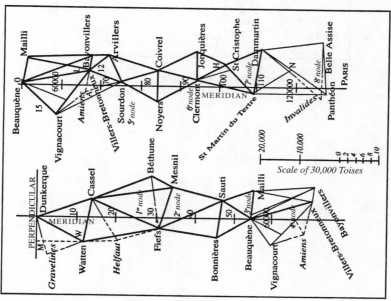

Measurements in Spanish territory

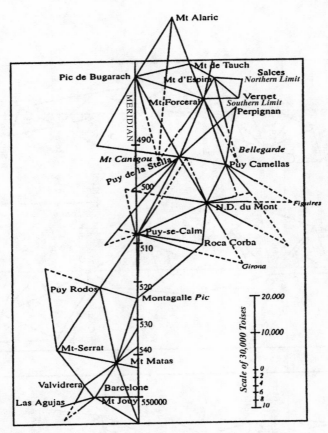

Measurements in Spanish territory *(continued)*

The Repeating Circle

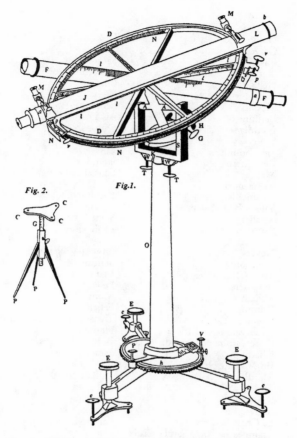

Drawing based on an illustration of the repeating circle in Delambre's
Base du système métrique, from the library of the Observatory of Paris

*Angles and azimuths were measured with Borda's repeating circle. The astronomers
had four such instruments available to them. The repeating circle was based on the
principle of repeating measurements as often as one wished without returning to the
starting point. The result was not read until the final measurement had been made.
The errors due to the instrument were thus divided by the number of observations.
The more observations one made, the smaller the error: repetition yielded greater
precision.*

*The baselines were measured with flat bimetallic rules made of platinum and
copper. The length of these rules was two* toises *(a* toise *was approximately six and
a half feet).*

Path of the Meridian in France, Station by Station

Dunkerque
Gravelines
Cassel
Watten
Helfaut
Fiefs
Mesnil
Béthune
Bonnières
Saulty
Fiefs Bonnières
Beauquesne
Mailly
Vignacourt
Bayonvillers
Villers-Bretonneux
Arvillers
Sourdon
Coivrel
Noyers
Clermont
Saint-Christophe
Jonquières
Saint-Martin-du-Tertre
Dammartin
Dôme du Panthéon
Observatoire de Paris
Observatoire de la rue de Paradis
Châtillon
Brie-Comte-Robert
Montlhéry
Torfou
Saint-Yon
Malvoisine
La Chapelle-la-Reine
Étampes-La Forêt-Sainte-Croix
Bruyères-le-Châtel
Pithiviers
Bromeilles
Boiscommun
Orléans
Neuville
Haut de Châtillon
Méreville
Châteauneuf-sur-Loire
Sully-sur-Loire
Saint-Germain
Torfou
Melun
Lieursain
Chaumont
Vouzon
Lamotte-Beuvron

La Courdieu
Soême
Sainte-Montaine
Ennordre
Oizon
Mery
Morogues
Ais-Dam-Gillon
Dun-sur-Auron
Bourges
vaisselai
Issoudun
Chezal-Benoit
Morlac
Béthune-Charost
Culan
Saint-Saturnin
Arphevilles
Laage
Orgnat-Villemonteix
Sermur
Mendren
Le Puy
Mont-Dore
Felletin-Bordes
Truc-Courtine-La Fagitière
Herment
Bort-les-Orgues
Meimac
Puy Violan
La Bastide
Aubassin
Monsalvy
Rieupeyroux
Saint-Mamet
Rodez
Albi
Montredon
Montalet
Saint-Pons-de-Thomiere
Narbonne
Nore
Carcassonne
Castres
Castelnaudary
Grugies
Alairac
Montréal
Tuchan-Tauch
Narbonne
Béziers
Forceréal
Perpignan

Deposit of the Meter

L'AN sept de la République française, une et indivisible, le quatre messidor, trois heures après midi, le citoyen *Pierre-Simon Laplace*, l'un des ex-présidens de l'Institut national des Sciences et des Arts, remplaçant le citoyen *Bougainville*, absent pour cause de maladie, président actuel; le citoyen *Louis Lefévre Gineau*, le citoyen *Antoine Mongez*, secrétaires de l'Institut; les Membres nationaux et étrangers de la Commission des poids et mesures: savoir,

LES CITOYENS

Darcet, de l'Institut national;
Fabbroni, envoyé de Toscane;
Van-Swinden, envoyé de la République batave;
Mascheroni, envoyé de la République cisalpine;
Vassalli, envoyé du Gouvernement provisoire de Piémont,
Aeneae, envoyé de la République batave;
Lagrange, de l'Institut national;
Méchain, de l'Institut national;
Multedo, envoyé de la République ligurienne;
Pedrayes, envoyé de l'Espagne;
Ciscar, envoyé de l'Espagne;
Legendre, de l'Institut national;
Trallès, envoyé de la République helvétique;
Delambre, de l'Institut national;
Brisson, de l'Institut national.

(*Est à observer que les citoyens Laplace et Lefévre-Gineau sont membres de la Commission des poids et mesures.*)

Les citoyens *Lenoir* et *Fortin*, artistes, adjoints à la Commission;
Le citoyen *Garran-Coulon*, membre de l'Institut national;

Après avoir présenté à l'un et l'autre Conseil l'étalon du mètre et l'étalon du kilogramme, l'un et l'autre en platine, se sont rendus aux archives de la République, pour y faire, en exécution de la loi du 18 germinal an 3, le dépôt des deux étalons, renfermés chacun dans une boîte fermant à clef.

Le citoyen *Armand-Gaston Camus*, membre de l'Institut national, garde des archives de la République, a reçu les deux étalons, l'un et l'autre en bon état, et sur-le-champ il les a renfermés dans la double armoire en fer fermant à quatre clefs.

De ce que dessus, le présent procès-verbal a été dressé en double minute, dont l'une, après avoir été scellée du sceau des archives, a été remise au citoyen président de l'Institut; et tous les citoyens comparans ont signé avec le garde des archives de la République.

Signé, LAPLACE, ex-président de l'Institut national; L. LEFÈVRE-GINEAU, secrétaire; Antoine MONGEZ, secrétaire; BRISSON, DELAMBRE, FABBRONI, LAGRANGE, MULTEDO, H. AENEAE, VASSALLI, LEGENDRE, CISCAR, PEDRAYES, MÉCHAIN, J. H. VAN-SWINDEN, FORTIN, DARCET, TRALLÈS, LENOIR, MASCHERONI, J. Ph. GARRAN, CAMUS.

Observatory of Paris

4 Messidor, Year VII (June 22, 1799). After being shown to the Council of Ancients and the Council of Five Hundred, the standard meter and kilogram were deposited in the Archives of the Republic. The "meter of the Archives" is a flat platinum rule with a rectangular cross-section of 25.3×4 mm. It is an end-to-end standard (that is, its length is defined as the distance between its two end faces).

From the Meridian to the Standard Meter

On March 26, 1791, the National Assembly accepted the advice of the Academy of Science and of Condorcet in particular and adopted the quarter section of the earth's meridian as the universal standard of measurement. In other words, they chose the earth itself as the standard—the earth, shared by all men, invariable, and universal. The Assembly also decided that the ordinary unit of measure would be one ten-millionth of the quarter meridian, which would be called the *meter*, from *meson*, measure.

More than that, they decided that various measurements should be interrelated, that they should form a *system*. This system was to be based on the meter. From that unit of length would be derived other units for surface area, volume, and mass. The unit of mass was defined as the kilogram, this being "the mass of a cubic decimeter of distilled water at maximal density." Multiples and submultiples of the basic units were to be based on a decimal scale. In this way the foundations of the decimal metric system were laid.

The Meridian of Paris was chosen as the basis of the meter. The arc chosen for concrete measurement was that which stretched from Dunkirk in the north of France to Barcelona in Spain. It offered certain advantages: namely, it extended almost symmetrically north and south of the 45 degree parallel, the median parallel of the northern hemisphere; it was of sufficient amplitude, just over ten degrees; and its two endpoints stood at sea level.

The actual measurement was carried out by two astronomers, Pierre Méchain and Jean-Baptiste Delambre, and took six years.

Chronology

1788
Convocation of the Estates General.

1789
May 5: Opening of the Estates General.
June 27: The Estates General become the National Constituent Assembly.
July 14: Taking of the Bastille.
July 25: Proposition of Sir John Riggs Miller to the British House of Commons.
Night of August 4: Abolition of privileges.
August 26: Declaration of the Rights of Man and the Citizen.

1790
January 21: Principal of equality of punishment for all.
February 5: Prieur's speech to the Assembly on weights and measures.
February 15: Uniformization of the territory, abolition of the provinces, creation of eighty-three *départements*.
March 9: "Proposal on the need and means to make all measures of length and weight uniform throughout the kingdom," submitted to the National Assembly by Talleyrand.
March 15: Fees charged for the use of standards of measurement of weight are abolished.
April 13: British House of Commons creates a committee to look into the standardization of weights and measures.
May 8: The Assembly issues a decree "urging the King to write to His Britannic Majesty to request that he ask the Parliament of England to cooperate with the National Assembly in establishing the unit of weights and measures." A proposal is made to adopt as the standard unit of length the length of a simple pendulum with a period of one second at a latitude of forty-five degrees.
October 21: The tricolor flag replaces the white flag with fleurs-de-lys as the emblem of France.
December 3: The English reject the French proposal to establish a common unit of measure.

1791
February 16: Borda proposes that the Academy appoint a commission "to discuss the bases on which one ought to establish standard weights and measures."
March 19: "Report on the Choice of a Unit of Measure," submitted to the Academy by Borda, Lagrange, Laplace, Monge, and Condorcet, who proposed a quarter of the meridian as a unit of length and the base of a new system of weights and measures.

March 26 and 30: The National Assembly approves a decree embodying the proposals made in the report submitted on March 19. With the law of March 30, 1791, the National Assembly adopted the quarter-meridian as the base of the new system of measurement and opted to base the whole system on the decimal scale. It also issued orders that a series of operations be carried out.

April 2: Death of Mirabeau.

April 3: The Church Sainte-Geneviève becomes the Pantheon.

April 13: Nomination of five commissioners to work on establishing the decimal metric system.

August 9: The National Assembly proclaims France indivisible.

September 30: Last session. The National and Constituent Assemblies separate.

October 1: First session of the Legislative Assembly.

1792

April 15: For the Festival of Liberty the slogan "Liberty, Equality, Fraternity" is devised.

April 25: In Strasbourg, Rouget de L'Isle creates his song for the Army of the Rhine, which will become known as *La Marseillaise.*

June 20: The people of Paris invade the Tuileries.

June 25: Méchain leaves for Spain, where he is to carry out his first measurements.

July 11: Proclamation: "The Fatherland is in danger." In a report to the Academy by Laplace, Lagrange, Borda, and Monge, the word "meter" is used to denote the unit of measure on which the new system is to be based.

August 10: Capture of the Tuileries by the people. Fall of Louis XVI.

September 20: Victory at Valmy.

September 21: First session of the Convention. The monarchy is abolished.

September 22: Proclamation of the Republic "one and indivisible." At midnight begins Year I of the new era, the republican era.

1793

January 21: Execution of Louis XVI.

April: Méchain's accident. He lies in a coma for a week. Broken ribs and shoulder.

April: War with England.

April 6: Creation of the Committee of Public Safety.

June 2: Arrest of twenty-seven Girondin deputies and two ministers. Closing of the Bourse.

July 13: Assassination of Marat.

August 1: The Convention passes a law establishing a uniform system of weights and measures throughout the Republic. It institutes the provisional metric system. The length of the provisional meter is set by the Academy of

Science at 36 *pouces* 11 *lignes* and 44 *centièmes* of the *toise de Pérou,* and the provisional kilogram at 2livres, 5 gros, 49 grains, or 18,841 grainsof the *marc moyen* of the *pile de Charlemagne.*

August 8: Abolition of the Academies.

August 10: First Festival of Reason on the Place de la Bastille.

September 11: Creation of the Temporary Commission on Weights and Measures, chaired by Borda.

October 5: Adoption of the republican calendar.

November 10: Second Festival of Reason at Notre-Dame.

November 24: Law of 4 Frimaire, Year II, makes the decimal division of the day compulsory.

December 23: Delambre, Borda, Laplace, Coulomb, and Brisson, all of whom are working on the establishment of the decimal metric system, are dismissed from their posts for signing a letter in support of Lavoisier.

December 25: Christmas gift from the Convention: school is made compulsory.

1794

Winter: Interruption of measurement of the Meridian.

Winter: Méchain makes hundreds of observations at the Fontana de Oro.

March 25: Provisional meter is stored at the National Archives.

March 28: Condorcet's suicide.

April: "Lessons on the measures deduced from the size of the earth, uniform for the whole republic, and on calculation of their decimal divisions," drafted by Haüy of the Temporary Commission.

April 5: Execution of Danton.

May 8, 1794: Twenty-eight farmers general are guillotined, Lavoisier among them.

July 27 (9 Thermidor, Year II): fall of Robespierre.

1795

March 1: "Report of the Committee of Instruction on the need for the previously mandated new weights and measures and on the means of introducing throughout the Republic," by Prieur.

April 7 (18 Germinal, Year III): Law establishing the new metric system. The new measures are called "republican." Article 2: "There shall be only one standard of weights and measures for all France. It shall be a platinum bar on which shall be traced the meter, which has been adopted as the fundamental unit for the entire system of measurement. The measures shall be marked with the seal of the Republic. In each district there shall be a checker in charge of applying the seal."

May 16: Treaty of the Hague with Holland. Maastricht becomes French.

June 7: After a hiatus of seven months, Delambre resumes his measurements in Bourges.

October 25: End of the Convention.

October 25: Creation of the Institute. The mathematics class is almost entirely composed of scientists involved in the weights and measures operation.

Constitution of 1795: Article 1: The French Republic is one and indivisible. Article 2: The universality of French citizens is sovereign. Article 371: There shall be uniformity of weights and measures in the Republic.

October 26, 1795: Installation of the Directory.

1796

April 6 (17 Germinal, Year IV): Manifesto of the Equals.

1797

May 27: Gracchus Babeuf is executed.

July 3: Talleyrand proposes to the Institute that an expedition be sent to Egypt. Decree of the Directory's executive concerning the completion of work begun on the republican measures.

1798

June 3 (15 Prairial, Year VI): Completion of measurement of the Melun baseline.

October 16 (15 Vendémiaire, Year VII): Date of the expected arrival of the first foreign scientists named to the International Commission to verify the measurements and calculations connected with the standard meter.

1799

June 22 (4 Messidor, Year VII): Proclamation by the International Commission of the results before the Legislative Body and deposit of the standard platinum meter and kilogram in the Archives of France.

November 9–10 (18 Brumaire, Year VII): Bonaparte's coup d'état and beginning of the Consulate.

**Le mètre mesure 3 pieds 11 lignes 296 de la toise
du Pérou à la température de 16°1/4**

C'est à toi, cher Delambre, à diriger ma route ;

toi qui sais réunir, par un double pouvoir,

les beaux-arts au calcul et le goût au savoir.

Ce fut au bruit des vents déchaînés sur nos têtes,

quand la foule appelait les publiques tempêtes,

quand le sol ébranlé s'entrouvrait sous nos pas,

que Delambre et Méchain, armés de leurs compas,

des sables de Dunkerque aux rivages de l'Ebre,

sur la terre marquait cette ligne célèbre

qui du globe inégal mesure les degrés.

J. Delille, *Les Trois Règnes de la nature*, Paris, A. Nicolle, 1808

**The meter measures 3 feet 11 lines 296 *toises*
of Peru at a temperature of 16 1 /4 degrees**

Your job, dear Delambre, is to guide me on my way, you who are doubly blessed with the fine arts of calculation and the thirst for knowledge. It was to the howl of the winds unleashed upon us when the mob called for public storms, when the shaken ground opened up beneath our feet, that Delambre and Méchain, armed with their compasses, marked this famous line on the earth from the sands of Dunkirk to the banks of the Ebro and measured the uneven globe's degrees.